PRAISE
FOR JORGE VOLPI

"Jorge Volpi will be one of the stars of Spanish literature of this century."

—Carlos Fuentes

"Every generation or so a writer comes along who liberates his peers from oppressive expectations of what Latin American fiction is supposed to be. Jorge Volpi's *In Search of Klingsor* woke everybody up!"

—Francisco Goldman

"An ingenious literary journey into the world of science, cloaked within a spy thriller."

—Alan Lightman, author of *Einstein's Dreams*

SELECTED WORKS BY JORGE VOLPI

IN ENGLISH TRANSLATION

In Search of Klingsor

IN SPANISH

El fin de la locura

La guerra y las palabras

La imaginación y el poder

El jardín devastado

El juego del apocalipsis

Mentiras contagiosas

La paz de los sepulcros

A pesar del oscuro silencio

Sanar tu piel amarga

El temperamento melancólico

JORGE VOLPI

SEASON OF ASH

A NOVEL IN THREE ACTS

TRANSLATED FROM THE SPANISH
BY ALFRED MAC ADAM

Originally published by Alfaguara, Madrid as *No será la Tierra*, 2006

First U.S. edition, 2009

Library of Congress Cataloging-in-Publication Data:

Volpi Escalante, Jorge, 1968-
[No será la tierra. English]
Season of ash : a novel in three acts / Jorge Volpi ; translated from the Spanish by Alfred Mac Adam. — 1st U.S. ed.
p. cm.
ISBN-13: 978-1-934824-10-8 (pbk. : alk. paper)
ISBN-10: 1-934824-10-0 (pbk. : alk. paper)
I. Mac Adam, Alfred J., 1941- II. Title.
PQ7298.32.O47N613 2009
863'.64—dc22

2009035395

Printed on acid-free paper in the United States of America.

Design by N. J. Furl

Open Letter is the University of Rochester's nonprofit, literary translation press:
Lattimore Hall 411, Box 270082, Rochester, NY 14627

www.openletterbooks.org

For my ornithologist.

For them have I woven this vast shroud
Out of the sad words I heard from them.
—Anna Akhmatova, *Requiem*

There are women born in a moist earth.
Each of their steps is a sonorous sob,
and their vocation is to accompany the dead
and to be the first to greet those who come back to life.
—Osip Mandelstam, *Voronezh Notebooks*

CONTENTS

PRELUDE

RUINS

(1986)

Enough rot, howled Anatoly Diatlov. The alarm went off at 1:29 A.M. Moving at 300,000 kilometers a second, the photons passed through the screen—rendered brick-colored by the dust—pierced the air saturated with smoke from Turkish cigarettes, and, following a straight line through the control room, smashed into his pupils just before the blare of a siren, traveling at a mere 1,200 kilometers per hour, reached his eardrums. Unable to distinguish between the two stimuli, his neurons generated an electric whirlwind that engulfed his body. While his eyes focused on the scarlet iridescence and his ears were thrashed with sound waves, his neck muscles tensed, the glands in his forehead and armpits accelerated the production of sweat, his limbs stiffened, and, without the assistant to the engineer noticing, adrenaline infiltrated his blood stream. Despite his ten years of experience, Anatoly Mihalovic Diatlov was dying of fright.

A few meters away, another chain reaction was following a parallel course. In one of the side panels, the mercury was flying to the top of an old thermometer, while the iodine and cesium particles were becoming unstable. It was as if those inoffensive elements had plotted a revolt and, instead of being suspicious of each other, had joined to destroy the bars and torture the guards. The creature wasted no time in taking control of Reactor Number Four in an open challenge to the emergency rules. It was taking revenge and accepting no excuses: It would execute its captors and establish a kingdom of its own. Ever more powerful, it sped to conquer the plant. If the humans did not take immediate steps, the massacre couldn't be contained. Thousands would die. And the Ukraine, Byelorussia, perhaps all of Europe, would be forever devastated.

Flames were devouring the horizon. Far away, the Pripiat shepherds, accustomed only to events as severe as meteor showers, confused the columns of smoke with artillery practice or the celebration of some victory. Makar Bazdaiev, tending sheep, became tongue-tied as he watched the sky—an aftertaste of vodka in his throat—not knowing it heralded his death. Nearer to the fire, engineers and chemists, builders of stars, recognized the nature of the cataclysm. After decades of alarms and vigilance, the unthinkable had actually occurred, the often-postponed curse, the feared surprise attack. Old people still dreamed of German tanks, impaled children, and rows of graves: The enemy would decimate the forests again, burn the shacks, and drench the altars with the blood of their children.

At 1:30 A.M., Diatlov decided to do something. He'd always hated spring—the sunflowers, the songs the townspeople sang, the need to smile for no good reason. That's why he stayed inside the plant, safe from the euphoria. Only vodka and extra work enabled him to survive the holidays. And now this! The wise men of Kiev and Moscow, cities of wide avenues, had sworn that nothing like this would ever happen. A Party boss had reproached him once upon a time: There is no room for error. You have the manual in front of you, just follow instructions.

The manual was now useless. The needles were spinning wildly, like helicopter blades, and the protective barriers erected thanks to the indefatigable will of socialism—thousands of workers had built the secret citadel—were collapsing. This is how Sodom must have looked. The night was pierced by shouts; the air was filled with the stink of scorched flesh, and panting dogs blocked the side streets. The peasants confused the black smoke with the angel of death. And all because of a whim: the desire to test the resistance of the plant, to go beyond standard precautions, to surprise the Minister.

Only a few hours earlier, Diatlov had ordered the cooling system disconnected. Just routine. Within seconds, the reactor fell into a lazy sleep. Who could suspect it was faking? Its breathing became slower and its pulse was barely perceptible: less than thirty megawatts. Finally, it closed its eyes. Fearing an irreversible coma, Diatlov abandoned common sense: We must increase power again.

The technicians retracted the barium carbon rods, which restrained the beast, and it recovered its powers. Its vital signs stabilized. It was breathing again. The technicians cheered, not knowing that those rods were the only thing that protected them: The manual stipulated fifteen as the lowest acceptable number, and now there were only eight. How stupid! That error would result in thousands of casualties. The monster's heartbeat quickly reached six hundred megawatts, and in the blink of an eye it had enough strength to demolish the walls of its cell. Its roars shook the fir trees of Pripiat like the howl of a thousand wolves. Sand crackled and steel blistered. The nucleus of Reactor Number Four had almost attained the heat of the stars—magma pouring from its jaws—but Diatlov stubbornly insisted on floating above the void. Let's go on with the test.

The beast took no pity on him or his crew. It attacked its guards and devoured their guts; then, angrier and angrier, it began its pilgrimage across the plant's galleries, spreading its fury through the ventilation system. Disregarding orders from his superiors, Vladimir Kriachuk, a thirty-five-year-old technician, pushed the AZ-5 key to stop the entire process. Two hundred carbon rods cascaded into the body of the intruder—vainly. Instead of succumbing, it went back on the offensive, becoming even more dangerous.

It's out of control! Olexandr Akhimov, the team leader, wasn't lying: The monster had won. It plucked out Yuri Ivanov's eyes and smashed Leonid Gordesian's skull like an almond shell. Two explosions signaled its victory. Reactor Number Four ceased to exist.

The plant was the pride of the nation. In secret, over the course of toilsome months, an army of workers, supervised by hundreds of functionaries from the Ministry along with various security groups, built the reactors, the electric transformers, the water distribution system, the telephone lines, the workers' houses, the schools for the workers' children, the community centers, the firehouse, and the local centers for the Party and the secret service. A city in miniature, an example of order and progress that was self-sufficient; a perfect system erected in a place that didn't appear on any map—a genuine utopia, proof of Communism's vigor.

Besieged in the rubble, Diatlov ordered the activation of the emergency cooling system (his hands were trembling like wheat in a gale). He thought that water, as it did in ancient eras, would defeat the fire.

Comrade, the pumps are offline. It was the voice of Boris Soliarchuk. Diatlov remembered that he had ordered them disconnected only the day before. What is the radiation level? The maximum our instruments can register is one millirem, and we went beyond that hours ago.

That was a hundred times the allowed norm. Diatlov furrowed his brow and imagined a cortege of cadavers.

Viktor Petrovich Briuhanov, the director of the plant, slept a sticky sleep. Every night he tossed and turned without waking up: His conscience was as fluffed up as a goose-down pillow. When the telephone rang, he was dreaming about a toy ambulance: He only answered after the third ring. But he heard no one at the other end of the line. Finally, Diatlov's voice stuttered to life with a justification of his mistakes. How can anyone explain that he's opened the doors of hell?

Briuhanov buttoned his shirt. He thought: It can't be that serious. Then: There has to be a way to fix things. As he walked out of his house, his optimism disappeared. The columns of smoke, as high as skyscrapers, were threatening to fall on top of him, and the wind was clawing his lungs. He travelled the three kilometers from Pripiat to the plant thinking he was living in a nightmare; only the heat, the heat which would ultimately kill him, kept him from losing his way.

Diatlov was waiting for him at the command post, his face covered with soot and shame. Olexander Akhimov and Boris Stoliarchuk didn't bother to let him ask. In their opinion, the catastrophe was irreversible.

Once the damage was confirmed, Briuhanov ran to the telephone and dialed the Ministry; then he called the Regional Committee and the Central Committee of the Party. He mumbled the same sentences over and over, the same formal greetings, the same excuses, the same pleas: We need help—something terrible has happened in Chernobyl.

As the nuclear fuel burned, the bureaucrats in the Ministry could only repeat the news to one another. Briuhanov addressed his subordinates, demanding calm, fortitude, and faith in socialist destiny, but he couldn't believe his own words. Someone in Moscow, the city of wide avenues, would know how to stop the meltdown. (At the other end of the plant, in the turbine room, half a dozen employees were fighting the fire. Protected by useless conventional fire equipment. They were trying to protect the gasoline supply. Their fingers were falling off piece by piece.) Briuhanov bit his lip: His city was collapsing. For some reason, he remembered a tune from his childhood and began to hum it. Indecisive, he waited several hours before authorizing an evacuation. Only when every watch said it was 3:00 P.M., and the radiation had infiltrated the cells of his subordinates, did he order the building emptied. At his side stood Diatlov, Akhimov, and Stoliarchuk, resigned to the fact that their mothers would have to receive their Hero of the Soviet Union medals.

From Pripiat, the plant seemed wrapped up in celebration. A beam of blue light rose from its center like a mast. The only things missing were the scarlet banners, the military salutes, the hammers and the sickles.

Far, far away, in a tranquil meteorological outpost in Sweden, a group of scientists confirmed the readings from the meters. There was no doubt. The radiation invading the Scandinavian forests was not coming from their reactors. A disaster must have taken place behind the iron curtain.

That same day, long-haired Paisi Kaisarov found out he would indeed fight in a war. He slipped out from under the sheets silently, in order not to disturb his woman: He would soon be the father of a little girl. Until then, his work had seemsed slow and boring. His comrades were overjoyed whenever they put out a fire. But now the enemy was taking them by surprise. What was he supposed to think, when the Pripiat firehouse itself had been burned to the ground?

A few hours later, the eleven members of his squad were shoulder to shoulder, fighting the flames around the plant. By then Reactor Number Four was a mirage, and in its place stood a foreshortened image of an overcast sky. They would have to fight to the death to defend Reactor Number Three. Doomed to defeat, Kaisarov and his comrades trained their water cannon on the beast, but all the water in all the seas wouldn't have been able to bring it under control. The flames might die, but a shard of graphite was all it took to reanimate its fury. The firemen swallowed the smoke, and their veins swelled up like snakes. They all fell on the battle field.

It took time for the reinforcements from neighboring republics to converge on the outskirts of Pripiat because they were unable to communicate with one another, as if a curse had put a spell on their radios. Two regiments of Ukrainian sappers camped around the town. Who could have imagined them fighting the wind when they'd been trained to fight in trenches! Their commanders set the attack plans, checked the maps, and calculated the losses. The fights took place one after another all afternoon—the squads demolished by invisible hands—until the fire finally seemed under control.

Matvrei Platov, officer in the Seventh Air Army, flew over the vicinity of the plant without knowing who the enemy was. Despite his insistent questions, his commander had refused to reveal the nature of his mission. Platov felt the clouds and stopped wondering, fascinated by the Ukrainian plains—that yellow ocean—unable to imagine the plague that was being scattered over them. This time his mission would not be to spy on NATO aircraft or to frighten the Japanese or the Chinese. This time his plane was loaded with enough sand to build a stockade, and his mission was to defeat discharges no one could feel. Matvrei Ivanovich, an expert watchmaker, dropped a storm of cobblestones on the beast's incandescent skin. Hundreds of pilots dropped their bomb loads through the air in the same mission.

In their improvised headquarters three kilometers away, Colonel Liubomir Mimka drew a star each time a load released by one of the pilots hit the target. At midday on April 27th, Mimka informed the appropriate person in the Government of the total success of the offensive. The radiation had diminished to tolerable levels. But the cheering didn't last long. A messenger revealed the bad news: The monster was caged but was still alive. And wounded, it is even more dangerous.

Reactor Number Four was a dormant volcano: Everyone knew that there were still 190 tons of Uranium-235 in its guts, enough to generate a miniature big bang.

The radio broadcast fiery speeches, like Stalin's harangues against Hitler: Old people, children, and women must mobilize in defense of the nation. Meanwhile, the air force continued the bombardments, adding borax and lead to their loads. After sweeping their objective, the pilots would return to base to be disinfected. Unlike those who lived around Pripiat, they could use an iodine solution to weaken the effects of radiation.

The town turned into a field hospital. The bodies were piled up in plastic bags—shiny Communist shrouds—and, told nothing, the wounded silently waited for the helicopters that would carry them to Leningrad and Moscow. Most had their stomachs eaten away, the skin burned off their chests, and wounds on their hands. None would last more than a few weeks. In Polaskaie, 150 kilometers away, mothers and widows were not even allowed to see the faces of their sons and husbands. The military sealed the corpses in zinc coffins and buried them in secret.

Routine took control in Pripiat and the surrounding area. Those living there got up before dawn, put on asbestos suits, and, after a breakfast of bread and milk (the only food their stomachs could tolerate), went off to do the day's work. Their families, exiled to the outskirts of Kiev and other cities, passed the time doing crossword puzzles or watching ballet on black-and-white television.

In Moscow, the Party silenced all rumors. They told the international media that there was a minor leak, no reason for alarm. The vigorous Secretary-General even crossed his arms when an Austrian journalist dared to ask about the number of dead.

On May 9th, 1986, thirteen days after the leak, the monster seemed liquidated. Yet another triumph of Communism! The Party ordered the shops stocked to the rafters with vodka and Georgian wine so the pilots, bombardiers, and liquidators could dull their consciences a bit. Glasses burst in mid-air amid insane cheers and long-lives concealed the absence of the fallen. To your health, comrades!, toasted Boris Chenina, chief of the government commission in charge of the catastrophe.

Suddenly it was as if nothing had happened. Around Pripiat, the birds again slipped through the sky and the hillsides displayed their bushes and trees while a red sun tranquilized the anguish of the deer. If it hadn't been for the smoking ruins of Reactor Number Four—and the mysterious absence of voices and songs—anyone might have imagined it was paradise.

On May 14th, at noon, the Secretary-General again held a press conference: The situation was under control, there's nothing to fear. And then, using the same rhetoric as executioners and traitors, he attributed the rumors of a tragedy to the dark forces of capitalism. But the victory was an illusion. Though the beast had been chained up, its venom was spreading across the globe. Wind and rain were carrying its humors toward Europe and the Pacific, its dregs were piling up in lakes, and its semen was filtering its way through the geological strata. The monster was in no hurry. It was patiently planning its revenge: Every baby born without legs, without a pancreas, every sterile sheep, dying cow, every rusty lung, every malignant tumor, and every eaten-away brain would celebrate its revenge. Its curse would go on through all eternity. Ultimately, the explosion would leave 300,000 hectares of land in a putrefied state, seventy towns emptied by force, 120,000 people expelled from their houses, and an incalculable number of men, women, and children contaminated.

Mikhail Mikhailovich Speranski, with intense gray eyes, had just joined the Armada. Held back in school because of mathematics and spelling, and prone to bullying his brothers, he celebrated his recruitment: He was seventeen years old, and the only things that mattered to him were money and women. When a sergeant suggested he join the special labor force that was working in the Ukraine and Byelorussia, and promised him extra rubles every week, he abandoned the wide-cheeked girl whose bed he shared and went off in search of adventure.

Transported in obscure military trains, he reached his objective after three days: an improvised encampment on the Ukrainian plain. By then, hundreds of volunteers were dreaming of long hours of combat. A tall, thin sergeant explained the mission to his squad. At 5:00 A.M., an army truck drove him and four of his comrades to a spot seven kilometers form Pripiat. The moon was shinning through the trees. Their orders were blunt: They were to kill every animal and clear the land—that's right, the whole place—to free it from the plague. They were no longer soldiers but butchers. The local peasants called them liquidators.

Speranski almost wept when he shot his first deer, a doe only a few months old, but after a few weeks of constantly emptying his rifle, he barely took note of his victims. The corpses of sheep, cows, cats, goats, chickens, ducks, and hounds carpeted the meadows before being doused with gasoline and burned like heretics. The liquidators had to eradicate everything the monster hadn't devoured. Within a radius of ten kilometers, all cities and towns were demolished, the trees cut down, the animal life decimated, the grass taken away. The only way to guarantee the survival of the human race was to make the plain into a desert. Mikhail Mikhailovich went about his task with the same blankness as the executioners who put his grandparents to death in the Kolyma camps. After contributing so faithfully to the massacre, Speranski found life less than attractive. Soon after the fall of the Soviet Union, he would be executed for armed robbery.

Piotr Ivanovich Kaganov, from a village in Byelorussia, was ordered to remove the debris on the roof of Reactor Number Three. Wearing a rudimentary astronaut suit, he was carried by a combat helicopter and abandoned in that swamp dotted with balls of incandescent graphite, each one of which weighed ten or twelve kilos. His job was to pick up as many as possible in the time allotted to him, but after a few seconds his boots burst and his skin cracked like clay. The army had tried to execute the maneuver with small Japanese robots, but their circuits melted instantly.

Piotr Ivanovich summoned up all his courage and dropped onto the roof like a child riding a sled. Despite his precautions—he'd put sheets of lead in his socks—the soles of his feet burned as if he were walking on hot coals. His breath became short and, trapped in his helmet, he could barely make out the shape of his hands. He used up his time before he could move a single ball of graphite. The helicopter reeled in the cable he was attached to, and Kaganov rose up into the sky, defeated and half dead. Luckily, hundreds of conscripts were standing in line to replace him.

After weeks of racking their brains, the wise men of Moscow finally came up with a plan to stop the disaster. A team of engineers drew up the plans over the course of four days and nights before submitting the project to the scrutiny of their superiors. Architects, physicists, geographers, and other experts gave their blessing to the project: The only way to conquer the beast was to bury it. Designed at top speed, the building would look like a shoe box, and it would have to be built from a distance—the radiation made it impossible to work in the immediate area—with the help of scaffolding, cranes, and other heavy equipment. Three factories began to manufacture enormous slabs of cement eighty meters high and thirty centimeters thick. Bulldozers, cranes, and tractors came to Pripiat from every corner of the nation, while more than twenty-two thousand liquidators were assigned to the actual construction. A new phase of the war had begun: To carry out the promises of the Secretary-General and the Party, the fortress would have to be finished in only a few weeks.

Valery Lagasov had dedicated his life to atoms. As a boy he'd fallen in love with those tiny universes, and for years he did nothing but draw scale models. As a member of the Kurchatov Institute, he'd unceasingly praised the virtues of atomic energy and had convinced his superiors to build more and more nuclear plants. Instead of using atomic energy for evil, as the allies did at Hiroshima and Nagasaki—he constantly repeated—the USSR had the obligation to illuminate hundreds of cities. Thanks to his persistence, scores of reactors appeared on the maps.

When he found out what happened in Chernobyl, Lagasov gave an interview to *Pravda*: He conceded the seriousness of the damage, but at the same time said he was convinced that the catastrophe would make Soviet industry stronger. Exactly one year after the explosion, on April

27th, 1987, the scientist composed a document titled "My Obligation is to Speak," in which he contradicted his earlier statements. He was wrong: The nuclear industry was not only a danger for the USSR but for the entire planet. After signing it, Lagasov blew his brains out.

The government commission ordered a rapid investigation of the events. After accumulating evidence, hundreds of items, a special group within the KGB arrested Viktor Briuhanov, the Director of the plant; Nicolay Fomin, Assistant Director and Chief Engineer; Anatoly Diatlov, Assistant Engineer-in-Chief; Boris Rogoikin, head of the night guard; Olexandr Kovalenko, in charge of Reactors Two and Three; and Yuri Lauchkin, Inspector for Gosatomnadzor, the company responsible for developing the Ukrainian plants. The six were tried in secret, accused of carrying out the tests that led to the disaster without receiving authorization from Moscow, of not taking the measures necessary to bring it under control, and of waiting too long to call the rescue teams. The former directors testified, but the judges had no need to listen. Briuhanov, Fomin, and Diatlov were sentenced to ten years in prison; Rogoikin to five; Kovalenko to three; and Lauchkin to two. As far as the Party was concerned, they were the only guilty individuals.

To Lieutenant Mavra Kuzminishna, a demolitions expert, the ruin of Reactor Number Four, surrounded by cranes, looked like a tarantula. Its amazingly high legs folded around its mouth, feeding it borax as its only food. An amateur climber and member of the weight-lifting team of the Eighth Land Army, she came to Pripiat to supervise the laborers. The gigantic wall was going up piece by piece around the plant: More than 100,000 cubic meters of cement. The project was moving along right on schedule. Soon no one remembered the dead, the explosion would be forgotten, and families from Siberia or the Caucasus would repopulate the area around Pripiat. Mavra Kuzminishna thought that, if the world were different, she too would like to live in the area. The prefabricated slabs piled up like a child's blocks; the cranes raised them up—counter-balanced by sixty-ton weights—and placed them on the remains of Reactor Number Four. Lieutenant Kuzminishna thought of an ancient temple. The satellite photos showed a very different image: an eighty-meter-high sarcophagus. The final legacy of Communism.

ACT ONE

WAR TIME

(1929-1985)

THREE WOMEN

1.

Moscow, Russian Federation, December 30th, 2000

Those aren't her eyes. As frozen as the mosaics in that place, her tone defies contradiction. Who would have the nerve? It's hard to know what she thinks or feels: This is one of the great mysteries of our race. Irina Nikolayevna Granina remains locked in her silence. She devours the doctors with her black eyes and memorizes their names in order to denounce them later. Where do they get off insisting like this, with such urgency, making her get up in the middle of the night? The end of Communism has not changed them, she thinks (or so I believe she thinks): Now they wear crisp uniforms and gloves, but they're still the same executioners who spit on Arkady Ivanovich in the past, the same cowards who classified him insane and dangerous, the same bastards who filled him with sedatives. They still have the souls of policemen, she grows enraged.

Irina clutches her handbag as if it were a safe conduct pass. She'd like to leave as soon as possible, to return to the whiteness of her sheets and the silence of daybreak, to the dream that consumes her nightly: a dense sea without a shore. Ever since she separated from Arkady (or to put it more clearly, ever since she abandoned him after thirty years of sharing his life), no one protects her from the shadows. Now she has to stare into them alone, with the same determination that allowed her to go on living and rescue him.

Look at her again, Irina Nikolayevna, please.

The woman steps back a few paces, her pulse accelerates, and someone raises the curtain—it's white, like the rest of the furniture. Under halogen light, human skin acquires a greenish tone, but Irina Nikolayevna doesn't raise her eyes. She has no need. A mother is never mistaken.

Those aren't her eyes. She'd like to shout it again and again, not her eyes, not her eyes, force them to shut up and beg her forgiveness, convinced that this dull green gaze is not the one she loved so much. But the words do not leave her lips. The temperature rises at a dizzying rate. Some air, please! Outside, the rain beats against the storm windows. The nurses offer her a glass of water which Irina contemptuously rejects. Finally she collapses onto a plastic chair. We know how painful this is for you, Irina Nikolayevna.

The little boy with violet shadows under his eyes doesn't know whom he's dealing with: Thanks to her, to her tenacity and strength, Russians now are free to say whatever they like. Now they can buy Italian ties or sleep with teenage girls from Thailand. Now they live without fear of being arrested. So how do you dare doubt her word? Perhaps it would be better to wait for Doctor Granin.

Arkady Ivanovich? Were they going to pester him too? A bitter smile materializes on Irina's face. During the past few months, she hasn't had the right to bother him, but these good-for-nothings can call him in at dawn because of a bureaucratic error! She is almost pleased that someone has disturbed the tranquility of Arkady Ivanovich Granin, illustrious member of the Russian Academy of Science, once a candidate for the Nobel Peace Prize, and has returned him to the land of the living. She imagines him in his pajamas, obese and ridiculous, getting ready to walk out into the blizzard. It might be worthwhile waiting around a bit to contemplate his bloated face. Arkady Ivanovich? We've just called him. He'll be here in a few minutes.

How naïve they are, Irina thinks, or perhaps she whispers it. They clearly don't know him: Like all victims, Arkady feels obliged to exhibit his martyrdom. He accepts every invitation, all homages, turns up at every gathering to celebrate any praise whatsoever of his person, but at the end of the day, he always gets his way. How long has it been since Irina last saw him? Six months, seven? He'll be furious when he finds out it's an error, and he won't rest until the guilty are punished.

Irina has no fears about her daughter. She has no idea where she might be, it's been months since she's had a letter from her, but she isn't worried: Whatever they say, that is not her body lying on that slab. After so many fights and reconciliations, Irina has almost gotten used to her absence, to that mixture of hostility and cowardice that keeps her on the other side of the planet. She's certain that the same fate which made her fragile and violent will also protect her from danger. The poor thing doesn't deserve to die so young.

Irina Nikolayevna remembers caressing her daughter's bloody face. Oksana, seven years old at the time, had just fallen from a third-floor window, but miraculously (though of course Irina did not believe in miracles) she only suffered scrapes on her forehead and knees. As a good scientist, the socialist scientist she was obliged to be, she rejected supernatural explanations and convinced herself of the strength of her family: The girl's genes, present in her mother and grandmother, would make her invulnerable.

May I leave? One of the pathologists shakes his head negatively. Let's wait for Doctor Granin, please.

Irina Nikolayevna seems fated to wait: For years she waited for Arkady to return from exile; what can a few minutes matter to her? Her yellowed fingers dig around in her bag until they find a pack of cigarettes. She takes one out, lights it, and carefully inhales (a strange ceremony). Nicotine accentuates her sadness. She repeats the action again, and then again.

Where is she? Irina recognizes her husband's voice. Ash slips between her fingers. Where is my daughter?

Arkady doesn't look fatter or older, but solid and majestic, with a carefully clipped beard. The master of the situation. Even now, he can't stand inelegance: He's wearing a dark suit, a freshly-ironed shirt; no one would imagine that for years he wore the same suit and the same underwear, holes and all. Irina conceals her spite and yields to her husband's confidence (yes, he's still her husband). Arkady Ivanovich Granin is no ordinary man; he's a moral reference point. A symbol. Or at least he was until the scandal erupted. The scandal she herself provoked.

He doesn't even bother to say hello and follows the doctors, who show him the body with a deference that that used to be reserved only for high-ranking Party officials. Arkady can't stand the spectacle and quickly nods. He hopes to resolve the matter as soon as possible; for him this death is nothing more than an undeniable fact. He's neither sad nor surprised, just resigned. His daughter was possessed by uncontrollable violence, a delirium that made her abnormal. Oksana died long ago (at least in his heart), when she ran away from Moscow and joined the other dropouts who were lost in the dark streets of Vladivostok, the ghost port.

Arkady whispers a few words to the director of the morgue and gets ready to leave. Irina stops him. As if he feared the raucous presence of the reporters who've been tailing him since the DNAW-Rus scandal became public, he gives in and hugs her. Irina Nikolayevna clings to his body. Arkady notes with disgust that she's dyed her hair blond and then feels dizzy after inhaling her sugary perfume.

It's not true that it's Oksana, it's not true that it's our daughter, right? Arkady remains silent. He's always been afraid of his wife's outbursts. He knows her determination, her daring, her courage, and he doesn't want a scene. The newspaper vultures will be there any minute now, the autopsy and the burial must both take place as soon as possible. The cause of death? Arkady asks the chief pathologist. He leads him to the slab and shows him the wounds: We'll take care of covering them up. Oksana finally got what she wanted, thinks the biologist.

Arkady stands tall, but Irina begins to collapse. Neither cries, but for different reasons. All he wants is to leave, while she remains incredulous. Those are not her eyes, isn't that so? Arkady doesn't answer. Tell me those aren't her eyes, that those aren't the eyes of our Oksana. Tell me, Arkady Ivanovich.

Calm down, Irina, it was inevitable. Those words condemn him. The woman glares at him furiously and then rushes toward the body of her daughter. Irina approaches the slab, overcomes her own resistance, and touches the lifeless body. She won't dare to look at her face and simply caresses her neck on top of the sheet. Then she seizes her daughter's right hand, small and covered with scabs, her childhood hand. When she realizes she hasn't touched it in years, she kisses it again and again. Finally she kneels and makes the sign of the cross.

Arkady Ivanovich rushes through the paperwork. He's not willing to break down now, after all he's suffered. After contributing to the liberation of 200,000,000 people, he cannot allow himself to weep over one. A long time ago, when his fights with Oksana became unbearable, he made a decision: The death of his daughter would not be his death. As simple as that. Even so, he smashes his fist against the wall, his only display of rage or grief. Calmer, he decides to wait until Irina finishes praying to the inert body of his daughter, that part of him which defied him all her life and which now has taken the cruelest revenge.

2.
New York, United States of America, December 30th, 2000

Jennifer opens and closes the kitchen cabinets, fascinated by the sound of the doors: The touch of the wood calms her nerves. Wearing that black skirt and that blouse, with its peter-pan collar, she looks like a schoolgirl. Either she hasn't had time to put on makeup or she's decided to skip it in order to accentuate the drama in her face. The kitchen tiles sparkle in the sun filtering through the windows. In the distance, the skyscrapers delineate a grayish labyrinth. It's been a long time since the city looked so bright, so immobile, Jennifer thinks (I want her to think) as she turns on the water and rinses her hands for the umpteenth time. She's always adored cleanliness—the shelves are packed with Brillo pads, rags, detergents, soaps, disinfectants, insecticides, bleaches, deodorants, rolls and rolls of toilet paper, napkins, and spot removers—but today she will not allow even a speck of dust, which is why she will not stop dusting and rinsing her hands under the water.

Finally, Jennifer plops down onto one of the armchairs in the living room, a purple model with no pleats that must have cost Wells a fortune, and contemplates the void stretching out before her eyes. From this observation point, a Park Avenue twentieth floor, the world doesn't look like a battlefield. There are no tanks in the streets, no rotting bodies on the sidewalks, no land mines in the garbage dump, no machine gun buzzing, no dynamite exploding. But the war is there, everywhere, without anyone's seeing it.

For Jennifer, peace is merely an image (like the idea of the world economy taken as a totality), a deception only the uninformed or indigent believe in. All you have to do is kick a hole in that anthill, demolish its mechanisms and springs, to reveal the cruelty of its battles. Most people prefer to dissimulate, to convince themselves that nothing is happening, that here in the heart of America it's possible to be safe, far from the stray shots that murder children and old people in other places on the planet. They're wrong. The fighting is everywhere, even in this tower just a short distance from Central Park. Sitting like this, her legs crossed, barefoot, Jennifer can barely tell the difference between herself and the irresponsible masses teeming down below. Her apparent indifference makes her resemble the models whose flesh carpets Manhattan's billboards. Like so many women of her age and social class, she could simply accept being just one more victim of fashion and indolence. She would almost like to be as ignorant, as pure as those women: That way she wouldn't have to appear charming, she could massage her feet for as long as she wanted, could watch soap operas, exercise, do yoga—or pay a psychoanalyst—with no fear of being frivolous. That's not her fate. She chose to belong to the exclusive club of those who guide, who order. Of those who *know*.

At the International Monetary Fund, the altar of the planet's economy, Jennifer learned to imagine herself commanding an army. Except that her soldiers don't carry weapons, don't besiege cities, don't fight guerrillas or terrorists. But their mission of pacification is not really different from those carried out by tanks or infantry. Her conquests are more subtle, but no less violent (and no less necessary, according to her). She's never doubted the morality of her goals. Even if hers is a dirty job—fighting against those who disturb the freedom of markets—she's convinced that someone has to do it. She has no regrets. And certainly isn't sorry.

Jennifer is dying to light a cigarette (she hasn't smoked for twenty years), but she doesn't. Instead she just opens one more bottle of mineral water, takes a sip, and puts it on the table next to her cell phone, her fetish. It hasn't rung in over half an hour. The truth is, she doesn't know what to do or how to behave. Actually, what she doesn't know is how to break the news to Jacob. Should she explain that it was an accident and perhaps use the word *tragedy*? Or would it be better to skip the details and launch into a sermon about the existence of Heaven and the angels? And if she were to tell him the truth, that Allison was stupid, that for years she been taking senseless risks, that she'd always been irresponsible, cynical? How do you tell a ten-year-old boy that his mother would not be coming home, and, the hardest part, how do you make him see that it's the best thing that could have happened to him? Jennifer will need all her diplomatic skill to convince him, but there's a reason she is the Fund's star negotiator. Jacob is clever and has begun to take on the same defiant attitude all the Moores possess.

For the first time since she learned what happened to her sister—the ambassador's voice is still echoing in her ear—Jennifer can't manage to hold herself together. Which sensation is stronger, pain or relief? Her puritan temperament forces her to erase that comparison. She will never admit they were not a model family, as they presumed, but a pair of fighters, of rivals. One part of her always wanted to get Allison out of the way: That weepy girl was a permanent bother, an obstacle to her plans for independence. Jennifer had to slip out of the yoke imposed on her by her father, Senator Moore (that's what both girls called him), and to do that she invented an intimate, barely perceptible revolt that Allison put at risk. That's why she preferred having her far away, why she detested taking charge of her, spoiling her, watching over her, scolding her. She had work enough taking care of herself.

Jennifer withdraws to the bathroom, where the mirror reflects her devastated face. Perhaps if she'd been less beautiful when she was young, less perfect, she would be less unhappy now . . . She fixes her hair as she does every morning, untangles her long blond tresses, rubs her eyes, and washes her hands again. With horror, she confirms the fact that yet another wrinkle has appeared at the corner of her mouth. How much time will pass before the telephone transmits the news? She'll have to explain things to Jacob before that happens, before she hears the buzzer, and the neighbors burst in with their condolences.

Jennifer picks up the phone and dials Jack Wells. It rings several times before he answers. What do you want? In the background she hears the noise of motors. Where are you? What? Something's happened . . . Can't you go someplace quieter? Is this better? The racket goes on at the same pitch. Allison is dead. What? She's dead, Jack, damn it all. The stupid fool. What are you saying, Jennifer? If this is a joke . . . She's *dead*, are you listening to me? I understand, I'll be right there.

Jennifer takes another sip of mineral water and discovers Jacob's eyes at the other end of the kitchen. Was he listening? The boy's face is bleary, his hair a mess. She goes over to him without touching him. I want hot chocolate. Jennifer sighs. At this time of day? Please. Jacob looks like a cartoon character in his green and orange stripped pajamas. He's biting his left thumb. I've told you a thousand times never to go barefoot in the house!

Decked out in slippers decorated with bears in several colors, Jacob again takes his place in the kitchen. He's prudent rather than timid, and by now he's learned how to manage his aunt's temper. Jennifer hands him his hot chocolate. Then the cellphone rings, and she jumps. What if it's a reporter. What am I supposed to say: Yes I am Allison Moore's older sister, yes I'm very upset, yes it's a horrible tragedy? Her knees are shaking.

I'm almost there, says Wells, any news? Jennifer sighs. No. I've got Jacob here with me. Have you told him? Not yet. Pretty soon your place is going to turn into a circus, maybe it would be better to go down to Philadelphia. It would look as if we were running away. Can you imagine what people would say after all that's happened? You can always say you're overcome with grief.

Wells cannot imagine the world without an order, a hierarchy, a plan of attack. Jennifer is convinced he must have even calculated the death of his own parents. The poor bastard. People who think he's only interested in money are wrong. His only goal in life has been to foretell the future and to control those around him. It's no coincidence that over the past few years his enemies have grown in number, too many people would like to see him disgraced. Finally they're about to get their chance.

Are you crying, Jen? Jacob doesn't try to interrogate her or expose her, but Jennifer explodes. No. And now go to your room, and don't come out until I call you. Understood? The boy leaves without a grumble, accustomed to his aunt's mood swings: He knows her only too well, and, even though no one believes it—at times not even Jennifer—he loves her. He really loves her.

Jennifer reviews her options: too many exposed flanks. Allison's death. Jack. The DNAW scandal. The press. Condolences from friends and politicians. The paperwork involved in repatriating her body. The funeral. What if there were a humanitarian foundation created in the name of her sister? A few thousand dollars would be enough to satisfy public opinion . . . No, she can't concentrate.

After using his own key to open the door (the rat promised to give it back months ago), Wells comes in, self-satisfied and relaxed. He kisses Jennifer on the cheek. I've talked to everyone, he says, may I have a whisky? Jennifer almost admires his insolence. You know where it is, get it yourself. Arthur promised to do whatever he can . . . Pack some things and take Jacob with you. I've already told you I have no intention of leaving. Don't be stubborn, Jen. Think about the boy. For God's sake, Jack, my sister is dead, I can't just walk out. Not now, and you know it . . . With the accusations made against you, it would be prejudicial for *both of us.* You have no idea how much pleasure people are going to get seeing you on television all broken up because of your sister. She had to pull this dirty trick on us even at the end. The blood rushed to Jennifer's cheeks. If Wells stays one more second, she'll explode. It would be better if you left. He checks his watch: Just as you like. If something happens, please call.

The same parents, the same schools, the same friends. How could they have followed such opposite paths? How did they turn out to be so different? Why in the hell did her sister do her best to become her mirror image? Did she envy Jennifer as much as Jennifer envied her? At what point did they separate? When did their war start? Now that she's gone Jennifer realizes that in fact she's not at all worried about what happens to Allison's body, with her work at the Fund, with Jack's fraudulent deals, with the human genome, with the stock market, or with the economic crisis once again wreaking havoc in the Third World. Because now she has what she always wanted, what she always loved, the only thing that matters to her.

3.
Rockville, Maryland, United States of America, December 30th, 2000

One dawn, after we made love, Eva told me that feelings were the lingering misgivings of evolution, a pathology of intelligence, in the best case a self-preservation manual. Drunk and naked, she kept pouring it out: Love is the glue of reproduction, rage a detonator in the face of danger, fear a substitute for pain and perhaps for death. She never tired of repeating those phrases, as if they were aphrodisiacs. She had fun hectoring me that way, bursting into my private zones, assaulting my passivity or my silence, and then she'd laugh without letting up and throw herself on my ribs and my sex, the victim of the euphoria that carried her away after every period of melancholy. I loathed her bragging, I found her provocations puerile and irrelevant. In her lack of subtlety—of malice—it was obvious we came from different cultures.

Sitting here on the bench, to the side of the spectacle—the cameras and microphones never give me a break—besieged by that mob that either damns me or sympathizes with me in a foreign language, her opinions about natural selection sound like real garbage to me. Within me reigns an undefinable bond, a bond that's separate from my will or my desire. Maybe Eva was right: At this moment, I wouldn't know how to say what it is that oppresses me, how much I'm suffering, or how sorry I am. When we were together, we both showed how proud we were of our I.Q. (the only thing that makes us alike, she would goad me), but ultimately it too was useless.

Who am I? A warm-blooded mammal who lives on land, a biped, male, omnivorous, with a rather complex cerebral cortex, given the size of my skull. My nervous system resembles a power grid (I'm startled by the slightest provocation) and at the same time, at least in theory, my senses have reached a high level of subtlety. My pupils dilate, my heart pumps ceaselessly, and my sweat glands work frenetically. A powerful dose of hormones irrigates my tissue. In sum, I'm a cornered animal, sad and sick. An animal that, despite the infinite advances of science—that progress to which Eva used to contribute—doesn't manage to understand itself.

Strange logic! Is there really someone inside me? Why do we humans persist in being unique individuals, taking on a personality that anchors us permanently? The idea of being many, of being legion, terrifies us. To recognize the different voices that inhabit us would mean accepting a new detour every day. In order to be admitted into society, we have to show that we're always lucid, masters of an impeccable logic, capable of moderating our impulses. That's why they tell us that consciousness has no fixed limits, that it's merely a complex computer program, the product of an algorithm executed in our brain. I never accepted that hypothesis. Moreover, for months I did nothing else but oppose it. I am *not* a machine I shouted a thousand times at Eva, who never tired of annoying me with her calculations and theorems. I was convinced that the soul was not the product of nerve endings. It came from some other place, maybe not from God, but certainly from a cosmic force that determined the essence of what it is to be human. The mind cannot be explained, as I see it, by the simple combination of biology and chemistry.

No sooner do they take off my handcuffs than I show how defiant I can be. Ignoring the advice of lawyers and psychiatrists, I refused to enter a plea of temporary insanity. I'm still convinced that in that instant, when what happened happened—provocation, blindness, the accident—I was myself and not someone else. That certainty terrifies and perturbs me, and it confers on me one last reason for living: to understand, to understand myself, to decipher myself. I turn around in my chair, I look down and collide with the glitter of my shoes. I cross my legs. A man is sketching my profile, emphasizing the shadows under my eyes and my weeks-old beard. A clerk announces the arrival of the judge, a stout woman dressed in purple and black with a bitter grimace on her face. Everyone present rises, but I don't until one of the guards gives my arm a hard squeeze. My wrists ache. A clerk reads out the indictment.

I have to accept the facts: Eva will not rise from the dead. Her body, profaned by the forensic surgeon's hands, has been buried for weeks. The court rejected my appeal to attend the funeral. Klara used all her influence to stop it: She was not going to allow her daughter's murderer to corrupt her grief. I almost understand her. A mother's grief is sacred. I also despise her. I always felt jealous of that part of Eva that her mother possessed, the part I could never possess. Mother and daughter shared a bullet-proof complicity—they even invented a secret language whose meaning was completely obscure to others. None of the other men who passed through Eva's life—and there were many—managed to separate them. They formed an unbreakable, extremely powerful duo that others had to respect and obey. Klara is right to curse me with all her might. She's even willing to protest the sentence: I was never part of her family; she never approved my union with her daughter, I do not deserve her mercy.

An accident.

Those were my words, the only ones I managed to pronounce, the only words that were—and still are—true. What is an accident if it isn't the actualization of the improbable, an occurrence neither sought nor desired, disorder that erupts into everyday tranquility, a proof of the irrationality of the future, the name we humans give to entropy?

An accident, I repeat.

A lie! There are no accidents, only coincidences, fatality, bad luck . . . An almost empty room. Minds clouded by alcohol and who knows what other substances. Too many words. Voices from the past. A howl in the heart of the forest. And then nothing. *Nothing* . . . These are all the elements in the drama, I'm omitting nothing, but they aren't enough. The explanation remains in the margins, in silence, in those ungraspable details. Eva had lost consciousness, she didn't react to my caresses, she was only a body, a body emptied of soul (that soul in which she did not believe) with its legs twisted and blood on its cheeks and lips. The algorithm of her mind had stopped, there had been a glitch in the computer program that kept her alive.

I sit down again. My palms are sweaty. What's going on before my eyes seems alien to me, as banal as a film. Is this justice? All these shysters do is follow a pre-established script set down in useless and deaf laws. What punishment would they be able to impose on me? The electric chair, the gallows, the guillotine? No punishment would repair what I did, none would rehabilitate me. So? Those functionaries will never enact justice: In my case, crime and punishment are one and the same thing.

The monotonous voice of the clerk reels off the summary of the case. I sob when he says the name of the woman I loved: Eva Halász, born in Budapest in 1956, who resided at 34 George Washington Street in Rockville, Maryland, Assistant to the Chief of Celera Biocomputer Programming, dead by reason of a cerebral hemorrhage—no other cause was possible—on June 27th, 2000. I pay no attention to the rest of the summary, don't even listen to the account of my own acts. I don't need it.

When I recover consciousness, the judge is asking the members of the jury if they've reached a verdict. A bald, portly man—a novelist it turns out; I imagined that he was a baker—hands a note to the clerk who passes it to the judge. He reads it and gives back to the clerk, who returns it to the foreman of the jury. No one expects a surprise.

The foreman of the jury will read the verdict, I hear. Just what I needed: to be turned into a character from a detective novel, that dross of the imagination, that literary virus, I who had always gone out of my way to insult that phony, irrelevant genre. I loved Eva, and Eva loved me. We both knew it. Both of us had abandoned everything just so we could be together. That is the incontrovertible truth, the only truth that counts. But now Eva is dead. Dead because I, Yuri Mikhailovich Chernishevsky, wanted it that way without wanting it.

An accident.

The jury foreman had a different opinion: We find the defendant guilty of homicide in the second degree. Nothing new there. Even so, I find myself weeping, moved by a blast of repentance that I myself don't understand. My fate doesn't matter to me (my destiny was decided that night). The future (the absence of any future for me) doesn't matter to me either, but I can't hold back my whining. Furious, I promise not to cry again. I have to face the consequences of my act and live without her forever.

I stand to listen to the sentence. The people in the courtroom stare at me in horror. Someone points out the contradiction between my public fame and my intimate brutality. Outside, overflowing the steps into the Court House, a crowd of reporters, gawkers, and militants from organizations that protest against domestic violence gets ready to jeer. I, who was a hero for that vehement and radical left, have become a symbol of infamy: the independent writer who stood up to Yeltsin and the oligarchs, the defender of just causes, the scourge of the powerful and corrupt, was just a nasty, perverse *machista* like so many others.

The judge stares at me with a severe air. From the start, I knew she would be against me: Who could sympathize with a jealous, alcoholic, violent man? No one forgives a man who beats and murders a woman like Eva Halász, one of the most respected scientists in her country, a woman responsible for decoding that chimera, the human genome.

Fifteen years.

Klara jumps out of her seat and cheers. My defense team tries to soothe me with their devastated faces and angry gestures, their juridic passion and their tricks. We will appeal, they whisper to me, but it no longer matters. I only want to return to my cell. I'm almost happy. Fifteen years to understand what happened during those hours. Fifteen years dedicated to Eva and what Eva pursued. Fifteen years to reconstruct his history and the history that led us to the river-side cabin. Fifteen years to untangle the skein that tied me to her and the women around her. Fifteen years to write a book, the only worthwhile book—not a novel or a personal account. And it wouldn't be a confession or a memoir, just a settling of accounts. Fifteen years to write *Season of Ash*.

IRINA NIKOLAYEVNA SUDYEVA

Union of Soviet Socialist Republics, 1929-1953

The assault troops begin the siege ready to die in the fight. Only one of them will take away the victory, and that in the best of cases, but even so, they engage in the battle with determination. They don't doubt or worry. They are nervous war machines stripped of reason and common sense. One after another they are repelled—fallen angels—without the number of casualties having the slightest effect on their fury. After hours of skirmishing, one of the intruders finally slips into the enclosure, rips open the protective mesh, and, completely ignoring the magnitude of his sin, fuses with his victim in an interminable struggle. That's how Irina Nikolayevna Sudayeva was conceived—and that's how all humans are conceived. Through this pure act of violence. No matter how much men and women pretend to love each other, within them there is no accord of any kind: Masculine genes and feminine genes will betray one another until their extinction.

On May 15th, 1932, Irina was born in Leningrad—earlier Saint

Petersburg, then Petrograd, and then once again Saint Petersburg—on the shore of the Baltic Sea. Her father, Nikolái Serguéivich Sudayev, once a political commissar, had been shot in a prison camp in Perm a few weeks earlier. Irina barely weighed one kilo 600 grams, and her mother had her baptized by an alcoholic *bátiuschka* in conformity with the ritual of the Orthodox church, which was being persecuted at the time by the Communists. To give the tone of the period, a novelist would write "those were difficult times," but since I'm not a novelist (I'm fighting against being a fraud), I won't try to camouflage the arrests, summary trials, and executions that were a part of everyday life because the lord and master of all the Russians, a Georgian named Iósif Dzhugashvili, but who liked to be called the Great Leader and Teacher—or Little Father of the People in his tender moments—thought that he could only retain his authority if he liquidated millions of supposed enemies.

The tiny Irina Nikolayevna did not die of pneumonia or anemia. Her cells, those cells that fascinated her so much as an adult, continued their ceaseless multiplication, guided by the blind will which animates the universe. As time went by, she became a skinny girl with a severe and somewhat aloof look in her eye. She wasn't pretty, but she did possess a certain languor that wasn't wholly devoid of allure. Though Irina always denied the authenticity of the anecdote—only her grandmother persisted in repeating it—her charms caught the eye of Stalin himself who, during a visit of school children to the Kremlin in 1946, patted her on the cheek, never thinking she was the daughter of the traitor Sudayev. Irina never confirmed the episode, but whenever someone mentioned it she felt an itch on her right cheek, as if the scratch on her skin made by the Little Father of the People had not healed.

Like all children of criminals, conspirators, and enemies of the people, Irina Nikolayevna was torn out of her mother's arms when she was four, just at the moment when the Germans began their surprise invasion of the Soviet Union. Irina was transferred to an elementary school in western Siberia, in Sverdlovsk, bastion of ice, called Yekaterinbug both before and after. Yevgenya Timofeia was not granted authorization to emigrate, so she remained in Leningrad while the city suffered one of the bloodiest sieges of the war. Famous for her beauty—green eyes and a sharply outlined profile—she became a ghost with downcast eyes, arms reduced to threads, and a broken voice. Irina only saw her once more, when she was summoned to her deathbed in 1947. Neither recognized the other. Out of decency, or a trace of filial goodness that hadn't been erased by the cold, Irina closed the eyes of that unknown woman with a vague motion of her hand: Her fingertips were impregnated with her mother's smell for weeks.

Irina Nikolayevna was a model student, an example for Communist children. Her skill with numbers—she could do seven figure operations in her head—and her way with animals foretold that she would get the highest grades in a scientific *semiletka*. She would have preferred to study philosophy or literature, but those disciplines were not very attractive when the country urgently needed scientists to transform itself into a technological power. Irina never expressed her desires. Forced to serve a greater cause (the well-being of humanity), she simply obeyed her instructors. The greatest Soviet virtue, she'd been told, was to repress all traces of egoism.

As an adolescent, Irina took no interest in politics. If someone had told her the world could be different, or that on the other side of the ocean people saw things differently, she would have thought that they were provoking her. She was never a rebel, and her own history made her flee any predicament whatsoever. For example: When Soviet troops invaded Hungary in 1956, Irina was oblivious, though she believed nothing of the official propaganda that insisted on the friendship between the two nations. At fifteen, she joined Komsomol, the youth wing of the Communist Party, favored only by her grades. The exterior world only aroused her indifference.

That afternoon, looking at herself in the mirror, Irina noted a small mark in the center of her forehead. After scratching it and confirming that it did not disappear, she hid the wound with her hair, continued her ordinary activities—she was carrying out an experiment with mice—and didn't examine herself again until the next day, under the shower. By then the mark had doubled in size. Doctors had always inspired terror in her: In her infantile universe, doctors played the same role the police or the secret service played for adults. Soviet doctors, like all the doctors in the world, had neither modesty nor tact: For no reason whatsoever, they made her take off all her clothes, touched her with a coldness that gave her goosebumps, and made her carry out the most shameful acts—urinate, defecate, reveal her intimate parts—as if they were foremen in a factory.

Three days later, the bump had become a wound half a centimeter in diameter which inspired jokes from her classmates. Irina finally went to the infirmary in the *semiletka*, where a slovenly male intern made her wait hours before seeing her.

Even though the infection was on her forehead and not her backside, he made her strip, made a point of looking over her breasts, actually those small protuberances that would soon become her breasts, and ordered her to stretch out on the examining table. He took a magnifying glass and analyzed her forehead as if she were incubating a worm. He then determined it was a rash, prescribed some kitchen oil—in the USSR ointments were reserved for serious burns—and ordered her back to class.

In less than twenty-four hours, the false rash had spread like the plague. Irina felt a sudden itch on her ankle, then on her right thigh, and soon her stomach was invaded by red pustules. Her navel was surrounded, as was her back, her shoulders, and her neck. Horrified, she locked herself up in the bathroom. By then her body was covered with pustules, and she felt an enormous weight in her legs and arms. A torpor in her joints made it impossible for her to move. She could think of no other option than collapsing next to the latrines.

The girls in her class turned her in: Something is wrong with Irina Nikolayevna. She's on the bathroom floor curled up like a baby. The head of the school slapped her, not to bring her back to consciousness but to punish her. She brought Irina back to the infirmary. She'd been irresponsible and egoistic: Out of fear, indolence, or carelessness, she'd put the health of everyone in the school at risk. She not only deserved that pain but the punishment awaiting her when she recovered. The young intern also did not hesitate to reproach her.

Irina was delirious, but the scolding was bursting her eardrums. Every move the intern made seemed to her a reprisal, as when he stripped off her clothes by force or when he stuck a needle into her forearm. After several hours of torture, a nurse transferred her to the rear section of the dispensary, a desolate, yellowed room. Then she locked her in. She was to be held under strict quarantine until a definite diagnosis could be made. Irina had always heard about the spies that infiltrated Soviet society with the mission of undermining it—secret powers, viruses—but only now did she understand the reality of her fears. She had become a pernicious element, an infected body. She deserved isolation and punishment.

The next morning, or perhaps the next night—Irina had lost any notion of time because the room had no windows—the young doctor was replaced by an older physician, a tall, severe man with enormous eyebrows and a gritty voice who was no friendlier than his colleague. He asked Irina a long series of questions, most of them absurd or impertinent (who were her friends, what had she eaten during the previous week, about her personal hygiene, even if she'd had her period or sexual relations), and forced her to reconstruct her past and reveal her secrets. Irina could not understand what use that might have in curing her. Only later would she realize that the doctor wasn't trying to help her or prevent the spread of the epidemic but instead was trying to get to know and dominate her. While her body was stuffed with medication, her mind was absorbed by this guardian of health. Do I have chicken pox? The old man just went on examining her legs: I'm the doctor here. He didn't even have to raise his voice, because in his soft, concise words Irina discovered a terrible nuance that was much colder than the needles.

When she was alone again, wrapped in sheets of an indecipherable color, she began to cry. First silently, almost out of shame, and then hysterically. In that room, no one would hear her shouts, no one would come to console her. She imagined the worst, an army of microbes, bacteria, and germs attacking her tissue, destroying her little by little, devouring her. And she was unable to defend herself in this invisible, parallel world: The sickness made its home in her viscera. Irina only noticed the consequences of the struggle—fever, wounds, fatigue—but not the causes. She felt guilty and dejected. Perhaps she wasn't responsible for her suffering, but by the same token she hadn't managed to fight it off. The enemy had defeated her.

We humans are ambiguous creatures, structured after the double helix planted in our cells. Which explains why couples seem so obvious, so necessary to us, and which explains why we fabricate that stupid belief—that fraud—which makes us see ourselves as incomplete beings who are forced to chase after our lost other half. While she deserved the attention of other men, Irina Nikolayevna always thought herself a part—perhaps the least attractive part, but certainly the staunchest—of Arkady Ivanovich Granin.

Compared to her, he had an almost normal childhood. Let's be more precise: *Normality* is one of those inventions that have no connection with the facts, a generalization whose objective is to diminish our terror in the face of differences. In the USSR, normality was even more precarious, even by statistical standards. Arkady was born in October of 1929. His early years coincided with the high point of Stalinism, so he witnessed, or at least was a contemporary of, the great purges of 1936-1938. He must have heard about the 1939 visit of the Nazi minister Joachim von Ribbentrop to Moscow on the radio, and he had to flee Moscow at the outset of the Great Patriotic War in 1941. At the end of 1944, when he was fifteen, he entered the Red Army. Seen in this way, there was nothing ordinary about his childhood—it was caught up in the fluctuations of History—but if we consider that his father, Ivan Tijonovich Granin, never lost his position as an adjunct to Lavrentiy Beria, the all-powerful commissar of the NKVD, we may better understand why Arkady enjoyed myriad privileges—clothing, food, education—that had been denied to others his age.

Ivan Tijonovich Granin was neither coarse nor savage. An ethnic Russian, he'd nevertheless spent most of his life in Georgia, where, at the age of twelve, he started working for a mining company. When the Revolution broke out, he joined the Bolsheviks, fought against the nationalists in the civil war, and became an assistant to the feared Beria. He wasn't an executioner or a butcher, but a perfect bureaucrat, and the future *apparatchiki* would be based on his pattern: a severe, hardly majestic figure, always dressed in gray and hidden behind tiny glasses that made him look like a raccoon.

He never witnessed an interrogation in the NKVD basements, never stained his hands with blood, never wanted to learn about the fate of the millions of Russians, Ukrainians, Georgians, Moldavians, Balts, or Germans who were executed in his boss's dungeons. Ivan Tijonovich signed orders and memoranda, compiled archives, answered letters, took telephone messages, and commented on reports with the meticulousness of a craftsman. If some papers implied the execution of an enemy or of tens of thousands, he never revealed he knew a thing. Lavrentiy Beria thought his assistant was not very intelligent—that in fact he suffered a certain spiritual slowness—and never doubted his loyalty. He kept him at his side even during the period when, under orders from Stalin, he executed half of his collaborators.

In his memoirs, Arkady Ivanovich describes his father as an empty, inexpressive shadow, shut up in a will-to-perfection. Tall, sober, immaculate, Ivan Tijonovich survived his comrades thanks to his invisibility and his silence, and even when his old protector was accused of treason and executed at the order of the Politburo, he was never called to account; he retired with a pension that allowed him to continue his life as a shadow.

Ivan Tijonovich never spoke to his son about his work; actually, he never spoke to him about anything. For a long time, Arkady thought his father a mystery. Very belatedly he discovered that, behind his mortuary mask, his enormous dewlaps, his opaque gaze, and his fatigued movements there was no hidden internal struggle, no contradiction, only a creature dying of fear, willing to do anything to survive. Ivan Tijonovich showed he was more skillful than his colleagues, but his success did not depend on his intelligence or luck but on his ability to adapt. The old bureaucrat died when Arkady was thirty, in 1959. His death was as methodical as his existence: That day, he got up, dressed, and, when he was ready to have breakfast, fell asleep and switched off forever.

If his father was a kind of visitor who would sit in an armchair to listen to the radio or leaf through the paper, his mother, Yelena Pávlovna, was just the opposite: Loquacious and irritable, with enormous black eyes, younger than her husband, she suffered long periods of melancholy that would prostrate her for weeks. Arkady always knew his mother was a *sick woman*: That was what her husband called her and that was how neighbors and family members, with a certain veiled contempt, defined her. Whenever she sank into one of her depressive states, Yelena Pávlovna stopped being herself—her personality would change, and she would become someone else. Each of the features that made her jolly and lively would invert: Instead of being chatty, she would become impertinent; her enthusiasm bordered on delirium, and the intensity of her character would dissolve in the screams and tantrums of a child. The worst part, at least for those who lived with her, was her paranoia: She would lock herself in her room or in the bathroom, convinced that someone wanted to rape or murder her. There was no power on earth that could make her listen to reason, unless someone was willing to engage in hand-to-hand fighting with her, a hardly-recommendable course of action given the strength of her teeth. Yelena, apparently, did not suffer from any mental pathology—for most months of the year she was in perfect control of herself. According to the diagnosis given to Ivan Tijonovich by the Kremlin doctors, her attacks were the result of an infection she'd contracted during her childhood in Dagestan. It had been improperly treated, so the fever returned and drove her insane.

Accustomed to the mood changes of Beria and Stalin, Ivan Tijonovich treated her as if nothing was wrong. When his wife took refuge under the sheets or locked herself up in the bathroom, he would remain on the sidelines, ignoring a problem that was not his responsibility. For his three children, on the other hand, it was hell. Forced to comply with their father's strict discipline, they also had to take care of the domestic chores Yelena had abandoned. From the time he was five, Arkady took charge of his two brothers. Used to being the leader of his group of pioneers, he attempted to solve conflicts in the same way. He always acted in a rational way and did not allow an instant of doubt. No situation, no matter how risky it might seem, escaped his control. Only he was able to keep his family from falling apart.

In secret, Arkady lived a destroyed life. He could refuse to listen to his mother's howling and forget his father's indifference, relying on his gifts as an actor and on his almost military discipline, but he accumulated a growing resentment against both. The two of them were responsible for his rage, she because of what she did and he for what he didn't do. He found himself unable to forgive them. His idea of becoming a doctor was an act of pure revenge. Arkady was committed to overcoming sickness, any sickness, as if it were a personal enemy. As a soldier, as the Communist soldier he had to be, he took an interest in vaccinations, drugs, medicines, and medications with the goal of training himself with the arms necessary to face the enemy. In diametric opposition to Irina, Arkady always thought science was a battle field.

Ivan Tijonovich Granin educated his three children according to the dictates of the Party: Arkady was destined to be a perfect *Homo sovieticus*. According to the pedagogues and official scientists, Communism would construct a new type of human being, free of the errors, awkwardness, avarice, and meanness of our species. While architects remodeled the bombed-out cities and politicians reformed the social structure, Soviet educators tempered the youth. The discipline that controlled their intentions was not biology and not, as was thought in the West, sociology, but engineering. The Party ideologues conceived of man as a machine—blessed with pulleys, nuts, motors, and screws—to be studied and reformed. Just as a bridge or a dam is built (Stalin ordered hundreds of works like those without giving a second thought to the cost in human life), it was also possible to build a society where there was no room for capitalist egoism. *Homo sovieticus* would be one step forward, proof of our ability to improve.

Like millions of other children, Arkady Ivanovich was a guinea pig at the service of this dream, part of a gigantic experiment to prove the Party's theories. But, unlike his schoolmates, he suffered fewer privations, wrapped as he was in his father's privileges. Ivan Tijonovich's family had always lived in a small apartment, never in a *barak*, and they never had to share a bathroom or kitchen with fifteen or twenty strangers. While it can't be said his family was rich (wealth in the Soviet Union consisted in the absence of disgrace), the Granins enjoyed meat and milk even in the greatest periods of famine. In the classless society the USSR pretended to be, they belonged to that tiny elite that, as the jokes of the period put it, were more equal than others. When his father ordered him not to grow presumptuous about his advantages, Arkady had his first inkling about the fissures in the system. At the age of eight he joined the pioneers, and at thirteen he became a member of Komsomol. His father had indoctrinated him to believe the Party would take him in as his only and true home, and it was true. Many years later, forced to defend himself against accusations in the press, Arkady would finally recognize his youthful militancy. In his own defense, he would plead that in those days it was only possible to prosper within the structures of the Party.

Moved by the example of his father, or secretly trying to contradict him, Arkady set himself only one goal: to be the best. The best *in everything*. Or at least in everything possible. The best pioneer. The best student. The best scientist. Let's recall the scene: Arkady is wearing his pioneer uniform, proudly showing off his badges as he strolls through a yellowish plain. He contemplates the horizon and, as if it were an Eisenstein film, suddenly feels illuminated by the immensity of his surroundings, a Russian immensity that surpasses him, envelopes him, and devours him.

The young man kneels, but not to pray—the existence of God doesn't concern him—but to hold a leaf of Soviet grass between his fingers. He carefully studies it and finally says to himself in a low voice that some day he will understand its mystery and its silence, the silence of the world. The episode derives from the memoir Arkady wrote more than half a century later, and although the passage is saturated with romanticism, it transmits a central trait of his character: ambition. Arkady felt different, something separated him from other men and, contradicting his faith in socialism, made him irreplaceable. He was one of the chosen. He was to bring a great task to fruition, though he as yet did not know which. History would summon him by name.

Like Irina, Arkady Ivanovich never stopped being an *otlichnik*, an A student, the best student of his generation. His classmates would mock his arrogance, no matter how hard he worked to seem charming and generous. Arkady took advantage of another favorable circumstance: his success with women. The young pioneer wasn't simply brilliant, sensitive, and tenacious but attractive as well: From childhood on, his blond curls and frozen eyes—his mother's genes—fascinated his female cousins, and very soon he began to suffer the unsought-attention of the older girls. Arkady gave the impression he didn't take flattery seriously, but in fact he sought it out and wanted it. Western historians depict the socialist world as a watery cavern full of misery and rot, deprived of even a beam of sunlight, but even in such caverns human nature could prosper. Arkady always remembered his early years with tenderness, not for the things he had but for the possibilities that opened before him. It must be said: Arkady Ivanovich was a happy *Homo sovieticus.*

When Arkady met Vsevolod Andrónovich Birstein, an ungainly boy who had also matriculated in medicine at the Moscow Central University, he thought him a twin soul. A born leader needs a right hand man, a faithful companion, a shadow, and Vsevolod seemed created to occupy that position. Born in a peasant family, he had only come, thanks to his talent, to Moscow, that city of wide avenues, a few months earlier. Unlike Arkady's, his motives for studying medicine were more altruistic. He was concerned about the health of the people in his region and determined to prolong their lives.

Arkady and Vsevolod became inseparable. They spent long hours chatting, studying for examinations, or dissecting and classifying bones and tissue, their favorite pastime. To say they chatted would be a gross simplification: Arkady would launch into interminable speeches, and Vsevolod would absorb it all with a smile, ready from time to time to insert a critical note. The contrast between their temperaments was ideal: Arkady was extroverted, intense, tyrannical; Vsevolod astute, shrewd, and sardonic. Together they could conquer the world.

Why do you want to be a doctor, Arkady Ivanovich? I don't get it. You could have studied mathematics, physics, engineering, philosophy—anything. So why medicine? This question—they were spending a few days together at Vsevolod's father's dacha—stopped him dead in his tracks. Why not? That's no answer, Arkady Ivanovich. Well, just because. *Reductio ad absurdum.* When you're nineteen, any discussion becomes transcendent: to save humanity, concluded Arkady.

Vsevolod let one of his sardonic grimaces play over his face and didn't say another word. A typical Arkady statement, which reflected the difference between the two of them: He wanted to study medicine to save a few real people, while Arkady could only dream about the human race.

In 1948, the same year Arkady began his studies at Moscow Central University, an event took place with unexpected, not to say tragic or terrible, consequences for the future of medicine, biology, and science in general in the USSR. Without knowing it, Arkady was linked to the catastrophe. Between July 31st and August 7th that year, an extraordinary congress of the Academy of Agricultural Sciences of the Union took place. From that moment on, the Academy became the exclusive property of a man who didn't even bother to attend the meetings but who controlled them from a seat which was kept empty in his honor: Trofim Denisovich Lysenko. Despite some disturbances provoked by a few believers in formal genetics, the plenary meeting of the Academy imposed a credo for the nation's biologists, botanists, zoologists, and agronomists—the theories (to call them that) of the venerable academician. The order brooked no appeals of any sort: Throughout the Soviet Union, biology must be taught according to *michurian* criteria, the term Lysenko used for his ravings.

Gloomy, tough, devoid of the ability to smile, Lysenko had been planning his victory for twenty years. An article published in *Pravda* in 1927, "Fields in Winter," had brought him out of the shadows. According to this publication, which included a grim image of his face, Lysenko had cultivated varieties of wheat that were able to grow before the first frosts, wheat that would keep millions of peasants alive. As he confessed to a reporter, Trofim Denisovich had at first applied the theories of Gregor Mendel, but his non-conformist spirit made him see that the power of the genes and chromosomes was a bourgeois lie.

Mendel and his followers in the West asserted that the characteristics of living beings derived from inheritance, forgetting the environment. Frauds! Formalists! He on the other hand asserted that inheritance was a secondary factor and that external conditions determined the survival or extinction of plants and animals. Lamark was right: Learned traits could indeed be transmitted from parents to children. Lysenko's method, known as *vernalization*, consisted in applying various doses of heat to seeds until he succeeded in making the winter varieties turn into spring varieties. Unlike capitalist biologists, he, a poor agricultural technician, had discovered the secrets of evolution. He became famous overnight. Combining dialectical materialism with the ideas of the forgotten Russian agronomist Iván Michurín, Lysenko had discovered (or so he believed) the great error of Darwinism: There was no competition among species. Only imperialist scientists could declare nature a battle field—that was the source of Nazi perversions—when it was a fertile environment for cooperation.

As Director of the Odessa Genetic Institute, starting in 1929, Lysenko began his crusade for proletarian biology. One of the first to recognize his genius (to call it that) was the academician Isaac Prezent, who became the spokesman and official philosopher of Creative Darwinism, as he re-named Lysenko's nonsense. Meanwhile, Lysenko, puffed up with conceit, proclaimed his new articles of faith: No one knew what a species was. Or: The environment is the crucial factor in life. Or: Within a species there is no such thing as class struggle. According to him, species mutated in great leaps thanks to external conditions and their ability to adapt, not because of the slow modification of their genes (which implied, as one of his critics pointed out, that over time a house cat could give birth to a Bengal tiger.)

In 1935, the Little Father of the People attended one of Lysenko's conferences. At the end, not restraining his enthusiasm, he howled: Bravo, comrade, bravo! This was the equivalent of receiving the USSR's highest medal. Now Lysenko not only had the power to run Soviet scientific life but to determine *the fate of Soviet scientists.* In 1937, his supporters cancelled the International Genetics Congress, which was to be held in Moscow, and soon any argument in favor or Western genetics was considered a betrayal of the nation and the Party. The arrests of Lysenko's rivals took place starting in 1938, after the patriarch of proletarian biology was anointed as President of the Academy of Agricultural Sciences. It's at this point that this story gets entangled with Arkady Ivanovich's.

On July 16th, 1939, a few months before the start of World War II, Beria passed a memorandum to Ivan Tijonovich; it was for Stalin: a request for the arrest of Nikolai Ivanovich Vavilov, Director of the Plant Cultivation Institute and of the Institute of Genetics, a bitter enemy of Lysenko. Ivan Tijonovich used his harsh, cold style:

> *The NKVD has reviewed the materials relevant to the naming of T. D. Lysenko as President of the Academy of Agricultural Sciences. N. I. Vavilov and the bourgeois elements in the so-called*

> *school of "formal genetics" that he directs are organizing a systematic campaign to discredit Lysenko as a scientist.*
>
> *For this reason, I request your approval for the arrest of N. I. Vavilov.*

Demonstrating its efficiency, the Soviet security service detained Vavilov hours before Beria signed the document. With no notion that a plot against him was underway, Vavilov is on an excursion to the Carpathian Mountains, in search of rare plants and mushrooms for the Institute's collection. We can imagine him that way, alone and defenseless, classifying the various herbs, when two thugs in gray suits with harsh expressions on their faces surrounded and threatened him. The murderers punched him in the chest and on the nape of his neck, taking advantage of his weakness and his fear, and dragged him like a sack to the anonymous vehicle that delivered him to prison.

Vavilov was interrogated and tortured by the local NKVD agents for the remainder of the year, but his nightmare had hardly begun. In August of 1940, he was transferred to the Lubyanka, in Moscow, that city of wide avenues. Under orders from Beria, again prepared and transcribed by Ivan Tijonovich Granin, Lieutenant Aleksandar Jvat, famous for his brutality, took over the case.

Jvat felt no respect for the professor of biology: He'd spent the past several years destroying man after man, barely noticing their faces or personal histories. As he would confess forty years later, Vavilov's features never registered in his memory. Jvat carried out his labors with precision, moved by innate savagery. An expert on bacteria, Vavilov became bacteria himself. Jvat was trained to leave him alive, but he tried to destroy his resistance. Every night, an agent pulled Vavilov out of his cell, dragged him to the torture chamber—the *Kamera*—and left him in the arms of his executioner.

When the biologist was able to make out Jvat's face, he thought Jvat was stronger than him, a creature with greater possibilities of survival, but one who lacks that virtue, compassion, which makes humans human. Jvat was not a sadist, he took no pleasure, no delight. He twisted the skin and broke the joints until his victim vacillated, doubted, withdrew. When he'd transformed him into a wreck, when no more words, no more bile, no more blood spilled from his guts, when he was on the verge of fainting, Jvat returned Vavilov to his cell, where the biologist recovered over the course of the day, eating bread and a few sips of soup, only so that at seven the next evening the torture could begin again.

Jvat was systematic: In his notebook, he listed Vavilov's 215 interrogations, the 215 times he cornered him with questions, the 215 times he slapped him, the 215 times he kicked him in the testicles, the ankles, smashed his wrists, the 215 times he accused him of being a traitor, a dog, a coward, a weakling, an agent of imperialism, a renegade, a monarchist, of being one of Bujarin's accomplices, a rat, a worm . . . Vavilov didn't last long; his body demanded it, that body which is a dishrag, a piece of skin. At first, the scientist denied the accusations or at least dodged them, but after a few weeks he repeats the accusations word for word. Vavilov said: I am garbage. He said: I deserve death and more than death. He said: I am the most vile of creatures, the most miserable, the most unworthy. He said: I am no longer Vavilov the academician but Vavilov the renegade, the conspirator, the impious. The biologist confessed everything, even that he was the founder of, or that he sympathizes with, the Workers and Peasants Party, the regime's nightmare, even though it didn't really exist and was only an invention of the NKVD. Finally, Vavilov was no longer Vavilov. He was copy of Vavilov, the remains, the dregs of Vavilov.

If most of his colleagues and friends had stopped mentioning his name or had openly confirmed his treason, one of his old professors, the academician Príshniakov, had not forgotten his star student, and, putting his own life at risk, demanded he be set free. On two occasions, he visited Beria in Lubyanka, where—of course—the somber Iván Tijonovich Granin received him. Thanks to his efforts, or perhaps because Stalin and Beria think of using him as an example, they appointed a commission to evaluate his scientific contributions. And who was put in charge of approving the members of the commission? Lysenko, of course. Despite the protests of some members of the Academy, only *michurians* were included.

On May 9th—the German invasion was underway—the Military College of the Supreme Court of the USSR passed judgement on Vavilov. On July 4th, Vavilov signed his confession, prepared for him by the NKVD under the supervision of Ivan Tijonovich Granin. The accused was declared guilty and sentenced to death. The system followed its own rules and allowed Vavilov to appeal again and again, as if no one wanted to leave him in peace, as if the objective of Beria and Stalin was not to execute him but to burn him over a slow fire. The war altered daily routine, but it didn't annul sentences or condemnations. With the advance of the German troops, the Lubyanka prisoners were transferred to the Saratov jail.

Vavilov no longer remembered who he was, what he'd done: Fever was eating him up. Only when Ivan Granin informed Beria that the biologist was at the end of his rope did Beria order the torture stopped. Then, with infinite magnanimity, he dictated a new order, commuting the death sentence to a life sentence in prison. This time the efficiency of the NKVD left much to be desired: The message didn't reach the Saratov prison until the academician Vavilov, or at least the bacteria Vavilov, had already died of dystrophy. The prison doctors agreed that the cause of death was a fulminating lung infection.

Arkady learned of this story much later, when he himself had become a dissident. But his father's subterranean work managed to contaminate him, as if Lysenko had been right and the traits acquired by Ivan Tijonovich—his passive evil and his talent for survival—had been transmitted to his son. At the end of 1952, Arkady and Vsevolod were taking their final courses before being sent as residents to a rural hospital. Both had received the highest grades and were thinking of requesting a joint transfer. Despite the oppressive climate of the times—Stalin was sinking even more deeply into his paranoia—the two were sure they'd go on together.

Jew bastard! Arkady heard that expression in the corridors of the university just when he was getting ready to meet Vsevolod. The insult took him by surprise: He'd never thought about his friend as a Jew, doubted he really was a Jew, was sure his mother was Ukrainian . . . A few days later, in a pathology class, he noticed that the professor, a stuttering doctor named Márkov, allowed all his students to experiment with cadavers, all except Vsevolod.

Why does Márkov ignore you like that? I guess he doesn't like my face. I don't get it. What else could it be, Arkady Ivanovich? My last name isn't Petrov or Popov or Granin; it's Birstein.

The ominous signs piled up. First, the death of the actor Solomon Mijoels in January of 1948, then the dissolution of the Jewish Antifascist Committee, and finally the campaign against *cosmopolites*. As in practically every country in Europe, anti-Semitism was a common sentiment among Russians, but the ideas about equality put forth by Communism—and invented by a Jew—restrained their public expression. After what had taken place in Nazi Germany, the USSR could only allow itself to be *anti-Zionist*. But secretly, Soviet authorities erased all vestiges of Jewish culture from public life: They closed Jewish schools and theaters, abolished Jewish musical groups, threatened and jailed Jewish journalists, prohibited Jewish associations, and harassed Jewish leaders. By express order of the Little Father of the People, hundreds of Jews were expelled from public service, the army, scientific institutes, and universities. In August of 1952, twenty-four Jewish writers were locked up in the Lubyanka. The Great Leader and Teacher's suspicion of Jews spread to his subordinates, and soon the order to fire or jail Jews circulated through the Party's lines of command. Its echo reached the cells of the Moscow Central University.

They have no roots. They flirt with the West. They're traitors.

Such accusations were not directed at Vsevolod but at Arkady Ivanovich himself. His schoolmates surrounded him, imitating one another like monkeys. Those same students who had seemed more concerned about examinations than politics became beasts overnight. Arkady felt their inquisitive and severe little eyes scrutinizing his movements, trying to figure out if he too was a *cosmopolite* like Vsevolod: Only traitors were friends of traitors. If he wanted his rise to continue, he had no choice but to renounce his friendship: I had already noticed the cosmopolitan inclinations of Vsevolod Andrónovich. He isn't a bad Communist, but he ought to subject himself to a self-criticism and recognize that he's made a mistake.

While Arkady's words were an attempt to save Vsevolod from a dire fate—torture, exile, death—they carried the weight of a denunciation. The Party hyenas were only waiting to see a tiny scrap of carrion so they could all jump on it. Arkady had just sold out his friend, but the most serious dimension of it was that it hadn't cost him much work. Vsevolod Andrónovich Birstein was expelled from Moscow Central University only one year before he was to receive his medical degree. Arkady didn't even accompany him to the station to catch the train to Gorka, the city of his ancestors.

Many kilometers from there, in the Urals Polytechnical Institute, in Sverdlovsk, the bastion of ice, Irina Nikolayevna Sudayeva was getting bored. The School of Biochemistry was not what she'd imagined: Her classmates, 95% of them men—there was another woman but Irina never got to know her—were only interested in practical life, in getting a degree so they could work in some state-run business in the city.

Science wasn't their concern. For them, biochemistry was a pretext, a step in their road to being functionaries or, in the best case, directors of state-run businesses. They were not focused on research and did not feel any love for the organisms they were studying. The professors were no more attractive than the students: While the Urals Polytechnical Institute was reputedly one of the best universities in the nation, it suffered from an intolerable somnambulism. Irina did not want a mediocre or easy career. She wanted to explore life deeply. Perhaps if she'd had the influence necessary to matriculate in the biochemistry departments in Moscow or Leningrad, cities of wide avenues, her concerns would have been rewarded, but her condition, the daughter of a traitor, forced her to remain in Sverdlovsk, bastion of ice, where nothing was what it seemed.

Founded by Peter the Great with the name of Yekaterinburg, the city was always linked to war. From the surrounding mountains came the copper to make the cannon the Czar needed to defeat the Swedes. From that time on, the citizens had imposed a severe, detail-obsessed lifestyle on themselves, very distant from Moscow's pride or Saint Petersburg's elegance and dominated by a faith in work. Renamed in honor of one of Lenin's old comrades, the city, even before the Great Patriotic War, had become the seat of the country's war industry. Located in one of the richest mineral fields in the world—its inhabitants boasted they walked on soil where Mendeleev's entire periodic table of elements could be found—it seemed the ideal place to develop new weapons.

Around 1950, it was the third most productive region in the USSR, and hundreds of military and civilian businesses grew up in its suburbs. Sverdlovsk, bastion of ice, remained closed to foreign visitors, and its inhabitants had to pass through innumerable control points before leaving the city. It was a kind of miniature Soviet Union leaning against the Ural Mountains, where its virtues and vices were both exacerbated. Even so, the citizens showed their roots proudly, convinced they were an essential part of the country's progress.

Irina, on the other hand, felt like a prisoner. Luckily her introverted nature saved her from creating problems for herself: If she ever dared express her thoughts, she would never have been able to leave Sverdlovsk. Even though her comrades thought her odd, several tried to conquer her. Among her suitors, there was a vain, outsized rhinoceros, the captain of the volleyball team, a man she'd meet again in the future: Boris Yeltsin, a man with strong arms. But, like most of her admirers, the thickset sportsman did not satisfy her burning desire to learn.

Irina had just turned twenty—it was 1952—and she'd never kissed a man. She thought herself a pure substance, cloistered in her microscopic habitat, distanced from society. As paradoxical as it may sound, the field that interested her most was reproduction: All bacteria needed was a bit of food for them to multiply, overflowing the petri dishes where Irina kept them like pets. Those creatures seemed to have no other objective. With what avidity and spirit did they split, with what elegance did they separate, with what efficiency did they start the process anew! Irina would have liked human reproduction to be that simple, that orderly. What force made life so fragile and ubiquitous? At that time, it would never have occurred to Irina to contradict Lysenko's postulates, but she never doubted that genes governed evolution.

If Irina Nikolayevna was so free, so passionate about science, so eccentric when compared to the models of her era, and if she had managed to steer clear of men for so many years, why did she fall in love in such an absurd and immediate way with Yevgeny Konstantinovich Ponomariov? What did she feel when she discovered the industrial engineer, eight years her senior, adjunct professor at the university, handsome, luminous, and a bit devious, that would make her renounce her other obsessions? It's hard to know. One of the greatest enigmas of our species resides in our abstruse notions of pairing: When we choose our partner—that is, when we seek the other half of the DNA necessary for reproducing ourselves—we don't follow criteria that are biological or rational. Falling in love functions like voluntary blindness, a blemish or a fever that takes control of our minds and transforms us into zombies. As a justification, Irina told herself that a biologist could never understand mitosis if she didn't explore the meaning of carnal desire for herself.

Looking for a less complicated explanation, I'd dare to suggest that Irina fell in love with Yevgeny Konstantinovich because he didn't take the slightest interest in her. Unlike other boys—Yeltsin included—Yevgeny was only concerned with himself. He was arrogant and brusque, traits Irina found attractive. The engineer's overwhelming confidence disarmed her. Even so, she was the one who made the first move: Allow me to introduce myself. My name is Irina Nikolayevna Sudayeva. He told her his name, they exchanged a few conventional remarks—she detested empty small talk, *baltovnia*—and they said good-bye. That was that.

Irina dedicated herself to spying on Yevgeny as methodically as she supervised her bacteria. She soon learned that he went out with several girls, the most popular or pretty in the university. That didn't matter to Irina, because by observing his pairing rituals she would be able to determine his future reactions. Yevgeny never suspected he'd become his schoolmate's guinea pig. Overly self-absorbed, he lacked the intuition to realize he was being watched. Irina, accordingly, accumulated infinite notes about her *homo sapiens* in which she took account of his daily life, his schedules, movements, tastes, defects, and obsessions—he adored mirrors, covered up a slight limp, and got drunk on Friday afternoons—as well as his love affairs. After a while, Yevgeny did not seem so unreachable. He was one of those weak personalities that pass themselves off as strong—like those insects that develop stingers without venom—a rather common boy, blessed even with a certain sweetness, who did not have the courage to dig deeply into himself. Soon Irina decided the moment had come to put her theories into practice.

Yevgeny fell into the trap, but the transition from observer to active participant turned out to be harder than Irina imagined: He was uncontrollable, ardent, and awkward. He never stopped to think about her lack of experience, being used to the uninhibited girls he regularly saw. After a week, Irina ceased to be a virgin—the experience was more painful than interesting—and at the end of 1952, Yevgeny asked her to marry him. She accepted without giving the matter a second thought, convinced that this was the natural conclusion to her research. With that problem resolved, she could return to her microbes in peace.

If Irina behaved like an ascetic in the service of science, Arkady was just the opposite: a scientist with extraordinary talents who did not have to work to stand out. With a few hours of study and a few more in the laboratory, he got results that were more valuable and spectacular than anyone else's. Blessed by his militancy in the Party, his conciliatory character, and an almost ritual calmness, Arkady took delight in leading a parallel life, one that complimented his public life. In the Moscow of the mid-twentieth century there were few ways to have fun freely, even for someone who belonged to the *nomenklatura*, but Arkady made very sure he took advantage of every opportunity that turned up. While the majority of the citizens wore themselves out in fear, boredom, or alcoholism, he let himself be led by chance and passion, certain he was one of the chosen of the gods.

That night, Arkady felt a touch on his leg. Professor Kárpov, his host and preceptor, was offering his best food, even a bit of excellent caviar, and his guests smiled placidly at his anecdotes, which were more melancholy than amusing. Vodka heightened Russian sentimentality (I know whereof I speak), and, after a few seconds, Arkady again felt that subterranean friction: The thick thigh of Olga Kárpova was pressed up against his. The wife of the illustrious professor was much younger than her husband, had cobalt blue eyes, and a wide, clear forehead. When the other guests left the dining room, she slid her hand along Arkady's cheek. What a taste for risk! Ilárion Bogdánovich locks himself up in his laboratory every Tuesday between eight and five, she whispered in his ear.

Prostitution did not exist in the Soviet Union (at least according to the authorities), homosexuality became a crime in 1932, and a law dictated by Stalin in 1935 prohibited the publication, circulation, and reading of pornography. The ironclad morality of the Great Leader and Teacher was to be imitated by his subjects: Frivolity was considered a bourgeois vice and punished severely. Even so, the libertine spirit would materialize in the gaps of the closed system. Distanced from religion, young people had sexual relations beginning at the age of thirteen or fourteen, resulting in myriad pregnancies or abortions, while adultery was an unwritten law of social life.

Arkady gave Olga a self-possessed look and went back to the affected seriousness so characteristic of him: The other guests thought he was bored. The next Tuesday, at two in the afternoon, the young doctor escaped the university, dashed to Professor Kárpov's house, ran up the stairs, and knocked. Olga Serguéievna offered him a cup of tea and led him to her room. Every Tuesday Arkady would repeat this ceremony with the same zeal he studied pharmacology or attended Party meetings. *Madame* Kárpova became his best course: He learned more from her, from the subtlety of her voice and the heat of her cheeks, from her languid embraces, and loving pleas, than from all the classes he took from her husband.

Did he love her? The word never entered his mind. In 1953, the Soviet Union did not tolerate romanticism. Years later, a young woman would admit it: In the Soviet Union sex doesn't exist. Even so, he missed Olga, was obsessed by the scent of her hands, by her voice, by the tenuous conversations they had before and after sex. She listened to him intently, and her comments were never condescending, uncertain, or stinting. At the age of thirty-eight, Olga Serguéievna possessed an interior peace Arkady had never felt. What was it that determined a person's character?, he wondered. Why are some people, Olga for instance, prepared to face up to exterior difficulties while others seem condemned to wander endlessly? Was it environment, will, or education? Or was the truth about each of us inscribed there, within the body, in the cells?

There they lay, next to each other, or, rather, one on top of the other—Arkady on top of Olga, Olga receiving Arkady's body—when she said with her soft, implacable voice: We can't see each other any more. Arkady stood up. I'm sorry, Arkady Ivanovich, it's not possible. Circumspect, he looked at her—not asking anything, not questioning her decision, not wondering if Professor Kárpov's suspicion had grown or if she no longer desired him. Olga, worn-out and sad, did not accompany him to the door. They said good-bye and not see you next Tuesday. Then, when Arkady walked down the stairs for the last time, he realized two things: First, that he couldn't live without her, and then, that he was mistaken, that there was no doubt that he could live without her. He didn't know which of the two certainties was more painful.

During her time at the Urals Polytechnical Institute, Irina Nikolayevna never heard any of her professors express interest in genes, and, of course, no one spoke to her about DNA (identified midway through 1941 by Oswald Avery, Colin MacLeod, and Maclyn McCarty) as the repository of inheritance. Or at least not with the proper enthusiasm. Irina was no fool, so it wasn't long before she began to pester one of her professors, Mstislav Alexándrovich Slávnikov, an old student of Vavilov, to reveal the secrets of this new science to her. Though Slávnikov fled any polemic, he kept up to date on what was happening in the United States and Germany and was only waiting for Lysenko to die to make his discoveries public.

Slávnikov tried to avoid this problematic student, but Irina kept after him until the biologist, who was then seventy-one, accepted her as his student. Thanks to him, Irina found out firsthand about the dramatic history of Soviet genetics—Slávnikov talked to her for hours and hours about Vavilov—which, thanks to Lysenko, survived as a secret sect. Of all the possible chemical mixtures, the most explosive and dangerous is the combination of science and politics, the old man warned her.

Faithful to her Communist principles, Irina could not understand how science could turn into ideology: It was just the opposite, a neutral, pristine space beyond quotidian disputes. For her, Marxism-Leninism rested on a scientific foundation, and for that reason she could not stand

Lysenko's felonies. Comrade Stalin had to be ill-informed, otherwise he would never have supported a liar, a bad scientist.

Advised by Slávnikov, Irina specialized in microbiology. When she was in her laboratory, the outside world ceased to exist, and the cells became her only reality. Yevgeny Konstantinovich, her fiancé, did not understand this isolation (actually he understood nothing), but he thought that after the wedding, Irina would become like other women. The ceremony was set for March 10th, 1953. Neither Irina nor Yevgeny could imagine that a terrible and ominous event—a misfortune, a catastrophe—would force them to reschedule the wedding until April.

Six hours had gone by since the last signal, and Gori Zautashivili feared for his life. From the moment he began working for the Kremlin, he knew that something like this could happen: No matter what he did, he would ultimately be blamed, reprimanded, and perhaps even put on trial. He bit his lip. The alternatives were simple enough, either burst into the interior rooms without orders from above or just wait. Either decision could lead him to a court martial. If he dared to interrupt his boss (who wasn't a boss but a monster), waking him out of a sound sleep or disturbing his reading, his punishment would be obvious. If, on the other hand, he did nothing, if he stood there paralyzed and waiting as he had been during these six hours, perhaps something terrible or irreparable might happen. Zautashvili didn't dare to think about it. And then he wouldn't only lose his job but would end his days in a Gulag or in front of a firing squad. No one would help him choose the correct option: If he used the telephone to ask the opinion of Colonel Statírov, the colonel would wash his hands of the matter. Who in the world would want to bear this burden?

Zautashvili stared at the control panel: A greenish glow illuminated his face. What a relief!, he thought. Everything in order, the boss has finally gotten up. What a fright. He got ready to go on with his routine. But something wasn't right. The seconds passed, and the damned glow didn't disappear. Kúntsevo's alarm system constantly monitored the steel doors that protected the man behind them. A bulb went on when they opened and then went out automatically. But now the signal stayed on. Zautashvili stopped doubting and communicated with Statírov. Are you sure it isn't just a technical problem? Do you know what happens if you bother the boss for no good reason? Statírov trembled. Let's wait and see, he added, then we'll figure out what to do. And he added, as a kind of prayer, maybe it's nothing.

Zautashvili spent the longest hour of his life staring at that greenish glow. Once the test time had passed, he called Statírov again. He ordered Zautashvili to force his way into the dacha. Colonel, you have a higher rank, he excused himself. Statírov promised to come immediately (his stomach was aching), but in the meantime, Zautashvili would have to enter the leader's bedroom. The attendant approached the sacred room, the sanctum sanctorum of the Soviet Union, and kicked the door open. His legs refused to function, as if his muscles had atrophied. A few steps away, Stalin, or what was left of Stalin, a sick, weak version of Stalin, was stretched out on the floor, unconscious, perhaps dead. The Teacher was hugging his legs, his face buried on his knees. Statírov arrived at that moment. After making sure he was still breathing, they dragged the body and placed it on a divan in the center of the room. Then Statírov called Semion Ignátiev, the Minister of State Security, who ordered him to inform Beria of what had happened. Having been threatened by Stalin, Beria could not contain his joy. His orders were explicit: No one else must know of this.

Beria reached the Kúntsevo dacha at 3:00 A.M. on March 2nd, 1953. Contemplating his former comrade, his boss and enemy, the man who controlled the destiny of millions and who for months now had been thinking about destroying him, he felt relief. Perhaps fate had changed its mind, and he would not only escape execution but would occupy Stalin's place. Or at least keep a powerful position in the new government. To achieve that, Beria would have to pull all his strings as soon as possible, in order to recover control of the KGB and keep the respect of the presidium.

The doctors Beria had urgently summoned from Moscow—the greater part of the Kremlin medical staff was in the Lubyanka—arrived at 9:00 A.M. When they recognized Stalin, or what remained of Stalin, the doctors began to tremble. One approached to check his pulse, tripped over the rug, and broke his Baumanometer; another began a routine examination, but his hands wouldn't move. After a rapid inspection, they announced their verdict: the Great Leader and Teacher had suffered a hemorrhage in the left cerebral hemisphere. Very serous, yes, very serious, we do not think he will recover, how terrible, no . . . Beria was exultant.

While the higher-ups in the Party were being informed of the seriousness of Stalin's situation, Beria was recovering control of the apparatus. Having moved into Kúntsevo, he was the only one who spoke, the only one who decided, the owner of an inexhaustible energy (fueled by lots of alcohol). Khrushchev and Malenkov visited the Teacher that afternoon: Malenkov actually took off his shoes so he wouldn't disturb Stalin's sleep and approached him on tiptoe, as if he were a baby. By then Beria was tearing apart the last orders given by the tyrant, the arrest of Jewish doctors and the arrest of his own men. Speaking to a group of military men just released from Lubyanka, Beria did not hesitate: The pederast is dead! He couldn't believe that the others didn't share his joy.

All it took was for him to return home, where his wife was crying her eyes out, to realize the mystical control the Little Father had over his subjects. You really are odd, woman, he reproached her. If that miserable bastard dies, you and I are saved! Fear was encrusted on all hearts, emptying them of strength and courage. Only he, Beria, another Georgian, realized the vicious character of that mourning. If his plans became reality, Malenkov would become President, and he would see to it that the Soviet economy was reformed. He would eliminate the cult of personality and even pull the Red Army out of Germany. Under his command, the USSR wold finally be a modern nation. And no one would ever mention Stalin again, the dog.

Beria returned to Kúntsevo that afternoon, accompanied by Dr. Lukomski, a specialist on respiratory illnesses. Beria never stopped talking while the doctor conducted his examination. Can you assure me that Comrade Stalin will live? Lukomski whispered into Beria's ear: This man is a lost cause. To show he was willing to do the impossible to save the life of his boss, Beria summoned Dr. Nogovksy and his wife, Dr. Chesnokova. Both had founded reanimation studies and were considered experts in terminal cases. Their skills were of little use: Stalin was dying.

When Beria made his next visit, he found Svetlana Alliluyeva prostrate at her father's feet. What a moving scene, he thought, the loving daughter who, despite the infinite torments she's suffered, reconciles with her father at the end. If there was anything to be said in favor of Stalin, it was that his brutality made no exceptions for relatives: His family had suffered like any other, scores of his family members languished in jail or in exile, and just as many had been shot. Their crime? To know the Little Father of the People at too close a range.

Stalin no longer looked like Stalin. He'd gone back to being a Georgian seminarian, now old, dying, and rotten. His lips had acquired a blackish tinge, were full of cracks; the condition of his skin was no better, his cheeks and neck were covered with pustules and scabs, his swollen veins tracing out a labyrinth, his brow sweaty. His gray hair revealed large areas of his skull. But the most painful thing was his breathing: The air fought to stay out of his lungs. His wheezing sounded mechanical, inhuman, as if a bridge had collapsed inside him and the sound of the clattering nuts and bolts was escaping from his mouth.

When Vasili, Stalin's stupid, drunk son, burst into the room screaming his head off, the scene became grotesque. Those bastards killed my father, he shouted. Beria made a sign, and the security forces took him away. Just at that moment, the lips of the Great Leader and Teacher suddenly opened; no speech or economic meditation, no reflection on Slavic linguistics or dissertation on historical materialism came out of his mouth, not even a few words that might constitute a testament or epitaph, just a torrent of blood and bile. The clocks were striking twelve noon. For Beria, it was the long-awaited sign, the proof that there would be no going back.

Stalin's intimate circle gathered around his deathbed. From twelve noon until nine that night, the Little Father of the People died. His dark, almost black, face showed that decomposition had begun even before his death, as if the microbes and worms that inhabited his guts didn't want to wait another second before devouring him. Moved by a spasm or a final distillation of his will (a beast was still hidden inside that carrion), Stalin opened his eyes and looked at those present one by one, contemplated them with rage and fear, especially with fear. Then he raised his left arm and cursed them. His hand fell. His breathing stopped. One of the physicians leapt onto the bed, quickly administered a heart massage, and, as if the doctor were death, opened his mouth and kissed his lips. Nikita Khrushchev, furious, howled. Leave him in peace! It was 9:40 P.M., March 5th, 1953.

While in the corridors of the Kremlin the Party leaders conspired against one another to seize power—ultimately Beria would be shot, and Khrushchev would take Stalin's place—the lives of Arkady and Irina were also in turmoil. On April 2nd, Irina Nikolayevna and Yevgeny Konstantinovich went to the *Zags*, the omnipresent Registry of Vital Statistics, to validate their marriage. They had a party attended by scores of the groom's family members and friends, relatives from Moscow, the city of wide avenues, and even one from Vilnius (no one came from the bride's side). Irina and Yevgeny danced all night, got drunk, and fell asleep without making love, on opposite sides of the bed. Irina moved into Yevgeny's parents' house while the authorities went through the process of assigning them an apartment (in Sverdlovsk it took less time than in Moscow). Irina did not adapt well to these circumstances, but she tried to be courteous. She greeted everyone in the morning and spent the rest of the day holed up in her laboratory, obsessed with a life—microbial life—that was perhaps not so very different from her own.

About that time, Arkady had graduated and was studying to take the residents examination when a thickset and expansive man with leathery hands and an unequivocal gaze visited him at the university.

Comrade Granin. Yes. His visitor's skin looked like plastic. What a pleasure, comrade. Everyone talks about you. Everyone? Arkady didn't have to be very clever to intuit who this thug was. I won't beat around the bush, Arkady Ivanovich . . . We've examined your file, and we're convinced that you are perfect. Perfect? Extraordinary. Exactly the kind of person—in terms of character I mean—we're looking for. I don't like speechifying, Arkady Ivanovich, so I'll get right to the point, if that's all right with you? *All right with me?* Whatever you say.

Allow me to introduce myself. Lieutenant Colonel Gennady Isaácovich Petrenko. I'm a soldier, but, though I don't look like one, I'm a doctor. I'd like to invite you to work with us. The salary will be higher than you can imagine, but of course for a true Communist money doesn't matter. Only serving the nation, correct? *Correct?* Of course, Gennady Isaácovich. You will have at your disposal the best laboratories, you will be able to carry out your experiments as you could nowhere else. Science at the service of Communism, comrade. What more could you ask? *What more?* Nothing, comrade. I knew we could count on you, Arkady Ivanovich. I wasn't mistaken. Of course, the only inconvenience is that you will not be able to discuss this with anyone, not even with your family. Are you married, Arkady Ivanovich? No. Better, much better. Soon we'll have the relevant papers delivered to you, and in a few weeks your appointment will be ready. Wait for our instructions. Agreed? This time Arkady did not wait for his interlocutor to repeat the question: Agreed.

Thus, without thinking about it, without meditating for even a second, Arkady Ivanovich changed his destiny. Many years later he would recognize, in an act of public contrition, that at that moment he had sold his soul. And the worst thing was that he did so without expecting immortality or eternal youth in exchange for it. He considered himself a good soldier and a man of the Party. Two weeks later, he left for Sverdlovsk.

JENNIFER MOORE

United States of America, 1929-1970

It's already closed, sir. And? We've recovered a bit, sir. Jeremy Hammer's telephone voice became as squalid as his body: We can't sing a victory song, but we've gotten by this one. The worst is past. Are you sure, Hammer? Hundreds of kilometers away, Eddie sucked in his cheeks. Yes, Mister Moore, and, as if after consulting the teletype he himself didn't believe it, he added: We will survive. It was midday, October 26th, 1929, and Eddie Moore, baptized Edgar J. Moore, Jr., but known to his enemies as "Mad" Eddie, had spent all morning on the telephone from his country house on the outskirts of Philadelphia. Edgar had studied at Cornell, had been a soldier in France during the Great War, and was only concerned now about one thing: the future. And now the future, *his* future, was on the verge of disappearing. The Moore Utility Investment Company, the love of his life, was in danger of collapsing.

Edgar had just turned thirty-four, and, like all his ancestors, he was rich. Very rich. That's what the employees and operators in his business, his friends on Wall Street and in the government, the social column writers, and the finance analysts, and, of course, his wife Mary Ann all believed. But perhaps that wealth was an illusion, perhaps his mansion in Philadelphia, his yacht, his ten cars, the subsidiary offices of the MUIC scattered across the country, and the very farm where he was now drinking a Martini to calm his pounding heart were a mirage, a charade. Because, if his fears were confirmed—the ominous signs went all the way back to 1926, but like thousands of investors he too had ignored them—he was at risk to lose it all, *all*, in a few hours.

Moore was rather fleshy, though his back still did not have to support the 120 kilos he would weigh in old age. He had a reddish beard, and he wore Scotch cashmere suits even during summer. More than fear, he was beset by impotence: The market had recovered during the morning, but no one could guess what would happen when it reopened on Monday. Contrary to what Hammer was suggesting, the close might be just a pause. Moore knew human nature, and he feared that despair, fatigue, and anguish would settle on the investors as they thought things through over the weekend. People like him were usually avaricious and egoistic, even when their egoism led them to ruin. Confronted with the possibility of paying for their losses, they were fully capable of going insane and digging their own graves.

Moore lit a cigar with the same dexterity as his father. He didn't like cigars, but they represented that mixture of power and dandyism that had defined the Moores for generations. Imbeciles! he thought, how did we get to this point? Why didn't anyone foresee it, why didn't anyone have the balls to stop it? Stupid questions: Well-informed people knew the splendor of the market couldn't last, knew the tricks of brokers and analysts, or at least intuited them, and instead of worrying about the consequences—the infamous weight of the future—had taken advantage of the bonanza right down to the last second, squeezing the teats of capitalism until there wasn't a drop of milk left. No one in the government or on Wall Street had had the courage to fight the vices of the financial system. Sacrosanct liberal principles decreed that markets would regulate themselves—rather than intervene, the state should restrict itself to contemplating the debacle from a distance and simply *laissez-faire*. If there were mistakes, disproportions, abuses, the market should correct them on its own. The problem was that time had run out! The only future that existed was the opening of the market on Monday!

On tiptoe, Mary Ann entered the library where Edgar checked bills and received teletypes. Rather than walk, she slid along the floor with the stealth of a snake. Her only desire was to be liked by others (she said it herself), especially her husband. Every Sunday, at four in the afternoon, she entered his sanctuary, put on his slippers, and offered him a cup of tea: the perfect wife. Edgar loved her, even if he suspected that his wife feigned a happiness she would never experience. Everything all right, Eddie? No, we're up to our necks in shit, sweetheart, he thought to answer her. But instead he said, yes dear. A bit more tea, darling? No, thanks. Cookie? No. Should I open the curtains a little? I'm fine, Mary Ann. Sure? Damn it! Can't you see I'm busy?

Mary Ann fled, trembling. Now Edgar would have to dedicate several hours to consoling her. It would have to be later: For now, he had to concentrate on the financial condition of Moore Utility Investment. According to statistics, it was the eighth largest electrical company in the United States. The numbers were there, but something did not calculate, and Edgar knew it. He knew it!

The New York Stock Market had grown steadily since the end of the war—the Computing-Tabulating-Recording Company quintupled its earnings in five years, for example—but the measure, the gentlemanly behavior that had regulated financial life in other eras had vanished. That idiot Thomas Cochran, star analyst of Wall Street and proud friend of J.P. Morgan, had started the bubble of August 2nd, 1926. Instead of shutting up, he insisted on declaring General Electric an avatar of fiscal solidity. That very day, G.E. stock went up 11.5 points. Six percent of its value! So words could work miracles. It was so easy to become a millionaire! Only idiots hadn't made a fortune during those months.

Moore, who by that time had founded several companies, had created the MUIC at the end of 1924. His numbers rapidly grew, and when he finally placed stock in the New York market, it rose 7% in a month. Meanwhile, thousands of doctors, engineers, lawyers, university professors, and housewives, who until then had kept out of speculation because they thought it risky or perverse, hastily invested their savings. Edgar hummed the stupid ditty George Olsen had made popular during those days:

I'll have to see my broker
Find out what he can do.
'Cause I'm in the market for you.

There won't be a joker,
With margin I'm all through.
'Cause I want outright, it's true.

You're going up, up, up in my estimation,
I want a thousand shares of your caresses too.

We'll count the hugs and kisses,
When dividends are due,
'Cause I'm in the market for you.

The song described the spirit of those years, the Jazz Age, the age of Rudolph Valentino, Greta Garbo, Douglas Fairbanks, and Al Jolson: Everything was allowed, especially making money. The minor inconvenience was that paradise did not agree with the numbers.

In Autumn of 1928, Hammer delivered the preliminary report on MUIC and its monstrous losses. I'm afraid we're in the red, sir. But don't worry, I've found a way to fix it. Fix it? Yes, sir. This year hasn't been a good one, but that doesn't oblige us to compromise the future of a business as brilliant as this one, don't you think? If you authorize it, we can make a small adjustment in the company books.

If not illegal, those manipulations were suspicious: Edgar wasn't fooling himself, but he'd been born to conquer the future, not to lose it in a day. As he put it in a lecture at New York University, the value of a company should not be looked for in the cold numbers but in the men who were running it. Ultimately, he accepted Hammer's suggestions. On paper, the trick looked almost inoffensive. It was a matter of deferring a few long-term debts, assuming they'd be taken care of by next year's earnings, and calling the funds obtained from selling some property earnings—the old offices of the company in Columbus, Dayton, and Albany. Lots of companies—National City or Electric Power & Light—did their accounting in the same way. No one had any reason to be suspicious of the maneuver.

But Edgar was not sleeping peacefully. He had a sixth sense for business and felt negative vibrations. When, on Thursday, October 24th, 1929, investors lost their senses simultaneously and more than twelve million shares changed hands in just a few hours, Moore realized his worst fears had been confirmed. The stock exchange turned into a zoo: The screams of the brokers filled the hall, and the teletypes stalled, blocked up by an avidity that exceeded all predictions. The managers of the exchange closed the visitors gallery to keep the mob from pouring onto the trading floor. One word described what happened: panic. Panic over bankruptcy, panic over losing a lifetime's savings, panic over the prospect of poverty, indigence, the demands of wives and children, jail. Panic in the face of the abyss.

At lunch time, the losses diminished a bit, as if the cadaver of the U.S. economy were capable of reviving. MUIC stock, valued at $35.00 that Thursday, fell to $13.00 by midday and closed at $28.00: perhaps it was a false alarm. On Friday, trading volume fell to six million, and at the end of the day the flood receded. The crisis had been controlled by the market, just as the theoreticians expected. During the short time it was open on Saturday, the market performed without radical leaps and slept almost sweetly. Edgar was not tranquil: His instincts told him it wasn't over, that the situation would get worse, much worse.

On Saturday afternoon and on Sunday morning, Moore gave in to the evidence: Like a good Methodist, he accepted that what had happened had to happen. He apologized to Mary Ann, read Emerson, strolled through town, and, for a few moments, while he played poker with the Jenkins', he almost forgot his misfortune. After church, and after a lunch of cabbage soup and roast turkey, Edgar called his car to go back to New York, navel of the world. He had to be there on Monday, bright and early, to witness his salvation. Or his fall.

Hammer had been waiting for him at the MUIC offices since six that morning. The shadows under his eyes, and his hollow cheeks, did not promise anything good. The teletype hadn't stopped since the market opened. Just as Edgar feared, the volume was again extremely high, more than nine million shares. At the end of the day, the debacle looked unstoppable. Astonishing. Unlike Thursday, there was no recovery this time, only losses. Losses, losses, and more losses. MUIC stock closed at $12.00, a dollar less than the previous Thursday. Edgar considered getting drunk or killing himself, inaugurating the epidemic that would extend over the following four years, but that wasn't his style. He stared at the sunset along with Hammer, who never stopped jotting down numbers in his notebook. Moore went to bed at nine with a glass of brandy, his only concession to melancholy. He was unconcerned about the future.

On Tuesday, October 29th, 1929, more than sixteen million shares were sold. The stories of weeping, nervous breakdowns, instant madness, and suicide became ordinary, plunging the nation and the entire world into despair, poverty, and fear. Unable to meet its credit obligations, the Moore Utility Investment Company declared bankruptcy in December. Edgar J. Moore did not become poor (or at least not as poor as the majority of his contemporaries): He kept his house in Philadelphia and his fat bank account, but his dreams of glory vanished.

Under the pretext of mutual incompatibility, Mary Ann left him in March. In 1932, when the congressional hearings to determine who was responsible for the collapse began, Jeremy Hammer confessed that he was guilty of malfeasance and spent two years in jail. Though there was speculation about the possibility of arresting Moore, no charges were made against him. While his relationship with MUIC and Black Tuesday would mark his character for the rest of his life—his exuberance turned into acrimony and his prudence into hard conservatism—Edgar quickly reconstructed himself: He founded a candy factory (which he later sold to a holding company for a pot of money), joined the Republican Party in 1939, just before Pearl Harbor, was elected to Congress in 1946, and to the Senate in 1954.

Despite his experience during the crash, he always maintained solid ties with the finance community and Wall Street. When he was about to become a nationally prominent figure, he married his secretary, Ellen Bancroft. In 1945, his first daughter, Jennifer, was born, and in 1948, the second, Allison. While he was in the habit of lecturing them with anecdotes and moral tales, he never told them anything about the MUIC, the 1929 bankruptcy, or his first wife.

Senator Edgar J. Moore died in 1969, at the age of sixty-four, in an automobile accident that took place as he travelled from New York to his country house outside of Philadelphia. Along with several bank accounts, stock in various companies, investments, and property in three states, Senator Moore's daughters inherited his violent, ungovernable temper, his self-centered nature, and his fury. Also, a bullet-proof egoism. He died, but his greedy, savage genes were more active than ever, trapped in his daughter's slim bodies.

I hate saving her, I hate solving her problems, I hate the fact that she takes advantage of me. Jennifer shouted while Wells drove at top speed. The wind tangled her hair, but she insisted on keeping the window open: I'm suffocating, she shouted, I can't stand feeling locked up, I don't give a damn if you're freezing to death, understand? With an acquiescence he'd acquired over the years, her boyfriend gave in to her whim.

She always does the same thing, Jack, she went on without realizing he'd stopped listening to her. Allison's always got her excuse ready, she's younger, she blames all her problems on my father, encouraged by some stupid psychoanalytic thing. And when's all said and done, it's me who has to pick up the pieces. Don't you think enough is enough?

Jennifer had asked the same question several times, but she always needed to reconfirm the fact that Jack agreed. Anyone else would have run away from that combined avalanche of energy and doubts, but John H. Wells—everyone called him Jack—was different. No one was more stable (or as hypocritical), and it didn't bother him that Jennifer was as foolish as she was pretty, as intelligent as she was insecure. The first time they dated—he was still an undergraduate at the University of Pennsylvania—he knew he wanted to sleep with her, marry her, have children with her, spend the rest of his life with her. What was the source of that certainty? He was attracted by Jennifer's dry stare, her athletic legs, her magnetism, her fragile, violent nature, her attacks of jealousy, her indefatigable spirit, and her name (above all, her name). She was a whirlwind, and he had a special weakness for challenges: Wells hated tedium, and with Jennifer he could tear himself to shreds, be wounded, kill himself, or enjoy a reconciliation, but he would never be bored.

This is the last time. Allison's old enough to take responsibility for herself, don't you think? Before she wasn't like that. As a little girl she was sweet and even-tempered.

Wells knew that was untrue: Mrs. Moore had told him more than enough stories about the untamable sisters. They were only alike in their admiration and fear of their father and that interior strength, that inflexibility and persistence which made it impossible to argue with them. When they thought they were right, they let themselves be carried away by their burning desire for justice without taking anyone else into account.

Are you listening to me, Jack? Yes. It doesn't look that way. Wells focused on steering clear of the potholes. Obsequious as always, he put his hand on Jennifer's thigh: We're almost there. If we don't get back before ten, the Senator will kill you. *Me*? You're the only responsible adult around here. Jennifer's humor seemed controlled by some hidden force; sometimes she thought she was a tiger, others an ostrich.

The snow was falling in tiny, uniform—almost phony—flakes. Jennifer got out of the car and ran toward the police station. Her high heels sank into the mud while Wells followed, a few meters behind.

Allison had been held for more than seven hours after taking part in a protest march against the war in Vietnam. She gave the impression of being younger than the nineteen she was: Her hair was blond, like her sister's, but a bit finer and straight, cut even with her ears. But her childlike air concealed an uncontrollable fury. As soon as Jennifer entered the dimly-lit hall, she spotted her sister sitting between a pair of whores (that's how she defined them at first sight); her face didn't evinced a speck of contrition, she behaved like the mythological warrior women she would draw in her notebooks: stylized, amazingly beautiful amazons wearing gold and silver armor, always ready to fight mangy, always masculine, monsters. Before her sister could scold her, Allison kissed Wells on the lips.

While Jennifer finished up the paperwork—the desk sergeant trembled when he heard the Moore name—Allison pestered Wells with sexual innuendo: Sorry, Jack, I didn't want to interrupt you. I imagine you were, well, you know . . . Though the situation was one that had been repeating itself for years now, Wells blushed (the jerk still retained a pinch of modesty in those days). Time to go.

Jennifer grabbed her sister's arm and dragged her to the exit. In the car, when she was getting ready to launch into another sermon, Allison bellowed: I only ask one thing of you, dear sister, no more speeches, okay? Jack is tired and has to concentrate so we don't get killed. If our father knew what you've done, Jennifer reproached her. He won't find out, unless you tell him, and in that case you'd have to explain what you were doing with Jack at that hour. Your sister is right, Wells intervened, all three of us should calm down. Let's listen to some music. The radio was broadcasting a song by The Temptations:

I've got so much honey,
The bees envy me.
I've got a sweeter song
Than the birds in the trees.
Well, I guess you'll say
What can make me feel this way?
My girl,
Talkin' 'bout my girl.
Oooh,
Hoooo.

As little girls, they both submitted to paternal dictates, pretending to be the well-mannered rivals he was trying to shape. Because she was the older, Jennifer had to start the race—according to Allison their father treated them like horses—and from the very beginning she satisfied the Senator's requirements: In first grade, she got A+ in all her courses, won the spelling bee, came in second in mathematics, acted the part of the princess in the end-of-the-year play, and became the pet of Miss Connolly, the head of the school.

It was also about then that Jennifer began to show signs of hyperactivity, getting out of control at the slightest provocation, unable to control her fits of anger—on one occasion she almost poked out the eye of another little girl who made fun of her dress—though she tried to be charming. Her yearbook pictures show her as languid and pretty, conscious of her attractiveness, and at the same time showing a tendency toward terror or surprise, while her long, carefully-combed curls covered half her face. Her favorite day was the first of every month, when she would come home and brag about her prizes and special mentions. The Senator would stop working and hug her until she was about to faint: Excellent, sweetheart, excellent.

Those words would turn Jennifer back into the happiest girl on earth. A few steps back, her mother nodded. And, hidden under the table, little Allison admired her sister with her enormous violet eyes. When they began to go to school together—they were only a few years apart—the real competition began. Senator Moore always painted the world as a life-or-death struggle. Jennifer thought her sister was robbing her of the leading role she'd won over the years. Allison seemed cleverer, prettier, and nicer, and Jennifer was afraid she wasn't as good as Allison. By the same token, Allison thought Jennifer, whom she perceived as distant and unreachable, was out of her league. Allison only aspired to imitate her. Her goal was not to outdo her older sister but to make her proud of her efforts.

At the end of the fourth grade, Jennifer's nightmare came true: Her sister got the highest grades in the school, stealing her crown. The Senator didn't even notice the tiny percentage separated his daughters grades. Puffed up with pride over their performance, he lectured them as usual and celebrated their triumph with a pair of identical dolls. I never made distinctions, he would tell Allison years later, during one of their quarrels. And he really believed it. He always gave them the same gifts, the same number of kisses, celebrated their birthdays in similar ways, praised or punished them in the same balanced way. He proclaimed his fairness to anyone who cared to listen: to Ellen, to his friends, and to his diary. It wasn't a belief but a dogma of his personal religion, a norm he'd established when Allison was born.

But it wasn't true. Or it was, but only for him, because everyone else knew that Jennifer was his favorite. That disparity was not the result of a conscious decision made by the Senator but to an intimate weakness, expressed in little winks, isolated sentences, and those little slips that only family members know how to decipher. Jennifer's birth changed his life and gave him the strength to overcome the colon cancer that had left him hopeless: His first-born's little hands brought tears to his eyes. But by the time Ellen gave birth the second time, he already knew the meaning of paternity and did not experience the same joy (aside from the fact that he'd been hoping for a boy), though he always tried to hide his feelings.

By the end of the fifth grade, things had returned to normal. Jennifer was a few percentage points ahead, perhaps because Allison preferred the serenity of second place to the inevitable confrontations of first place. Allison did not seek perfection but love. Meanwhile, Jennifer had begun the slow process of remodeling her character. Though she always said she remembered having a rich and full childhood, she turned into an unsociable and irresolute adolescent. She felt as if someone was forcing her to commit imprudent acts or to hurt others for no reason, a typical trait of the Moore clan. Tormented by her own fear, Jennifer kept Allison out of her intimate space. Allison, not understanding anything, only suffered.

When she turned sixteen, Jennifer withdrew to her room, and began reading, astonished, shocked, and a bit horrified by the diaries she'd written when she was ten. The world she remembered was simply not there: Instead of the idyllic environment full of tenderness and well-being she'd wanted to describe, she discovered a solitary little girl, changeable, banal, standoffish. . . and ambitious. Her father had convinced her that the most important thing in life was to pile up her winnings, physical and sentimental, as if they were chips in a poker game.

She spent a week hidden away between the sheets—claiming she had a cold and violent headaches—more irritable than ever. Allison watched her from the doorway without daring to bother her. The one time she did try to talk to her, Jennifer threw her dolls in her face and shouted *whore*, a word little Allison didn't know (and which would soon obsess her). That time, intimidated by her abuse, Senator Moore didn't dare to scold her.

But Jennifer's anger vanished as rapidly as it had appeared. After five days, she got out of bed, spent an hour dressing, and went off to school as if nothing had happened. She'd made a decision: She would not go on suffering. As simple as that. And to a certain degree, she achieved her goal. Her outbursts may not have diminished, but she at least began to enjoy them. Little by little she learned to control herself. But to do that—to survive—she had to pay a price: She had to renounce her family. She loved her parents and her sister, but it was they who were responsible for her pain. Only by distancing herself from them would she be able to be at peace with herself. At eighteen, she'd become an iceberg.

You think that rich bitch is going to take you seriously? Theodore Wells raised his head from the desk: a tortoise. His eyes were bloodshot and his skin covered with warts, though Jack couldn't tell if they were the result of his insomnia or his drinking. His pen shook in his left, ink-stained hand (both of them were left-handed), Even though he spent his entire day in his office on Moravian Street, the old man would go home loaded with invoices, bills, accounts, and financial statements that he would check over until dawn. Forget her, Theodore poured him a shot of bourbon, before she forgets you. She'll use you, my boy. You don't belong to her class.

Jack was boiling: I'm going to marry her. His father eyed him sarcastically. Don't talk nonsense. You're not marrying anyone. Do you really think a woman like that would want to marry you? Listen to me, Dad, I'm going to marry Jennifer Moore.

Theodore got up and poured himself another drink. Want one? It would do you good. You know I don't drink, Dad. How long have you been going out with her? Three weeks. And how old is she, if you don't mind my asking? Seventeen. The old man roared with laughter: And you think Senator Moore is going to let his seventeen-year-old daughter marry a . . . a . . . marry you? I'm in no hurry, dad. I'll marry her five years from now, in exactly five years. Want to bet? Theo went back to his accounts. Have fun if you like, but I'd suggest one thing: Don't fall in love.

Theodore Wells had never been expansive or open, but since the death of his wife he'd lived like a mole. It was his fault that Jack hated numbers: Those bugs ate neurons. He'd seen first-hand how they'd eaten away his father's brain, how they'd excised his emotions, how they'd left him an invalid. Days, weeks, months, years, the same arithmetic, the same numbers, losing his sight and his reason. Boys dreamed about being firemen or doctors, even lawyers, but never *accountants*. . . The very word made Jack nauseous, and the worst part of it was that his father never even earned enough to buy himself a tie. If counting money was a lamentable thing, counting other people's money bordered on the shameless.

After years of being last in his class—and putting up with his father's bitter jokes—Jack decided one fine day that he couldn't go on that way. Little by little he improved his grades until he had an honorable average. In his last year of high school, he sent applications to the best universities in the country. After several rejections, he received a scholarship from the University of Pennsylvania and took a solemn oath: He would study to become rich—and to conquer Jennifer Moore and all the other women who crossed his path—but he'd never dirty his hands with other people's money.

Introduce me to that girl, he asked one of his classmates during a party for new students. But that's Senator Moore's daughter. He'd be hearing that remark repeated endlessly all his life, transforming him first into the boyfriend of Senator Moore's daughter, then into the fiancé, of Senator Moore's daughter, and finally into Senator Moore's son-in-law. To him it never mattered.

Up close, Jennifer didn't seem so imposing. Aren't you bored? Until a second ago I wasn't. Want me to tell you something that will amuse you for the rest of the evening? The girl was wearing a white dress, her shoulders bare. As always when she felt threatened, she bit her upper lip. I'm listening. You're going to think I'm nuts, but today, November 23rd, 1961, I want to tell you that you're going to end up marrying me. You're right. You are nuts. Let me finish: In a few years, you and I will be man and wife, we'll have children, and be happy, very happy. Somewhere inside Jennifer's laugh there was a dash of fear. What absolute stupidity.

Senator Moore's daughter turned her back on him and tried to avoid him for the rest of the party. Jack didn't lose heart (you've got to recognize the fact that the fool was persistent), and from that day on he did everything he could to be near her, showering her with roses and letters. He chased after her as she left school and finally cornered her at another party. She had neither the courage nor the desire to refuse to speak with him: For heaven's sake then, pick me up on Friday. But let's get one thing clear: It will not be a date. What then? We'll have dinner together and that's it. What's the difference between a date and a date that isn't a date? Jack Wells, you really are an idiot. At seven. And don't ring the bell, I'll be on the porch.

Jack had to wait forty minutes until she deigned to leave, wearing a horrible magenta dress. What distinguishes a date from a date that isn't a date is that at the end you will not be allowed to kiss me, she clarified. Wells brought her to a French restaurant, ready to spend every cent he had. The investment paid off. And why not? Do you always ask such stupid questions? Wells ate an enormous steak while Jennifer nibbled some of her salad. Before she went back into her house, she kissed him. You weren't allowed to do it, but I am, and this is still not a date.

For a few moments, Jack stood outside the Moore mansion—opposite the Phrygian columns, the triangular lintel over the door, and the beautifully-tended French garden—in ecstasy. And, without a trace of shame, said to himself: Some day, all this will be mine.

Allison, instead of trying to amuse herself, attempted to change the world. For weeks she'd been devouring the books Susan had lent her: Wilhelm Reich's *The Function of the Orgasm*, Emma Goldman's *The Tragedy of Woman's Emancipation*, and Rose Pesotta's *Bread Upon the Waters*. Then, on the radio, she heard a speech by Noam Chomsky denouncing the war, and she thought she could no longer go on doing nothing. Susan was fascinated by her plan: They would become *real* revolutionaries. Both of them imagined themselves as female reincarnations of Sacco and Vanzetti, with the responsibility to arouse revolutionary consciousness among the haughty students of the Philadelphia High School for Girls, the institution which had been proudly forming the mothers and wives of the city since 1848.

Senator Moore had always wanted his daughters educated there. When his wife forgot about the application deadline, he intervened, convincing the head mistress, Miss Connolly, to allow Jennifer to enter late. There was no need for him to intervene in Allison's case: the Philadelphia High School for Girls was inscribed in her destiny. For the younger Miss Moore it was a nightmare. Aside from being her in sister's shadow, she had to put up with a code of conduct that had been handed down from the nineteenth century. At first, her timidity kept her from confronting her teachers—she liked to push things to the limit but without putting her grades at risk—but the day finally came when she could no longer contain her disgust. Until that moment, her teachers had lamented the fact that she lacked her family's spirit, though they did appreciate her sincerity and expansiveness, and the fact that her character seemed less wild than Jennifer's.

The arrival of Susan eliminated her timidity. Adopted by a family of shopkeepers, her friend did not look like the other girls in her class. She was fat, insolent, and rude. She didn't care about her appearance and did nothing but read thick books by improbable authors (books she acquired from an obscure downtown shop). Allison overcame her repugnance at Susan's muddy shoes and bitten-down nails: This extraterrestrial fascinated her. I'm an anarchist, said Susan by way of introducing herself. An anarchist? Yes, stupid, and she immediately handed Allison one of her favorite works, a collection of Lucy Parsons's speeches from 1910.

In those bilious pages, Allison found a new way to view the world. She instantly adored the author, that turbulent labor organizer from Chicago whose real name was Lucy Ella González. And her admiration only grew when she discovered, in an old encyclopedia buried in the basement of the public library, that Lucy's husband had been sentenced to death for placing a bomb in Haymarket Square in 1886. Allison memorized the farewell letter Albert wrote to Lucy from his cell.

> *My dear wife,*
>
> *Our verdict this morning cheers the hearts of tyrants throughout the world, and the result will be celebrated by King Capital in its drunken feast of flowing wine from Chicago to St. Petersburg. Nevertheless, our death sentence is the handwriting on the wall, foretelling the downfall of hate, malice, hypocrisy, judicial murder, oppression, and the domination of man over his fellow man. The oppressed of the earth are writhing in their legal chains. The giant Labor is awakening. The masses, aroused from their stupor, will snap their petty chains like reeds in the whirlwind.*

But what she liked most was the ending: "Wife, living or dead, we are as one. For you my affection is everlasting. For the People. Humanity. I cry out again and again in the doomed victim's cell: Liberty! Justice! Equality!" Allison wept each time she repeated those words. Lucy's battle to defend her lover's ideals seemed so romantic! Comparing the fate of Lucy and Albert with her own—the heroism and commitment of that couple against the frivolity surrounding her—she felt obtuse and wretched. How blind she was, how stupid, how egoistic: While she wallowed in luxury, millions of people suffered.

In addition to carefully studying the books Susan recommended—anarchism became their secret—Allison began to read newspapers and take an interest in news broadcasts. The two girls turned the Philadelphia Public Library into their barracks. When school was out, they set up shop in the long reading rooms and memorized stories of heroes and villains. While their classmates adored The Beatles or watched *Bewitched*, they thought themselves the heirs of Thomas Paine, Bakunin, and Che Guevara. In no time they realized that if they really wanted to change the world, they had to oppose the war in Vietnam. (At no time did Allison recall that she was the daughter of Senator Moore, one of the principal instigators of the war in Southeast Asia.)

Digging in the library stacks, they came on a worn-out volume that contained instructions for making Molotov cocktails. It was a clear signal: They'd blow one up in the Philadelphia High School for Girls, that model of authoritarian power. Putting the bomb together was as much fun as a puzzle—both girls would remember that winter as the most exciting time in their lives—but they were not so naïve that they didn't take into account the consequences of their challenge. In a meticulous ceremony, which partook equally of an initiation rite and scout pledge, they pledged eternal loyalty to each other.

Following a careful plan, they put their threat against the military-industrial complex (in their case, the academic complex) into effect on April 15th, 1965. At 6:30 A.M., when the school was still empty, they threw four bombs from a roof. The fire spread through a bed of azaleas and tulips planted by the third-grade girls. They had nothing against flowers or little girls, they told each other, it was simply a military objective. The janitor put out the fire with no difficulty, but the scandal was huge. The head mistress suspended classes. In the halls, it was rumored that the guilty parties were Communists, but Allison and Susan knew that their act would be meaningless if it was taken as a joke or a provocation. So, forced to vindicate it, they sent the head mistress a *Manifesto against the War*, a summary of their desires for peace and a statement of their opposition to the barbarities being committed in Vietnam "by young people like us."

As soon as she recognized the handwriting, Miss Connolly almost fainted: One of the authors of the attack was the younger daughter of Senator Moore. Now she not only had to worry about the institution's good name but also about the reaction of the irascible politician: The fault lay with that pal of hers, Susan Anderson. We never liked that girl, the state forces us to accept all kinds of people. Moore listened to her in silence. I'm very sorry, Senator.

Moore's voice sounded frozen, from beyond the grave: What do you suggest, Miss Connolly? She'd been head of the school for twenty years, and nothing like this had ever happened: Allison is a good girl who's been led astray by bad influences. We wouldn't want this incident to be a stain on her record. At the same time, we can't overlook such a serious trespass. You'll have to agree with me, Senator: Your daughter will have to think things over. We can't let her throw her future out the window. I'm listening, Miss Connolly. If Allison publicly apologizes to her teachers and schoolmates, I will re-admit her. It's the only solution, Senator. So be it. We knew you'd understand, Senator. Moore got out of his chair: And what about her friend? Oh, Senator, that girl is hopeless.

Allison expected shouts, a thorough dressing-down, even a beating from her father. But the Senator seemed worn out: Long shadows under his eyes darkened his face. He showed no rage, just disillusionment. You'll have to apologize, Allison. Never! That wasn't a request. You will have to recognize your error, and that will be it. What about Susan? Susan will have to find someplace else to study. Then I'll go with her! The Senator sounded depressed: I'm sorry, but I won't permit that.

Allison did not understand her father's unusual calm: She'd never seen him so alone, so sad. If Susan is expelled, I'll go with her. Tomorrow you will deliver your apology, the Senator concluded. And that is what happened. Allison did not dare challenge him. She'd prepared herself to resist his threats but not to face his melancholy. That night, the longest in her life, she tried to convince herself she wouldn't betray Susan, but fear made her abandon her principles.

Yes, I confess. Yes, I confess. Yes, I confess.

Allison swallowed her words, and then, standing before the entire teaching staff, broken by fatigue and guilt, she asked forgiveness. But the worst punishment awaited her at home, in the eyes of her father. That day broke the link between them: Allison did not lose the Senator's affection but something more valuable and undefinable. He always told her he'd forgiven her, but he never again looked at her in the same way (he never again looked at her in the way he looked at Jennifer). Unable to stand this silent disillusionment, Allison saw to it that Miss Connolly was forced to expel her a few months later. The Philadelphia High

School for Girls was now behind her, and this time it didn't even occur to her father to intervene on her behalf.

Of course I love you. When it came to sex, Jack Wells had yet to learn the art of cynicism. While he massaged the feet of Lynn, the waitress he'd recently been seeing, and while he focused his full attention on her pubis, he really believed it. If someone had asked him what he felt for Jennifer, to whom he'd gotten engaged three months earlier, he would have answered with no remorse: I love her. Both propositions were not contradictory for him. When he was with Lynn, or, rather, on top of or inside Lynn, he thought of no one else. The rest of the time, when he was showering, having breakfast, attending classes on finance or statistics, watching film, or writing his intricate weekly letters, Wells thought only about Jennifer, the woman he wanted to marry as soon as he finished his degree at Wharton.

Lynn straddled Wells. Every time he slept with her, he felt liberated, as if instead of trapping him between her thighs, that seventeen-year-old blond were breaking his hips. With her, sex was a game, a mere rotation of positions. Sex with Lynn was the best possible arrangement: Docile, vibrant, reckless, she made him enjoy himself in exchange for very little. A very small investment—dinner at Harry's, a couple of beers, a few flattering words—allowed him to take control of her body with no reservations. Jennifer, on the other hand, was a high-risk investment: Perhaps more exciting—getting her out of her clothes was a challenge—but the results varied according to her mood.

While at first Jennifer rejected all physical contact, hiding her conservatism behind all sorts of rationales, she had, since the engagement, made an effort to satisfy the carnal desires of her fiancé. In bed, Jennifer behaved as though outside herself: Nervous, imperious, a bit awkward, but despite all that endowed with an innate sensuality. Her firm body, without a gram of fat on it, drove Wells wild. She kissed him sweetly and let herself be caressed violently, but she suffered with penetration. Like an orchestra director, she never stopped telling her lover to change the rhythm and tempo of his movements. The end of her orgasms, if she managed to have them, left her paralyzed and half asleep, indifferent to what was happening to him.

If making love to Jennifer resembled buying stock in a start-up, Lynn comported herself like a government bond. Following his lessons at Wharton, Wells tried to diversify his portfolio: If the price of the first dropped, he could always make up his losses with the second. He had no scruples about his double life: Jennifer would never find out about his peccadillos; that was proof of his love. He could sleep with Lynn, Maylis, Samantha, or anyone he chose, as long as they belonged to a different social class: That way there was no possibility his fiancée would find out.

As luck would have it, Jennifer wasn't even living in the same city. Though she could have gone to college at the University of Pennsylvania or Penn State to be closer to him and to her family, she had applied to four Ivy League universities, all of which accepted her. She opted for Harvard where, despite her father's reservations, she hoped to become John Kenneth Galbraith's student. Jennifer wanted to lay the most solid of foundations for her future, as if she were building a fortress. She loved Jack, but she would never sacrifice her professional life for anyone, especially not a man. They were at least united by parallel ambitions; like him, Jennifer also wanted *everything*: a happy family, and an invulnerable professional success.

Wells said he regretted the separation, but he took advantage of its advantages. Once a month he travelled to Boston, but he dedicated the rest of his time to his only desire: accumulating the capital necessary to start his own business. All his energies were focused on the stock market, that battle ground. At the time, Wells had a hero, Gerry Tsai, formerly a star at Fidelity Fund and, since 1965, Director of the Manhattan Fund. Born in Shanghai, Gerry was the new wizard of the New York Stock market—a wonder-worker according to his clients—and perhaps the best investment manager in the business. He'd become famous not only for his gains—he always bet on glamorous businesses like Polaroid or Xerox—but for his fascination with risky sports and his mania for flying helicopters. At least until a forced landing in the Hudson River made him give it up.

Like thousands of small investors, Wells confided blindly in Tsai. But he was interested more in the logic that enabled Tsai to make money than in actually making it himself. In the financial world, people said Tsai was inscrutable, and as soon as he bought or sold a stock, his competitors rushed to copy him. Wells knew *Security Analysis* and *The Theory of Investment Value*, the classic handbooks on the subject, by heart and had spent years studying the valuation of stocks, convinced that sooner or later he would find out how to decipher the success of his manager.

Tsai intuited that the markets were not efficient, a theory the experts espoused. Inspired by their faith in capital, economists believed that stocks would always end up acquiring their *real* value. According to that model, no individual could outwit the collective intelligence of millions of stockholders. Tsai, on the other hand, thought that perhaps in a perfect world markets would also be perfect, but in the world he happened to be living in—a world of inequality, where a few had a great deal and the majority almost nothing—information was not distributed in an egalitarian way. In certain moments, a few people could know more than others. It was then that the most astute (the fittest in evolutionary terms) could make spectacular profits. The problem was to guess the exact instant in which to buy or sell, before the market's invisible hand corrected the inequities in information. As in sex, winning in the market was simply a matter of time.

At the outset of 1966, while he was studying for his final examinations at Wharton, Wells managed to accumulate $15,000, thanks, in good measure, to a loan from Jennifer's father. He decided to put what he thought he'd learned from Tsai to the test. If his prognostications were correct, the technology sector would have a spectacular growth spurt that year. Senator Moore was not convinced by his explanations, perhaps because they greatly resembled the very ones he'd used before the 1929 crash, but he went ahead and supported his daughter's future husband. Jack didn't seem a good match to him, but at least they spoke the same language.

On February 9th, Jack's prophecies seemed to come true: The Dow Jones reached 1,001.11 points and the stocks of Ling-Temco-Vought, the company Jack invested in, went up almost a dollar. LTV was one of the first conglomerates to appear in the United States, and James Ling, its CEO, was the most fashionable of executives: He'd just bought a $3,000,000 mansion in Dallas which included a $14,000 bathroom. He admired Field Marshall Rommel, and his name turned up more often in the gossip sheets than in the *Wall Street Journal*. But Jack's optimism deflated very soon: The economic cycle had reached its peak in 1965 and then went into decline. The Dow Jones went down 20% in the following months, recovered slightly in 1967, and went down 30% in 1968. The market may not have been efficient or perfect, but it wasn't child's play either. After he paid back Senator Moore, Jack saw that while his loses weren't outrageous, they were certainly revelatory: His dream of a technological business would have to wait for better times.

In the fall of 1968, Jack, forced by circumstance, accepted the position of chief of purchases with Lockhead Pharmaceuticals, a company that specialized in the manufacture of stethoscopes, baumanometers, and other medical devices. It was based in Trenton, New Jersey. A few weeks before starting his new job, on September 14th, 1968, he married Jennifer in a glamorous ceremony held at the Moore residence. There were more than two thousand guests. His riskiest investment had paid off.

Open your mouth. I don't want to. You can rely on me. Cameron leaned over her lips as if he were going to kiss her again: Good, what a good girl. Allison felt a bitter aftertaste in her mouth and tried to swallow the pill as soon as she could, afraid she might vomit. In the three weeks she'd spent in public high school, she'd learned more about reality than she had in all her years at the Philadelphia High School for Girls. Life was not how her strict, embittered schoolmistresses had painted it and not, of course, how the Senator sketched it for her: There was more variety and wealth, conflicts and disturbances than she had ever imagined in that jail. Her father saw her as a rebel, but in her new environment she was practically a lamb.

Allison felt a violent dizziness and then a sensation of absence, as if she'd been left alone. As if objects were dancing at top speed. She was afraid. What she saw and heard and felt didn't resemble the experiences described by her schoolmates: She didn't see psychedelic forms, colors did not become more luminous, and she felt no happiness whatsoever. Cameron had warned that to enjoy her experience, she should relax and remain calm: A bad trip could be horrifying. *A bad trip*. Bewildered and terrified, she was leading herself directly toward that goal, and now she would not know how to how to get back.

Cameron held her hand, embraced her, caressed her hair, and finally kissed her. Allison was indifferent: Her body was living a life of its own, and she merely contemplated it from a distance. She barely listened to her friend's words: Don't worry, sweetheart, I'm here. She didn't even realize it when he unbuttoned her blouse, struggling to reach her breasts, or when he finally did. One part of her, perhaps the most powerful, enjoyed being touched. You've never done it?, she heard Cameron's voice and found herself saying no, but that she'd like to do it, to try everything with him, there, right there, surrounded by those people she didn't know rolling around on the floor. Are you sure? Yes, stupid, yes, now, *now*! Cameron pulled off her shoes and socks and then fought to pull off her jeans. Allison could barely see her friend's milky skin. She felt pain, a pain that was not localized anywhere, in her sex or her stomach, but spread all over her, from her feet to the back of her neck. Something was shaking inside her, making her shake. Cameron was moaning. Allison understood she shouldn't worry about his cries, he wasn't wounded—she had only wounded herself.

When she recovered consciousness—it was 3:00 A.M.—her joints, her stomach, her nipples all burned. She dressed as quickly as she could and called a taxi. Cameron didn't wake up, or pretended not to wake up, and let her leave in the middle of the night. The Senator was waiting for her at the door, wearing a ridiculous scarlet robe; he welcomed her with a slap: Again that pain, that same pain. She didn't want him to stop, hoped he'd beat her until he got tired of beating her, until she fainted, until she sank into oblivion. But the Senator stopped. He looked at his swollen hand, and two tears glistened in his eyes. Allison was shaking: because of the cold, because she was afraid, because of her crying mother cringing on the other side of the hall. Why, Allison?

She didn't answer, didn't even dare to look him in the eye. She ran upstairs. Jennifer watched her from the doorway, an expression of sorrow on her face. Allison slammed the door to her room and collapsed. What was wrong with her? She didn't know, didn't *want* to know. Her father had forced her to abandon the protected universe of her childhood, her misbehavior was his fault. Now she had no choice but to behave like her new friends, become more rebellious, aggressive, and insolent than they: It was the only way she could manage to survive. Jennifer and her mother were very mistaken if they thought she would stop now. She'd never apologize again. The Senator had educated her to be the best, and now she would be the best of the worst. She'd forget the restraints of the past, let herself be carried along by Cameron and his friends and by anyone who would guide her into that hell she now considered hers, only hers.

The next morning, the Senator decreed that Allison would not be able to leave the house. She didn't have the slightest intention of obeying him. It was the first time she prepared to challenge him. She needed to break the last chains that tied her to the Senator, to her mother, and to Jen. It was the only way she would be able to be herself. That night she came home after midnight: Her father had to recognize her challenge. But this time he wasn't waiting for her. Indignant, Allison went up to her room.

Why do you do it?, Jennifer asked her. You know our father isn't in good health, don't you have any consideration? Allison couldn't control herself: Leave me in peace! Get out, get out of my room! And she slammed the door in her face. She immediately repented, but it was too late. The consequences of her act weren't visible until the next day. At dinner time, the Senator cruelly told her off. Without showing any anger, the old man's exquisite voice and razor-sharp words only showed his disillusionment. If Allison continued behaving that way, she'd never be anyone. That would be her fate: *to be no one*. He then informed her that starting Monday she would visit Dr. Farber, a psychologist who specialized in adolescents with problems. And that was all. He then went back to conversing, praised Ellen's apple pie, and blessed the fine September weather.

Dr. Farber turned out to be an obese and hairless Californian who looked nothing like Sigmund Freud. The psychoanalyst simply listened to her, asked her to clarify a few details of her story—especially the sexual parts—and sent her off with a hug that was hardly orthodox. She never noticed any improvement, she was as impulsive as ever, and the tension between her and her father didn't diminish. Perhaps the only significant change was the slow erosion of her timidity. If she could thank Dr. Farber for something, it was for having given her the courage to say what she thought, as if those sessions had been lessons in oral expression.

Allison managed to graduate in 1967. Despite her revolutionary faith, she followed in her sister's footsteps, and sent applications to various universities, even though her grades gave her no hope of being admitted to an Ivy League school. Thanks to the secret intervention of the Senator, she was accepted at Penn State. Moved by inertia, she majored in business. Her mother, always worried she would waste her life, convinced her that at least she'd have her future assured. Allison held out for almost two years before her activism against the Vietnam War obliged her to give up college, along with a half dozen other militants, after becoming one of the organizers of the huge protest march that took place at the outset of 1970. By then, her father had already been dead for a year. No one wept for him as much as she did.

EVA HALÁSZ

Hungary—United States of America, 1956-1980

I do, she heard herself say: The syllables remained there, solid and indelible; her brain filled with serotonin, and a whirlwind whipped through her uterus. Eva felt vibrant, dumbfounded, and, yes, perhaps happy. Interesting, she thought. She hated behaving like those hysterical female scientists, who even in the most emotionally-charged moments—and marriage was one of them—study themselves like laboratory rats facing a new test. So she tried to eliminate her self-consciousness and to concentrate on the figures on the altar.

While Philip's lips rested on hers—that was not a kiss, a real kiss, but a simulacrum to delight the guests—Eva felt the gold ring strangling her finger and tried not to trip over her ridiculous white dress (another incongruity, she thought: I should be wearing red). An avalanche of images clouded her eyes: photos of her mother and grandmother in their Magyar costumes, scenes from the romantic films that fascinated her as a girl, snippets from the countless weddings she'd witnessed.

So many memories kept her from leaning on Philip's arm when he invited her to walk toward the church doors through the rustic notes of the wedding march. Curious, thought Eva: Just a couple of simple words, I do, for me to stop being myself, for Eva Halász to turn suddenly into Eva Putnam, even if Eva Putnam doesn't exist or exists only in the imagination of others. Who was this man escorting her along the red carpet? Eva barely dared ask herself. Why am I getting married? And why to *him*? How crazy, she chided herself.

She felt neither fear nor regret—Curious, she muttered again—only a kind of intoxication. Alcohol made her marry Philip, that was the only explanation for her folly. But she didn't remember having drunk anything and certainly did not feel the heaviness of being hungover. Perhaps she'd married for no good reason at all, because that avalanche of memories dulled her mind and obliged her to repeat the fate of her ancestors, even though she didn't have the slightest desire to marry and much less marry someone like Philip.

Love (no word was more cloying) was not an issue for Eva. It was a mask for disguising an evolutionary necessity: the desire to trap a man forever, or at least for a few years, with the aim of turning him into a supplier of genes and food. Then Eva thought that perhaps her skepticism, her lack of sentimental ties, was the reason for her marriage. She was uniting herself with Philip for no good reason: a caprice, a whim. The simple desire to be with someone, so she wouldn't have to go to the movies alone, so she could have someone with whom to split the electricity bill, the supermarket expenses.

The ringing bells destroyed her soliloquy. Her American cousins tossed rice at her head, her Hungarian relatives lined up to congratulate her, Klara, wearing a horrible pink hat, stared at her, disapprovingly, from a distance. And there, as the final element in the decorations, she saw the Cadillac that would carry her to the reception. Thank you, thank you, thank you, she heard herself repeat left and right, a knot in her throat. You look very beautiful, what a pretty ceremony, the groom is handsome, what a lovely dress, how old can she be? Best wishes, best wishes, *best wishes*! Those phrases drilled their way through her ears, distracting her from her mission: To become the happiest woman on earth. Eva hastily got into the car, at least there she's have a few moments of calm—with Philip next to her?—before getting to that other hell, the reception.

Even if she had agreed to get married (what silliness), she should at last have fought to have things done her way: No pomp and circumstance, in a country church with thirty guests and a red dress. Concentrating on a thousand projects, she did not have the heart to defeat her mother—who didn't even approve of the groom—or Philip's parents and perhaps even Philip himself, who declared himself an agnostic but ultimately showed he was charmed by the ceremony and pomp.

You always have to do everything before the proper time, Eva scolded herself: You learned to read at two, to multiply at three, and to do square roots at five, you read Attila József, Sándor Petofi, Lázló Kalnóki, Endre Ady, and János Arany at seven, you finished lower school at eight, and high school at twelve, you entered university at fourteen, graduated with honors at fifteen, and you obtained your doctorate at seventeen. You learned Hungarian at two, English at three, German at ten, and Russian at thirteen: That was the only reason for marrying at seventeen, of course it is. You're the typical child prodigy, Eva whipped herself on while Philip caressed her hand: the most intelligent young woman on the planet and also the stupidest, mature when it came to following the wandering paths of her intelligence, but inept in choosing a partner, in thinking over decisions, or attaining some serenity. I love you too, she said to Philip: He needed these doses of reaffirmation and tenderness. Deep down, he wasn't a bad person, even though at times he seemed stupid, and therefore intolerable, to Eva.

The place where the reception was held was sadder than she'd imagined it could be, and she had imagined it sordid and decadent: Huge pink ribbons hung from false marble columns, the tables boasted mammoth bouquets of petunias, one of those mirrored balls hung above the dance floor—the rhythms of Donna Summers singing "Love to Love You Baby" resounded in her head—and at the entrance someone was handing out little porcelain cups with *Eva & Philip* (like that, without the accent on the E). The scene was so grotesque that she almost enjoyed it: a couple of glasses of champagne and two good glasses of *tokay*—Klara had insisted on introducing some local color—and finally the critical and sarcastic Eva stepped aside, allowing another Eva, playful and irresistible, to take over.

Alcohol gave her the energy to dance without getting tired. She even tried a couple of *czardas*, and she didn't get depressed until very late at night, after her mother had already left. Then Eva became the other Eva, the one who overwhelmed or destroyed her partners (for now, Philip was the exception). So that may be the reason why you married him.

Genius had its disadvantages: melancholy, French spleen, Portuguese *saudades*, sourness, the *búskomorság* that usually whipped her after a period of euphoria. When dejection invaded her body and her spirit—or not her spirit, but her cerebral cortex—Eva would spend days or weeks in bed, and no one would be able to get her out. Luckily, it seemed that this time her sadness would not turn out to be an abyss or beyond her control; it was more like a cold than pneumonia, and she wouldn't need more than a week to recover.

Get me out of here, she asked Philip. A few guests are still here. I'm begging you. Philip was no fool, at least in practical matters: He knew that energetic tone and knew how to read the signs of alarm. Philip loved Eva (he never wondered about the semantic content of the term) and whenever she collapsed like a doll, he became her nurse and took care of her as no one else could. Yes, dear, let's go, he said, and they began making the rounds to say good-bye. It's late, and we start traveling early tomorrow morning, please have fun. Thanks, sweetheart, she whispered, and this time she was thankful for his concern and patience.

When they reached their hotel, and their impersonal, anodyne room, Philip helped her take off the wedding dress; it was a more complicated job than he'd imagined. The hilarity of the scene (she was half-naked, and he was fighting with her stockings) helped dissipate the melancholy and even made her laugh. Philip thought that this night, their wedding night, would not culminate with a sober good-night-dear but with a tender embrace, but Eva had no intention of being conquered, not that night. She jumped on Philip, kissed him, bit him, bit him a thousand times as though her life depended on it, fully intent on losing consciousness, on knowing nothing more about herself, on celebrating her night of madness and stupidity. She worked him over, scratched him, and didn't rest until she saw a line of blood flow from his lips and a purple wound on his neck. Those marks would remind her that on that occasion she'd triumphed, that for once she'd conquered her *búskomorság*.

Seeing him there, stretched out and fragile, at her mercy, Eva recognized that this was the beauty she sought: There was nothing like contemplating a naked man—with wide shoulders and a stomach flattened by exercise, a Greek athlete or a Roman gladiator—transformed into a puppy. Eva didn't do it on purpose. When she caught sight of a potential lover, she never thought about using or hurting him. And besides, it wasn't she who looked for them; they who approached her, imagining she'd be easy prey. Eva did not feel responsible for her desires or frustrations: In the game of love—because, dear-oh-dear, love for her was always a game—the players entered the arena with the same will, aware of the risks: It was their fault, and their fault alone, if at the end they were wounded or even dead.

Her strategy was simple: let them act, arouse their passions, and then abandon them. Some, the luckiest—or the most miserable, depending on your point of view—she not only came to appreciate and drive mad but also to need (it was the closest she could get to tenderness). But most were one-night-stands, or a-few-week-stands at most, identical and interchangeable. She couldn't avoid it: Besides science, sex was the only passion in her life. Science and sex fused to the point that she couldn't distinguish the pleasure of controlling another body from her pride at assembling a cybernetic device.

Are you sleeping with Philip too? Steve's extremely high-pitched voice did not seem to emanate from his enormous chest. His tone revealed jealousy and a touch of anger, not because he thought it impossible that Eva, whose reputation as an easy woman had spread throughout the university, might have had sexual relations with his best friend, but because she confessed it to him after making love, as if it were a comment on the weather.

Right from the beginning I warned you about two things, she retorted: *Primo*, my personal life is mine and mine alone and, *secundo*, that I'll never lie to you. I've kept my word about both things. But you on the other hand told me you weren't jealous, and just look at you.

Steve remained in bed, tense and sweaty—and, in Eva's opinion, exceedingly handsome—not knowing how to react; perhaps he should just get dressed and walk out indignantly. Eva was walking back and forth in front of him, barely covered by a pink bra—Steve always fantasized about her dominating character and discovered she wore the kind of underwear favored by teenaged girls—brazenly exhibiting her backside. But . . . but . . . Steve stuttered, trying to control the effect Eva's nakedness had on him, why did you have to tell me? And now, after what happened between us? And what did happen between us? I'm not naïve, I know you liked it too. You're right: It was wonderful, Steve. Well? Wasn't it special? Slightly exasperated, Eva put on an orange blouse and began to button it. How could Steve be *so* handsome and *so* dumb? Special isn't the same as unique: understand? Steve stood up and covered his sex with his hand: Now I see that what everyone says is true. Is that right? And what do they say? That I'm a whore? Well, that's what I am. You already knew that, Steve. I knew you were a whore, not that you're a bitch.

For the first time, Steve was showing some spirit. Eva almost took advantage of it. Steve, Stevie, there's no reason for us to get like this. You know I'm cleverer than you and could say even more offensive things. I like you. I like you *a lot*. But that's it. Is that so hard to accept? Eva sat down next to him and ran her fingers over his sex; I really don't understand you. I thought I was every man's dream: a woman who does everything you want without commitments. What are you complaining about? Steve put his enormous hands on Eva's thighs: We all like to be exclusive. But I don't. I never asked you to be faithful. Come on, now. Tell me. Have you slept with anyone else recently? With Eliza perhaps? Eva stared at him with such force that Steve had to confess: I'm sorry. Don't be sorry, enjoy it.

They gathered up their clothing and dressed in silence. Look, Stevie, sexual networks function like any other network. A single principle regulates the neuron connections, social contacts, electrical and telephonic systems, the circuits in computers and even the football teams you adore. To function, networks require that most of their elements be connected only with one or two of their same kind and that there be a few that concentrate a much larger number of connections. See what I mean? Not really. Oh Steve, how dumb you are. There are two kinds of people: the faithful and the more-or-less faithful, the immense and bored majority and those that function as connectors. I'm a connector. My mission in life is to sleep with as many men as I can, in order to connect circles that would otherwise never find one another . . . Okay?

By then, Steve had stopped listening to her and was concentrating on his own thoughts (perhaps the referee in the game between the Steelers and the Jets). That's the way it always was for Eva: No one valued her sophisticated sense of humor or, even less, her talent for popularizing science. In a muddle, Steve tied his shoes and opened the door. It made him uncomfortable not knowing how he felt, whether humiliated and sad—*omne animal triste post coitum*, Eva had recited to him—or just dazed.

He dropped the key to the room at the hotel reception desk and headed for his car. Eva followed a few steps behind, not knowing if he was going to leave her there or drive her back to the university. Steve thought of himself as a gentleman, another trait Eva found amusing in that mastodon, and did not hesitate to stay with him. Will I see you on Thursday? she asked as they said good-bye. Still in a daze, Steve hurriedly said yes.

Eva remembered having heard the story hundreds of time, from when she first began to think. Her father told it with a mixture of pride and anger, and in his later years with a certain nostalgia, as if at the end he saw that episode as the only valuable part of his life. At the time, Ferenc Haláz was only twenty-three years old—he was born in Kolcse, a village near the border with the Ukraine, near the Carpathian Mountains, in 1933—and he was a modest engineering student at the Technical University of Budapest, where his family moved after the war because his father had fought in General Béla Miklós's militia.

A bit slow and dissipated, Ferenc was more concerned about his examinations than the political situation. It would have been hard for him to recognize the photo of Mátyás Rákosi, the all-powerful First-Secretary of the Hungarian Workers Party—the MDP, the name the Communists had adopted with Moscow's blessing—or that of András Hegedüs, the first minister named by Rákosi to take the place of the mutinous Imre Nagy in 1954. Naturally Ferenc would have been unable to explain the maneuvering and misunderstandings brought about by the various Party men during the preceding five years. Every day he crossed the city from one side to the other to attend classes, leaving the miserable room he shared with his family on Tuzoltó Street, so he had no time for social life. He participated in no study group and had not joined the Young Communists. Eva thought her father was one of those shadows that pass through classes and garner neither glory nor disapproval, a solitary individual whose only pleasure consisted in taking long walks in the country or dancing at country fairs.

Ferenc barely noticed the brief reform interlude the nation passed through in 1953 under the leadership of Imre Nagy. Even if his schoolmates did nothing else but talk about it, he never even glimpsed Nagy's projects, didn't understand what the "New Way" referred to, was unaware of the refreshing atmosphere that had settled in after Stalin's death, and wasn't even concerned about Rákosi's forced resignation, his exile to Moscow, or his return, in a new period of Soviet hardening that took place at the end of 1954. Like everyone else, he thought Nagy honest and brave, more human, or less savage, than others, but he felt toward him the same distrust he felt for all politicians. As long as he was allowed to continue his studies, find work in a factory, find a good wife, and entertain the possibility of returning to the country, Ferenc wasn't interested in politics. He did not share the other students' enthusiasm for the revolution, had never read the libertarian poems that Sándor Czoóri and Istvan Orkény had published in the magazine *Irodalmi Ujság*, and didn't have the slightest idea what the Writers Union was or who the members of the Petofi Circle might be.

For him, having gone to see *Richard III* in the National Theater in 1955 did not constitute a political act, and he never stopped to consider the similarities between Rákosi and the English king. No, he was only concentrated on caressing the hand of Klara, the young nursing student he'd just met and fallen in love with. And of course he did not understand Rakosi's departure, or his return. Rakosi only made him fearful, but then he was removed from office again in July of 1956.

Right around that time, Ferenc's relationship with Klara had not only prospered but Klara, somewhat perplexed and somewhat delighted, informed him (at the start of January) that she was pregnant. The situation was not convenient—the couple had no money and no prospects. The future looked gray, not luminous. In the event, they decided to go ahead: The unexpected appearance of the child—who would be a girl, Eva—filled them with hope. They married in Kölcse on September 8th, in one of those peasant parties that Ferenc liked so much, indifferent to the struggle for power that was shaking the Central Committee of the MDP, indifferent to the authoritarian stupidities committed by the nation's new strong man, the yellowish Ernő Gerő. Three weeks later, on September 29th, Klara gave birth.

The university Ferenc went back to was now a seething cauldron: The students were organizing demonstrations and gatherings without getting approval from the authorities. Ferenc would have preferred taking his usual classes, but he soon found himself attending forums where he heard things he thought could never be said in public. The speakers not only demanded the restoration of Nagy but, recalling the tragic revolution of 1848, called for democratic elections, a multi-party system, the withdrawal of the Soviet Army, and the dismantling of the Warsaw Pact. While Ferenc did not understand all the subtleties of the speeches, he was immediately sympathetic to the cause and decided to take part in the October 22nd protest against the recent repression in Poland (it seemed there had been a massacre in Poznan a few weeks earlier).

That morning, while Klara was breast-feeding Eva, the voice of the minister of the interior was heard on the radio. He said that the students were being manipulated by the forces of imperialism, and he forbade their nationalist march. Ferenc convinced himself of the probity of his act and, ignoring the pleas of his wife, went to the Polish Embassy along with his friends. The revolt had spread to the city, with gatherings on every corner, and Ferenc soon learned that a column was marching from the liberal arts school to the Petofi monument.

At around 7:00 P.M., the demonstrators met outside of parliament and chanted: Nagy, Nagy, Nagy . . . Ferenc was carried away, raised his fists, waved tricolor flags, and shouted along with them Nagy, Nagy, Nagy, as if the name were an ancient prayer. At 8:00 P.M., the shocked and distant former prime minister, now turned into the personification of the revolt, appeared before the crowd. Nagy was certainly brave, but he never stopped being a rigorous Communist.

Comrades! he shouted. The spirit of the demonstrators instantly deflated: They hadn't come to hear that Communist rhetoric but to listen to the echoes of the future. Comrades!

Nagy urged the students to calm down and tried to convince them of the need to re-initiate the reform program established by the New Way in 1953. The crowd felt betrayed, and the demonstration dissolved in a disheartened cloud. A few decided to march to the monument to Stalin and knock it down. Ferenc was among the first to throw stones at the stomach of the Little Father of the People. Soon a pair of cranes arrived, and amid chants and cheers the students smashed the nose and mustache and rolled the head along the ground.

At the same time, in another corner of the city, Gerő picked up the black telephone that communicated directly with the Soviet Embassy, and without going through formalities, demanded that the ambassador, Yuri Andrópov, have troops immediately dispatched to the Hungarian capital. In Moscow, that city of wide avenues, the situation did not seem so simple: After the events in Poland, Khrushchev was unwilling to send military forces unless there was a formal request from the Hungarian government. Besides, he was deeply unsympathetic to both Gerő and Rákosi, whom he considered Stalinists of the worst sort. After several hours of discussion, the Central Committee of the Communist Party of the Soviet Union made a decision worthy of King Solomon: They would send troops to Hungary and remove Gerő, but without stripping him of his title of First Secretary of the MDP. Imre Nagy would become prime minister.

While the Soviet tanks rattled across Budapest, students, professionals, and workers organized the resistance. On October 24th, Ferenc joined the forces of Per Olaf Csongovay on Tuzoltó Street, very close to his house, where Klara was dying of fright and Eva was learning to tell colors and sounds apart. On the 25th, more than 100 demonstrators were murdered by Soviet troops and Hungarian security forces outside the parliament building. Nagy could do nothing to stop it.

Fearing they might provoke a revolt, the Kremlin approved the resignation of Gerő, and János Kádár became First Secretary of the MPD. Elevated to a position of power, Nagy negotiated the withdrawal of the Soviet Army and the removal of the Stalinists from the Party: The students had won. A glorious and ephemeral victory. Hungary became a rebel nation, part of a different planet, where it was possible to speak freely. On October 28th, Nagy decreed the end of the occupation; on the 30th, he accepted the creation of a multi-party system and ordered the release of political prisoners; on the 31st, he announced Hungary's withdrawal from the Warsaw Pact and petitioned the United Nations to have his country considered neutral. Strikers went back to work, and political leaders revived the parties that had existed in 1946. Carrying his daughter in his arms, Ferenc imagined a transparent future for his daughter.

But on November 1st, a plane secretly left the military airport in Budapest for Moscow. It carried two old politicians who only a few days earlier had joined the new Hungarian Socialist Workers Party founded by Nagy: János Kádár and Ferenc Münnich. Nonplussed by the rapidity of History—they were willing to reform the nation but not to hand it over to the bourgeoisie—they prepared to do what any good Communist would do: ask advice from the Kremlin. Khrushchev seemed fed up with the democratic experiment taking place within his empire, so he agreed to comply with his guests' wishes. He would send the army back to Hungary, but this time it wouldn't leave until benign Communist order reigned supreme in every household.

On November 4th, while the plane with Kádár and Münnich was landing at a field near Budapest, sixteen divisions of the Red Army began marching along the avenues of the capital, smashing the cobble stones, bursting the hydrants, and dismantling the electrical system. The tanks stood at the corners and fired on anyone who dared to challenge them. Ferenc saw how bullets were flying by him, how his comrades in arms were falling, how children and women were wounded in the smoke, how the invaders not only destroyed the city squares and towers but also its pride, how all resistance was crushed. It was then he turned his face toward Eva and thought that she'd been stripped of her promise-filled future, that now Eva would be the daughter either of a prisoner or a dead counterrevolutionary. So, while Imre Nagy and his government asked for asylum at the Yugoslavian embassy in Budapest, never imagining that Marshall Tito would quickly turn them over to Khrushchev, Ferenc and Klara packed up what little they had and fled toward the Austrian border.

First by car, then on hired carts, and finally on foot, they crossed Hungary's mountains and plains, its rivers and forests, helped by peasants, hungry, cold, avoiding police check points and escaping patrols in their search for that future which had been snatched away from them. Klara carried Eva in her arms, feeding her though she had no more milk, and made her pap with stale bread and raw milk.

On November 20th, two days before Nagy and his collaborators were betrayed by the Yugoslavians and sent to the Rumanian town of Snajov where they would be handed over to Kádár, Ferenc, Klara, and Eva crossed a moor that led them to Austrian territory, salvation, and life. A few months later, thanks to a cousin of Klara's who had emigrated to Boston during the thirties, the three made their way to the United States, where Ferenc found a job in small refrigeration company;he worked there until his death in 1970. Nagy did not have the same luck: After a summary trial, Kádár ordered his execution on June 16th, 1958. His last words were: I ask for no mercy.

Starting more-or-less at the age of ten, when she confirmed it was impossible for her to communicate with children her own age, when she fell for the first time into a long period of weeping, Eva discovered that her intelligence and brilliance, which made her different from others, made her special, wasn't a blessing or a miracle but a condemnation. What good was it to be the smartest, as her mother assumed? She didn't ask for this gift, it was something that had been imposed on her: She'd willingly give it up, if only she could be normal, happy. I want to be stupid, she shouted to Klara one day, stupid, stupid, stupid, and she smacked her head against a wall. Her mother did what she always did: She called Dr. Ormandy, listened to his advice, and complained in silence.

At fourteen or fifteen, Eva recognized the nature of her suffering: Intelligence was something like a little man lodged inside her head who forced her to think about things that didn't concern her, to remember banal facts, to carry out absurd mathematical operations. When she discovered that to explain the functioning of consciousness some recent theories made reference to the existence of a *homunculus*—a term derived from alchemy—Eva was horrified: This animal or cyst, this parasite, inhabited her. Later, thanks to Wiener's *Cybernetics*, she came to believe that if she wanted to understand herself, if she wanted to hunt down the *homunculus* living within her, she would have to study computers.

Eva wasn't yet sixteen when she walked into the MIT artificial intelligence laboratory that John McCarthy and Marvin Minsky founded in 1958. With her hair cut even with her ears and wearing a pinafore, she looked like a grade-school child. Old Minsky, the astute dragon, asked her if she'd gotten lost.

Professor, my name is Eva Halász. I'm a student here. I want to learn everything I can about artificial intelligence. Minsky looked her up and down suspiciously: He knew—and detested—child prodigies, computer fanatics, the usual pests. By then, he lacked the patience to be able to deal with adolescents, no matter how clever they were. Let's see, tell me what you know. I've just read Wiener's *Cybernetics*. Minsky turned his head to one side. I'm afraid to tell you, you're way behind, my dear. The road Wiener opened was important, but it doesn't lead anywhere. Current research is going in another direction. I'm sorry. What about mathematics? Eva gave a detailed account of her progress: The old man was impressed. Very well, you may attend my class next Tuesday. That way, we'll find out if you're up to the work.

Eva was taken aback. Aside from being one of the founders of the discipline, Minsky was famous for having advised Stanley Kubrick during the filming of *2001: A Space Odyssey*. He'd suffered an accident on the set that almost cost him his life, and he told thousands of anecdotes about it. The old man also boasted about being a caustic polemicist: Anyone who cast doubt on his theories should watch out. At MIT, he was considered the pope of artificial intelligence. A week later, Eva listened devoutly to his lecture.

The real founder of artificial intelligence was neither a mathematician nor a psychologist but a philosopher, our good friend Thomas Hobbes, Minsky recited. He was the first person to say . . . The rest of the class, with the exception of Eva, answered in a chorus: *Reasoning is the same as computation*. Correct! Therefore, what is a computer? A formal system? And what is a formal system? A combination of procedures and rules.

Let's be more precise. The professor squinted mockingly at his students: Let's say that a formal system is a game. A game like chess or checkers. That is, a game with players, pieces, a group of rules and, though you don't always see him, a referee. All of this was both unknown and fascinating for Eva.

And now write this down. It's said that two formal systems are equal when: (a) for each position of a piece in the first system, there is another piece placed in the second; (b) for each movement in the first system, there is a corresponding movement in the second; and (c) the initial positions corresponded. Minksy swallowed. Let's see, Miss Halász, give us an example of two equivalent formal systems.

She felt her classmates wanted to eat her alive: the brain and computers? Splendid answer, Miss Halász! Except that you forgot to add one *almost* insignificant detail. At least until today, we are not sure that the mind and computers are equivalent. I'm sorry. So we'd have to say instead that our brain and computers . . . *perhaps* . . . Perhaps are formal equivalents. If we study one of them in depth, we may perhaps understand the other. In other words, if we successfully program a computer to be intelligent, we may perhaps understand something of our own intelligence.

This was exactly what Eva had come to hear.

I'm sorry, Eva, really, I'm sorry. She stared into his bleary face, not believing a word, always suspecting that his pain was an act, a final bit of courtesy or amiability, the final request given to criminals in jail. Eva considered that expression—*I'm sorry*—the worst possible excuse: To be sorry about something, without specifying what, was an insufficient means of eliminating responsibility, just as a plea was unable to cleanse the soul. What did Philip feel? Guilt, remorse, shame? He'd just revealed that he no longer loved her, that he no longer wanted to be with her, that he would rather run away—though, with his usual tendency to use euphemisms he actually said he needed time, that things hadn't worked out properly, that perhaps it would be better to separate—and all he hoped was that she wouldn't make a scene in that faux-French restaurant.

Idiot! Eva had no intention of fainting and had learned to control her impulses, so she didn't slap him across the face like a bad actress and didn't throw her wine in his face. No. Eva was interested in calibrating what was going on in her brain. Curious, she said to herself, as usual: Eva felt she was suffocating, but she wasn't suffocating, as if she were seeing only the shadow of that pain and that suffocation. Things hadn't been going well between them for a long time—why should she fool herself: They were never compatible. Their marriage was coming to an end, but Eva thought she would be the one responsible for ending it. And this miserable fool had beaten her to the punch! She always thought she'd abandon Philip, but never guessed she'd be abandoned by him. I don't understand, she heard herself mutter.

Philip accentuated the pathos in his mournful expression, insinuating that their break was following an irrevocable law. Poor Philip, Eva thought, he doesn't even try to justify himself, doesn't even have the courage to take responsibility for his decisions. Why had she married him, why had she said *I do*, why had she moved into his house, why had she given in? For eleven months and three days she'd avoided the answer, assuming that life with another person, with any other person, was a blunder, and, such being the case, there was nothing to do but mask routine, giving in to the power of the genes and their silly will to perpetuate themselves.

Unlike the other men she'd slept with—by then, oh dear, the number had risen to thirty, maybe thirty-one—Philip was the only one who hadn't questioned her sexual life, the only one who had not used her past to insult her, the only one who hadn't bombarded her with questions about her other lovers, the only one who said he was willing to put up with her. He was the only man, of the thirty or thirty-one whose bodies she'd known (I can barely write it), who'd allowed her to be free. And now Eva was discovering that his generosity and his unselfishness—his apparent lack of egoism—were vices instead of virtues, manifestations of the apathy Philip showed for everything unrelated to football and business. The tears that suddenly began to run down her cheeks were not the result of disappointment, not even because of her smashed pride, but because she realized Philip wasn't the stupid one. He was what he was: handsome, insipid, unimportant. She'd wanted to transform him. What and idiotic idea, Eva Pygmalion.

Please, Eva, don't cry. Things will work out, you have the strength to achieve whatever you want. To Eva, those words stopped sounding like pretexts: Philip couldn't say anything else. His intelligence would never let him find more original words. Perhaps she'd chosen him because he said the most banal phrases with total conviction. That's how Philip was. You're beautiful, intelligent, young . . . You've got your future ahead of you. No doubt about it: *That* was Philip. Yes, yes, don't worry, I'm going to be fine.

As he listened to her, his face lost its severely pained expression, and his muscles relaxed. Eva helped him through this rough patch. They sat in silence, their fingers interwoven, and their gazes fixed, as if it were a first date: two people learning to love each other and not man and wife negotiating their divorce. And what's her name, Philip? Who? The woman you're seeing. Debra. Do I know her? I don't think so. Good. And what's she like? Let's not make this more painful. Tell me, Philip. How did you meet her?

Eva waved over a waiter and ordered a bottle of champagne. At first, Philip was reluctant to talk about Debra, but alcohol loosened his tongue, as if he weren't talking to his wife but one of his fellow party animals. He told her she was blond and tall, the same age as Eva; she worked in a furniture store and dreamed about becoming an actress. Philip had met her in a bar on one of the many nights when Eva had stayed in the MIT laboratory. She always said her greatest virtue was being a good listener, and she proved it. She did not hesitate to ask Philip details about her rival, about the size of her breasts, the way she made love, her expectations for the future.

Rather drunk, Eva and Philip went home, kissed, and took off their clothes with an eagerness and desire they hadn't felt for quite a while, as if other minds had usurped their bodies, as if they hadn't consummated their break, as if Philip weren't in love with Debbi, as if Eva didn't hold him in contempt. They awakened disconcerted but serene, and after showering together, Philip actually helped her pack. Good luck, they said at the same time, shortly before Eva got into the taxi that would deliver her to her next lover.

None of Minsky's students advanced as quickly as Eva. Even though she'd foreseen it, because of her skill in mathematics and her memory, the Old Man was always shocked at her rigor, her will to work, her need to show herself worthy of his laboratory. Minsky realized that Eva's obsession obeyed secret reasons, some special need, but he never dared ask her any personal questions. Their relationship remained on an abstract plane, two minds communicating by means of a cable, two brains without intimate lives that had established an empathetic connection.

How can we know if we have constructed an intelligent machine?, she asked the Old Man one day. For centuries, philosophers and scientists have been unable to agree about what intelligence is. Some say one thing, others the opposite. Thank God, a solution exists. When I was a graduate student here at MIT during the '20s, the unfortunate Alan Turing imagined a test for intelligence that depends neither on metaphysical theories nor on abstract concepts; it turns out to be very convenient, at least for our purposes. Turing called it the imitation game.

Eva listened to Minsky and at the same time imagined Turing, who became famous during the Second World War for deciphering Nazi codes, walking the MIT hallways fascinated by the bodies of his colleagues while he elaborated his theories. The imagination game was certainly ingenious. Three players were required: two behind a curtain and a third who was able to communicate with them. It was that simple. The first player was supposed to be a machine and the second a human being. The third, called the judge, could ask the others all kind of questions, the most elevated or the most absurd or insignificant (the answers were to be written down). A computer could be considered intelligent if the judge couldn't guess if the author of the answer was a person or a machine. This means that physical, biological, chemical, and simple engineering differences didn't matter, concluded Eva. The Old Man nodded: Everything that looks like intelligence *is* intelligence. In our field we don't have to prove anything else.

I do, Eva heard herself say it once again, although now the words sounded so different, as if they'd barely been born, free of memory. I do, she repeated, corroborating their full meaning, imprinting on them a permanence that at this point in her life seemed already distant or impossible. Not even two years had gone by since she spoke those words for the first time, in another place and to another man, and now she was again in the same situation, or at least in a very similar one, though she did everything she could not to compare them, trying to forget the wilted flowers, Mendelssohn's wedding march, and the white dress she wore then in order to concentrate on the elegant bone-hued dress (again, she didn't dare wear red), the minimal decoration, and the silence. No, marrying Andrew O'Connor wasn't the same as marrying poor, immature Philip Putnam—in fact, he was seated in the first row, alongside Debra, his lamentable wife. Even if in her heart of hearts Eva recognized the lie, she repeated to herself: You'll see, it will be different, Eva, you won't make the same mistakes, you'll be more patient and less fickle, experience must be good for something.

At least Eva could smile naturally now, almost innocently.

Her marriage with Philip, or the failure of her marriage with Philip, had taught her something: She didn't want to be alone, she needed to share her emotional strength. Despite the previous fiasco, Eva was a staunch defender of matrimony: The rite had been invented for a reason; people who lived alone ran the risk of going mad. Yes, matrimony was a nightmare, a crime, but it was worthwhile: It legitimized a transgression, sanctioned one person's interfering in the decisions of another, sanctioned stealing their space and their freedom. What challenge was there in sporadic sex? What knowledge could be derived from mere physical contact or relationships carried out at a distance?

As she looked him over, at the point of kissing him, he could not look more different than her first husband: Between Andrew and her there existed an intellectual complicity identical to their physical synchronicity.

He too was a scientist, with a Ph.D. in mathematics from Harvard—there was no competition—twelve years older, sensitive, and handsome, perhaps not as handsome as Philip, but doubtlessly more attractive than the sickly mathematicians she'd met at the university. His passion was rowing, and his biceps revealed years of training. Regattas and mathematics are very similar, he explained: games that lack a precise goal, where the only important thing is to be faster than your rivals. A bit conceited, yes, but it gave Eva confidence to be able to talk with someone who was her equal. Eva quickly kissed him, and the slightly acid taste of his saliva permeated her mouth, activated her nerves, and she soon felt that her sex was moist under the bone-colored dress. A good sign, she said to herself. She embraced him vigorously, and they walked out of the courthouse together: She deserved an ovation for marrying a second time, like an athlete who has broken his own record.

This time she had supervised the details of the reception herself: There were no petunias, no azaleas, just a sunflower at each table. The dance music bore no resemblance to the melodies Klara or Philip's parents had chosen. Each detail had her personal touch. Andrew found her sudden interest in souvenirs, food, and flowers amusing; he thought Eva detested practical life, but she had shown herself to be more earthly than he.

During the first months, the relationship between Eva and Andrew was, as she'd expected, not perfect, because perfection was itself unsettling. But it was lively and even simple. They spent hours telling each other about what they were working on—theorems and hypotheses, paradoxes and anomalies, axioms and algorithms—and they moved on to sex as if it were the natural consequence of their calculations. Andrew wasn't as passionate or curious as Philip, but at his side Eva felt calm.

Problems, the inevitable problems, began three or four years into their married life in the most unforeseeable way (Klara had warned Eva that Andrew was wrong for her too). While Eva had made an effort not to repeat the arguments she'd had with Philip, she suddenly found herself playing her usual role. When they married, Andrew barely knew her and showed himself to be firm and sensible, but as soon as he saw himself dragged along by her changes of mood, her delirium, and her anguish, by the constant turmoil of her mind—the *búskomorság* she hated—he fell in love with her and became almost as stupid as Philip. He began to behave like a father, a nurse, or a priest, always concerned about her sanity.

She felt spied upon, overwhelmed, and it wasn't long before she sought an escape. Until then, she'd felt no need to seek other men, but now she got involved in a long series of sporadic relationships. Andrew quickly became suspicious, but his reaction confounded her expectations: Instead of getting angry or dying of jealousy, he only seemed interested in Eva's lovers.

What's wrong with you? Tell me. You know you can tell me everything. She'd always dreamed of a man who would love her and leave her free, but now she was feeling chills. I don't know what you're talking about. I know you're seeing other men, Eva. That's not a reproach. I always knew it would happen; you told me right when I met you. I told you that? Something along those lines. And I accept it. As long as you love me, I accept it. What exists between us is stronger. There are those, like me, who are content with a single partner and others who need—I don't know how to put it—variety. I love you, Eva. And I respect you. That's why I want you to tell me everything. Otherwise, I couldn't live. Eva got out of bed. Do you realize what you're asking me to do? You demand I tolerate your adventures; all I ask is that you tell them to me.

That request sounded absurd and disgusting to Eva. But at the same time, Andrew's argument seemed rational: *quid pro quo*. How could she phrase things so that her words weren't a burden, didn't hurt, didn't destroy. This is the worst thing that ever happened to you, she said to herself: It will be terrible. You've got to make him understand. Impossible. At first, it was enormously difficult to confess her conquests, and even harder to describe them in detail, but he didn't rest until, little by little, he extracted the stories from her. Her infidelities didn't put an end to their sex life, but it did make it more languid and pathetic. In the eyes of others, they were an ideal couple, the envy of friends and neighbors, ideal accomplices in that community of divorced and neurotic scientists. The marriage of Eva Halász and Andrew O'Connor went on like that, with its hidden rhythm of permitted betrayals, insecurity, and voyeurism for almost ten years, until late in 1987.

I've spoken about Irina Nikolayevna Sudayeva, Arkady Ivanovich Granin, and their daughter Oksana, about Jennifer Moore and her sister Allison, about the infamous Jack Wells, and about my beloved Eva Halász (the threads of this tangled skein), and now all that's left is for me to introduce myself. I hate writing out my name, Yuri Mihháilovich Chernishevsky, as much as I hate the first-person singular and that insipid pronoun, *I*, that reveals my presence in these pages. How I would like not to be the narrator of this story, of this heap of stories—of accidents—and vanish without leaving a trace of my passage over the Earth! Impossible. I will only be able to expiate my guilt, or at least erase it for a few seconds, if I give a rough sketch of these lives and provide a glimpse of their subterranean powers.

Eva once told me that only six links are necessary to connect a person with any other person on earth. This phenomenon doesn't derive from a coincidence but from the topology of humanity, from the thing we could call its *form*. Now I understand: I pursue that architecture, I persist in discerning it here in this grave on the fringe of the present moment. Because of an inscrutable principle, Irina Nikolayevna Sudayeva, Arkady Ivanovich Granin, and their daughter Oksana; Jennifer Moore and her sister Allison; the infamous Jack Wells; and my beloved Eva Halász formed an immaterial network, mere points on a Cartesian plane. In this model, I became the miserable cartographer who had to connect them.

I was born in the port city of Baku, in what was then part of the Soviet Union and which later became part of the Republic of Azerbaijan, on the shores of the Caspian Sea (which is not a sea but a salt-water lake), on July 10th, 1958. My parents were ethnic Russians and could barely mutter the odd word in Azerbaijani. My father, Mihail Petróvich, had worked as a technician in a petroleum plant since the start of the

'50s, and my mother, Sofiya, was a grade-school teacher. A typical Soviet family, as unfortunate as many. But neither my grandparents, my aunts and uncles, nor any members of my immediate family were victims of the Revolution or Stalinist horror. None were condemned for treason or sent to a Gulag, or at least no one ever spoke about it. I joined Komsomol at the age of ten, but I never joined the Party.

I began my studies at the Baku State University. Engineering, of course. The city was always subject to the dictates of oil production. Alfred Nobel amassed his fortune there, the fortune that enabled him to finance the prizes baptized with his name. Just to be clear: I never liked engineering. Just to be sincere: I hated it from the first moment, but at the time I didn't even realize it because the profession was so deeply-rooted in my world and in my expectations. At the age of nineteen, I had to go on active duty in the Army, and when the Soviet Union invaded Afghanistan on December 24th, 1979, I was among the first to cross the border.

I was there for over two years, until August of 1982. I was wounded twice, first in a leg and then in my left eye. The second wound put an end to my military career. I received the Afghanistan-Soviet Friendship Medal, which on the back says "with the gratitude of the Afghan people"—the same people who shot me. The worst aftermath of my time at the front was not my partial loss of vision, not the bits of shrapnel lodged in my muscles, but my irrepressible appetite for alcohol and opium, and a muted inclination toward violence which I attempted in vain to repress over the course of the rest of my life.

Back in Baku, I became an employee of Azmorneft, the state industry that was developing the Neft Dashlari oil field, one of the richest in the world. To fight tedium, I began to keep a diary. Later I produced some stories I had circulated in *samizdat*. In 1984, I married an Azerbaijani girl, Zarifa, who'd been a neighbor of my parents since childhood. My marriage to her, weighed down by the ethnic conflicts that ravaged the zone—along with my frustration and rage—ended abruptly in 1988, right in the middle of perestroika.

I continued writing, ceaselessly, more and more disenchanted by the drift of the country. I left Baku when the heartbreaking conflict between Armenia and Azerbaijan began and moved to Moscow, that city of wide avenues. I got a job at the illustrated magazine *Ogoniok*, one of the first to take advantage of the freedom of expression brought in by Gorbachev, the shepherd of men. I published many articles about the forces that were tearing the Soviet Union apart, and which would end up burying it. Because of my denunciations, I was victim of an attack that put me in the hospital for several weeks, just before the coup d'état of August 1991, whose failure I watched from the front line.

The publication of my Afghanistan memoir heightened hostility against me, both in the government and among the veterans of the war (one of the most reactionary groups in the nation). In 1995, my second book came out, a denunciation of the irresponsible draining of the Aral Sea and the corruption that dominated the privatization of state industries. Again I was insulted and persecuted, now by Boris Yeltsin and the oligarchs who took over the former Soviet factories.

Burned out, I set about sketching a novel, *In Search of Kaminski*, a political thriller about the new Russian moguls (Kaminski was the code name of Mihail Khodorkovsky, the owner of Russia's largest oil company, Yukos). I received scores of threats, but the book sold thousands of copies and was translated into twenty languages. Overnight, I became a celebrated author, because of one damned novel! My face appeared in the press and on television, I gave lectures at universities and book fairs, I traveled from one place to another as if someone were after me (perhaps someone was after me), and my voice became a reference for ecologists and critics of neoliberalism. For months, I was unable to write a single line, hemmed in by my fame, my relative and awkward fame, and the ghosts of alcohol. It was then, intent on escaping that swamp but sinking more deeply into it with each day that passed, that I traveled to New York, navel of the world, and in the autumn of 1999, I met Eva Halász for the first time.

THE STRUGGLE FOR SURVIVAL

Union of Soviet Socialist Republics, 1953-1985

Carried by the afternoon wind, the infectious agents scattered throughout the plant. No one noticed their escape, no one saw them enter the ventilation system, slip through the filters, or disperse into the atmosphere. Bad luck. Meanwhile, they mercilessly attacked their first target: a ceramics factory across the street. Ignorant of the threat, the night-shift potters spun the wheels, modeled the clay, heated the ovens, and painted flowers and patterns on the porcelain without realizing that the spores were invading their mouths, noses, and ears. The strategy was vile but effective: The virus let itself be trapped by the defenses of the immune system—a miniature Trojan Horse—but once inside it exploded like a time bomb. Then it stole nutrients from its host and reproduced relentlessly. Worn out, the human cells burned.

The potters went home with sore throats, convinced they had colds, but within a few hours their symptoms worsened: a dry, insistent cough, watery eyes, congested respiratory passages, extremely high fever. The virus had secreted proteins that poisoned the antibodies attempting to devour them. First they generated an edema and then forced the antibodies to produce cachectin (or TNF and interleukin-1-B, two substances that work to induce inflammatory reactions but whose accumulation in the pleura and lungs provokes a septic shock).

Beginning on Sunday, April 1st, 1976, the workers from the ceramic plant entered, one by one, the nearby hospitals. Diagnosis: an acute infection by the *Bacillus anthraces*, gram-positive bacteria ranging in size from one to six microns, discovered by Robert Koch in 1877, the cause of anthrax, a sickness that infects lesser herbivores but sometimes, especially when there is a biological plant across the street, infects humans.

The first thing Arkady Ivanovich Granin thought when he was informed of the outbreak (he received the news at five in the morning) was: I hope I'm not the guilty party. Luckily he wasn't, but as Scientific Director of Installation Number 19, he knew that they would be looking for a scapegoat.

Though he was forbidden to talk about his work with Irina—she'd given birth not even two weeks earlier—panic distorted his face. All he said was: I have to go. She stayed in bed, more lethargic than tender, with Oksana's mouth at her breast. She got no pleasure from breast feeding: Afterward, her chest burned for hours. She still had three weeks of maternity leave left, but she already couldn't stand being at home. Even there, in her room, interrupted by her daughter's crying, she only dreamed of techniques she would soon put into practice in her laboratory. Is something wrong? she asked. Nothing serious, muttered Arkady. I'll be back later. He didn't even come over to her to say good-bye: He was repelled by that animalistic act.

The bustling city was still ignorant of the anthrax epidemic. But at 11:00 A.M. the first victim died, a watchman at the ceramics factory. Arkady visited one clinic after another to observe the patients first-hand. Then he went to Installation Number 19, which he found guarded by the special forces. Frustration and fear, the double fear of the epidemic and the reprisals, floated in the air with the same acrimony as the virus.

Installation Number 19—code name for the Military Institute of Technical Problems, a dependency of the Fifteenth Directorate of the Ministry of Defense—was in charge of producing anthrax for military purposes. Arkady Ivanovich Granin had begun to work for Biopreparat, its mother company, at the end of the '60s, invited by General Piotr

Burgasov, who now acted as chief of medical services for the Ministry of Health. Like other scientists involved in the biological weapons program, to accept the position he had to convince himself that he would be creating new antidotes and finding new ways to respond to enemy attacks. In reality, he was producing stronger and stronger viruses—anthrax, tularemia, meliodosis, glanders—and continually improving the agents capable of dispersing them. For a long time he did the impossible, brutally silencing his conscience's protests about the perverse nature of his experiments, but now, as the number of victims rose, he could no longer conceal his regret.

Just as it would happen in Chernobyl ten years later, the bacteria leak in Sverdlovsk, fortress of ice, had been an accident. A damned accident, like everything else in this story! For the anthrax to be used as a weapon, it had to be subjected to a risky manipulation that was carried out by three technical teams who rotated over the course of the day. Each one had to dry and pulverize the cultures so they could be scattered by aerosols. When the process was finished, a few spores would inevitably remain in the air, so the staff was vaccinated and the ventilation system was protected with thick filters. That afternoon, when the refining machines were disconnected, a technician discovered that one of the filters was torn. Aware of the danger, he informed Colonel Nikolai Chernishov, on the evening shift, of the problem. Fatigued, Chernishov forgot to write down the information in the log, so the man in charge of the next shift simply turned on the machines without knowing there was a failure. Thousands of spores escaped from Installation Number 19, crossed the sidewalk, and attacked the ceramics factory. Within a few hours, they had expanded over a radius of several kilometers.

All the units connected with Project Ferment—or Project F—were moved to the city, despite the risk of arousing the suspicions of spy satellites. Arkady Ivanovich set about organizing the decontamination of the plant, implemented a program of emergency vaccination, supervised the care of the most at-risk patients, and informed his superiors of the deaths. Whenever a death occurred, a special unit from Biopreparat picked up the cadaver, delivered it for autopsy, then placed it in a lead coffin, and buried it in secret.

Arkady didn't return home until 5:00 A.M., and only to shower and rest for a few minutes. Irina was waiting for him, awake and frightened. He understood her nervousness: What if something happened to Oksana? She was too young to be vaccinated.

There's been an outbreak of anthrax, he confirmed to his wife, anticipating the official story: It seems to be the result of a shipment of contaminated meat. Is it serious, Arkady Ivanovich? Don't leave the house, and above all don't go downtown.

Arkady could fool the ignorant—many western epidemiologists would swallow the lie—but not his wife. She too was a biochemist and, supported by her lack of confidence in Soviet institutions, had always harbored suspicions about the plant where her husband worked. She was sure that her own laboratory, charged with making sulfa, was a subsidiary of the military-industrial complex.

Tell me the truth, Arkady Ivanovich. That's all I know. Irina followed him to the bathroom: We have a daughter, I know what's going on. You know nothing! No more lies. Tell me what's going on. Arkady washed his immutable face. An accident? Yes, an *accident*, he exploded. There are dozens of infected people, I don't know how many will die. Irina came up to her husband and embraced him over his shoulder. It's perverse, Irina, perverse, he whispered, but right now there's no time for feeling sorry.

Irina understood, understood very well. He wanted to reveal everything, express his impotence and rage, but he still was unable to do so. He lacked the courage to make her into his accomplice, to share his doubts or criticism with her. Even though they'd been married for seven years, he still had doubts about Irina.

The number of cases rose at an alarming rate: It was the worst outbreak of pulmonary anthrax ever recorded. To top things off, no reliable statistics existed in the Soviet Union, and not even Arkady Granin, who held an important job in the biological program, could rely on official estimates. According to the figures released by the Ministry of Health, ninety-six people had been infected and sixty-six had died. Following his own calculations, Arkady raised that number to 115.

A delegation composed of Colonel Yefim Smirnov, Commander of the Fifteenth Directorate of the Ministry of Health, and Piotr Burgasov, Arkady's old boss, came to the city a week after the accident. Boris Yeltsin, of strong arms, the thick and punctilious First-Secretary of the Sverdlovsk *oblast*, greeted them. The Party board room became their command post.

At your orders, comrades, Arkady Ivanovich saluted them. Skip the circumlocutions, doctor, Yeltsin blurted out, what do you recommend? Analyze the reports on the dead, determine the type and development of each infection, and carry out a complete study of the victims and the contaminants. Do you see, comrades? shouted the First-Secretary, standing up like a bear: We have to work calmly to ensure that nothing like this ever happens again. With all due respect, the Ministry of Defense is not cooperating with us to resolve this crisis in the most appropriate fashion, he added. I disagree with you, Smirnov interrupted, we cannot allow anything to be known about this event. The most important thing is to act with efficiency and discretion. Thank you for your words, Doctor Granin, you may leave now.

Arkady would have liked to support Yeltsin's arguments, but Smirnov stopped him. The firmness and sincerity of the First-Secretary, rare virtues among Soviet bureaucrats, impressed him. Honoring his own reputation, Yeltsin visited Installation Number 19 with his bodyguard and demanded to be let in. He was not going to tolerate the military's lack of support. Sverdlovsk, fortress of ice, was his responsibility: I have no intention of leaving here, he thundered.

A soldier delivered a message: By order of General Dmitri Ustinov, Minister of Defense of the USSR, no civilian is authorized to enter the plant, and that included him, comrade First Secretary of the Sverdlovsk *oblast*. Two weeks later, Ustinov himself came to the city, so there would be no doubt about his control. Meanwhile, the television news reported that various butchers and meat distributors had been arrested for not supervising the quality of their products.

What happens now, Arkady Ivanovich?, Irina asked. Maybe nothing will happen, as usual, or perhaps we've learned a lesson.

That wasn't the case.

Three years later, in October of 1979, a Russian-language newspaper published in Germany by a group of exiles revealed the anthrax outbreak in Sverdlovsk. How did those dogs get the information? bellowed the KGB officers attached to Biopreparat as they pointed to the plant's scientific team. Ultimately, they were unable to find the guilty party. In January of 1980, the same newspaper published new details about the case, asserting that an explosion had provoked the epidemic. The *Daily Telegraph* in London and the Hamburg *Bild Zeitung* republished the story, and the United States re-directed its satellites toward the zone. Ronald Reagan, then a candidate for the U.S. presidency, declared that the USSR was, without a doubt, an evil empire. On March 24th, 1980, Arkady read an article produced by the TASS news agency in *Pravda*, "The Germ of the Lie," that re-asserted the truth of the contaminated meat account and went on to accuse the agents of imperialism of calumny against the Soviet Union.

Since it was impossible to go on using Installation Number 19—the city had become a permanent target for western espionage—Leonid Brezhnev, the cunning mummy, ordered the plant closed in 1981 and transferred all the researchers connected with the biological program to a small Biopreparat laboratory on the solitary plains of Kazakhstan, not far from Stepnogorsk.

Stepnogorsk! shrieked Irina Nikolayevna. That's what the orders say. When would we have to go? Arkady exploded: Never, I don't intend to accept. He spoke those words with a firmness she did not recognize. I've thought it over a lot, Irina. We're not going to Stepnogorsk. Maybe you can request a transfer to another planet . . . You haven't understood. I'm not going anywhere. Arkady furrowed his brow: I'm going to resign.

It was insane. He'd never be allowed to do it. Do you know what you're saying? What I've done until now is unworthy of a scientist. They'll come after you, Arkady Ivanovich, they won't leave you in peace. I don't intend to cause them trouble. I just want them to let me work in a civilian laboratory. I don't care where. I want my work to be useful, to save lives, not end them.

The next morning, Arkady brought the subject up again: I've requested an appointment with Yeltsin. Maybe he can do something. The First Secretary was sympathetic, but his hands were tied. Arkady knew too much, and the KGB would never let him leave Biopreparat. Despite Yeltsin's advice, both Arkady and Irina agreed to face any and all consequences, the infinite and terrible consequences that would result from their decision. Oksana had just turned five: They didn't want her to be ashamed of them in the future.

I'm with you, Arkady Ivanovich. We'll fight side by side!

General Piotr Burgasov clapped his hands to his head, more out of incomprehension than anger. Arkady had gone to the Ministry of Health in Moscow to visit him. Though his position was subject to the Fifteenth Directorate of the Ministry of Defense, he'd preferred to communicate his resignation directly to his old boss. After all, he was the one who'd invited Arkady to the Military Institute of Technical Problems in Sverdlovsk.

I'd like to dedicate myself to pure research. I have a family, general. And a responsibility as a scientist. No one will understand it that way, comrade. I'm prepared to justify my decision. I consider myself a good Communist, General. I just want you to transfer me to a civilian laboratory.

Do whatever you like, Arkady Ivanovich, but never come back here again.

That was the first of the many reprimands, accusations, and threats that would rain on him. Not even his friends or fellow workers sympathized with his cause. Vadim Krementsov, whom he'd known since university, tried to explain things: It was an accident. You shouldn't feel guilty.

Arkady Ivanovich did not resign from the Ferment Program because of the 100 dead in Sverdlovsk, fortress of ice, but for a more intimate, more profound reason, one perhaps he himself did not suspect. He'd reached the point of no return. But, following Krementsov's advice, he agreed to wait until the end of summer. In August, he went to the family dacha with Irina and Oksana. The heat and humidity did not calm his nerves. He went off by himself, indifferent to the desires of his family, and locked himself in his office.

Will you play with us, Daddy?, Oksana repeated every midday. Yes, yes, you get started, and I'll catch right up to you. But he never did. He had to find a way to reconcile his obligation and his conscience, a task that was too arduous to be set aside for walks and riddles.

The family returned to Sverdlovsk on August 28th, 1981. Arkady was supposed to be in Stepnogorsk on September 1st. That day, he took refuge in his room, drinking tea and vodka until late at night. No one came to arrest him; he'd received no calls from his superiors. Only silence.

On September 7th, Oksana saw three armed men in front of their house, but they disappeared without leaving a trace. On the 13th, Arkady received the order to appear in the KGB office that was attached to the Military Institute for Technical Problems. For the first time, he kissed his daughter on the forehead as if he would never see her again. Irina walked him to the door and whispered encouragements to him. Arkady did not feel like a hero. He was simply incapable of moving to Kazakhstan. Perhaps that was all: apathy, disenchantment.

The KGB officer got right to the point: Comrade, you have an obligation to the state, an obligation you cannot refuse to carry out. Your responsibility is enormous, comrade. If you wish, take a few days off, a week perhaps, comrade, but don't put yourself in a difficult situation. Quitting your job may be interpreted as an act of rebellion, or even treason, comrade. Treason. He held out a firm, glacial hand. And if I were to ask for a medical absence?, thought Arkady. That would only prolong his uncertainty.

Starting on the 25th of September, he was summoned to make statements every day, from 8:00 A.M. until 2:00 P.M., as if this were his new job. His interrogators took turns in a regular way; sometimes they were military men, others agents of the KGB, scientists, functionaries, and members of the government or the Party. He could barely tell what rank they were; they all seemed to be variations on a single person, a single prosecutor. At first, the interrogations maintained a certain level of courtesy because no one as yet had made a formal accusation against him, but friendliness soon gave way to suspicion, then to hostility, and finally to violence. Those men did not listen to his justifications; they only wanted to ascertain his plans and break his spirit (his memory of his father became more vivid than ever). Arkady not only had to explain his decision to abandon Biopreparat but justify every act in his life, make an inventory of his career, reveal his character and his manias, reveal his secrets.

I can't go on any longer, Irina, maybe none of this is worthwhile . . . She contradicted him: You can't go back now, Arkady Ivanovich, you have to be strong.

The prosecutor general signed the order of arrest on November 3rd, 1981. He was not only accused of abandoning his work but of anti-Soviet activities as well. The order of arrest noted that when his dacha was searched, the police found documents that had been illegally removed from the Military Institute of Technical Problems, as well as a text that put state secrets at risk (these were the notes Arkady had jotted down during the summer). Just as he recounts in his *Memoirs*, that same day he was arrested and taken to a military prison. Oksana watched him walk away from the window. The child would never forget that image: Her father, until then a man protected by the *nomenklatura*, arrested like a common criminal.

Locked in a cell with two other prisoners, Arkady was still not convinced he'd made the right decision. He didn't want to harm his country or Communism, he wasn't a rebel or a dissident like Sakharov—he always distrusted scientists who got mixed up in politics—and much less an enemy of the USSR like Solzhenitsyn. He simply had principles and wasn't willing to ignore them any longer. For fifteen years he had contributed to the production of biological weapons, weapons that could kill thousands or millions of people, and he just didn't want to go on doing it. There was no resistance in his act, or at least he did not perceive any, it was simply an ethical challenge. He was prepared to defend his position to the end. To the end? Arkady had no idea what that could mean—the possibilities were terrifying—but after discussing it with Irina he decided to stay firm, not to renounce his convictions, and to go as far as was necessary.

Meanwhile, Irina mulled over her own anguish: She had encouraged her husband to challenge the system. She had backed him up, she had raised his spirits. If she'd remained silent during that summer at the dacha, perhaps Arkady would have forgotten his pretensions and would now be alongside her and their daughter. But instead of keeping silent, she'd focused her rebelliousness through him, had turned him into an instrument of her frustration and rage (a rage—even he had to recognize it—that she'd also directed toward Arkady). During the twelve years of their marriage, they'd never had a fight, had never raised their voices. Their shared life had been, at least from the outside, perfect.

She'd been separated from Yevgeny Konstantinovich for five years when her friend Svetlana Dubinskaya introduced her to Arkady in 1965. He had been married to an Army engineer from the Military Institute for Technical Problems for three years. She fell in love with him on the spot: Irina had no idea what chemical reactions Arkady stimulated in her body, but she simply could not stay away from him. They slept together that very day, but from then on she avoided him: She did not want to be in love with a married man. But Arkady was relentless and, obeying the dictates of his genes, did everything he could to conquer her. He sent her fiery, almost pornographic, letters, swore eternal love, pursued her day and night, tempted her, pestered her relentlessly, and finally got what he wanted.

They began seeing each other secretly two or three times a week. After each meeting, she would say: This will be the last time, Adrkadi Ivanovich, good-bye. Despite the advantages of the situation—she had unlimited freedom and could spend hours and hours in her laboratory without being recriminated by anyone—she could not accept being merely his lover. Every night she promised to leave him, and every night she did the same thing. After a year, Arkady's wife got fed up with his tricks and demanded a divorce. He begged her to reconsider: It would not look right to the Party if such a promising scientist—he'd already taken his doctoral examination and had been promoted in the

Institute—separated from his wife. But the engineer was adamant.

Irina Nikolayevna and Arkady Ivanovich appeared at the *Zags* to formalize their union in February of 1969. By then he was another man, as if after achieving his objective he'd lost all interest in Irina (which is how masculine genes behave). More than forgetting her, he went back to concentrating on the only thing that really interested him: himself. Irina accepted the new situation without complaining: Her love for Arkady, her admiration of Arkady, and her devotion to Arkady were so intense that it didn't matter to her that she'd become his wife, assistant, secretary, lover, and servant. She could spend hours listening to him analyze every conceivable topic—especially if he was talking about biology—and speculate with hypotheses and theories. She wasn't bothered by this subordinate role. As long as he talked to her about science, she was content to resolve all the practical issues. Irina was as certain of Arkady's greatness as he was himself: Her husband was destined to occupy a place of honor in Soviet science.

The years did not undermine that shared opinion, though they did moderate it. While Arkady was considered a brilliant biochemist, his position at Biopreparat limited his perspective. He was not authorized to write any articles related to his research, and only rarely, after subjecting himself to the judgement of myriad bureaucrats, would his bosses allow him to publish notes of marginal importance unrelated to the biological program. The benefits of his position were obvious—his salary was extremely high by Soviet standards, and he received a house in downtown Sverdlovsk—but glory was both dim and distant. To what extent did this lack of opportunity, visibility, and recognition influence his resignation from Installation Number 19? Irina never doubted her husband's sudden attack of conscience, but she believed his professional frustration also played a role. For Arkady, anonymity was the worst sentence he could receive.

Her unreserved admiration, her tenderness, the trust and faith Irina felt lessened a bit when their daughter was born. The creation of an authentic life, one independent of her bacteria and protozoans, took her by surprise, but from the moment the doctor informed her of her pregnancy a series of abstruse biochemical processes altered her personality. Science stopped interesting her, or only interested her if it helped explain how the cells multiplying in her womb were going to turn into a human being. She didn't consider life a miracle—it wasn't a magic trick but a brilliant series of accidents—but when she imagined the infant beginning to inhabit her, when she thought she was no longer one but two, her resistance to sentimentalism vanished.

For Arkady, both Irina's pregnancy and the actual birth were inconvenient, if not abominable. He perceived something monstrous in his wife's inflamed body, and the idea that his daughter carried half his genes neither comforted him nor made him proud. Or, as Irina came to think, perhaps he was simply jealous. When she reached the fifth month of pregnancy, he stopped touching her (sex had ceased to be one of his passions), and he limited himself to asking about her health in an aseptic tone. His coolness increased when Irina gave birth. Arkady did not know how to behave with his daughter. From the first day, he was reluctant to hold her, got into a terrible mood because of her crying, and stayed far away when his wife rocked her to sleep or changed her. He didn't perceive this distance, liked to present himself as a good father, and took every opportunity to show her photo, but he couldn't stand to smell or cuddle her.

The accident at Installation Number 19 widened the separation between Arkady and his family. While Irina rushed to confirm her solidarity with him and encouraged him to go further with his revolt, it seemed to her that Arkady had found the best excuse for forgetting about Oksana. The threat hanging over him made everything else irrelevant. Paternity would have to wait for better times. Ultimately, Arkady's arrest ended his relationship with his daughter. Irina found herself torn between two contrary sensations, the need to support her husband and the rage his negligence provoked. In prison he would have to endure myriad tests, but she and Oksana would hardly find life outside easy. You're a phony, Arkady Ivanovich, Irina recriminated him in secret: You finally got what you wanted, to be the center of the world.

The same day Arkady was taken off to jail, Irina went out in search of help. Defying her husband's instructions, she made contact with activists from the human rights movement. Arkady reasoned that an alliance with dissidents would prejudice his cause, but Irina no longer felt obliged to follow his orders. Thanks to the good offices of a friend, she met Sofiya Kalistratova, a lawyer who was friendly with Andrei Sakharov. She was well-known for having defended several dissidents, like General Piotr Grigorenko (stripped of his Soviet citizenship in 1977), the poet Natalia Gorbanevskaya (in exile in Paris since 1975), and the activist Ivan Yajimovich (locked up in a mental asylum). While Kalistratova had, since 1970, been deprived of her right to help political prisoners—she was now a tough seventy-four-year-old lady—she was still linked to the movement and formed part of the Moscow section of the Observers of the Helsinki Accords. She showed Irina the unknown side of Soviet reality: Since the Khrushchev thaw, the number of dissidents and political prisoners had only increased.

I'm afraid Arkady Ivanovich will be one more name on the long list of scientists the government holds in jail, in internal exile, or in psychiatric hospitals, she said. Do you know the case of Sergey Kovaliov? He was arrested in 1975, sent to prison in Perm, and then in Cristopol. He now lives in a Siberian town where the average temperature is fifty below zero. I don't want to frighten you, Irina Nikolayevna, but you should know the possibilities. If you want to get background, take a look at the *Chronicle of Current Affairs*, founded by Kovaliov.

Sofiya dug into the false bottom of a drawer and showed her a *samizdat* copy; it registered all the violations of human rights in the USSR during the past decade. The regime passes through periods of relative tolerance, the lawyer explained, but then the repression increases savagely. We now find ourself in a critical phase, which began with the arrest of Sakharov in 1980. From then on, everything has gotten worse . . . Your husband picked the worst moment to rebel. Andropov claims to be a reformer, but we cannot forget his years as Director of the KGB. Nor can we forget that he called Sakharov the nation's public enemy number one.

Just as Arkady feared, Irina's contacts with the activists increased the pressures against him. Where before there was no proof of his anti-Soviet activities, the prosecutors would now have no trouble proving his treason. But the charges against him were so vile and nonsensical that Arkady finally stopped opposing his wife's strategy. Even if he remained suspicious of the movement for human rights, he was, in fact, a dissident.

In mid-February 1982, Arkady Ivanovich wrote a long letter to Leonid Brezhnev, that cunning mummy, sending copies to the Academy of Science and the Ministries of Defense and Health, urging them to close down the USSR's program in biological weapons and to comply with the 1972 Convention on Biological Arms. No one answered him. His case finally appeared in the May, 1982 issue of *Chronicle of Current Affairs*:

> *From March 13 until March 25, the Sverdlovsk Court, presided over by A. Shalayev, heard the case of Arkady Ivanovich Granin (born in 1929; arrested on November 3, 1981), and sentenced*

> *him according to articles 70 and 190-I of the Penal Code of the Socialist Soviet Russian Republics. The prosecutor was K. Zhiranov, the counsel for the defense V. Shvirinsky. Verdict: Arkady Ivanovich is declared guilty of all charges.*

Accordingly, in April of 1982, Arkady was removed to Special Camp for Prisoners Number 35, in the *oblast* of Perm. While Arkady believed himself ready to face the tragic and glorious destiny that awaited him, he very quickly discovered that his body couldn't tolerate imprisonment. Nothing in his previous life had prepared him for mistreatment, oblivion, and despair. Unlike most of the prisoners, he had benefited from the privileges of the elite, had enjoyed a life full of comforts, and hadn't even suffered the shortages of the Stalin era.

Wearing the same grayish uniform worn by all prisoners, Arkady shared his cell with Aleksandr Ajutin, a dissolute and crazed young man who insisted on introducing himself as a civil rights activist. The space occupied by the two men was only nine square meters, barely room for two beds, a tiny table, and a minuscule sink. The lavatories were outdoors, and it was only possible to use them with permission from the guards. Aleksandr had spent the past five years going in and out of the camps and tried to appear welcoming, but Arkady could not stand his presence. He'd imagined jail as a lugubrious, atrocious place, but a solitary one, a place where he at least would be able to analyze himself, discover his interior truth. The presence of another prisoner ruined his plans. The system stole what he prized most highly: his privacy.

The first weeks in Perm were the worst. Aleksandr never stopped talking, and when he finally shut up, he amused himself by massaging his toes, picking his nose, or humming noisy, incomprehensible songs. There was no way for Arkady to stop hearing and seeing him and his obsessive tics and manias. The frozen nights subdued his intolerance. He never became friends with Aleksandr—he never managed to understand him—but his company became an indispensable part of his imprisonment. For a scientific mind like his, the worst aspect of jail was its lack of new things: Every day was identical, as if time were a dense, inert sphere.

In his *Memoirs*, Arkady gives a detailed account of his routine: The lights came on at 6:00 A.M.; Aleksandr yawned and cursed his fate. Then a guard led them to the dining room for breakfast, after which they were forced to go through two hours of exercise. After that came six hours of forced labor (the quotas promised by the camp director had to be met). In the afternoon, Arkady made for the library, which held only old Marxist manuals, the complete works of Lenin, and two or three novels by Jack London, which he reread very carefully. At 8:00 P.M. the lights went out. That way week after week, month after month . . .

By January of 1983, Arkady, who was now fifty-four years old, looked seventy: His hair had gone gray, his skin had acquired a wrinkled consistency, and his eyes had lost their shine. He hated to look at himself in the mirror: He couldn't stand seeing himself so old. In less than one year he'd become a wreck, even though he'd heard so many stories about prisoners who'd resisted the much more severe conditions in Tomsk or Magadan. Disgusted by his own lack of will (he was a walking cadaver, he later wrote), he led, during his second year in the Special Camp for Prisoners Number 35, a revolt to demand improvements in the food. The prisoners only had the right to a greasy, insipid broth. Perhaps his action would lead to nothing, but at least it would give him back his self-confidence.

The result of his complaints was that both he and Aleksandr were sent to the *Kamera*. Tossed onto a frozen floor, Arkady Ivanovich once again was forced to recognize his excessive pride. In that space, only four square meters, there was neither bed nor table, paper and pencils were prohibited, the only light came from a spotlight that barely formed a faint halo, and in one corner there was a foul-smelling hole that served as a latrine. That was all. The world had shrunken to that grave, that black box. At first, Arkady tried to order his mind, review his life, observe the road he'd chosen, but the humidity and the cold deadened his ideas. The solitude, the darkness, and the stench were transforming him into an animal. On the verge of delirium, he understood that now his only objective was to not go insane.

To escape from that time without time, where there was not difference between morning and night, Arkady invented a new routine: He exercised during the morning (he made hundreds of laps around himself), scratched (uselessly it seems) the stones and holes in the walls in search of a piece of paper or a cigarette, awaited the broth that came at midday, and, in the afternoon (or what he imagined to be the afternoon), meditated on scientific subjects—evolution, the struggle for survival, the vitality of genes, the mechanisms of inheritance, the work of proteins, the cleverness of nucleic acid, the memory of the mitochondria, cellular death, the survival of the strongest.

When the guard dragged him out of the *Kamera* two weeks later,

Arkady was no longer Arkady. That immersion in nothingness had extracted something from him, he didn't know what, his humanity, his pride, his character. He no longer felt the same, could no longer be the same. His challenge revealed itself to be a lost bet, a misunderstanding, a stupid thing. He no longer wished to be there, no longer wanted to rebel, no longer wanted to be a dissident, a prisoner, a hero, a martyr. He longed to return home, to recover Irina's eyes, Oksana's laugh, his own past. Impossible: He'd gone beyond a limit and, as he himself might say, there was no going back. He would remain there who knows how many years, would get old, and perhaps die in this dump, on the margin of history, evoked like a number, a footnote in the *Chronicle of Current Affairs*.

Stretched out on his cot—how he missed that musty mattress!—Arkady was slow to discover that he was now alone in his cell. And Aleksandr? Was he still in the *Kamera*? He did not appear either that day or the next, and the guards refused to discuss his whereabouts. Might he be sick? At times tuberculosis or pneumonia were good news. The camp clinic had certain advantages—hot food, light, attention. Another prisoner revealed the truth: Aleksandr, the unstable, febrile, maniac Aleksandr, had found a wire in his punishment cell and had hung himself with it. Arkady listened indifferently to the news, perhaps because suicide seemed the natural consequence of his cellmate's temperament. But after a few hours he could not keep himself from crying. He had convinced that dimwitted, stuttering young man to back his protest; he had dragged him to his death. That night, Arkady Ivanovich discovered he'd been beaten, that he was dead. He'd finally been defeated. He could stand no more, no more.

Irina Nikolayevna found out about Arkady's crisis thanks to Kira Gorchakova, another militant in the human rights movement. In June of 1983, Arkady was moved from the Special Camp for Prisoners Number 35 to a psychiatric hospital on the outskirts of Sverdlovsk, fortress of ice. Why? According to Gorchakova, he had begun a hunger strike after the death of a cellmate. Concerned about his health and the political repercussions of his act, the camp director decided to subject him to a psychological test—they diagnosed delusional paranoia (or something like that): it was a pretext for removing him from the camp and placing him under the authority of the KGB.

During the last few months, Irina had barely maintained contact with her husband. Two agents followed her everywhere, her letters were opened and checked, and her telephone was tapped. On more than one occasion she'd been forced to make statements in the offices of the KGB, and she never stopped receiving anonymous threats. Oksana was barely eight years old and had become a nervous, hypersensitive child, unable to stand the bullying and jokes of her classmates and teachers, who humiliated her in public and amused themselves by telling her, in detail, about the punishments the enemies of Communism deserved.

No matter how hard Irina worked to convince her that her father was right, and that she should be proud of him, the pressures around her became too strong. Oksana refused to accept her pain and spoke of her father as a ghost. Dark and thin, with enormous black eyes, Oksana was a phantom, always lost in her daydreams. Whenever Irina tried to explain Arkady's reasons, Oksana would hold her ears or sing as loudly as she could. Too absorbed in her own struggles, she simply observed how the child sank deeper and deeper into herself: a stranger with whom it was painful to live.

Soon after learning about Arkady's psychiatric confinement, Irina received a call from Oksana's school: You must come here immediately, comrade, the principal ordered her in a cutting voice. When she reached the office, she found Oksana sitting in a chair, silent and firm.

What happened? Sit down, please, said Comrade Smolenska. The principal looked at her with a sour expression: Your daughter has always behaved oddly, but we assumed that was because—how to put it, comrade?—of her family situation. But what happened today is intolerable. What happened? Why don't you ask your daughter yourself, comrade? Irina turned toward her daughter, who immediately averted her eyes: Oksana . . .

The girl just sat there silently, humming inaudible phrases, fragments perhaps of the songs she liked so much. We understand that the girls fight from time to time, comrade, it's normal. But it is not normal (the principal turned the word into a dagger) that one girl send another to the hospital. Oksana pounded Olga Makaninova against a wall until she knocked her out. It took fifteen stitches to close the wound, comrade. Fifteen stitches! Does that seem *normal* to you? I'm sorry, comrade, but I'm obliged to expel your daughter and send a report to the Ministry. In my opinion, she needs psychological help. I hope you take the appropriate measures, comrade, otherwise I'll have to do it myself.

Irina took Oksana by the hand and left hastily. Her daughter had done something terrible, true enough, but the principal was using the fact to increase the persecution of Arkady's family. Did they really want to send her daughter to a psychiatric hospital as they'd done with her husband? How far would they go?

Why did you do it? Why did you hit that little girl? Oksana whistled, indifferent. Please, honey, we're in a very difficult situation . . . Nothing. Oksana, please, I need your help. Together we can move forward. The girl's expression never changed. How could anyone guess what was going on inside her? How could anyone break through that wall? Sometimes she wanted to slap her or shake her so she'd see the light, so she'd break out of her apathy, and give herself over to her, to the one who loved her so much, the one who only wanted what was best for her. But Irina had other things to worry about: After Arkady's arrest, her colleagues at work had shown, if not solidarity, at least a certain understanding. But new directives from the company created an atmosphere of distrust toward her. Even in her laboratory her colleagues had stopped looking at her sympathetically. Soon she received the order to give up her personal research—her artificial life project—and was forced to concentrate on routine, mechanical preparations.

In December of 1983, she received the first bit of encouraging news in many months. Despite his own delicate health, Andrei Sakharov had found time to write a letter to Brezhnev, "In Defense of Arkady Granin," which had begun to circulate in the west. It was the first time Arkady's name had been mentioned outside the Soviet Union. But the plea was of little use, and 1984 began horribly. It was the date chosen by the dissident Andrei Almarik in his book *Will the USSR Survive until 1984?* to signal the end of Communism. But at the time, no one in his right mind thought the end of the Soviet Union was right around the corner.

On February 9th, after being Secretary-General of the Communist Party and President of the Soviet Union for little more than a year, Yuri Andropov died of a liver illness and was replaced by the walking corpse of Konstantin Chernenko, an old favorite of Brezhnev and an advocate of immobility. The reforms set in motion by his predecessor were forgotten, and the Soviet machinery moved only because of inertia. The rise of the elderly *apparatchik* represented a new blow to the movement for human rights. On May 6th, 1984, Sakharov began a new hunger strike to protest the arrest of his wife and the increasing repression.

At around that time, Irina finally received permission to visit Arkady in the hospital. She could barely recognize him: An obliqueness in his eyes recalled the vigorous man she'd married, but the rest of his body was a bad copy. His thorax was extremely thin, and his hands trembled uncontrollably. Despite his physical appearance, Arkady Ivanovich had begun to recover his courage. Aleksandr's suicide had caused him to hit bottom, and from then on he'd begun his slow climb toward the light. Now he did not feel conquered but simply fatigued and, as he said to Irina, he'd soon be ready to return to the struggle. A new struggle, more vehement than ever.

How is Oksana? Fine. Really? I shouldn't lie to you Arkady, she's had lots of problems in school. I don't know what to do, I barely manage to communicate with her, at times I don't recognize her, all this has had a huge effect on her. Arkady consoled her: This can't go on, Irina, soon we'll be together. Did you hear about Sakharov? The hunger strike? I hope someone convinces him not to go all the way, it would be the worst thing that could happen to us.

Irina stopped sobbing. She could not break down: We'll move forward, Arkady Ivanovich, she exclaimed. I'll have a talk with Oksana, I'll find a way to reach her, I promise. At that moment, neither of them could guess that within a year Chernenko would also die and that a 54-year-old Party member would take his place—a man whose destiny would be not only to reform the Soviet Union but to lead it to its destruction.

THE WEALTH OF NATIONS

United States of America—Zaire, 1970-1985

Despite the chaos, the stench, the mud, the traffic jams that could last for hours, and even despite its crude buildings and dark inhabitants (that part she couldn't share with anyone), Jennifer didn't want to be anywhere else on earth. As soon as she landed at the Kinshasa international airport, a den of jackals, and took a look at its shanties, its badly-painted walls, and its unpaved streets, she realized that accepting Dr. Blumenthal's invitation, without even getting Jack's consent, had been the right thing to do. This decision would separate her from her husband for an indefinite period of time, but they had agreed to respect each other's job opportunities above all other considerations. Do you really think it will be advance your career, Jen? mocked Wells when he found out. Africa? The Congo? Mobutu?

Jennifer retorted with one of her verbal cascades: Of course, Jack, don't you get it? It's a unique opportunity, do you think that I'd be so excited to accept if it weren't? Blumenthal is one of the greatest economists of our time, and he's asked me to accompany him, and not as his assistant but in a directorial position. In practical terms, I'll be the Vice-Director of the Central Bank of Zaire. I know that doesn't impress you, but for me it represents a formidable challenge, to civilize those savages, the task is grandiose, imagine the experience, to direct a nation . . .

Could you live without Bloomingdale's or Saks? For God's sake, Jen, just think about it. Is there a *more* horrible place on earth? His sarcasm was useless, Jennifer had already made an airline reservation. During the following weeks, she carefully packed what she'd need—including her stiletto high heels—so she wouldn't feel abandoned or miserable in Africa. *Africa.* Jennifer repeated that word to herself as a mantra, convinced she was embarking on a trip to the heart of darkness.

As the departure date approached, Wells became even more unbearable. Night after night he asked Jennifer if she'd been vaccinated against this or that horrifying sickness (and he would then describe its effects), and he would not stop lecturing her, as if he were a consummate explorer and not a vulgar executive whose closest contact with the Third World took place on the beaches of Acapulco.

How long will you be away? Don't worry, darling, I have no intention of settling down in Zaire, and you can visit me any time you like. A little adventure would do you good.

Adventure was what the jerk needed least: Not only had he begun a passionate affair with his obsessive secretary Laura, but Merck seemed interested in acquiring Lockhead Pharmaceuticals. The merger was almost a fact, but he didn't know what would happen after it took place. The idea of losing his position as head of purchasing sent more adrenaline through his body than fighting off a lion.

I'll come see you as soon as possible, he lied, maybe we can go on a safari.

A safari! No matter how adroit he was in business matters, Jack at times could be *so* infantile. Jennifer was on the verge of taking a significant step forward in her career, in Zaire—yes, Zaire!—and the only thing he could think of was hunting animals for sport.

Her husband's snobbery and banality practically disappeared when Jennifer moved to Kinshasa, den of jackals. While he supervised the number of syringes distributed in New Jersey, she was occupying a suite worthy of a pharaoh in the Gran Hotel, whose huge windows allowed her to watch the flow of the Congo, symbol of the vital current that was carrying her along. Worn-out by the flight, Jennifer sank into the tub, opened a bottle of champagne, and tried to calm her nerves. She woke up at 4:00 A.M. There were so many projects going through her mind that she decided to get up, call for a *ristretto*, and put some order into the notes she was to present to Blumenthal that morning.

At seven, she bathed again, put on makeup, and chose the ideal outfit for the occasion, something formal but sexy that would show her authority without diminishing her freshness. Jennifer spent hours choosing the perfect skirt and blouse: She preferred black, blue, or gray to brown or beige—colors for clerks she would say—but she was never satisfied, certain she could always look better.

Erwin Blumenthal, a cold, scrupulous German, the stereotypical high-ranking bank executive—he'd been President of the Deutsche Bundesbank—didn't see her until seven that evening. By then, the heat had ruined her hairdo.

Professor, she said in her sophisticated East Coast accent, before we get started, I'd like you to guarantee something . . . Blumenthal froze: This woman was speaking to him as if he were her subordinate. What's that, Jennifer? There no use in my being here if I can't work freely. I need you to guarantee that you'll support all my proposals and that I'll always be able to tell you what I think.

The German held back his laughter. He'd already been warned that the daughter of Senator Moore had a demonic personality, but he never imagined she could be so determined, so irreverent . . . so pretty. I'm sure we'll understand each other well, he calmed her down with a tone that left no room for arguments, I like to speak clearly myself. Jennifer relaxed: I want to thank you for your confidence, Professor, I won't disappoint you. Are you all set up? Is there anything I can do to make you feel more comfortable in this country? To tell the truth, there is. Jennifer went back on the attack: My office is intolerable, it doesn't even have any ventilation, and I need another secretary. The poor lady helping me is a dolt . . . I'll see you're moved to an office with more air, but I fear you'll just have to get used to the secretary.

During her last few weeks in the United States, Jennifer had locked herself away in the Harvard library to study, or rather dissect, the repugnant beast that was the economy of Zaire and Zaire's principal operator, owner, and beneficiary, the no less nauseating General Mobutu, he of the foul-smelling smile. That horrible personage, who in every single photo is wearing a leopard-skin cap (the height of kitsch) was responsible (in 1961) for the arrest and execution of Patrice Lumumba, the father of independence. Four years later, Mobutu had enthroned himself as boss of the nation. Much given to ostentation and grand spectacles, he decided one fine day to change the name of the country and to Africanize all proper names. He renamed himself Mobutu Sese Seko Nkuku Ngbendu wa Za Banga, which means something like: The All-powerful Warrior who through His Perseverance and Inflexible Will to Triumph Will Move from Conquest to Conquest Leaving Fire in his Awakening. How about that?

Thanks to the support of the CIA, which was attempting to stamp out the Communist plague in Africa, Mobutu transformed the once prosperous plantation of King Leopold of Belgium—the Congo was not only one of the biggest nations on the planet but one of the richest in natural resources—into his private preserve. At the suggestion of the International Monetary Fund, he introduced new currency, the zaire, to replace the Congolese franc and committed himself to maintaining equilibrium in the balance of payments. But those maneuvers only masked his true objective: to make himself infinitely rich. During the mid-'70s, per capita income in the nation was about $200.00, one of the lowest in the world, and the majority of the populace lived in the most abject misery.

The *matabiche* was the law of the land: Any service or license had to be paid for, and the thievery carried out by Mobutu's clan spread like an epidemic. Corruption was not only conspicuous, but Mobutu, he of the foul-smelling smile, had created a criminal network that allowed him to benefit from all the outside capital that flowed toward the country. An example: The Zaire Society for the Commercialization of Minerals was controlled directly by the President, without Congress or even its own administrators having the remotest idea of the transactions it carried out. The same held true for the Central Bank, which, until the arrival of the mission from the IMF, was nothing more than the President's piggy bank. He could dip freely into its reserves. With that money he built himself a replica of Versailles in Gbadolite, his home town, acquired scores of leopards and cheetahs for his gardens, and set about organizing the World Boxing Championship of 1974 (Jennifer recalled Norman Mailer's acerbic article about the fight between Muhammad Ali and George Foreman). According to several intelligence services, his personal fortune, deposited in dozens of accounts abroad, was more than four billion dollars.

Squandering on such a scale meant bankruptcy for the nation, and by 1975 Zaire could no longer pay its foreign debt. After renewed pressures from the IMF, Mobutu found himself obliged to devalue the zaire by 46%. One year later, the Club of Paris approved the restructuring of his credit, and international financial institutions forced the President to introduce drastic reforms. Fully aware of his power—the United States supported him unconditionally—Mobutu agreed to everything and carried out nothing. Or he carried measures out in theory while continuing to dole out the nation's wealth to his bureaucrats. By the outset of 1978, the IMF and the World Bank were finally fed up with his evasions and sent him an ultimatum: He would either initiate a rapid process of privatization, devalue the zaire, and commit himself to adjusting expenses, or sanctions would be imposed immediately.

At this point in the story, Jennifer could already foretell Mobutu's reaction. The fawning leader again agreed, accepted the presence of foreign advisers and inspectors, and agreed to privatize various strategic industries. These stopped belonging to the State (that is, to Mobutu himself) and passed into the hands of private owners (that is, Mobutu's relatives and friends). That was the tipping point. The United States threatened to cut back on military support if Mobutu again reneged on his promises. To guarantee the success of the measures, the central bank would cease to be under the President's control and would be a direct responsibility of the IMF and the World Bank. Which is how it came about that on August 17th, 1978, Erwin Blumenthal was named de facto President of the Banque du Zaire with Jennifer as his second-in-command.

As soon as she'd returned to her office after the harsh interview with her boss, Jennifer Wells assembled her team, some ten individuals, including her inept secretary. It was 10:00 P.M.

I want to thank you for staying on until this late hour. The first thing you have to know is that I'm a hard-working woman: I will not tolerate laziness. And much less negligence or betrayal. But I do know how to listen and to recognize my errors. I want this office to become an example to the country. Zaire has changed, and we will be the advanced guard for that change. Remember: For me, mediocrity is an unforgivable sin.

Despite the fact that her voice was too high-pitched, compared with the rumble of Zairian French, Jennifer's colleagues applauded her words. Most were young people who desired modernization.

You can count on us, Doctor, answered Jean-Baptiste Mukengeshayi, her chief of advisers, a tall, thin boy who had studied economics in Brussels. We won't disappoint you. If you'll allow me . . . That's what I wanted to hear, Jennifer interrupted him, unwilling to give up her starring role. We need that enthusiasm. Enthusiasm and honesty! You can see me whenever you want, I'll always be ready to listen. Good night.

As the others left, Jennifer signaled Mukengeshayi to stay: Jean-Baptiste, I have to ask a favor of you. Tomorrow, first thing, you have to give me a report on the performance of each of your colleagues. If it's necessary to throw them all out, it doesn't matter to me. I only care about efficiency and loyalty, understand? Yes, Doctor, but . . . See you tomorrow, Jean-Baptiste.

Jennifer was often accused of being rude, but she thought she possessed two capital virtues: sincerity and perseverance. Even if these simpering Zairians complained about her character, they would ultimately be thankful for her firmness.

This isn't a country, it's a casino, she complained to Blumenthal during their second interview. It's incredible what Mobutu's clan is doing with the people. They think they're entitled to every penny, and meanwhile millions are on the verge of starvation. We knew our task would be unpleasant, Jennifer. It's worse than I'd imagined. I can't understand how the people put up with it. Why don't they revolt? Calm down, Jennifer. Over the course of my career I've seen myriad cases like this one. But you are right about one thing: This is the worst. What we have concentrated here are all the defects of colonization and barbarism. Like you, I think we can't put up with Mobutu's trickery, so I'm going to give you a special assignment. I need a detailed report on his foreign bank accounts along with all the businesses he owns directly and indirectly. We've got to shake up this mastodon by force.

That night, Jennifer called Jack: Blumenthal is beginning to trust me. You can't imagine what this place is like. A swamp or something like that, a bog . . . I miss you. Me too. Wells was expecting another call and didn't want to waste time. Merck just announced the purchase of Lockhead Pharmaceuticals to the press. When are you coming to see me, darling? As soon as I can, Jen, things are red hot here. You want to hang up? I'm busy . . . You always do that to me! Anyway, good-bye.

They couldn't manage to come to an agreement with thousands of kilometers separating them. A few months earlier, during one of their daily fights, she had considered divorcing him, but had ultimately rejected the idea, convinced that neither of them would be able to survive alone.

Jennifer fought with her assistants, scolded them for their inefficiency, made them work twelve-hour days, and tormented them with sarcasm and threats—I'm going to fire you right now, she skewered each one—until she got what she wanted. Two weeks later, she delivered her report to Blumenthal. He listened to her in the presence of other members of his team and the representatives of the U.S. State Department and the CIA. Ninety percent of Zaire's exports and, therefore, the foreign capital derived from them, is concentrated in the hands of fifty companies, all of which belong either to President Mobutu or his clan.

For the next hour, Jennifer recited an exhaustive list of companies, pointing out their earnings and the links that connected them to power. As long as a small group continues to control the natural resources, the process of modernization cannot move forward. This regime is not a democracy, or even an oligarchy: It's a kleptocracy. The high functionaries, without exception, are dedicated to theft and graft. This is the depressing and sad reality.

Blumenthal nodded: Gentlemen, it's time to do something drastic. He adjusted his glasses: Are we in agreement?

The next day, the Banque du Zaire, supported by the IMF, the World Bank, and the United States, decreed that the fifty businesses inventoried by Jennifer would be disqualified from receiving state loans and excluded from international commerce. The measure took Mobutu, he of the foul-smelling smile, by surprise and angered his family. In the twinkling of an eye, they'd been stripped of their most lucrative businesses and offered nothing in exchange: it was a declaration of war. Hours later, Litho Moboti, the President's cousin and head of the clan, appeared at the offices of the Banque du Zaire (until then his back room) and burst into Blumenthal's office without even announcing himself. Moboti was a thick, fierce gorilla stuffed into a shirt of loud, clashing colors, wearing a cap identical to the one his illustrious relative wore.

An outrage! he screeched in terrible English. An attack! Zaire's sovereignty: Where did it go? You don't understand. You're stripping the people of their resources. Ignominious. Ignominious. I won't allow.

It took Blumenthal a few moments to recover his composure. Cold and serene, the old German fixed his eyes on the intruder and with an impatient wave of his hand pointed to the door. Before leaving, Moboti cursed again and again. Blumenthal confessed to Jennifer that his knees had been shaking the whole time: That man wasn't a negotiator. He was a criminal. That afternoon, he and Jennifer agreed that the final details of the plan would be executed around dawn: Dozens of accounts in the name of Mobutu and his surrogates, to the value of five million dollars, would be sequestered simultaneously in Europe and the United States.

Jennifer popped open two bottles of champagne with her team to celebrate the coup. They also felt proud to be sabotaging the kleptocracy, though they never stopped deploring Jennifer's tyranny.

What's wrong with them, Jean-Baptiste? Why do they look so apathetic? I really don't understand them. That's why they can't escape this misery, they don't have the nerve.

Mukengeshayi carried out Jennifer's orders to the letter—but he felt a mixture of respect and pity toward her, The poor woman lives a tormented life, he explained to his colleagues, she has no personal life, and now she suspects her husband is playing around. But sometimes she drove even him mad. Jennifer never realized how much she was hated, convinced as she was that she was carrying out great work. She could easily have been in the United States, augmenting her collection of jewels and fur coats, unconcerned about poverty, but instead she preferred the heat, insecurity, and mosquitoes of Kinshasa. Her only objective was to help its mangy inhabitants. All she expected from them is that they show some understanding for her mood shifts.

Mukengeshayi was right: Perhaps this time his boss did deserve more compassion than acrimony. Every time Jennifer returned to her suite in the Gran Hotel Kinshasa (she refused to move to the diplomatic neighborhood) she turned on the TV to pretend she wasn't alone, spent hours rubbing creams into her skin, tried to do 100 sit-ups every day—with this food I'm going to turn into a pig, she always said—and stuffed herself with tranquilizers and sleeping pills.

Her relationship with Blumenthal wasn't entirely negative, but she suspected he avoided her, fed up with her caprices. She had no friends and felt she could rely on no one in this shit hole. It never even occurred to her to have dinner with Mukengeshayi. She appreciated his efficiency, his deliberate, introverted manner, and his willingness to resolve any conflict. But he belonged to another world. They would never be equals; that was the truth, and Jennifer preferred not to analyze it. She didn't try to get her employees to agree with her proposals; she hoped only for loyalty, that they not slander her behind her back, and that they respect or, at the very least, fear her.

The last straw came when Jennifer discovered that Jack was having an affair, as she confessed one day to Jean-Baptiste. This wasn't the first time in their seven-year marriage that she suspected the interfering presence of another woman, but now her disadvantage was obvious: Wells was going through a tense period, and she was thousands of kilometers away. How could she compete at such a distance, how could she fight for his love, annihilate her adversary? Jack's telephone calls became briefer and briefer and more and more sporadic: They sounded like reports. Even so, she was not ready to give up her post in Zaire so she could keep an eye on her husband. She'd never done so before, and this time would be no exception. But, since her anguish did not diminish, she finally delivered an ultimatum.

Either you come here to spend New Year's Eve with me, Jack, or I never want to see you again. You took yourself off to the end of the earth, he defended himself. You know I can't leave my job a single day, one bit of carelessness would destroy all *my* efforts. But you, sweetheart, can certainly take a short vacation. The Merck deal has just gone through, Jen. She wouldn't yield a single inch: Please, I need you here.

There was no escape for Wells: He had to fly who-knows-how-many hours to calm his wife down because she was threatening to unleash a new matrimonial crisis. The Merck business had become public, and Wells met with Roy Vagelos, the new research director. Vagelos not only kept him on in his old job but promised to promote him to administrative director. His professional career was finally getting the push he'd longed for. His wife was right, perhaps he could take a few days off to celebrate his promotion. That way he could also escape a bit from Laura, who already saw herself replacing Jennifer.

Wells's plane landed at the international airport at Kinshasa, that den of jackals, on December 23rd. Jennifer was there to greet him, more elegant than ever. They shared a long kiss, symbolic of their definitive reconciliation, and went to the Grand Hotel. They made love with that meticulous urgency Jennifer enjoyed so much, and to which Jack had become accustomed. Then, surrounded by candles, creams, aromatic salts, and champagne, they took a long bath. A perfect night, he thought bitterly, trying to banish Laura's hyperbolic youth from his mind.

Cheers, Jack, to us! Yes, cheers. All he could do was count the hours until he could return to Rahway, where Merck's corporate offices were located. Mr. and Mrs. Wells sat face to face in the tub, as separate as islands. Jennifer didn't care for Vagelos, streptomycine, or cortisone

(Wells's mouth overflowed with these delightful terms), in the same way that he was bored by Mobutu, Blumenthal, and Zaire's commercial balance.

Jennifer changed the subject. What have you heard about Allison? I had dinner with her a couple of weeks ago. In San Francisco? I was there for a day, on business. I took her to a magnificent Japanese restaurant. She's as crazy as ever; I can't understand how the two of you can be sisters. You can just imagine, hippy clothes, meditation classes, and anti-capitalist speeches. She was very excited about organizing a march, Take Back the Night or something like that, to protest the mistreatment of women. So now she's a feminist. Well, she never answers my letters. I found her in rather high spirits.

She's not a little girl any more, Jack. She could at least be more responsible; just look at how she's wasting her intelligence . . . Jennifer wrapped herself up in a towel: Do you know if she's seeing anyone? Your sister has never had a stable relationship. From what I gathered, she sees lots of people, men and women. Jack! Allison always thought variety was the spice of life.

Jennifer went over to the sink and began her slow nighttime ritual. In front of her stretched a line of creams of all colors and aromas. Jack . . . Yes? She paused: I want to have a baby. Jen, please, we've already gone over that. The risk is too great; the doctor's told you so a thousand times. Don't think about that, we have all we want, we're happy the way we are. Or aren't we? Happy . . .

His wife had no intention of letting up: Okay, we'll adopt one. Jennifer! I'm serious, Jack. Let's talk it over tomorrow, I'm tired. No, I want to talk it over now. Jen, please . . . I've just turned thirty-three, I don't want to be an old mother, I want to have the strength to play with him, educate him. A child, can you imagine? Actually, I can't. Do you want to be a lonely old man? What are we going to do twenty years from now in a gigantic, silent house? We wouldn't be able to stand it, Jack; we've got to put in the application right now. It's 3:00 in the morning, Jen. She went on with her sermon until her husband got out of bed, grabbed a pillow, and headed for the living room.

The same dynamic as always: She'd launch a subject, he would respond, she would get angry, he would contradict her, and so on until the insults and shouting would start. For Jennifer, maternity was an obsession; for Wells, torture. When they married, no one mentioned children—both gave the highest priority to their careers—but one fine day Jennifer became convinced that her genes had begun to demand it: The desire was unlike any she'd ever experienced. It wasn't one of those momentary, uncontrollable whims that came over her from time to time, but an urgency that affected her entire being.

At the beginning of 1974, Jennifer decided to become pregnant, but the weeks passed and again her period came, threatening and ominous, to underline her failure. At her insistence, they underwent medical examinations that revealed her sterility: The same genes that forced her to want a child kept her from producing one. According to the doctors, a hereditary defect kept the ovule from settling in the uterus. The possibility of her ever getting pregnant was minimal. But Jennifer would never give up, and after two years of taking hormones she achieved her objective. The gynecologist confirmed the miracle.

It was not an easy pregnancy. Jennifer had to take the utmost care of herself. She was supposed to refrain from exposing herself to strong emotions, an almost impossible task given her anxiety. During the final months, she requested a leave of absence form the IMF, spent her days indoors, and was transformed into a housewife, a role she detested. First, she tried to knit, then she amused herself decorating the room for Edgar or Cynthia—she'd already chosen the names—with pictures of ships, waves, and mermaids.

One afternoon, as she was drawing a miniature sailfish, Jennifer felt a dizziness and then a tearing. She woke up in the hospital six hours later, and the first thing she saw was Wells's face, tinged with an unbearable compassion. She didn't need his confirmation: I want to try again, I want a baby! The nurses administered a sedative. After her recovery, Jennifer concentrated more and more on her work, her only refuge. She went back to the IMF and climbed the hierarchy at astounding speed. If she couldn't be a complete woman, she could at least be a successful one.

Even so, she could not put up with the outrage (her definition) her sister inflicted on her during the winter of 1978. After giving up her business administration studies, Allison turned into one of those outrageous young women who let themselves be carried along from one side to another, from one idea to another, without will or order. She worked as a waitress, a telephone operator, insurance saleswoman, public relations officer in an electronics company, archivist, and secretary. She lasted two months in each place, earned enough to survive for a few weeks, got bored, and quit, relying on her good luck and good looks to find another job. Seeing her always in a good mood and expansive, so different from herself, Jennifer did not understand what had gone wrong in Allison, what error or detour made her so free and poor, so distanced from reality. The world doesn't exist, little sister, Allison mocked, only the prisons we make for ourselves. And you're an expert at living in them.

Jennifer tried to make her listen to reason: You need to choose your own path, time's running out, one of these days you'll find out you've used up your talents. But Allison only laughed at her: I don't want to *triumph*, I only want to survive. Don't be silly, Allison, you've got everything. Everything? That's the problem, the Senator always gave us everything, which is why I don't look for anything. Listen to me, Jennifer: I'm not looking for anything.

If Allison went quickly from job to job, she moved from one man to the next even faster. Jennifer counted up more than twenty boyfriends in one year, and she was sure Allison slept with many more than that. Like items of clothing, masculine bodies were interchangeable, Allison explained. Aren't you a great defender of the free market? *Laissez-faire, laissez-passer.*

Despite these arguments, the sisters did not get along badly. They lived in opposite dimensions, with very, very few points of contact, but on the rare occasions when they did coincide (when they recalled their childhood, for example), they were still able to reconstruct their infallible complicity. They lived equivocal existences, each one obsessed with the fate of the other, as if as children they'd exchanged bodies.

In 1976, Allison moved to San Francisco, the only more-or-less liberal city in this country of gorillas. There you can at least dare to be different without someone reporting you to the police, spitting on you, or murdering you, she explained to Jennifer. Of course her statement soon proved to be false: On November 27th, Mayor George Moscone and the militant-gay city supervisor Harvey Milk were murdered by Milk's predecessor, Dan White. And what do you intend to do in San Francisco? I know, I know, protest—isn't that right? It's so easy to complain about everything and do nothing to fix things. But what will you protest against? Discrimination against gays? Vietnam? Whale hunting? There's always a good cause. Or pretext I should say.

When racial violence took over The Haight, which until then had been the neighborhood that epitomized the gay liberation movement, the Victorian mansions in the Castro District began to be covered with multicolored banners. Allison moved into 10 Blanche Street, a dead-end block a short distance from Dolores Park. Living on her floor were a pair of lesbians, Teddy and Sonia, Teddy from New York and Sonia from a mid-Western evangelical family, Ge (Allison never did find out his or her real name—Ge was a beautiful transsexual with black eyes), and Victoria, an out-and-out elegant lesbian who by day worked as a lawyer in a chic office and chased after girls in the local bars at night.

Was Allison homosexual? Even though she was almost thirty, she did not know for certain herself. She'd had brief flings with women, enjoyed sex with them, but couldn't put up with them for long. Men, on the other hand, repelled her—too violent even when they wanted to seem tender. However, they were at least predictable. After years of torturing herself, putting up with the jokes of her male friends and the suspicion of her sister, Allison made a decision: She wouldn't have to decide. She'd let herself be carried along by impulse, the desire of the moment, forgetting the illusory and authoritarian barrier of sexual differentiation. She was intent on fighting against all boundaries—political, economic, social, gender. Maybe she didn't know what to do with her life, as Jennifer constantly scolded her, but at least she recognized her enemies.

Life in 10 Blanche Street confirmed her expectations, and San Francisco allowed her to forget she'd been educated in the straitlaced east. Every morning she got out of bed intent on seeking new adventures and beginning new projects, and every night she got into bed convinced that a better world was possible. Her relationship with her friends was almost perfect, and as soon as she explained to Victoria that she wasn't interested in her—I never sleep with friends, she lied—all tensions evaporated. Ge became her confidant, able to divide herself in half in order to advise her either as a man or a woman. Allison loved strolling with Ge through the neighborhood, stopping to buy flowers or handcrafts or sharing a bit of marijuana while they chatted about the stars or predestination.

Three weeks later, Victoria introduced Allison to Tresa, one of her old lovers, a smooth, silent girl of Chinese origin with almost translucent skin. A few weeks of combustible passion—Tresa turned into a dragon when she took her clothes off—were followed by a slow, incurable boredom. When Allison ended the affair, her languid lover went into her bedroom and, with truly oriental patience, tore up all her papers, letters, photographs, and bills, all in order to strip her of their shared past.

Distressed, Allison turned inward, even though, every night, Ge and Victoria urged her to go out. Tresa has nothing to do with this, she explained, I need a bit of air, a time to forget, don't worry about me, I just need time. She got a job working in a library (she'd loved them since her time in the Philadelphia High School for Girls), and in her free time she coordinated the efforts of, just as her sister imagined, a protest group. What did they protest against? Against everything. For example, now they were opposed to the Supreme Court Decision of June, 1977, that said states did not have to pay for voluntary abortions with money from Social Security.

Nothing in Allison's routine seemed to be leading her toward a new relationship, much less one that involved a man. But her well-ordered life as a librarian and militant feminist was shaken up when she met Kevin, if that was his real name. When she spoke with him for the first time—he was an assiduous reader—he seemed a Martian to her: Thirty-five years old, blond, with enormous hands and slow gestures, he was always dressed in gray and always wore a tie. Ever since she'd given up on university, she'd had no contact with the fussy students she'd known as a girl. There was something spontaneous and tender in Kevin that clashed with his clothes and manners, a kind of psychic fracture, a certain neediness that fascinated Allison (because it made her think of her own). He tried to pick her up the first time he met her, but he did it with a serenity that no yuppie possessed. Kevin evinced no haste, no urgency, did not overwhelm her with love talk, did not threaten her with compliments, and did not pester her with double entendres or stupid presents. He was simply there every day, asking how her day had been and taking an interest in her militancy. One day, Allison invited him out for a drink, and they walked around the neighborhood until midnight; they ended up making love in a cheap hotel (she would never have dared to bring him back to Blanche Street).

For the first time in years, perhaps for the first time in her life, Allison felt comfortable with a man. Not ecstatic, but certainly calm and, why not say it?, happy. Every Wednesday they repeated the date, always with the same tranquility and delicacy, as if instead of loving each other they were just getting to know each other. Kevin never asked her anything except what her name was (even that show of curiosity seemed an intrusion to her), and she too wanted to find out nothing. Maybe it's better this way, she thought, no shadows, no echoes, pure present. She began to love Kevin because he did not try to possess her, why would he want more? But Allison did want more. Whenever she returned to 10 Blanche Street, she wondered if it wouldn't be possible, if perhaps it wouldn't be better, if it wouldn't be worthwhile . . . That is, she had doubts. Like any middle-class girl, she would have liked to know who Kevin was, what he really did—he insinuated he was a doctor or veterinarian or something related to health—and fantasized about a future at his side, a future of wide horizons and no borders, the kind she liked, but, after all was said and done, a future.

At the end of March, 1978, while her group was preparing a protest against the Supreme Court Decision *Stump vs. Sparkman*—five members of the court had decided to grant immunity to a judge in Indiana who'd ordered the involuntary sterilization of a mentally retarded girl—Allison discovered she was pregnant. The damn pills had betrayed her! Now what? Should she tell Kevin, or was it better to say nothing? That was her only dilemma, because she never considered the possibility of *not* having an abortion: Bringing a child into this world seemed a crime to her. Finally, her sense of honesty prevailed over her fear.

Let's have it!, he said. I love you, Alli. I never had the courage to say it to you before. Leaving everything doesn't matter to me, leaving everything for your sake, for the three of us. Allison stared at him, horror-struck. Had he gone insane? What was it he would have to leave? Kevin confessed he was married, that he had a twelve-year-old son and a ten-year-old daughter, and that he was very unhappy. Why are you telling me all this, Kevin? What a son of a bitch! Couldn't you just keep quiet? You've ruined everything! I'm sorry, I never dared to tell you the truth. She couldn't contain her rage: He wasn't understanding, serene; he was a coward, just like all the rest. You don't understand anything, Kevin. It doesn't matter to me that you're married or that you have three children or five lovers . . . Bastard! I don't want anything from you, do you hear me. I never wanted anything, I never asked you for a thing! *Nothing!* Why are you doing this to me?

Kevin stood there, confused. Now all I want from you is to be left in peace. I never want to see you again. Allison, calm down, we can work this out together. You and I are not *together*, that fucking word doesn't exist, Kevin. I'm here with a parasite in my guts, and you're there. Nothing connects us, there are not wires, cables, no tubes, so don't you dare tell me what I have to do.

Allison caressed his face before running away. That very day she made an appointment at a clinic, and the next day the parasite was dislodged from her uterus. She never went back to the library, the only place where Kevin could find her. She hid in 10 Blanche Street, where

Teddy, Sonia, Ge, and Victoria consoled her as if she'd had an accident (her version of what happened). She never saw Kevin again.

As soon as Jennifer found out what happened, she exploded in rage. Allison didn't expect understanding or affection, but she certainly didn't expect that fury. She'd never seen her sister that way. Jennifer accused her of having the abortion simply to hurt her: I thought you were capable of anything but that. God! How is it possible that we're sisters? You're not only a whore but a murderer! Allison turned on her heel and walked out. For her, her older sister had ceased to exist. Jennifer, on the other hand, never understood Allison's exit. They'd spent their entire lives fighting and had always finally made up—theirs was the only friendship they'd ever known—it was absurd that Alli would take things so seriously, to the point of returning her letters and hanging up the telephone on her. In her opinion, she was the offended party: Allison had been unfeeling and cruel in not noticing her pain. How could she have sacrificed a living being, one of the Lord's creatures, when Jennifer needed one so badly?

Jennifer hated liberals like her sister because of their double standard. They said they were the defenders of the weak and abandoned, but they were unable to find real solutions for their problems. She, a proud Republican, did not think she was better than anyone, did not think about guiding the poor the sick, or the disabled, but she did more for them than all these armchair progressives . . .

Every time she remembered that scene, Jennifer became nauseous. But as soon as Wells got on the plane back to New York, navel of the world, she felt liberated. She'd achieved her objective, which was to twist her husband's will, but now she had to concentrate again on her job. The first half of 1979 was a time of battles. She lived day and night in her office, accompanied by her faithful Mukengeshayi, planning the campaign to overcome the corrupt military, the corrupt customs people, the corrupt businessmen, the corrupt functionaries, and the corrupt citizens of corrupt Zaire.

In April, Blumenthal received a confidential report on the first results of his battle against the *matabiche*. While it may have been true that new secret businesses were discovered every week and scores of individuals where arrested, neither of those factors was in any way reflected in the economic indicators. The draconian measures pushed by both were diluted in a network of tricks and secret deals, as if the men and women working for the IMF and the World Bank were living in an ideal world and their decisions had no repercussions in reality. Zaire was a hole.

The lack of incentives and the economic stagnation added to the increasingly obvious distance between Jennifer and Blumenthal. She sank into a state of anxiety that caused her to take three different kinds of tranquilizers. Little by little, she was losing the support of her superiors, while her subordinates were rebelling against her in the most subtle and perverse ways. They're all plotting against me, she complained to Mukengeshayi. I can't trust anyone. Blumenthal is a softy who doesn't want to get involved in any problems; I don't know if he's reached an agreement with Mobutu, but I wouldn't be surprised . . . And the others are just waiting for me to make a mistake to gang up on me—they can't stand the idea that a good-looking and successful woman is better than they are.

Jean-Baptiste had learned to ignore her flashes of paranoia, but he couldn't stand it anymore: What you say is false, Doctor. We've been killing ourselves for a year now just to please you, to move this project forward, and you've never taken us into account. How do you expect us to respect you? You, you're against me too, you too! Your only enemy is yourself, Doctor.

Jennifer ran out of the office in tears and hid in the bathroom. After a while, she again summoned Jean-Baptiste and apologized a thousand times over. She promised to change, told him she needed his support, that it was very difficult being a woman and having a job like this, that her nerves were a wreck, that she couldn't take any more, that she needed his help, please, please.

That afternoon, Blumenthal urgently called her to his office: Jennifer, I gave you my full confidence from the beginning. I've overlooked lots of things over the course of these months, but now I'm fed up. I can't put up with your suspicion or your insinuations. Professor, I never . . . You tell everyone, Jennifer. You shout over the telephone, your screaming even reaches my office. If you're not happy, leave. For the second time that day, Jennifer burst into tears, tried to explain, only blubbered, apologized, but Blumenthal would not relent: I'm going to request your transfer to Washington.

Suddenly everything was going badly. But the final blow against the IMF policies was delivered at the start of August. A new report revealed that the Zairian Society for the Commercialization of Minerals had just transferred $5,000,000 to the personal account of President Mobutu, he of the foul-smelling smile, in Switzerland. Five million: the same sum discovered by Jennifer and seized by Blumenthal's order months back.

Our work is useless! Blumenthal looked defeated. This job is impossible with Mobutu working against us. If you take it away from me here, I'll just take it from there! And what are we going to do? shrieked Jennifer, just give up like that? There's nothing else to do. After such a long time, they were both on the same team again, but only to share defeat. And the promises we made? What's going to happen to these people, to all the ordinary citizens who suffer under this dictator? Blumenthal took off his glasses and fell silent. I'm sorry, Jennifer told Mukengeshayi, Blumenthal has thrown in the towel, and I have to return to the United States. It's always the same thing, he pointed out, you people go, and we stay.

Jennifer cleaned out her desk while the rest of her team gathered around her. Some didn't hide their joy—they were finally getting rid of the ogre who'd enslaved them for months; others, Jean-Baptiste among them, understood that Jennifer's departure was an obituary for the nation. I'm really sorry, Jean-Baptiste. He insisted on accompanying her to the airport: Don't worry, Doctor, we'll survive. Overcoming her repugnance, she embraced him.

With Jennifer's help, Blumenthal wrote a report of his experiences: *Zaire: a Report on its International Financial Credibility*, the chronicle of their failure. Two years later, in June, 1981, the directors of the IMF turned a blind eye to the report and conceded to Zaire an extended arrangement for $912,000,000. By then, Jennifer had been living in Washington, axis of the cosmos, for some months, and, even though she felt betrayed, chose to remain silent. The world is at war, she consoled herself, and nothing could be worse than the expansion of Communism.

MUTUALLY ASSURED DESTRUCTION

United States of America—Afghanistan, 1970-1985

Even if I wasn't there, at her side, taking charge of her pain—we would not meet for another ten years—I can look on her sleeping face, her skin barely rippled by the current of her veins, the shadows under her eyes, her extremely black eye lashes, her half-open lips, the hardness of her cheekbones. Eva slept without dreaming, her hands over her stomach and her feet bare: a madonna. Nothing in her appearance suggested her condition, the minutes passed between life and death, her drastic way out. She opened her eyes. A misty space appeared before her, and little by little, she made out a few figures: the outline of curtains (white); an end table and a vase filled with flowers (also white); a few metal chairs, a commode, and a door (all white); and finally, hidden behind the curtains, a metal screen (white, always white), definitive proof that she was not in the usual kind of hospital.

Why did she do it? Why then and not five or ten years earlier? Why did she wait so long to flee? This eagerness for death lacked logic. Eva was renouncing life at exactly the moment when the pieces of her destiny were beginning to fit together. She'd been receiving offers from the best universities and corporations in America and Europe, her cybernetic nets were becoming more and more intelligent—more *human*—and then, after three years of collaboration with the government, she finally had time for herself. As if that weren't enough, Andrew was still with her; moreover, Andrew still loved her. Her life was normal. So? She inhabited a hostile, incomprehensible wasteland, and that wasn't going to change even if she accumulated all the recognition in the world.

November 12th, 1985 had been a day like any other. During the morning, she said good-bye to Andrew, grabbed her bicycle, and rode to MIT along her usual route. She spent three hours evaluating her progress and then had lunch with Michael Buxton, to whom she revealed her disquiet over the commercialization of personal computers programmed with LISP—the programming language designed by John Mc Carthy—because she thought their interpretative range very limited. She said good-bye to him—promising to continue the conversation the next day.

Back at home, Eva read for a while and watched an episode from a television series (Andrew would be having dinner with his graduate students and staying late); then she went to the kitchen, opened the refrigerator, and got out lettuce and tomatoes to make herself a salad. But instead of putting these ingredients in a salad bowl, Eva, or what was left of Eva, went to the bathroom, opened the medicine chest, and contemplated it as if she were a shrew. She lined up the boxes and jars of medicine on the sink and emptied them one by one, piling up the pills, granules, and tablets according to their color and size, forming a pyramid. She observed its composition, perhaps expecting a sign or warning that never came. Finally, she swallowed all those substances one by one.

Left lethargic by the mixture of Diazepam, Iproniazid, Xanax, Tegretol, Ritrovil, and Ativan, the remains of the drugs prescribed for her in the past, she dropped to the floor, her back on the tiles. Her drowsiness barely lasted a few seconds, because then the other Eva, the strong-willed and stable Eva, the sensible and irresistible Eva, the genial Eva—the Eva I would love much later—overcame her sick counterpart and managed to drag herself to the telephone. Before losing consciousness, she managed to dial Klara's number and tell her what had happened. The paramedics found her on the floor, pale but conscious. Eva fought them because they looked like shadows who would most certainly lead her to an operating room to surgically remove her sadness, the modern version of the stone of madness. She kicked and tried to bite them: Leave me in peace, damn you, how dare you touch me, how dare you put your hands on me, I called you, I made you come, I have the right to send you away, all my life I've put up with these crises, I can get better on my own, get out! Used to fighting with madness, the paramedics just tied her down by her wrists and ankles.

Eva always knew that something like this could happen to her: Her intelligence was shit, her neurons and genes sentenced her to an early death and an empty existence, a series of depressions and false hopes. Her brain behaved like a damaged machine that was plagued with short circuits. Sooner or later, she would end up in an insane asylum, just like her Hungarian grandfather: The jerk didn't leave her wealth or treasure, only an unknown homeland and that hereditary defect. The medics stuck a needle into her forearm. For years, drugs had been her only permanent company: Tranquilizers, analgesics, and sedatives for the periods of excitement or rage and stimulants, corticoids, and lithium capsules for anxiety, periods of inactivity, or boredom. Her spirit was traveling on a roller coaster; if she was going up to a peak, it was only so she could crash into the void. Her consciousness either inhabited hills or valleys, never plains or plateaus. Poor little Eva: I saw her that way or perhaps not that way, not in that state of desolation, but in very similar circumstances. And I never got over it. Her extreme lucidity made it impossible for her to put up with reality.

At a certain point I too considered suicide. To me, the world seemed a hostile and contemptible pit, but I never had the nerve to try. When I went back to Baku in 1982, after two years of fighting the mujahideen and other guerrillas in the Afghan hills, mutilated in body and soul, my life became a meaningless swamp, identical to the lives of thousands of soldiers who'd gone off to defend Communism, not knowing that Communism was by then just a mask.

Back in Baku, no one thought I was a hero. Soon I began to hear about other soldiers who'd come back from the front: To forget Afghanistan, our secret Vietnam, we all gave ourselves over to alcohol and idleness—and the most lucid among us to death—waiting for a recognition that would never come. In theory we were titans, but the government treated us like pariahs, uncomfortable witnesses of a debacle. No, unlike Eva, I never dared to attempt suicide, or rather I did it in the laziest and most hypocritical way—the way I did everything in my life—by letting alcohol destroy me little by little, letting its slow poison contaminate my reason and my thinking until it made me cruel and skinny.

In the months leading up to her crisis, Eva had also worked for her country's government, as part of the Strategic Defense Initiative or, as the ignoramuses called it, the space shield. At the outset of the '80s, the nuclear balance between the Soviet Union and the United States had tipped. The opinion of experts in the CIA and the Pentagon was that the nuclear non-proliferation treaty signed by both countries, Salt I, had only allowed the Soviets to augment their secret arsenal. Our war machine, controlled by the military-industrial complex, had developed rapidly, and by 1975 the USSR had achieved absolute superiority. President Carter, a devout Christian, based his arms policy on deterrence. At the end of the '70s, he made huge efforts with regard to the signing of Salt II, which was to reduce the number of nuclear warheads each country maintained in Europe. By contrast, Leonid Brezhnev, the cunning mummy, had less friendly intentions, as the Afghan invasion demonstrated.

At the time, it was easy to spot signs of U.S. weakness in every corner of the world: Communist regimes had taken control in Angola, Mozambique, and Ethiopia; the Sandinista guerrillas had triumphed in Nicaragua; and in Iran the Islamic revolution had exiled the Shah and established a theocratic regime that viewed the U.S. as the incarnation of the devil. As if that weren't enough, In November of 1979, an Islamic commando team burst into the U.S. embassy it Tehran and kidnapped a dozen people. Carter approved a rescue attempt that turned into a spectacular failure. The United States looked on itself as a humiliated power threatened by the Communism.

Ronald Reagan, sovereign of heaven, won the 1980 elections on the promise he would restore the United States to the place it deserved to occupy. As soon as he took over the White House, he asked if the superiority of the USSR was as worrying as he thought. The reports from the CIA, the State Department, and the Secretary of Defense confirmed his fears: The window of vulnerability—the possibility that the Soviets could launch a surprise attack and obtain an immediate advantage—was wider than ever. The old actor perhaps lacked experience in diplomacy and military strategy, but he certainly did know how to be as energetic as the cowboys he'd played in the past. All branches of government were to find a way to counter the disadvantage. Within a few months, he won the support of Congress and multiplied the defense budget tenfold.

On March 23rd, 1983, Reagan went on television to announce to the nation that the Strategic Defense Initiative would be set into motion. Yuri Andropov considered the announcement a provocation, as did various pacifist groups, and the Union of Concerned Scientists thought it was a ridiculous idea, but Reagan stood firm and named Lieutenant General James A. Abrahamson director of the project. He in turn asked two scientists, Fred S. Hoffman and James C. Fletcher, to conduct two independent studies to determine the program's viability.

A professor of technology and energy resources at the University of Pittsburgh, Fletcher recruited physicists, mathematicians, engineers, and computer experts from the best universities. Eva Halász, whom Fletcher had met years earlier, was among them. At the start, it seemed to him that she was the ideal person to develop the computer system for the SDI. At first, Eva felt uncomfortable about the project's military implications and the distraction it would be from her own research, so she declined the offer. But after a sleepless night, she contacted Fletcher and told him that as a former victim of Communism her obligation was to contribute to the defense of her country.

SDI implied a colossal technological effort: It required articulating a vast array of satellites located 36,200 kilometers above the equator that would keep the earth's surface under constant surveillance. The satellites would be equipped with infrared sensors that would be activated by the launch of an intercontinental missile. The information the sensors acquired would be transmitted to satellites equipped with defensive platforms and a complement of satellite-sensors. These platforms would contain weapons that would be able to intercept enemy missiles before they completed their ascent. And, in case some missiles got beyond the first phase of their flight, sensors in lower orbits would send the information to ground platforms which would launch projectiles to destroy them during their descent. Finally, ground missiles equipped with homing devices would attack any missiles still active before their entry into the atmosphere.

To make all this technology functional, a complex network of computers, along with software to control them, would have to be assembled. Fletcher assigned Eva to the area known as C\3 (command, control, and communication), whose function would be to coordinate the entire process and create cybernetic components that would react to external stimuli in fractions of a second. While the military engineers in SDI thought articulating extant technology would be sufficient, Eva made it her business to design a genuine artificial brain: The linked computers on the earth's surface and in space would become a gigantic brain, a simulacrum of God.

The final meeting of the SDI Study Group, led by Fletcher, was as stimulating as it was chaotic. Some thought the program would be too expensive, even for the United States; others thought the technology was still too primitive to guarantee its success. But at the end they all agreed to present the President a hopeful report.

The advances of the past two decades show great promise for a defense against ballistic missiles, Fletcher summarized. Fred S. Hoffman's team agreed with him: The technology for ballistic defenses against missiles, along with those that can identify in a precise and effective way nuclear and non-nuclear systems, has advanced rapidly. It presents opportunities to resist aggression and reduce the threat of conflicts that are more likely than nuclear attack.

Both speeches represented a great victory for Reagan, sovereign of heaven, although it must be said that reactions against SDI became more acid with each day that passed. Especially serious was the article published in *Science* by Hans Berthe, which rejected the conclusions reached by Fletcher and Hoffman. Later, the Union of Concerned Scientists published a study according to which SD would need to put 2,400 satellites into orbit. 2,400! The scientists associated with the project insisted on reducing the number to 1,000, 500, or even 45, though neither side could ever justify their figures.

From the moment when Senator Edward Kennedy mocked Reagan's project, calling it *Star Wars*, the space shield became a common topic of conversation in cafés and social gatherings. Andrew O'Connor himself, until then on the fringe of the dilemma, could not resist the temptation to annoy his wife. The idea is crazy, Eva, you have to recognize that. And what do you know about it? she retorted. Hundreds of us have dedicated ourselves to the project—I just don't understand why people make such superficial comments. You can't think that a Reagan idea can be a good idea, Andrew insisted. She had never sympathized with the President—politics seemed a distant and abstruse subject to her—but this time she felt obliged to support him.

Just imagine what would happen if we could eliminate the fear of a nuclear war . . . The Russians would stop being a threat . . . Or turn into a worse threat, her husband interrupted. Strategic balance of power has freed us from catastrophe. *Star Wars* may destroy that balance, and then . . . This is a legitimate defense issue, Andy: Over the past ten years, the Russians have built one missile after another, and we go on doing nothing. This is better than investing in nuclear missiles.

Instead of arguing, Andrew showed her the editorial page in the newspaper, where two caricatures appeared. In the first, "Buck Ronald & His Super Laser Cannon," the President appeared in a Buck Rogers costume. He fires his pistol, but he incinerates himself. But take a good look at the other one. It was titled "Research on SDI" and showed Merlin the Magician, surrounded by sacks filled with frogs' eyes and magic potions, stirring a cauldron inscribed "Strategic Defense Initiative." Eva, you've turned into the sorcerer's apprentice.

Andrew O'Connor's criticism did not enrage Eva, but it did undermine her spirit. While she still thought that SDI was both possible and just, she was no longer able to take on its challenges in complete freedom. She felt she was being watched, as if Andrew and his fellow critics were only waiting for a tiny mistake, an equivocation, or error to attack her. Around 1985, when the Soviet enemy was on the verge of taking a drastic step toward modernization (and its unforeseen and inexorable road toward nothingness), Eva's interest in SDI had waned, following the same logic that could sweep her from exaltation to depression in one fell swoop. It was not long before she left Fletcher's work group under the pretext of returning to her neural nets.

To celebrate her decision, Andrew suggested a trip to Europe: They might even go to Budapest, her parents' home town. Enthused, Eva reviewed Hungarian history and immersed herself again in Hungarian culture and the Hungarian language, as she had as a little girl. She even called her mother and invited her to go with them. Klara refused: I won't go there until the last Communist is dead.

Three weeks before their trip, Eva, my fragile and depressed Eva, emptied the medicine chest and stuffed herself with tranquilizers and antidepressants. Hungary, or the dream of Hungary, ended up sinking her. After two weeks convalescing in a Vermont clinic, the doctors recommended shock therapy. Eva tried to resist—she recalled *One Flew Over the Cuckoo's Nest* all too vividly—but the psychiatrist explained that the procedure had evolved considerably during the past few years and could be effective in a case like hers. Potential suicide cases, you mean, said Eva.

As she told me years later with forced briskness (I can barely stand the memory of it), they first gave her a muscle relaxant, then they anesthetized her, and finally they placed one electrode on her left temple and another on her forehead. The current passed through the cables for no longer than thirty seconds, and shortly after she was awake, dazed, but lucid. How do you feel? The psychiatrist's voice came to her from a distance. You may feel a bit confused, your muscles may be tense, but the effect will wear off quickly, I promise. It will be difficult for you to remember some things, but your memory will return in three or four weeks. Congratulations, Mrs. O'Connor, you've been very brave.

The same day she went home, Eva decided to ask for a leave of absence from the MIT Artificial Intelligence Laboratory, and she accepted an invitation from the Konrad Zuse Institute of Information Technology to spend a sabbatical year in West Germany. Andrew listened to her reasons silently: Though the offer did not seem very attractive to him, it did give him the opportunity to separate from Eva without remorse. While his wife was being subjected to electric shocks in Vermont, he had fallen in love with another woman.

ACT TWO

MUTATIONS

(1985-1991)

1985

1
Moscow, Union of Soviet Socialist Republics,
March 10th, 1985

It was 7:24 P.M. when the telephone rang at Number 12 Alexei Tolstoy Street. Raisa Maksimovna picked up the receiver and handed it to her husband, almost tenderly: In an oblique way, she wanted to feel she was the bearer of good news. Mikhail Sergeyevich's hands barely trembled. He'd spent too many nights rehearsing the scene, and his nervousness had vanished. The officer greeted him in his usual military voice, but there was something different in his tone, a minimal inflection or perhaps a certain obscurity. He didn't even have to listen to the details. Could the old man have suffered? It didn't matter much. After a week in a coma (not to mention months of agony), this was the best thing that could have happened to him. He couldn't even stand up; at the end he was a statue of salt and not a hyena, with his eyes sunken and his face splotchy, an insipid caricature of himself. Not even in his best periods had Konstantin Ustinovich Chernenko been a model of daring or wit, though at times he might show a coldness that some confused with valor. At the end he could barely swallow pap or sit down on the toilet—the Kremlin doctors helped him even in those maneuvers—and he was enclosed in the indifference that defined him so well.

Poor Konstantin Ustinovich! When the only thing that truly concerned him was breathing, Viktor Grishin forced him to pose before the cameras, made up like a wax mannequin, believing that way he'd become his heir. To be photographed with a cadaver! Only an imbecile like Grishin could come up with such a crude plan. But reflecting on the old man's sorrows was a waste of time. It was time to act. Mikhail Sergeyevich turned to his wife and whispered: He's dead. More dramatic, or less hypocritical, Raisa Maksimovna hugged her husband: You have to call a meeting of the Politburo tonight, she warned. I know what I have to do, retorted Mikhail Sergeyevich.

Two hours later, Gorbachev was in his car on the way to the Central Committee building in Staraya Square. Raisa Maksimovna did not send him off with a kiss on the cheek but with a firm handshake. The members of the Politburo soon arrived. After Mikhail Sergeyevich, the first was Grishin, General Secretary of the Moscow *oblast*. As lifeless and sordid as Chernenko—he'd just turned seventy—he was the quintessence of immobility: dry, corrupt, venal. Exactly what the Soviet Union did not need at this moment. Mikhail Sergeyevich greeted him with a hug, and both exchanged expressions of sympathy. Comrade Grishin, said the flattering Gorbachev, the important thing now is to organize the homage to our deceased General Secretary, and I think you're the ideal person. No, no, a thousand times no, Comrade Gorbachev, tradition dictates that the funeral be coordinated by a Secretary of the Central Committee and not by a Regional Secretary like me. I think the right man for the job is you, Mikhail Sergeyevich. An abundance of courtesy!

Little by little, the other members of the Politburo arrived. If we were to add up their ages, we'd reach prehistory, thought Mikhail Sergeyevich, though he immediately censored his own sarcasm. Those old men inspired both respect and fear. Even so, he recalled the joke he was told when he went to Great Britain in 1984. After returning from Andropov's funeral, Margaret Thatcher calls Ronald Reagan and says: Ronnie, you know, these Russians just get better and better at this funeral business. You can be sure I'll go back next year. But Gorbachev couldn't laugh, not yet.

Once the meeting of the Central Committee had been called to order, Viktor Grishin asked permission to speak and, carrying out his obligation—or perhaps looking for a dignified way out—proposed that Mikhail Sergeyevich Gorbachev be placed in charge of the funeral arrangements for Comrade Chernenko. Someone tried to oppose the idea, arguing that Grishin would be a better candidate, but no one seconded his motion. Everything is turning out perfectly, Gorbachev thought. But even if on the previous two occasions the man responsible for organizing the funeral had been enthroned as General Secretary, it was not an inexorable law. The definitive meeting of the Politburo was fixed for the next day, March 11th, at 3:00 P.M.

Mikhail Sergeyevich returned to Number 12 Alexi Tolstoy Street at 11:24. Raisa Maksimovna met him at the door wearing a long black robe. She could barely restrain her impatience, her anxiety to know. Her husband kissed her, and they both went up to their bedroom. Did you get it, Mikhail Sergeyevich? He took off his jacket and loosened his tie: Yes, they've put me in charge of the funeral. Raisa Maksimovna applauded: It had to be! But it doesn't mean a thing, her husband calmed her, it's only a sign. Of course it means something, Mikhail Sergeyevich, it's a fact, a *fact!* The Politburo votes tomorrow at 3:00. And? I can count on Ligachev and Rizhkov and, from what I saw today, I can also count on Gromyko and Chevrikov. Now let me work a little, I have to prepare a few words for the ceremony. I knew it, I knew it! murmured Raisa Maksimovna, we're very close, Mishka, very close . . . Just as she predicted, during the Politburo meeting the astute Andrei Gromyko made a fiery defense of the candidacy of Comrade Mikhail Sergeyevich Gorbachev, shepherd of men, a young and resolute leader, educated and open, with a child's smile and steel teeth.

2

New York, United States of America, March 12th, 1985

That's the word we have to remember: options. That's what he said to Jennifer during breakfast. Concerning ourselves with reality, with solid and tangible objects, isn't worthwhile. We have to think about the infinite realm of possibilities. We have to concentrate on the future, Wells went on, sipping his coffee. It's a conceptual change very few understand right now. Is your friend Andy Krieger one of them? she asked. You have to meet him, Jen. He's not only very rich, but also interested in Oriental philosophy. He's been to India several times and even knows Sanskrit, Wells insisted, choking on the corn flakes he stuffed down his throat.

For weeks Wells had been unable to talk about anything else: He quickly forgot the admiration he had professed for Roy Vagelos and Gerry Tsai, and now he only sang the virtues of Andy Krieger. That's how Jack Wells was: He let himself be carried away by first impressions, and while he tried to show he was sure of himself, he was in fact the most easily influenced man on the planet.

On the other hand, Krieger could have starred in a movie: He spoke in that soft and melodious tone adopted by those who thought themselves spiritual, declared that his greatest concern was the children of Calcutta, and in his moments of leisure studied the Vedas in the original. He was a vegetarian and a compulsive, and, as if that weren't enough, he'd also been a tennis champion during his university years. In under two years, he'd become rich without losing even a bit of his mysticism. Wells met him at a party on the Upper East Side, and after they discovered they'd both studied at Wharton, they spent the rest of the evening exchanging anecdotes about professors and students. At the end of the party, they agreed on one thing: Money was so disgusting that it had to be earned as soon as possible.

During their second meeting, in a coffee shop on 57th Street, Andy confided to Wells the magic word that would make them *very* rich: options. At that time, very few people on Wall Street bothered about those financial instruments, and most economists either disdained them or knew nothing about them, but in Andy's opinion they symbolized the future. An option, as Wells explained, is the right to buy or sell something in the future. It might be anything—tomatoes, computers, stocks, bonds—the important thing is to find the right moment to exercise your option.

During his years at Wharton, Andy had analyzed, in minute detail, all the ins and outs of the Black-Scholes model—the formula created in 1973 by Fisher Black, Robert Merton, and Myron Scholes which calculates the value of an option. He had developed a computer program that improved on that formula. Like Wells, he thought the market was neither perfect nor efficient.

At Solomon Brothers, Andy worked from dawn 'til dusk, energized by that faith which before had bound him to Hinduism. For him, there was no deity more worthy of veneration than Ganesha, god of material well-being. At night, instead of resting or celebrating his triumphs, he made myriad telephone calls so he could participate in the Tokyo stock market, though at times he still dedicated one or two hours to meditation. During his first year with Solomon Brothers, he earned more than $30,000,000 for the firm, and was quite disillusioned when, at the end of the year, his bosses only gave him a $170,000 bonus—more than any other broker in the company, but much less than what he was due, given his earnings index. But now Andy's frustration was a thing of the past. 1985 looked full of promise: He would earn more than any other executive in the history of Wall Street.

Jack, do you know the joke about the economist and the hundred-dollar bill?, Andy asked while he gobbled down his first bacon cheeseburger in five years. No? Listen: A classic economist finds a one-hundred dollar bill on the street and decides not to pick it up. Know why? Because according to the theory of efficient markets the bill doesn't exist. If it did, someone would already have picked it up . . . Andy giggled stridently. Get it, Jack? Luckily, we aren't classical economists, so we can pick up those stray bills without any problem, ha ha.

That's how the lunch ended. Two weeks later, Wells was getting ready to invest thousands of dollars in options that would be managed by his friend Andy. For that reason, he was the picture of health. If things went well, he could quit Merck and achieve his dream of founding his own company. Wells finished his coffee and kissed his wife before leaving. That same day, Andy Krieger put $30 million into currency options—the equivalent of a billion dollars in other stocks. A testimony of the times: A single man armed with a computer program and some intuition could control stratospheric quantities of money (at least in theory). Wells could rest easy: His money was in good hands, the economy was still rising, and he, with his executive position at Merck, was in no hurry. Everything was working out according to his plans. The '80s would indeed be the realm of the possible.

3

Sverdlovsk, Union of Soviet Socialist Republics, April 13th, 1985

Oksana promised herself not to cry. Comrade Smolenska became more and more agitated with each passing second, shouted at her, insulted her, but she resisted. Finally, in a fit of rage, Comrade Smolenska slapped her. A kind of itch invaded her cheek, but the girl kept her promise and didn't even sob. She clenched her fists and pursed her lips, and a few tears ran down her cheeks. That's all. Not a word, not a lament, not even a sound. Comrade Smolenska was a tall, slovenly woman with a pronounced squint and military manners (she was no different from other teachers). Oksana had never liked her, and the feeling was mutual. That explained why she'd been there, in her office, for over an hour, defiant. Furious because of this new challenge, Comrade Smolenska went on shouting: You leave me no choice, I'll have to call your mother in, she's to blame for all this, those parents of yours have no idea how to bring you up, you're a rebel just like them, so now all of you will have to pay the price, are you listening to me, Oksana Arkadyevna?

Seven hours and fifteen minutes had passed since Oksana had made an unbreakable decision: She would not speak again. When she did say something, no one believed her. The teachers marked her down as a liar, declaring she made things up, that she was only trying to get attention. Her mother was at work all day, and then in meetings and gatherings, always trying to learn the fate of the child's father—that ghost—so the best thing the child could do was keep silent. Keep silent and on the watch. Oksana did not think these things with such clarity; her decision had been vague and natural, the result of fear and horror more than a strategic plan. For her, silence wasn't a whim or a shield but a refuge.

In class, she disobeyed every order, forgot her homework, and answered questions in a surly way. Not because she wanted to rebel, like so many girls in her class, but because her nature made her act that way. Someone had injected her with that virus which told her to be cruel to animals, to be distracted, to show disrespect. Sometimes she tried to behave, tired of receiving one punishment after another, but in the end she could never manage to control herself. She hated the world. She hated her school and her teachers. She hated Comrade Smolenska. She hated her mother. And she especially hated her father, Arkady Ivanovich Granin, that absent spirit, that traitor who'd abandoned her, who'd never loved her, who'd never taken an interest in her. The only thing she liked in life—the only think that relaxed her or at least let her forget her problems—was singing. She could spend hours singing or humming popular tunes in a delicate and very high pitched voice.

Her mother came to Comrade Smolenska's office a couple of hours later, anxious and unkempt as usual. Oksana didn't even bother to look at her, concentrating on the photographs of Moscow that were hanging on the wall, next to the diplomas that accredited the pedagogic skills of the principal. Good afternoon, Irina Nikolayevna, I had no choice but to have you come here again, you have no idea what a bother this is, but I see no other way out. Oksana Arkadyevna is worse than ever, her personality is impossible, tell me what to do with her, Irina Nikolayevna, what am I supposed to do with a girl who refuses to speak . . .

Irina did not really understand the principal. Oksana hasn't spoken a word all day, as if she were mute! shouted Comrade Somolenska. Just try, and you'll see.

Irina went over to her daughter. Seeing her livid, expressionless face, she guessed it wouldn't work. Let's see, Oksana, tell me what's bothering you. Her daughter let out a sigh. Oksana, sweetheart, please, if you don't talk to me, I can't help you. Nothing. See? snorted Comrade Smolenska, she's been like that all morning, as if our teachers had nothing else to do but take care of your daughter: What selfishness, what a lack of . . . of . . . of everything, Irina Nikolayevna. The principal's face puffed up like a balloon.

I'm sorry, comrade, let me bring her home. Sorry! Sorry! always sorry, howled Comrade Smolenska. Well, Irina Nikolayevna, do whatever you can, but I'm warning you that if things go on like this, we'll have to send your daughter to a special institution. Do you understand me?

Yes, I understand you, comrade.

Irina took Oksana by the hand and dragged her out of the office. The child put up no resistance. At home, Irina made her some tea and tried again. Oksana, honey, tell me if something happened to you, I'm your mother, and I love you, I have to know what you're thinking. The two of us together can fix things . . . It was useless: Oksana never opened her mouth. All right, her mother said, it would be better if you took a nap. Oksana washed her face in silence, changed her clothing in silence, and silently went to bed, though she kept her eyes open, wide open, for a long time.

When she woke up the next morning, Irina had almost forgotten the previous afternoon, but in no time she confirmed that Oksana was still in the same mood. She ate her breakfast without saying a word and then got ready to go to school without even saying good morning. Oksana, I beg you, if you go on this way, they won't let you stay in that school, I've had to change your school three times in the past two years, I know this has been a hard time for you, but you have to make an effort . . . The girl pretended not to hear her, looking away or focusing on the void. Irina didn't know what to do, so she sent her to school in hope she'd change her mind.

The telephone call that interrupted her at 11:00 A.M. proved how wrong she'd been. Oksana is still defiant, said Comrade Smolenska, and I have to suspend her. I'll give her a week to reconsider, but that's all I can do. Irina had to ask permission from her laboratory to bring her daughter home. This time, she did not try to convince Oksana to speak. She knew it was futile. Perhaps if she left her in peace for a few days, the child would finally get bored. No one can stay silent forever.

Aside from her stubborn silence, Oksana seemed her usual self. She'd never been a communicative child; she had a day-dreaming, distracted side, and her attention always wandered. But Irina Nikolayevna was beginning to get worried. Arkady's arrest had affected Oksana more than she'd imagined. Besides, she had to face the fact that over the past months she'd barely paid her any attention, concentrating on the fight to free her husband. And now, what would become of her and her daughter? If Oksana went on like this, she'd have to be placed in a special school.

The following days were a nightmare for them both. Neither wanted to hurt the other, but their positions were so irreconcilable that there was no way back. Oksana stayed at home all day; when Irina came home in the afternoon, she no longer tried to force her to talk, convinced that she shouldn't behave like Comrade Smolenska. So she pretended her daughter's silence was normal. She would wait a reasonable amount of time before bringing her to see a psychologist.

Oksana felt more and more isolated, sadder and sadder. Now it wasn't simply that she didn't want to speak: She couldn't. The words clogged in her throat. When she was alone, she would try to shout or sing without success. It was as if an unspeakable confession was refusing to leave her body, as if not even she herself knew what was happening to her. She lost her appetite and secretly threw out the food her mother left for her. Soon she lost weight and contracted a fever. Irina brought her to the doctor; he prescribed some pills without evaluating her mental state. Irina couldn't stand to watch her daughter waste away before her eyes.

That morning, Oksana felt she couldn't stand it any more. She began to pound the walls with her fists and then with her head, as if she needed to break her body to free herself. Then she ran to the bathroom and smashed her hands against the mirror, trying to cancel out that image of herself—of that ugly, skinny Oksana—once and for all. Suddenly, almost surprising herself, she saw that blood was flowing between her fingers. Not content with that wound, she picked up one of the pieces of the broken mirror and cut her forearm open. Finally she heard herself scream with all her strength, with all the energy her lungs had been saving up.

Hours later, when Irina came home and found that Oksana's arm was bandaged, she thought a tragedy had taken place. But her daughter calmed her. Don't worry, mommy, I'm fine. It was an accident. Oksana was talking again! Irina hugged her with all her strength. Her daughter seemed relaxed, almost happy. She'd finally found the way to relieve her pain.

4

Auckland, New Zealand, July 10th, 1985

It had been months since Allison felt that peace. She'd spent much too much time incubating a rage she could never manage: She'd watched several of her dearest friends die one by one, devoured by a plague that was transforming San Francisco into a death ward. Ge, her confidant and pal, had been among the first to develop those horrible sores. After a few weeks, she'd lost all her equivocal beauty. The last time Allison went to see her in the hospital, she had a yellowish skin and her eyes were like marbles. Allison could not tolerate her grief and ran out. She didn't even attend the funeral. By then Ge's soul had separated from her body, ready to reincarnate itself in another living being, perhaps an ash tree or a carnation—her favorite flower—or in the fetus that would ultimately become a woman. Allison could not stand being in San Francisco. In December of 1984, devastated by her memories, she again quit her job, intent on dedicating herself to the only thing that mattered to her: other people.

As she contemplated Marsden Bay illuminated by the winter lights—the sky and the water joining together in the darkness, the rhythm of the tide, the masts like needles, the ominous absence of clouds—Allison felt transfigured. She needed to get rid of her past, forget her quarrels with Jen and her fatuous or unfinished love affairs, distance herself from that part of herself that only sought pain and battles. Who knows, perhaps her place was the sea—the ocean aroused contradictory feelings in her, took her breath away, and bewitched her with its roaring—that magma where life began.

How calm, she shouted, more for herself than the others, though Fernando responded with an affable, barely ironic grin. She liked that man. There was something fascinating in his manner, in his dense, minute gaze. As soon as they left Vancouver, he came over and invited her to have a beer on the deck. Well, she was the only new woman in the group—her training had taken several weeks—and the others had known one another for years. They'd sailed together from one end of the planet to the other. It was hard to find a way into the lives of a group that was used to spending so much time at sea. No matter how open and welcoming Jane, Albert, Susan, Marie-Pierre, Davy, or even Pete, the captain, tried to be with Allison, they were already too ingrained with one another to let her join in their complicity.

Allison was not discomforted by their distance because the solitude on board the ship was like a balm for her wounds. And besides, there was Fernando, who usually bombarded her with questions, always eager to mock her naïveté or her religious contradictions (she insisted on presenting herself as a Buddhist). Sometimes they spent the night on the deck of the *Rainbow Warrior* arguing about destiny, transcendence, or extraterrestrial life. Fernando was a ferocious atheist, indifferent to the spiritual world Allison pursued so fervently. I'm not doing this to save my soul, Fernando explained, but for the sake of my children, a pure act of egoism. You have no idea how annoying I find people who think that because they're good or altruistic they deserve applause or praise. Sometimes I think they're not very different from the politicians we're fighting.

Fernando had been a photographer for Greenpeace for many years. On a stormy night, off the coast of Samoa, he showed Allison some of the images he'd collected: Icelandic whalers, Orkney seal hunters, employees in California or New Mexico nuclear plants. He also had pictures of the French soldiers guarding the Mururoa atoll, where they were heading. The worst thing is seeing how closely all these men resemble one another: Just look at the faces of the fishermen and the gestures of the sailors, and you'll see the same greed, the same fear, the same ancestral stupidity. They only think about themselves, about preserving the absurd, criminal order they were born in to.

While living in San Francisco, Allison had worked with several ecological groups—she'd even traveled to New York, navel of the world, to take part in the historical demonstration against nuclear arms in Central Park on June 12th, 1982—and later had been an adamant adversary of Reagan's space shield, but she only decided to join Greenpeace after Ge's death. Ever since its reorganization in October of 1979, the group had constantly appeared in the news because of its spectacular protests against atomic testing, toxic waste, whale hunting, and environmental decay. Its activists had been persecuted or arrested, its ships fined or confiscated, but none of that stopped its efforts. Thanks to the vision of David McTaggart, a Canadian businessman who'd settled in New Zealand, Greenpeace had become an international network that was able to mobilize scores of teams to any point on the globe.

The *Rainbow Warrior*, named in honor of a North American Indian deity, was an old forty-four-meter-long fishing vessel which Greenpeace bought for £40,000 in 1978. This time its mission would be to block the nuclear test France was preparing to carry out in Mururoa. Allison felt proud to have been accepted as a volunteer, despite the fact that she'd only recently joined Greenpeace and despite the hastiness of her sea-training.

You'll see, everything will work out, Fernando cheered her on as they walked back to the ship after having dinner in a tavern in the port. Have you two seen Frédérique? Davy asked suddenly, distracting them from their own thoughts. Frédérique was a young blond with intense blue eyes who worked in the New Zealand section of the organization. Allison thought Fernando was attracted to her—he never took his eyes off her—but she never dared to ask. I haven't seen her for a couple of days, Fernando answered. Davy stared at him in disbelief. You're all wrong, Fernando exclaimed, I don't like that girl, not one bit.

The *Rainbow Warrior*'s masts stood out, arrogant and serene, and Allison thought they were the totem poles of her religion. The night was cool and calm, and everyone was tired, longing to go to bed or have one more beer in their cabins. One by one they went back onto the ship, like ants entering the anthill. Home sweet home, Marie-Pierre recited sarcastically. Good night, good night to you, yes, see you tomorrow . . . Allison and Fernando remained on deck chatting about this and that. Do you miss your children? Don't be silly, of course I do. They stared a while at the stars, and then Fernando said he was a bit tired, kissed her on both cheeks, and went off to bed. I'm going to stay here a while longer, get a good night's sleep, Fernandinho.

At 11:48 P.M. Allison fell to the deck, tossed by a violent tremor. Used to San Francisco, she thought it might be an earthquake. An earthquake in New Zealand, right here in the bay? She touched her forehead and felt the moisture of blood: She'd cracked her head against something. Time seemed to condense. She heard shouts and screams, the snapping of wood, and then she felt the boat keel over to the left. Her friends, some of them naked, came up on deck to see what was happening. We're sinking! shouted Marie-Pierre. Pete bellowed an order: Everybody off the ship, now! Then he asked: Is there anyone still down in the engine room? Susan took Allison by the shoulder and helped her walk to the dock. The darkness kept anyone from seeing their anger and surprise.

On the dock, they all saw how the *Rainbow Warrior* was listing, as if it were caught in a whirlpool. What was it? asked a confused Allison. Pete came back to the surface, soaked and panting: There's a hole the size of a car in the engine room, the water is pouring in. How could this happen? asked Marie-Pierre. Fernando ran back onto the ship: I have to save my cameras. Stop, Fernando! shouted Allison. Now time became slow, miserable, and the boat sank like a stone. Fernando, come back! Davy dove in, but the waves were now covering the deck. Marie-Pierre and Jane also dove in, uselessly. Then there was another, even more violent, explosion.

When the rescue boats finally came, the *Rainbow Warrior* was nothing but a chunk of wood floating in the middle of the ocean. Marie-Pierre was crying; Pete, Davy, Albert, Allison, Susan, and the rest of the crew were screaming. Fernando Pereira's body was recovered just after midnight. Allison looked into his face and gave him a cold kiss. My cameras, was all she managed to mutter. Such a stupid death. So useless.

Thanks to international pressure, the New Zealand police would discover that the two submarine crewmen who placed the bombs on the hull of the *Rainbow Warrior*, as well as the languid Frédérique Bonlieu—whose real name was Christine Cabon—and several of her friends, were actually agents of the French secret service under the command of Colonel Louis-Pierre Dilais. The New Zealanders arrested two of the men, but the rest escaped on a yacht, the Ouvéa, and took refuge in New Caledonia. Some years later, the French government would accept responsibility for the attack and indemnify Greenpeace to the tune of $8,160,000. But that would not bring back Fernando Pereira, who did not believe in the next world or in reincarnation.

5
Milton, Massachusetts, United States of America, September 9th, 1985

Eva Halász was free again. While she and Andrew had agreed not to divorce—we need to think it over, the conclusion they usually reached—both knew their relationship was over. Eva couldn't accuse him of abandoning her in her hour of need—Andrew waited until the doctor declared her out of danger to confess his passion for Bea, one of his graduate students. Even so, she felt betrayed. At the same time, she understood her husband: Who would want to live with a woman who went from euphoria to deep depression every three months? Who in his right mind would want to live with a potential suicide? He's no saint, Eva told herself, I can't demand he stay with me, I'm too difficult, much too difficult. She hated the idea that while she was in the hospital Bea had slept in her bed, used her shower, and dried herself with her towels, perhaps even used her toothpaste or soap. Why didn't Andrew take her to a motel? Didn't the university pay him enough? Bea thought Eva would never find out, but women have a special intuition and can identify a hair on the rug, sniff out the remains of perfume, guess what twists and turns were carried out on top of the sheets.

Eva decided to leave the house to Andrew and went to live in a cabin in the country, near the Neponset River, about an hour outside of Boston. Her leave of absence from MIT had begun, and there were still a few months before her job in Germany began, so she decided to avoid town and stay in that sanctuary where she could dedicate herself to doing what she did best: thinking. Do you really think it's a good idea to be so far away? asked Andrew. It's exactly what I need, so don't worry, she answered. I've learned a lesson, and, besides, there is a telephone. I'm not in the middle of a desert. And if that desire to end your life should come over you again? If I'd really wanted to kill myself, I would have done it. Her mother had insisted on moving in with her for a few weeks, but this time Eva refused categorically. Klara grumbled, but stopped insisting. After the months of working on SDI, that chimera no one dared to carry on, Eva felt the urgent need to reorganize her priorities.

As she strolled along the muddy bank of the Neponset, Eva thought that no machine had passed the test because the test itself was badly formulated. She stretched out on the grass and stared at the sky through the tree branches. She watched a couple of crows fly by, and then a plane left its wake between two cloud masses. And then she had an illumination (that's what she would later call it): There, reclining in the forest, she understood that Turing had made a mistake: in simplifying the definition of intelligence, he'd concentrated on the least attractive part. Contrary to what the English mathematician thought, intelligence could not be measured only by its external manifestations. Eva could remain there, immobile, mute, alone without ceasing to be intelligent: Inside her brain, chemical and electrical reactions that generated ideas, reflections, and doubts went on taking place. It was not necessary to speak or move to *think*.

That autumn day in 1985, Eva felt she'd been set on fire by a spark of lucidity. That idea was not only overwhelmingly convincing—and, like all great ideas, obvious—but disturbing. If she really wanted to build an intelligent machine, she should concern herself more with the relationship between the mind and reality than on getting computers to imitate human beings. She still hadn't imagined how to apply that focus, but at least now she knew—yes, she knew—what her predecessor's error had been.

6
Washington, D.C., United States of America, November 19th, 1985

While she was putting dozens of papers in their portfolios into order—she had to have everything ready to travel the next day—Jennifer never took her eye off the television. At the end of their first meeting in Geneva, Ronald Reagan, sovereign of heaven, and Mikhail Gorbachev, shepherd of men, were shaking hands heartily between grimaces and feigned smiles. Jennifer still did not know what to think of the new Soviet leader: He was, no doubt about it, younger and more charismatic than other Soviet leaders, but that aura of modernity and energy might be only a disguise, the pretty face of a regime that would never really open up. As a militant Republican, she was happy that there was finally a firm leader in the White House. No matter how much criticism was heaped on him, Reagan was solid.

To Jennifer, Reagan's polemical SDI seemed a master stroke. It made no difference whether the damned shield was useless or expensive or couldn't be completed until halfway through the twenty-first century: Its importance was not based on its operative capacity but on its symbolic character. Everyone in Washington, axis of the cosmos, knew that the Soviet economy was in one of its worst moments—only oil had kept it alive during the past decade, and now oil prices were plummeting—and that despite the declarations made by its military, the government would never match the United States' technological investments. Reagan's strategy was brilliant: Suffocate the Russians, not by means of a secret weapon, but by forcing them to spend millions on an arms program they could no longer pay for.

Jennifer knew that Gorbachev had caught on to the trick. That's why he'd come to Geneva: not to get to know his enemy at close range, but to find out if SDI was a sign, a Trojan horse, or a real possibility. Of course, Reagan would ruin his tranquility: SDI is only a defensive project, we have no intention of altering the balance, nor do we intend to turn it into an offensive weapon. We don't have the technology or the intention to unleash a nuclear offensive, blah, blah, blah . . . Beyond the chatter, he would maintain his threat: We have the resources and the technological ability to get this project up and running, while you . . .

On the screen were images of the press conference that followed the five-hour meeting at the Chateau Fleur d'Eau. When Jennifer started paying attention again, Reagan was rambling while Gorbachev focused on his own topic, the only thing that mattered to him: the economy. Jennifer found the exchange surprising: While the U.S. President talked about security and defense, the Soviet leader chattered on about "economic links." Of course! That was his only priority! Face-to-face with a bankrupt economy, the corruption of the *nomenklatura*, and the rigidity of his system, his only salvation was the economy. The *new thinking* did not mean a political opening, as Gorbachev went around crowing, but a final attempt to survive! Jennifer turned off the television. The sun was disappearing from her window, and she needed to finish packing. Her flight to Mexico would take off in a few hours.

During the past few weeks, the debt situation of the countries of the Third World had become critical. The danger of a payment suspension was real. In her new role as the IMF's executive for Latin America, Jennifer had convinced the lending banks and the finance ministers of the debtor nations—cultured, mellifluous bureaucrats—to restructure credits and adjustment schedules. The task was not simple: As she'd discovered in Zaire, sometimes the imbalances were so huge—and the legal systems so rigid—that genuine miracles were necessary to straighten out the balance of payments.

Just a few weeks earlier, on October 6th, Jennifer had attended a meeting in the Seoul Hilton, where James Baker, Reagan's Treasury Secretary, had outlined his new strategy for resolving the debt problem. In a session that lasted all morning, Baker ordered the IMF to impose greater controls on the debtor nations in its adjustment programs: That was the only way the banking industry would be willing to grant new loans.

As Jennifer said to her new boss, Jacques de Larosière, Director-General of the Fund, Baker's speech was a slap in the face, albeit by a white-gloved hand. In her opinion, the U.S. Treasury took too much of a role in these matters, relegating the IMF to a secondary position. De Larosière agreed with her and asked her to map out medium- and long-term projections for the countries that were deepest in debt. The results were alarming: If an agreement wasn't reached, Third World debt would become unmanageable.

On November 13th, during a meeting De Larosière called historic, the IMF decided to support the Baker Plan. Less than a week later, he called Jennifer to his office. After thanking her for her enthusiasm and perseverance, the Director-General asked her for help. Given her experience in extreme situations—the Zaire case was a perfect example—it would fall to her to take charge of a nation whose economy was on the brink of collapse after an earthquake had struck its capital just a few days before.

Jennifer closed her suitcases—she would certainly be charged for the extra weight—she checked her dresser and the drawers in the commode, took one last swig of mineral water, and turned out the lights. Mexico, she repeated to herself. A few years earlier, she and Jack had spent their vacation in Acapulco (she loved the beaches and hated the food), but she never imagined she'd be returning to Mexico in such radically different circumstances. A new challenge, she said to herself. She too was entering deeply into the kingdom of the possible.

1986

1
Merritt Island, United States of America, January 28th, 1986

Without knowing it, without even imagining it, the four of them stared at those images, horrified, each one associating them with his own terrors. Allison had been back in the United States, in Philadelphia, for several months. She'd returned after the explosion of the *Rainbow Warrior*, still in a state of shock because of Fernando Pereira's death. Jennifer had just returned from her first work trip to Mexico, a country as hospitable as it was opaque. Eva remained in her voluntary confinement on the banks of the Neponset, picking apart the concept of intelligence and getting ready for her imminent stay in Berlin, an island surrounded by cannibals. And Wells was chairing a work meeting in his sparkling Merck offices in Rahway.

The liftoff had been spectacular, but Allison, Jennifer, Eva, and Jack were not watching television at 11:38 A.M. and did not see it live. They also did not hear the countdown, weren't surprised by the flame and explosion, and did not share the pride of conquering space. Hours later, on the other hand, the four were horrified by the scenes on the afternoon news. Barely .678 seconds had passed after ignition when a gray sputum appeared in the sky; at .836 seconds, the stain turned black. Then, at 2.733 seconds, there was a dense, frightening explosion. The color of the smoke indicated that the elastic rings that sealed the connections of the boosters were burning out of control, proving that the faults, detected in 1984 in the Morton Thiokol rockets, should have been more vigorously attended to.

A light in the sky marked the end of the process: When it was fourteen kilometers up and traveling at mach 1.92, the space shuttle Challenger, pride of NASA, succumbed to an explosion—the hydrogen and oxygen atoms burned as soon as they touched. It disintegrated in a heartbeat. Allison's eyes filled with tears, as if that light had torn her cornea; Jennifer envisioned the economic consequences of the catastrophe (the Russians would be happy); Eva tried to imagine the causes (she made a rapid calculation); and Wells, as stingy as ever, only thought about the losses the market would report the next day.

2
Rahway, New Jersey and Washington, D.C., United States of America, March 20th, 1986

That night there was no one left in the Merck plant. Wells was always the first to arrive and the last to leave. Just a few weeks earlier, the board of directors had named Roy Vagelos CEO, and he had offered Wells the position of chief financial officer: The salary was generous and the possibilities for promotion enormous, but it wasn't enough for Wells. He was fed up with being an employee. His career at Merck had been long and successful, but he did not want to grow old there, dominated by inertia. He'd spent enough time immersed in the biomedical industry to know its possibilities. The future was there, waiting for him, but not if he stayed inside a giant like Merck. It would have to be in one of the small start-ups that popped up like mushrooms in California and New England. He didn't want to be part of a huge bureaucratic structure when he could create a professional and modern business—most importantly, a business that would be all his.

That was the dream Jack Wells wanted to share, so he considered every minute of every day dedicated to other tasks a waste of time and money. Now was the time to ride the wave. Thanks to Andy Krieger's audacity, he now possessed the means necessary to begin his adventure. His work at Lockhead and Merck had supplied him with the scientific contacts he needed. He was convinced: He would leap into the void.

Wells packed up his personal files, loosened his tie, and got ready to drive to Washington, axis of the cosmos, to join Jennifer. As he drove his Mercedes Benz 560 at top speed with a CD blasting a maximum volume—he was a fanatical fan of The Velvet Underground—he planned his next moves: He would call Harry Kleist, a Stanford biochemist who'd worked with Boyer and with whom he got along very well, and Walter Matthews, his lawyer, to set up a meeting as soon as possible. For months he'd been worried about registering—for only $5.00—the name DNAW, which combined DNA with the "W" in Wells to produce something pronounced *Di-Now*, and he had taken the first steps toward bringing his brain child to life. Founding a business was like conquering a woman, a tortuous and exciting process. Only someone with an iron will (and the cynicism to match) could risk giving up a secure job to leap into the void.

When he reached his house in Washington, axis of the cosmos, Jennifer was watching a rerun of an episode from *Dynasty*, a series about a family of Texas millionaires, the Colbys, whose greed had become emblematic of the era. Jack kissed her on the forehead and quickly made his calls, not at all concerned that it was midnight. Kleist was not at home—he was a fan of late-night clubs—so he left him a message. He could only speak with Matthews for a few minutes, having interrupted him during a romantic interlude. He set up a meeting with them for early Sunday morning.

When he went back to the bedroom, Jennifer was almost finished slathering on her arsenal of creams. Wells was surprised to note there were different creams for legs, toes, forehead wrinkles, eyelids, hands, as well as the stretch marks she'd discovered (to her horror) on her upper thighs. Wells undressed and, as if he were repeating some banal fact, said: I've decided, on Monday I'll talk to Roy. Jennifer did not understand: Talk about what? I'm going to quit my job at Merck, Wells replied, smacking his hand against the wall: I won't back out now! She stared at him completely baffled, too stunned to discourage him. This is the right moment, Jen! I'm going to set up DNAW even if it kills me . . . Are you crazy? I've always been crazy, he embraced her: You don't believe me now, but it's going to be the company of the century. With the help of Harry and Walter, I'll put together four million to start. Know what? Unlike those ex-hippies in California, I've decided to locate the business in Manhattan. Some day, you'll read on the cover of *Fortune*: "Biotechnology moves to Soho."

Jennifer didn't have the energy to fight: You're going to need more capital, she said. Why not convince Roy Vagelos and try a joint venture with Merck? Roy's a great guy, he answered, but he's not interested in biotechnology. I've watched dozens of scientists uselessly plead for a few cents. What about asking for a leave of absence, just in case something goes wrong? It will go right, I assure you! Wells stalked into the bathroom and slammed the door in a rage. Jennifer left her creams on the night table, put out the light, and closed her eyes. Another damn night of insomnia.

3
West Berlin, Germany, April 6th, 1986

Eva woke up feeling pain at the back of her neck, with bruises on her thighs, shoulders, and throat. Her lips burned, along with her nipples and sex. It took her a few seconds to remember where she was. She looked at her watch: 11:00 A.M. Then she looked over her body, twisted and naked, the sheets in a knot. She had to pee. She stood up quickly and looked at herself in the mirror. She barely recognized herself: her hair a mess, traces of blue eyeshadow and black mascara on her cheeks, teeth marks—yes, from teeth—on her left clavicle. For God's sake! What have you done? Finally, she gathered enough strength to walk to the bathroom.

She heard the sound of the shower and caught sight of a masculine figure washing nonchalantly. Only then did she recover some images from the pervious night. She had no memory of what he looked like—she'd barely been able to see him under the colored lights—but she did remember his smell and his sex. Ismet? That was it, yes, she was sure. A bit timidly, she perched on the toilet and let her urine slip out noiselessly. Eva? He opened the shower curtain, talking in a scratchy, accented German. I thought you'd never wake up. Eva observed his quiescent sex and the black hair that covered him. What a crazy night, eh?, he said as he went on soaping himself. Take all the time you want, she said, still in a daze, I need a coffee. It wasn't the first time she'd lived through something like this, but ever since leaving the hospital, she hadn't gone this crazy again.

Eva put on a T-shirt and went to the kitchen. She put the coffee into the pot and looked for an analgesic. The doctors had forbidden it, but she never for a moment considered following their advice. Ismet came up behind her and kissed her on the neck: Her cut ached. A bit savage, no? she said, pouring out two cups of coffee. And what have you got to say for yourself? he answered, showing her the scars on his buttocks and chest. Eva remembered nothing, but the cuts and bruises revealed the reality of their nocturnal combat.

Ismet stood there naked, uninhibited, a smile on his lips. Looking him over carefully—his muscular torso, his flat stomach, his red lips—Eva understood why she'd let herself go: He wasn't handsome, but he gave off an irresistible animal aura. What do you do, Ismet?, she asked to break the silence. I told you yesterday, I study business at the Freie Universitat. Ah. And where did you say you were from? You really remember nothing? I'm a Turk, but I was born here in Berlin, sweetheart.

Eva turned on the TV: cartoons, a cooking program, a documentary on wild ducks in Canada, and three channels broadcasting the same blurred images. Even if she couldn't manage to understand everything the news reporters were saying—her German was rusty—she understood that something serious must have happened. She could make out ambulances, smoke, bloody, and tear-stained faces, and she managed to translate: anguish, chaos, survivors, dead. Ismet, come here!

The Turk reappeared wearing jeans and a black t-shirt. He stared at the screen in silence, his nervousness increasing with every second. His face contorted. I've been there many times, he admitted, scared to death. It's a discotheque—the soldiers from your country go there a lot. Last week I went there with some friends, it's called La Belle, everybody knows it's a hangout for the Marines, good-looking women go there, you know, last night I thought we could go . . . Eva couldn't follow Ismet's hesitant English. Translate what they're saying. An attack, with bombs . . . They don't know who's responsible, Palestinians or Libya . . . Three dead: two American officers and a Turkish woman . . . Oh, no. Not now. Life is difficult here, Eva, and this is going to complicate things for people like me. What do you have to worry about? You don't understand, Eva, they'll blame us, you'll see, it's terrible, terrible. Calm down. Can I stay here? Here? Just today, Ismet insisted. I promise I'll leave tomorrow, please.

Some welcome to Berlin, this island surrounded by cannibals! A bomb in a discotheque and a guy hiding out in my house. She hadn't even finished unpacking her things, hadn't yet set up her office in the Zuse, and here she was, sharing her apartment with a Turk she barely knew. That's me, she said to herself, I just can't stay out of trouble. Okay, Ismet, you can stay here today, but—how can I put it?—I'm very possessive when it comes to my space, I don't like anyone touching my things, understand? Don't worry, sweetheart, I won't touch a thing. Fine, but one more thing: Never call me sweetheart again!

Ismet kissed her. She tried to resist, but when she felt his sex, she couldn't hold back. If she was going to have a man in the house, she should at least get something out of it. They spent the entire day in bed, making love and resting up to eat. Eva made an omelette, and he made it better with all kinds of spices. And they went on watching the news. There were three confirmed deaths and 200 wounded. By evening, the news reports had declared the Libyan President, Muammar al-Gaddafi, the guilty party.

See? Muslims, always Muslims. She had no desire to argue. She thought she had no racial prejudices—Ismet's presence was proof—but the fact was that most terrorists practiced that religion. Over the past few months, Palestinian commandos had taken over an EgyptAir flight and the Italian cruise ship Achille Lauro.

Just as she told Klara when she called her that night, as she looked over at Ismet next to her, calm and fragile, she wouldn't have the nerve to throw him out the next morning. Or, for that matter, the morning after that, or the morning after that. Resigned, she caressed the stomach of her new lover—of her new toy, because that's all he was—and got ready to go to sleep.

4
Baku, Union of Socialist Soviet Republics, April 26th, 1986

Finally, fear became flesh. Incubated for four decades in our hearts, terror found its reason for being in our land and right before our eyes. Just a few got the news, just a few found out the truth, but the disaster could not be covered up: The rot we bequeathed to our children, the nameless corpses, the amputated members, the dryness, the oblivion. Right here in the USSR. It didn't take an enemy invasion or a fantastic space weapon to defeat us. Just a drop of carelessness, another drop of improvisation, and a dash of pride—all it took to forge a catastrophe. That, no question about it, was the beginning of the collapse, the sign that things no longer worked, that we were living in apathy and backwardness. The abyss that separated facts from words had become so deep that only the biggest fools denied it. It had to be accepted: We'd been conquered. That radioactive cloud announced our capitulation. Even if no one dared to say it or even to whisper it, the wound was fatal.

Our leaders could go on and on about new thinking, transformation, opening: useless. Reality showed how sterile their excuses were. The rest of the world would soon realize the degree of our misery, and on that day we'd cease to be an empire, a threat (a diaphanous ogre) and become ragpickers, garbage men, a nuisance. It looked as if we were still controlling half the world, making a commotion with our outbursts, seated at the table of History, while in reality we were stumbling along on crutches, helped by insulin injections. Maybe the charade could go on for a few more years, even decades, but the results would be the same: a slow and ominous decomposition, the necessary step toward dissolution.

This part of the story has already been told: lack of foresight, pride, fire, bureaucratic ineptitude, unhealthy air, half of Europe contaminated, radioactive mist pushed along by the wind. An accident. In Baku. *Pravda* barely published the news, printing only an inert and inconsequential note at the bottom of the page: an accident at the Chernobyl plant that our brave firemen have brought under control. Long live Communism. Long live Lenin. Long live the USSR. That was all we needed to know. According to the official line, everything had returned to normal after a few hours. Despite his reformist anxieties and his desire to break decades of treachery and silence, Gorbachev, shepherd of men, behaved like his predecessors: He mumbled two or three lies, denied the facts, cursed the imperialists. Brezhnev, the cunning mummy, couldn't have done a better job. Let's raise a finger and blot out the sun. No danger, no danger, no danger, the USSR is stronger than the atom.

But people began to doubt. It was the first sign. Or perhaps they'd been doubting for a long time, but only now, with the noise of the explosion in the background, their doubts had been amplified. Even my Azmorneft companions, silent or submissive or wary, expressed their criticism aloud: They're hiding the truth from us, treating us like children. There, in the rich fields of Neft Dashlari, we could document, every day, the inexorable disintegration of our machinery. We weren't surprised that the catastrophe had taken place in Chernobyl: We survived almost by a miracle. Soviet industry—everything Soviet—was a stodgy mastodon. Nothing worked, even if the Five-Year Plans only described advances, achievements, attained goals. Double talk. Sumptuous phrases to fill the ears (and perhaps their pockets) of the bosses. Chernobyl revealed the secret: The Soviet Union was a fiction.

5
Mexico City, Federal District, July 8th, 1986

Mexico wasn't Zaire, but it seemed like it. Even if by then Jennifer had become familiar with the gigantic cities of the Third World, this city of ruins and vagrants disturbed her more than others. While one street of the capital resembled Frankfurt or Manhattan—absurd skyscrapers built on impossible sites—the next was a copy of Kinshasa or Calcutta: sheet-metal shacks, piles of garbage, and beggars. A year hadn't passed since September 19th, 1985, the day an earthquake flattened hundreds of buildings and killed some ten thousand people (the official figures were much lower, of course). Entire neighborhoods remained devastated—they reminded Jennifer of the bombed-out zones in Libya—and their inhabitants languished in the ruins, waiting for the help while the politicians lined their pockets.

The way in which the corrupt and ubiquitous Revolutionary Institutional Party (PRI), in power now for more than five decades, had dealt with the crisis was an example of the nation's condition: Instead of rebuilding demolished houses and alleviating the situation of the victims, the political bosses had hidden, fearful that the natural earthquake would produce a political tremor. President de la Madrid, a gray, nebulous technocrat, decided to lock himself away in his official residence, Los Pinos, instead of participating in the rescue efforts.

Within a few minutes of the catastrophe, TV reporters from the privately-owned stations rushed to see if the soccer stadiums had suffered any damage: Mexico was going to host the World Cup in 1986, and the only thing that disturbed the elites was a problem with their business. That was Mexican modernity: a mixture of mud and stainless steel, soap operas and fried food, luxury jewelry shops, and beggars. According to Jennifer, the image that best defined the nation was its violent, out-of-control, and broken-down microbuses. On two occasions she was almost run over, and on another two she fell victim to the pickpockets who were thick on the ground in the Zona Rosa. The worst part was the food: During her first visit, she spent three days in the hotel bathroom, languid and weak, unable to concentrate.

$730,000,000. Jennifer repeated the number in her head: seven-hundred-and-thirty-million-dollars. How was it possible that so much money could disappear just like that in a few months? The extent of the damage was formidable indeed, but no one could explain where it all had ended up. The bills the Mexican functionaries offered her were labyrinths. Fully aware of the material and human losses caused by the tremor, she had personally guaranteed that the Fund would approve a transfer of $330,000,000 from its natural disasters program; the Inter-american Bank for Reconstruction and Development had added another $400,000,000, but even so, the Mexican economy was sinking into a bottomless pit, into a jelly as thick as the character of the citizens.

The commercial balance was a pandemonium with a thousand shrieking voices, and the drastic fall of oil prices was driving the nation to the edge of bankruptcy. Mexico was a chimera: rich and buoyant on paper, always about to enter the First World, and a swamp of traps and half-truths in fact. As in Africa, the corruption, pride, and carelessness of its governing bodies were the principal cause of the situation. Here the *matabiche* was called *mordida*. Here too everything had to be paid for. Functionaries only functioned when "greased" with cash. The Treasury was a den of elegant thieves.

Able to chat with her about perfumes, golf, or luxury automobiles, her Mexican counterparts ignored the guidelines of the IMF. Gentlemen, Jennifer explained, if you really want to move forward, you must contain inflationary pressures and reduce the foreign deficit. A new adjustment is becoming *absolutely necessary*. Then they, showing off the suits they had had made in London or New York, would cover her with bubbles because they were incapable of getting to the point. We must also maintain growth, they would say, without explaining how or why, slipping along on the figures like skaters. Those polite and mellifluous bureaucrats were mocking her! If you go on this way, she warned them, commercial banks will refuse to finance you. Do you understand? *Cero acuerdo*, she shouted in Spanish.

Only then did the Mexicans become reasonable. After months of diplomatic give and take, they accepted that the new IMF program would include a contingency plan and that it would take the fight against inflation as an indicator of the adjustment. At least it's a start, thought Jennifer, foreseeing that in a few months those same men would present her with false or retouched figures.

Things stood that way, and starting in December of 1985, Jesús Silva Herzog, Treasurer, visited the offices of the IMF, the big commercial banks, and the Treasury Department again and again, intent on coaxing their functionaries to agree with him. He's an inveterate seducer, muttered Jennifer, as she listened to Silva Herzog's baritone voice. Too bad he's not my type. She had to tell him the truth: I'm sorry Mr. Secretary, but your country says one thing and does another. We want results, not good intentions. Drastic measures, not coverups. As Jennifer had foreseen, in March of 1986, Mexico entered yet another financial crisis: On the 21st, a debt of $980,000,000 with a commercial bank came due, and the government delegates had not managed to restructure it. Jennifer had no recourse but to intervene brutally—the Mexicans only paid attention to her if she shouted and stamped her foot: She sent them a severe letter of intention, and they had no option but to sign it. Only when the banks saw that Mexico had finally given in did they extend the due date for another six months.

Accompanied by her boss, the Spaniard Joaquín Pujol, Sub-Director of the Department of the Western Hemisphere, Jennifer visited Mexico twice in April of 1986 and collided with the same problems. A new fall in oil prices, inflation, and depreciation of the peso made it impossible to reach the agreed-upon goals. Even though the Mexican functionaries promised to carry out severe cuts in the finances of the government (that prehistoric tortoise), the deficit only rose. The matter is serious, gentlemen, Jennifer warned them. Either the deficit goes down 5 or 6%, or this thing explodes. Pujol approved her words. A new threat: Yes, the medicine was bitter, but Mexico had no other option. The Mexican negotiators languished and promised to try—*try* is a word I don't understand, shrieked Jennifer—for a 2.5% cut, half of what the Fund requested. Jennifer stormed out of the meeting room in a rage. *The deficit is the most important thing, damn it, not growth!* A few hours later, she flew back to Washington.

In May, the Mexican delegation returned to Washington, axis of the cosmos—they love to go shopping, Jennifer quipped ironically. But this time they did not want to talk with Pujol and even less with Jennifer. They wanted to speak directly with Jacques de Larosière. He supported his subordinates: Mexico would have to carry out a severe fiscal adjustment otherwise it would never reduce its dependency. This time, the Mexicans were unfazed: We're prepared to initiate negotiations with the creditor banks with or without the consent of the IMF, they declared. Another of their customary bravura tactics. Finally, they left Washington with empty hands. And to top things off, they'd wasted all their credibility. Mexico is digging its own grave, Pujol confided to Jennifer: Investors will stop believing in the nation, and then they'll run to beg us. His predictions were correct: At the beginning of June, the Banco de México announced it had lost $500,000,000 of its reserves and a total of $1.5 billion during the first half of the year: The alarm bell had rung. You were right, Jennifer said to her boss, now they'll come back on their knees, or it will be all over.

On June 9th, Paul Volcker, the new Secretary of the Treasury, made a secret visit to Mexico to convince Silva Herzog to resume negotiations with the IMF. Under pressure, he called de Larosière and promised to send a new negotiating team. But the Mexicans failed to keep their promise. Silva Herzog said he would travel to Washington, but he postponed his trip at the last moment for reasons that, once again, were not clear.

There is a storm in Mexico, Pujol revealed to Jennifer: With the specter of the suspension of payments, it must be war. More and more distanced from the center of power and blocked by the young and rising Secretary of Planning and Budget, Carlos Salinas de Gortari, Silva Herzog resigned on June 17th. Another technocrat, Gustavo Petriccoli, replaced him. He traveled to Washington on June 27th. To Jennifer he seemed more arid and less attractive than his predecessor: She preferred to have strong enemies. Now, in her visit to Mexico, she would again meet with him to prepare his second visit to the IMF, on July 11th. The situation could not be more tense: The future of Mexico—and her own future, and the future of the IMF—was hanging by a thread.

6

Sverdlovsk, Union of Socialist Soviet Republics, September 14th, 1986

Oksana was another person. At the age of ten, she had metamorphosed into a tall, slender girl with an intense stare, calm manners, and perturbing self-confidence when speaking with adults. Those meeting her for the first time usually thought she was thirteen or fourteen years old. Outwardly, she was a child—her breasts would never grow, conferring on her that androgynous aura she would later be so proud of—but even then there was something dark in her eyes, a certain disillusionment or fatigue that was uncommon for her age. Her temperament had sweetened, or at least she'd filed down its roughness. Comrade Smolenska and the other teachers never had much regard for her, but at least they left her in peace. Instead of considering her a source of embarrassment, they now found her odd and inoffensive: always alone with her books. Because Oksana had not only discovered the value of knives, pins, and razors—the sacrilegious joy of her blood—but also the music hidden in words.

Poets that had been demonized during the Brezhnev era were rehabilitated under glasnost, and Irina would regularly bring home books and magazines lent to her by her friends in the democratic movement. These Oksana read in secret, like a thief. Often she missed the subtleties of the poems, but their harmony helped her emerge from the darkness by granting her fleeting moments of joy. Oksana memorized the poems, like this one by Marina Tsvetaeva:

I know not where you are, where I am.
The same songs, the same chores.
Such friends, you and I.
Such orphans, you and I.

Together we get on well,
with no home, no rest, no one . . .
Two little birds: When we awaken, we sing,
two pilgrims: We feed off the world.

These syllables alleviated her suffering, allowed her to survive and move forward. To the point that whenever someone asked her, Oksana would answer that yes, she was happy, more-or-less happy, and she even came to believe it. She wasn't like the other girls, never would be, but at least she was close to a certain normalcy. Also, Oksana now had a friend, the first girl who'd ever approached her without reminding her of her father's fate. Her name was Galina, and she wasn't interested in poetry, but she made witty remarks and defiant statements that Oksana found *very* poetic. The only child of a peasant family from western Siberia, Galina was a skinny, slow girl who thought Oksana was a sibyl or a sorceress. Oksana took advantage of that inexplicable comparison and behaved as if she were those things.

They went everywhere together; they worked as a team, and visited each other on weekends. Unlike other girls, they barely played, and hated, sports. They preferred to invent sedentary, almost static games. They wove a secret language full of squints and sentences in code, and they laughed madly. Protected by their mutual complicity, they fled the real world—it frightened them—and exchanged it for an aquatic planet they invented, populated by monsters, sirens, tritons, and sunken ships. They saw themselves as queens in danger, damsels in distress who awaited the arrival of no prince—men were sharks—and preferred to defend themselves on their own from the dangers of the sea. Oksana's fantasy was so overwhelming that one day Galina said: You are a poet. *Poet.* At the time, Oksana hadn't written a single verse, but the word fell sweetly on her ears.

But suddenly something broke between them. That Sunday, Oksana and Galina had agreed to meet in the morning. The autumn was still warm, and Irina promised to take them to the country. When they finally came to a more-or-less pleasant meadow, Irina told them she would stay there to read while the two girls wandered around among the birches. She was concentrating on her papers—the general amnesty was growing more and more remote—when she heard Galina crying. The girl ran to her and held on tight. What's wrong? The child would not stop crying. Oksana appeared immediately. What's wrong with Galina? I don't know, said a severe Oksana. You don't know? No. I want to go home, Galina stuttered through her sobs. Did you two have a fight? No. All right, declared Irina. Let's go, but later you two will have to give me an explanation.

On the way back to Sverdlovsk, neither girl wanted to talk. They didn't even look at each other. Irina again demanded an explanation, but it was useless. Fights between girls, she thought, they'll probably make up tomorrow. That didn't happen. Oksana told Irina she never wanted to see Galina again. Their friendship was broken forever. Irina was sorry. Her daughter seemed too solitary, too tempestuous, and the company of other girls moderated her character. Oksana allowed no one to approach her for a long time. I don't need anyone, she shouted at her mother, when Irina dared to question her. No one. And she again took refuge in her books.

7
New York, United States of America, September 29th, 1986

I really don't want to go to this party, said Jennifer, trying on the tenth dress of the evening (all black and identical). That woman is a snob, walking plastic, no brains. She may be whatever you say, Jen, but she's got lots of money and the best contacts in New York. *Everybody* will be there, and you know that I need to make contacts now more than ever. Wells straightened his tie and waited for his wife to finish getting dressed. She had to be faking: Who would turn down an invitation to one of Christina Sanders's parties? Thousands of people would pay to get into Christina Sanders's house, to say hello to Christina Sanders, to have Christina Sanders's autograph, to rub elbows with Christina Sanders! Jennifer was too proud to admit it and tried her best to seem blasé and sophisticated; in fact, she was just as frivolous as any of the inhabitants of the Upper East Side. A few weeks earlier, Wells had found her leafing through *Informal Dinners* and *Casual Style*, two of Christina's bestsellers.

Wells met her at one of her benefit dinners. Christina sat next to him for a few minutes, and he gave her an instant summary of the origin and goals of DNAW. Against all expectations, she expressed great interest in the subject, asked him if it was truly possible to find a vaccination against cancer, and finally asked him to visit her offices on Fifth Avenue to go more deeply into the subject.

Christina Sanders personified the American dream: From a family of Czech immigrants—her real last name was Skvorecky—she'd worked as a publicist and then got her own television program. Within a few years, she became an icon, and her advice on domestic matters and fashion were followed by millions of women who venerated her as an oracle. Christina's success derived from her smooth talking, her simplicity, the way she whispered to housewives: You can be like me, you don't have to be an aristocrat, you don't have to spend a lot of money to cook like a chef, to look beautiful, young, and stunning. Her books made her rich, and she was surrounded by the most influential and chic people—movers and shakers in business, journalists, moguls, film stars, sports figures, and politicians: They all fought for the privilege of her friendship and affection. Because Christina was—and this was how her publicity presented her—the most understanding, the sweetest of women, the best friend, the ideal wife. Her concern about endangered species, AIDS-afflicted children, and single mothers—there were half a dozen foundations under her name—won her the sympathy of the whole world.

From the moment they met, she and Wells discovered an inevitable affinity: Both came from underprivileged backgrounds, both wanted to get rich at any cost, both worked to protect the vulnerable (at least that was what they said), and both adored sophistication and glamour. Besides, Christina was at a low point: Richard, her husband of twenty-five years, had just left her for a serpent who could have been his daughter. Abandonment made her even more sensitive and generous. And what Wells needed most was help, all the help possible. In July, he bought a broken-down loft in Soho, but the cost of transforming it into a first-rate laboratory was much higher than he'd imagined.

Wells confided his dreams and projects to Christina: His immediate aim was to produce new vaccinations and clone cytokines. After hearing his fabulous depiction of possible cures for diabetes, AIDS, osteoporosis, and cancer, Christina Sanders entered into a collaboration with her new friend and not only handed him a million dollars (in exchange for stocks in the future company) but put him in touch with several of her friends, who offered to study his proposals.

This is why it was so important that Jennifer and he go to Christina's party: While it was improper to discuss business at social events, Wells would have a chance to meet the men who could secure the future of DNAW. He had to avoid being eaten up by the multinationals and keep his independence. He was aiming high, his team would find and commercialize a wonder drug and transform the future. To accomplish all that and to reap the benefits of his own success, he needed a good infusion of cash.

Don't I look fat? asked Jennifer. Of course not, you're divine. And we'd better be on our way, or we'll be very, very late. Just let me choose some earrings. That could take you hours. It didn't: His wife chose some platinum pendant earrings, and they rushed out to get into the limousine that would take them to Christina Sanders's house, a splendid apartment on Park Avenue that she'd decorated to the exact specifications of *Elegance for Everyone*. As they went up in the carpeted, mirror-lined elevator, Wells felt happy. The world of appearances was his place.

8
Washington, D.C., United States of America, November 28th, 1986

How long had it been since they'd seen each other? Allison tried to calculate: eleven months, maybe a year? No: it must have been Christmas, 1984. Almost two years without seeing each other, with anodyne telephone calls: Yes, hi, how are you?, Fine, and you? Fine, and Jack's working as usual, oh, yes, oh, okay, stay well, you too, let's get together soon, yes, very soon . . . They'd become distant relations, strangers. What had made their worlds so alien, or, to put it more clearly, so opposite? Allison could not keep from getting angry at her sister's pride and vanity—Jennifer was like a blemish on her skin, a knife that reminded her who she was and whom she had to fight. Even with her Greenpeace comrades she felt the need to justify herself: Yes, I am Jennifer Wells's sister, but we're very different. I barely ever see her, have barely any contact with her, as if her connection to her sister were an anchor.

But she didn't hate her: No matter how silly, conceited, frivolous, and conservative Jennifer had become over the years, she was still her sister, and that word was sufficient to calm her down. They could fight, insult each other, even wound one another with the most powerful verbal weapons—the Moore genes at their best—but they would never separate forever because they were tied together by an invisible chain. Allison often found herself thinking: What would Jen do in this situation?, as if she were obliged to compare herself with her sister or get her consent. She'd turned down dozens of Jen's invitations, but she finally agreed to have drink at her sister's place, so they could sign yet another peace treaty (and thus be able to begin a new fight). They had both learned to keep cool or to select their fights with care; they no longer fought over unimportant matters, only over transcendent subjects, almost always political or religious. Allison could not understand how her sister, an intelligent and lucid woman, gifted with a will of iron, could be a spokesperson for capital.

It was 8:00 P.M. For once, Allison was on time. She pressed the buzzer and waited. Jennifer opened the door, as pretty as ever, as nervous as ever, dressed as if she were going to a dance (at least in Allison's opinion), wearing a revealing black blouse and a gold necklace. She immediately offered Allison a glass of champagne. Welcome, little sister! She hugged her (well, a half hug, she was worried she might wrinkle her blouse), what a great thing, you owed me this visit.

Allison dropped onto a gigantic black leather sofa, impressed by the luminosity—and bad taste—of the room. She'd never been in the house, but the pomposity of its inhabitants was evident everywhere. Refinement had given way to a kind of theatrical vulgarity: enormous, multicolored paintings (doubtlessly worth thousands of dollars) on the walls, extremely white furniture, maple-colored floors, designer kitchen, minimalist lighting: a clinic. Like it?, asked Jennifer, feeling herself studied. Impressive, answered her sister.

Jennifer sat on the arm of another armchair—Why there? To show how comfortable she felt?—and began to chatter in a relaxed way, as if they'd been together the previous day, about the weather, about how expensive things had become, about Aunt Susan and her maladies, about Jack and his new business. Allison was biting her nails: She was the sole spectator of a monologue. She'd promised herself to be patient, so she went on listening, or pretending to listen, more aware of the decor than the words. Then she poured herself another glass of champagne and drank it down in one gulp. The bubbles relaxed her.

But when Jennifer began talking about her job—her irritating Mexican experience, complete with stereotypes and complaints—Allison couldn't stand it any longer. Once again, it would be war. Both prepared their strategies and went into battle: Her sister's arguments were so foreseeable that Allison was almost ashamed. Jennifer declared that the only way to help "those people" (of the Third World of course) was by forcing them to respect the policies of the IMF. Allison declared the opposite: It was possible to find other roads to development and justice. Immediately after came the verbal rages, the hurt feelings, the ironies, and the ancestral jokes. By that point, the subject no longer mattered, and each sought only to destroy the other.

Jennifer opened another bottle of champagne, confident she would win. Allison changed the subject: How is Jack doing? Jennifer pretended to giggle (only she was capable of laughing like that, like a character in a movie): This is a marriage of convenience, little sister, we do what we like, as we like, when we like. I recommend it to you. Allison counterattacked: I can't believe you. And what do you want me to say? Jennifer reclined on the sofa like Canova's statue of Pauline Bonaparte, that Jack's probably running around in New York with yet another of his sluts? And that it hurts me, or affects me, or wounds me? No, Alli, I've decided not to suffer any more because of men. Jack can see anyone he likes, as long as he watches his step. What matters in our marriage is just that—marriage, stability, contacts, social forms. We use each other, like everyone else: The difference is that we at least recognize it.

Well, well, thought Allison, so her older sister was becoming a cynic. But she noticed a sediment of sadness in her words—there was as much lucidity as there was resignation. And are you sleeping with anyone else? Jennifer laughed again, less self-confident, less histrionic. Of course, who do you think I am? Really? Tell me all about it. Jennifer stood up and put her glass on the little glass end table: Okay, for the moment there is no one, but there could be . . . And why isn't there anyone? Because I haven't met anyone interesting, anyone at, how to put it?, my level. I'm beyond the age of fooling around. What about you, Alli? Bah, I don't know why I even ask, you've probably got dozens of lovers, as always. Isn't that right? You're wrong, answered Allison, I'm as alone as you. Why is that? No idea, maybe the two of us are growing up . . .

Despite the fact they were getting drunk, both noticed just how pathetic they were and fell silent. But Jennifer couldn't stand it, had to show she had everything under control, and found yet another subject likely to bring them into confrontation, the Iran-Contra scandal, the final chapter (she thought) of the persecution of Ronald Reagan, sovereign of heaven, by the liberals. As she said, Oliver North, responsible for selling arms to the Islamic nation and financing the opposition to the Sandinistas in Nicaragua, looked like a scapegoat, a hero in the struggle against Communism. For Allison, North was simply a mercenary, a criminal. Everything returned to normal.

Before leaving, Allison walked over to her sister, looking hopeless. Jennifer knew that look only too well: How much do you need this time? Five thousand dollars. Jennifer went to her room and came back with the check. Her younger sister folded it in half, put it in the back pocket of her jeans, and walked out without saying good-bye.

9

Moscow, Union of Soviet Socialist Republics, December 22nd, 1986

I saw him today, Irina wrote to her husband that same night. I saw Sakharov, maker of light, I was there at the door of his house on Chkalov

Street along with dozens of reporters, foreign correspondents, friends, and neighbors to celebrate his return, the return of a hero. It was incredible, a miracle. I saw him, Arkady Ivanovich, I spoke with him for a few seconds, I even embraced him, and he encouraged me, and seeing him I saw you, in his blue eyes, your eyes were sparkling, in his breath, I found your breath, and the scent of your skin in his scent. Oh, Arkady Ivanovich, his wrinkles made me foresee yours. He looked so tired—he'd only just arrived from Gorky yesterday afternoon along with Liusia, always hand in hand—he seemed so tremulous and thin, melancholy, and his voice metallic.

Oksana was with me, she witnessed that historic moment, the prefiguration of your freedom, Arkady Ivanovich. For the first time in a long while, I again felt that the struggle had been worthwhile, that the pain, the trouble, and your torment had been worthwhile, and I said so to your daughter, Arkady Ivanovich, I said: Oksana, take a good look at that man, memorize his words, never forget this day, Oksana Arkadyevna, never, because it's the first true day, the day that announces our victory.

She was listening to me, sticking by my side, the two of us united forever, the two of us longing for you, the two of us convinced that justice will be done and that soon, very soon, you'll be with us. I wept, I wept a lot, out of neither sadness nor joy, but out of a mixture of the two. And I wasn't the only one, Arkady Ivanovich, all the members of the movement were weeping, and some reporters were weeping, and I even detected tears in the eyes of Andrei Dmitrievich and Liusia. Finally they were going home, and not as fugitives but as symbols of a new era.

I trembled when they put the key into the lock and crossed the threshold of their old house. When they were inside, Arkady Ivanovich, we were told this: Gorbachev himself called Andrei Dmitrievich in Gorky to tell him he and his wife could return to Moscow. After Andrpov had accused him of being public enemy number one, after Brezhnev and Chernenko sent him into exile, Gorbachev was allowing him to return. But Andrei Dimitrievich did not simply thank him for that gesture; he actually urged Gorbachev to free other prisoners, told him that only that way could the injustices be repaired, that only that way could he escape opprobrium.

And Andrei Dimitrievich Sakharov, maker of light, mentioned your name. He remembered you in that historic conversation. Gorbachev promised to study each of the cases, including yours. It may not be much

Arkady Ivanovich, but I believe in him, I think Gorbachev will listen to the voice of his conscience, the voice of Sakharov, that he'll keep his promise and allow you to come home to us. We're waiting for you, Arkady Ivanovich, Oksana and I are awaiting your return, the day your rehabilitation is announced, the day you're returned to us. It won't be long now, keep fighting a little longer, be strong, the worst is past. It's the moment of change, Arkady Ivanovich, the moment of transformation, and soon everything will be possible, my love, everything.

1987

1

Sverdlovsk, Union of Socialist Soviet Republics,
April 16th, 1987

Irina didn't even have to hear his footsteps to know that it was Arkady in the hall; her heart gave a leap, she bounded out of her chair, and opened the door wide. There he was, or what was left of him: Dumbfounded, thin, more distracted than happy, surprised, immobile, *alive*. After five years, five months, and thirteen days of imprisonment—a hell—Arkady Ivanovich was finally home. Irina fastened her eyes on his, and embraced him. She held on as if he were an oak tree in the middle of a storm, a log floating on the ocean. She had to feel his body, the reality of his body, feel his warmth, his scent, prove to herself that it wasn't an illusion or a trap, that he'd returned forever.

She clung to his shoulders, ran her hands over his back and neck (marked by rings of tension), and touched his gray hair. He barely responded to her urgent need. An abyss was opening in Arkady's eyes, a blackness that made Irina tremble; those savages destroyed him, deprived him of everything, tore out what he held most dear: hope. She wasn't hugging her husband but a changeling, a mannequin, a scarecrow. She caressed his face, traced her finger over his features, felt his stiff, grayish whiskers, touched his hollow cheeks, his cold nose, his wrinkled eyelids, his forehead.

It's me, Arkady Ivanovich, she whispered. You're safe and sound at home. He pushed her away gently: He had to look at the interior of his house, the furniture, the curtains, the filthy lamps, the windows. More important than recovering people was his need to recover that setting, that lost everydayness. Irina let him walk in: From then on, she would be his guide, his guardian.

Oksana, come here, come see your father, she said to the child. Only then did Arkady notice her. They approached each other carefully, silent, each as frightened as the other, and they hugged without enthusiasm. Here I am, Arkady said, wishing that sentence were accurate, your father. Oksana studied his features; she made an effort to remember the man who abandoned her when she was a baby. Irina joined them, weeping hopelessly, all the pain and anguish she'd accumulated during those five years, all the fear and threats, the mockery, the oblivion, it all flowed from her eyes. Oksana was sobbing too, caught up in that contagious sickness, compassion. Even Arkady tasted the saltiness of tears, except that he knew the reason: No matter how much he might try, he would never be able to compensate for that time, he would never be able to have a daughter.

Who knows how long they stood there wrapped up in one another's arms, fearful of separating and confronting their differences. Oksana was the first to step away. She stepped back a few paces, wiping her face on her sleeves. Arkady took note of her extremely black hair, her white socks and brown shoes, her irregular fingernails, her long, pointed fingers, her compact, hard body, and her sad eyes. No, he did not know who this girl was. What would she think of him? When he was arrested, she was just over five years old, and now she was eleven; little by little she was becoming an adolescent, a woman: a stranger. What could be left of him in her memory? Irina tried to resolve the situation and bring it to an end. I'll just make tea, she said, as if Arkady were an unexpected guest.

Irina could not grasp the idea of having her husband around again. She looked at him without knowing what to say, how to transmit her joy and sorrow, the emotions she'd accumulated over so many sleepless nights. And would he ever be able to reveal what he'd lived through? Was it possible to sum up five and a half years of isolation and terror? Both seemed sentenced to that mutual ignorance, that impotence. What should they say to each other? How could they rely on words?

Arkady looked at his daughter and said: You've got my mother's eyes. Perhaps it wasn't true, perhaps he could no longer recall any eyes at all, but he needed to believe it, needed to toss his daughter a link. Oksana smiled without joy: thanks. And time froze again. Irina came back with the tea. So nothing will ever be the same, Arkady told himself. Irina was surprised by his slow, lumbering movements. No, nothing will ever be the same, she muttered as well, but we must move forward, build a new world, close up the wounds.

I want us to get out of here as soon as possible, Arkady announced, carefully pronouncing each syllable. This house is the past, a past that no longer belongs to us. Irina agreed: We have to start over somewhere else. Arkady spoke to his daughter, using a childish tone: How'd you like to move to Moscow? Oksana clenched her teeth. She didn't want to go anywhere, was afraid to losing her house, her hideouts, her universe, was afraid of living with this traitor who claimed to be her father. Arkady tried to put his hand on his daughter's forehead, but she slipped away to the bathroom. She wanted to hear nothing more, wanted to be alone, alone as she was before, alone as she always was.

Irina tried to justify her daughter's attitude. Don't worry, the three of us need time to get used to one another. *Time.* In prison, time was interminable, but now it seemed to slip through his fingers. There was so much to do—the country was changing from day to day, the old structures were creaking, the foundations shaking—and he was late for his meeting with History. Sakharov, maker of light, and the other old dissidents were waiting for him to go forward with the fight against the monster. Nowadays, the system looked like a benevolent façade—the face of Gorbachev, the novice idealist—but nothing can keep the ogres from coming back and claiming their due, as happened following the thaw Khrushchev started in the '60s. Everyone had to be on guard.

Irina and Arkady stayed there for hours, exchanging ideas about the future or meditating in silence, looking for points of agreement and avoiding arguments. Perhaps because she was more naïve or more thankful, Irina believed in Gorbachev, in his ability to renew the system from within. By contrast, Arkady had lost all illusions during his imprisonment: He owed that man nothing. His arrest was unjust and so was his freedom. The authorities had forced him to sign an agreement: he wouldn't speak about his activities in Biopreparat. He couldn't imagine breaking that agreement, but its mere existence was an outrage. We have to leave Sverdlovsk, Irina Nikolayevna, we haven't a moment to spare.

Irina agreed: It was her husband's first day of freedom, and she always thought they'd celebrate it like a rebirth. But there was no joy in the air. Arkady barely looked at her as he reviewed his plans, which he did aloud, used to the solitude of his cell, and thought about how to go about saving the nation. At no time did he remember that she too had fought, that she too had resisted hundreds of threats, or that it was she who'd sought out Sakharov in the first place. Arkady's gaze had become opaque, and his body had lost its strength, but there was something that hadn't changed: He was still convinced that he, and only he, had a mission to carry out.

2
Klamath, California, United States of America, May 1st, 1987

Allison felt neither curiosity nor fear, only an excitement that ran over her skin with the subtlety of a tarantula. In the moonlight, her long cotton tunic allowed a glimpse of the rosy tone of her nipples, the dark stain of her pubis, even the diminutive roundness of her navel, but none of the women accompanying her seemed interested in those notes of sensuality. She'd been told that members of other Wiccan groups customarily celebrated Beltane naked, but nothing like that happened with the feminist variety she'd joined. Her companions appeared more concerned with heightening their contact with the Goddess than with exhibiting their bodies. Even so, Allison was excited by the vague eroticism, the liberation of the senses that was heightened by the bonfires and dances. She did not believe in the witchcraft or the magic invoked by her friends, but she'd agreed to accompany them in their rite: She lacked faith, but since her return from New Zealand there was a void in her soul, and she felt compelled to seek any consolation. No matter how much her rationality kept her from getting involved in those practices, she was fascinated by the mixture of activism, feminism, ecological struggle, and direct action she'd found in the group.

She'd abandoned Greenpeace after the death of Fernando Pereira, disillusioned by the passivity of the group's protests—the leaders refused to approve violence, were anchored in a crude defense of private property—and ever since she'd wandered from one ecological group to another until she came upon Earth First!, which had been founded by Dave Foreman at the start of the '80s. Unlike other collectives, Earth First! wasted no time on chatter and went directly into action. Inspired by the characters in Edward Abbey's 1974 novel *The Monkey Wrench Gang*, where a group composed of an outcast Mormon, Seldom Seen Smith; a surgeon, Doc Sarvis; a feminist saboteur, Bonnie Absug; and a former Green Beret who fought in Vietnam, George Hayduke, try to sabotage the Glen Canyon dam. Its members sabotaged contaminating businesses and carried out acts of active resistance—"monkeywrenching"—against the police. Abbey, a desert anarchist, coined the motto *A Patriot Must Always Be Ready to Defend His Country from His Government*, and Earth First!'s battle cry was: *No Compromise in Defense of Mother Earth!*

For ten months, Allison had been attending the Earth First! meetings in northern California, was an avid reader of the group's newspaper *Earth First! Journal*, and had even taken part in the Round River Rendezvous, where she met dozens of men and women who, like her, were willing to do anything to defend nature. Some of them, like Jenna Sullivan and Marianne O'Connor had been in the organization for more than seven years and had taken part in the famous "Glen Canyon Dam Crack." In the spring of 1981, about eighty members of Earth First! gathered on top of the dam on the Colorado River and unfurled an enormous, one-hundred-meter-long banner with a huge crack depicted on it—in imitation of Abbey's novel.

For us, Jenna explained, the Earth is much more important than human beings, and she recited a poem by Byron that they used as a hymn:

There is a pleasure in the pathless woods,
There is rapture on the lonely shore,
There is society where none intrudes . . .
I love not man the less, but nature more.

Allison never imagined that, in addition to interfering with the construction of dams, stopping the loggers, blocking the construction of highways, arguing about anarchy or bioterrorism, planning new forms of protest, and mocking the authorities, its militants also participated in magic, or, as they said, "neopagan" cults. Jenna and Marianne belonged to a sect, the Number 1 Susan B. Anthony Society, founded in California around 1973 by the Hungarian-born witch Zsuzsanna Budapest. Within the sect there were feminists, radical ecologists, and women who said they had secret powers, had had visions, and worshipped Diana (the source of their name). At first, Allison tried to keep her distance from the esoteric wing of Earth First!, but her friends persisted until they aroused her interest in their beliefs.

Allison agreed to attend one of the sessions of the Number 1 Society at the end of 1986, and five months later she was initiated as a member in a ceremony held on the outskirts of San Francisco. And now she was attending her first Beltane gathering in a northern-California forest. Her head was spinning: If in fact all those rites seemed a bit incomprehensible to her, the planning and execution of small acts of terrorism—the destruction of a transformer or a gas station, the toppling of a crane—gave her a more concrete pleasure. Even so, as she observed those half-naked women singing and dancing around the fire, Allison thought that perhaps all those theatrics were not a fraud or a banal, histrionic exhibition but an authentic communion among women who, believers or not, witches or not, let their emotions flow and joined together without fear. After several hours of dancing in a circle, of reciting, shouting, and howling, being embraced and accepted, Allison abandoned her prejudices. She too had found her place.

3
Moscow, Union of Soviet Socialist Republics, May 29th, 1987

For Oksana, that lanky boy with the smooth face, almond-shaped eyes, and enormous black glasses was an angel. Sent from heaven, timid and withdrawn like her, a messenger from another dimension, a solitary friend who'd landed in Moscow, city of wide avenues, to visit her. It hadn't even been a month since her family had carried her off to the capital, and she already felt suffocated by that crowd of threatening and hostile faces, trapped in that cage—her new school—where she was supposed to stay all day. She hated the morning her father returned to

Sverdlovsk; or perhaps she only hated her father, that severe, immaculate man who'd snatched away her life.

Was he really her father? Oksana recognized his pouting lips, the way he raised his shoulders or rubbed his chin, his rancid smell, and his thick hands. But his watery, languid eyes were not his, as if they'd been exchanged for others, as if the originals had been pulled out and glass balls inserted in their place. Oksana tried not to look at his face; his nearness filled her with an intimate, obscure fear. Even if that man was her father, he was also a monster.

Whenever Arkady came near or made a joke, she backed away. Irina scolded her: He's your father, Oksana, and he needs your affection. He's a hero, Oksana, a hero. But why should she love him? She did not have a single affectionate memory of him, no caress, no smile, no shared game. Why? Akrkadi Ivanovich was a shadow. Besides, he didn't seem especially concerned about her. Oksana saw him dedicated to a thousand things, writing letters, making calls, receiving visitors by the score—everything was more important and urgent than her.

And to top things off, her mother had also forgotten her—she was busy helping her husband, that vagabond who said he was her husband. She spent hours at his side, how disgusting, totally distracted from what was happening with her daughter, not speaking to her, not asking her anything, not asking her opinion before setting out on that damned journey, his exile. Oksana was the real victim, not her father.

During their first days in Moscow, city of wide avenues, the three shared a room in the house of some distant relations. How much longer will we have to be here with these people?, she asked her mother without getting an answer. After three months, they moved to the house of other "friends," strange people who spent the day cutting up newspapers or copying manuscripts. They often asked her to help, but Oksana remained aloof, not wanting to be part of their conspiracy.

Her only consolation came from her poets. One day, while Oksana was trying to understand a line, she felt the gaze of Yulia Simeovna, a friend of her mother, on her head. She was an older woman, about sixty, with graying hair, a beautiful collection of colored bracelets; she was crippled in one leg. What are you doing, Oksana Arkadyevna? Nothing. Do you like poetry? Oksana looked at Yulia with contempt: Yes, a little. I like it a lot, the older woman replied and sat down next to her. I don't write, I never had the necessary sensibility, I'd love to, but I do know some poets. Really? Yes, I'm friends with a couple of them, very valuable women, very brave . . . Want me to show you their work? Yes, yes, howled Oksana.

Yulia got up with difficulty, went to her room, and came back with some papers that were much the worse for wear. Before, these texts were prohibited, she explained, and circulated only in *samizdat*. Why? Because to some people poetry seems dangerous. Dangerous? Yes, Oksana: Poetry can be a weapon, poetry can say things that can't be said in any other way, and that is troublesome. In other times, writing poetry was punished with imprisonment or even death. Oksana couldn't believe it. What harm can a few words do? Listen, this is by my friend Nadezhana Poliakvova:

You come toward me like all the rest
to drink tea like all the others.
It's as if nostalgia for a lost country
were gnawing at our hearts . . .

No, I won't call you or reproach you for anything,
for now we're neither friends nor enemies.
How sad and miserable and solitary
sound your footsteps there below.

And let's see what you think of this one, by another young poet, I don't think you know her, her name is Assia Veksler. Yulia recited in an incandescent voice:

For what purpose do we live?
After rejecting a heap
of excuses and insults,
this last question still comes near:

There, when unrepeatable life
is over,
What will we leave behind
the inseparable frontier?

Oksana was burning. Not only because of the poems, which had delighted her, but because she'd found a new friend, an accomplice, the first person she liked in a long time. They spend the afternoon reading and reciting poems by women—Bella Akhmadulina, Polina Ivanova, Marina Tsvetaeva, Yunna Moritz, Natalia Gorbanyevslaia, and the one who would become her favorite, her model, her twin soul, Anna Akhmatova—as if it were a rite of passage or a ceremony. Oksana felt free, renewed. That night she wouldn't have to lock herself in the bathroom with the razor blade, she wouldn't need to purge her pain.

And, as if it were of no importance, that angel had appeared. The adolescent, melancholic angel who landed in Red Square, next to the Kremlin, as smooth and luminous as his little plane, with his almond-shaped eyes and unruly hair, his sinuous hands and his mouse's nose. Oksana looked at his photo in the newspaper and nodded: Yes, that boy, Mathias Rust, was an angel, an emissary who'd come from Germany to bolster her courage, to confirm that one day she too would plow through the sky, mock borders, and fly toward another world.

4
Washington, D.C., United States of America, June 2nd, 1987

Jennifer slammed the door and shook the walls. She returned from a meeting on the Mexican case with an upset stomach: She'd spent two years fighting with the functionaries from that country, with their smoothness and courtesy, their simulation and duplicity, and she was fed up. She took each new excuse as a personal affront. Did they think she was stupid? They always came with new excuses, like children who invent the death of their parents to justify their laziness.

Harriet, the timid, clumsy secretary assigned to her two months ago—Louise, her previous secretary, had requested a leave of absence because of stress—came into her office. Jennifer could not stand her slowness or her typing errors, but once again the human resources administrator warned her there would be no replacement. Harriet was probably her own age, but instead of taking care of her figure, she wore floral dresses—what a nightmare—and combed her hair like someone's grandmother. Yes? asked Jennifer in that tone that only she did not consider violent. Your husband called several times. Why didn't you tell me? You were in the meeting, and I didn't want to interrupt you. So you make the decisions around here now, Harriet? I just thought . . . You just thought, you just thought. That's all you do: think. If instead you worked a little. All right, what did he say? Nothing, only that he urgently needs to talk to you. Very well, you may leave.

Wells only called her when he had bad news. Why had the world turned against her? The Mexicans insulted her, they hid the facts, they doctored the figures, and they still had the nerve to question the recommendations of the IMF. Her own team cheered their mistakes, united against her. And now her husband was going to give her even more trouble. Jennifer dialed the number. What the hell could he want?

Wells assured everyone he'd become famous and a millionaire, and said so during every one of the parties he gave in the Park Avenue apartment he'd just bought. Jennifer did not understand his finances: DNAW barely functioned (it had yet to earn a single dollar), but Wells acquired a gigantic apartment in the most expensive part of Manhattan, called limousines just to go a few blocks, hired planes in the name of the company, and even gave her jewels for no reason. At first she accepted the new lifestyle happily, but not knowing how her husband was paying for all that luxury made her uncomfortable. Her life was based on this stupid paradox: By day she negotiated the debts of Third World countries, and by night she tried to find out how her husband managed his.

Jennifer listened to the stupid voice of Jack's secretary: Mr. Wells is on another line, he'll call you as soon as he's finished. Jennifer hung up, frenetic. It had been a bad day. In May, the directors of the IMF decided to give Mexico another $510 million, despite the fact that it wasn't adhering to the guidelines they'd laid down. Jennifer thought it a grave precedent. Because of that, Citibank tossed out its adjustment program, adding three billion dollars to its reserves. Obviously! argued Jennifer, as long as the debtor nations won't tighten their belts, the commercial banking system will be reluctant to pay the piper. Mexico, on the other hand, continued its wheedling strategy. Guillermo Ortiz, the new Under-Secretary of the Treasury, declared that a great effort had been made to comply with the adjustment program but that the avarice of the commercial banks had ruined Mexico's objectives. Within the IMF, his colleagues accepted Ortiz's argument and even cheered it. Jennifer didn't believe it: The idea was not to donate money to developing nations but to transform them into responsible economies! No one listened to her: After so many arguments, they all wanted to celebrate the event, and at the end of the session Michel Camdessus, the new Director-General, even predicted a quick upturn for the Mexican economy. Absurd!

The telephone rang, and Harriet connected her with Jack. What's going on, Jack? He told her immediately: Good news! I've just signed two agreements, the first with a Japanese pharmaceutical company and the second with Schering-Plough, for $20,000,000. Also, Christina convinced one of her friends to advance us another five. And I've just signed a deal with a Stanford researcher to develop neurotrophins. It's been a fantastic day, Jen. She barely congratulated him: Great, the only thing I ask is that you be careful. Are you sure you've got everything under control? Of course I do! The markets are growing as never before, *The Wall Street Journal* is celebrating the upturn in technological businesses, DNAW has created great expectations, we're working with the most outstanding researchers, some of the best minds in the nation have joined our advisory board, and we finally have liquidity. So we've decided to have an I.P.O. in October, what do you think?

She was surprised: She supposed that her husband's company was barely off the ground. Microsoft had gone public the previous year, and since then scores of technology firms had imitated it unsuccessfully. Are you sure it's a good decision? Yes, yes, yes, Wells declared, it *is*. Walter has already negotiated a deal with Solomon Brothers to take charge of the I.P.O., so nothing can go wrong. I want you to come to New York this weekend. We'll have a big party, I need you with me. Jennifer hated her husband's social events (at least that's what she said), but she couldn't shirk her duty. Against all her predictions, the world seemed to be entering a new era of prosperity, and she did not want to be a wet blanket. Fine, she muttered, I'll be there.

5
New York, United States of America, October 19th, 1987

The damn computers are to blame for everything! That would be the most common explanation of the disaster, as if computers could think, make decisions, make mistakes, and send everything to hell! Wells had gotten up in an expansive mood. The television news concentrated on the military reprisal President Reagan had decreed against Iran; the weather report announced a sunny, warm day, and while stock analysts were expressing some concern about the decline in European and Asian markets, there seemed to be no reason for alarm: In October the Dow had broken a historical record.

Wells finished his tea, took a final bite out of his croissant, and started for his office. In the limousine, he called his broker Arthur Lowell to get his first report of the morning. With a trembling voice—that's how Wells would recall it—Arthur told him things were going well, fairly well. That *fairly* left Wells a bit nervous: The I.P.O. for DNAW was scheduled for the following week, and nothing should cast a shadow on it. Wells glanced at his watch: 9:00 A.M.

Banal problems distracted him for a while, but soon his discomfort became a genuine anxiety. He decided to call Walter: Bad news. The S&P 500 index out of Chicago had just plummeted 20.75%, and it was dragging down the other markets. I don't know how to say this to you, Jack, but I'm predicting a catastrophe. Just like that? Wells couldn't understand why his friend was speaking in such a resigned way. He again contacted Arthur, who'd already received scores of calls from clients obsessed with selling.

Wells turned on his TV. In New York, navel of the world, at 9:53 A.M., 273,700 shares of Coca-Cola were sold at a price 3.5 points lower than their value the previous Friday. At 10:40, 398,400 shares of Eastman Kodak opened 13.5 points lower than the previous day. And at 10:47, 1.38 million shares of Exxon fell 3.5%. Walter was right: a rout. If things didn't improve before noon, a recovery would be impossible.

By 11:00 A.M., the volume of shares traded had reached 154 million, an absolute record. The screens and tickers could not keep pace with recent transactions, with prices, or with volume. Meanwhile the sales floor was turning into a babel of shouts and laments.

Wells was pounding his desk with his fist. By then his office had filled up with the administrative and scientific staff of DNAW. At 1:09 P.M., the Dow Jones news system broadcast an ambiguous message: The new President of the Securities and Exchange Commission declared that he was not considering suspending trading *for the moment*. What an idiot!, Wells shouted. The traders won't wait a second to sell! Within a few minutes the Dow Jones fell from 2,018 points to 1,969 points. To correct its error, the SEC announced, at 1:25, that it was not considering the possibility of suspending trading. Too late: The damage was done.

Suddenly everything became calm—the strange silence that precede chaos. At 2:05, the Dow returned to the somewhat comforting level of 2,000, but by 2:35, all hope of a rise vanished. The innumerable transactions were processed by the market's system, made up of 200 microcomputers, each one of which had to execute more than 500,000 transactions. The machines could not keep up, which caused an ever-widening gap between the information that appeared on screens and reality.

When the trading day ended at 4:00 P.M., the market had registered the largest loss in its history. Much larger, Wells noted, than the crash of 1929. The Dow Jones fell 508 points, losing 23% of its value in six and a half hours. Wells repeated the figure in order to believe it: *Twenty-three percent in one day!* His stomach ached. The other employees of DNAW stared at him in stupefaction. And if there was a recession? The total volume of shares traded was almost 604 million! Never, *never* had anything like that taken place.

At 4:26, Wells received a call from Jennifer. Did you hear Reagan's message? He says the economy remains strong . . . Are you listening to me, Jack? He was in no mood to fight with his wife after losing hundreds of thousands of dollars. One thing was certain: DNAW's I.P.O. would have to be postponed. We'll talk later, Jen, I've got too many things on my mind. He hung up. Only then did he notice the NASDAQ results: The situation there was slightly better than at the Dow, only—he laughed as he said the words—11.35% instead of the Amex's 12.7% or the NYSE's 19.2%. Perhaps, but only perhaps, everything wasn't lost. When Walter called to give him a final balance of the situation, Wells told him to *go to hell.* All he wanted was some silence. He'd go home to his Park Avenue apartment, take a hot bath, open a bottle of wine—one of his best—and let himself sink into a soft, painless lethargy.

6
Moscow, Union of Socialist Soviet Republics, October 21st, 1987

Arkady was a living rage. Even though he'd begun to gain back weight thanks to Irina's care, he still had huge dark circles under his eyes and his arms were as thin as threads. None of that kept him from accumulating an anger that contrasted sharply with his lassitude. His wife, his daughter, his few friends—none of them recognized him: His good manners, his conciliatory spirit, and his prudence had all disappeared. Now he had a venomous and turbulent personality, would hear no contrary opinions, and would tolerate no ambiguous act. He shouted at the slightest provocation, carried away by an irrepressible fury. And what did you expect, Irina Nikolayevna?, he shouted during one of his attacks, that after five years of being buried in a concentration camp and a psychiatric hospital I'd be at peace? You have no idea what it is to be *there*, transformed into a non-human, into a beast. After a few months, you end up believing it, and after a few years you can't recover your former shape. Listening to him, Irina almost felt ashamed: It was true—she could not imagine the tortures or mistreatment he'd suffered. At the same time, she couldn't love him: She was afraid of his outbursts and attacks of violence, and she was especially afraid he'd lose control with Oksana.

The members of the democratic movement detested his mood shifts and deplored his radicalism. Unlike Sakharov and his circle, Arkady felt no regard whatsoever for Gorbachev. The Secretary-General had issued the order to free him and had allowed him to move to Moscow, but that seemed to Arkady a mere act of justice that did nothing to redeem the politician. Gorbachev had initiated perestroika and glasnost, but for months he'd been enmeshed in a bureaucratic spiderweb that kept him from controlling the old buzzards in the Party.

Perestroika is in a phase of stagnation, Arkady would say—to anyone who took the time to listen: The geezers embedded in the system sabotage the reforms; there is a real danger we'll return to the old model—generalized repression, totalitarianism. And it will be Gorbachev's fault, because he's become a haughty czar just like his predecessors. He's in love with himself, puffed up with the praise he gets from the West. Russia—Arkady refused to say Soviet Union—can't afford to lose more time.

Even when Irina agreed with his diagnoses, she deplored his lack of tact. Even the most impassioned members of the democratic movement felt intimidated in his presence. Arkady preferred to identify himself with Boris Yeltsin, of strong arms, because of the impression he'd made during the anthrax crisis in Sverdlovsk. Now, in his role as Secretary-General of Moscow's *gorkom*, he showed himself to be more receptive to democratic demands than Gorbachev.

Arkady had run into him in May, when a delegation from the democratic movement (which would later take the name Memorial) visited him to discuss the construction of a monument to the victims of the Gulag. At that moment, Yeltsin avoided any commitment, but his affable nature, his direct style, and his charisma again impressed Arkady. When the meeting was over, Arkady chatted with him. Boris Nikolayevich kissed him twice and told how happy he was about Arkady's freedom. At that moment, they established a mutual complicity, although it wasn't exactly an intimate friendship. That was the time when Yeltsin moved heaven and earth to curry favor with the *intelligentsia*, while Arkady wanted to influence someone with genuine power. With his frank and populist style, Yeltsin began to invite him on the tours he was making throughout the city, so Arkady could see the extent of his influence. Boris Nikolayevich possessed a bullet-proof clarity, and his desire to escape the rigid labels of the *nomenklatura* had already aroused the distrust of other party leaders. Yegor Ligachev, conservative and small-minded, linked to Gorbachev out of convenience, was intent on destroying him.

In his double position as Secretary-General of the Moscow *gorkom* and candidate for the Central Committee, Yeltsin made speeches everywhere, and while they reflected Arkady's points of view, they still did not step outside the rhetorical canon of the Party. Which is why what happened on October 21st during a plenary session of the Central Committee of the CPSU (Arkady would write in his *Memoirs* that he was one of the instigators of what took place) was so disconcerting. While the plan stipulated that Gorbachev would be the only speaker, Yeltsin insisted on making a statement. Boris Nikolayevich, used to preparing his speeches in order to mitigate his nervousness and mistakes, decided to improvise: He went from one idea to another, got lost, and went back again and again to the same arguments. Perestroika is faced with great difficulties, he said in a broken voice, the Party has created expectations that are too grand and unrealistic, there is an air of disillusionment, there are many advances but also many retreats . . .

The most conservative members of the Central Committee had no idea where the devil the Secretary-General of the Moscow *gorkom* was going, but Yeltsin, of strong arms, did not restrain himself: All this has me very worried, he insisted, and the attitude of some comrades, who are impeding reform and stopping change, seems unacceptable to me. In particular, I feel an enormous lack of support on the part of Comrade Ligachev. All eyes turned toward Gorbachev's second in command, who had already begun to chew over his response. And then, without anyone imagining it, without there being a single precedent, perhaps without calculating the impact of his words, Yeltsin concluded: Under these circumstances, I cannot continue with my work, so I present my withdrawal as a candidate for the Central Committee. I only hope that the Moscow *gorkom* will decide to retain me as Secretary-General.

Yeltsin's withdrawal speech sounded so crazy—no one had ever rejected the Central Committee—that Gorbachev was slow to react. When he did, his words were not soft: I don't know if I've understood correctly, Boris Nikolayevich, but are you intending to remain Secretary of the Moscow *gorkom* and divide the Party in two, or do you only wish to fight against the authority of the Central Committee? Yeltsin tried to respond, but Gorbachev silenced him brutally.

Ligachev requested the floor and began the barrage of discrediting remarks and insults Yeltsin had earned that afternoon. He called Yeltsin irresponsible, immature, a traitor. When he finished, a dozen speakers repeated the same accusations, the same insults. Who did Comrade Yeltsin think he was? How did he dare break Party discipline? What pride, what egoism! Yeltsin was immoral, primitive!

When the salvo of reproofs was over, Gorbachev closed the debate, but Yeltsin insisted on speaking again. This time, the bear behaved like a hare, muttering two or three apologies. Gorbachev, unmoved, rebuked him as if he were a naughty child. This is what Comrade Yeltsin had become: a wretch, a caricature. Gorbachev, shepherd of men, launched into yet another of his interminable soliloquies, presenting himself as the all-powerful and forgiving father: Perhaps we shouldn't ascribe too much importance to what's happened here; in Lenin's day, the arguments were sharper, the best thing would be to forget the matter and go on working for the success of the reforms. Just idle chatter. Yeltsin was sweating, hunched over because of a sudden pressure in his chest: He felt sick, very sick. From that moment on, he became like the plague, an untouchable. He'd gone beyond all limits. The curse of the Secretary-General would soon reach him: Nothing would again be the same for him or, for that matter, for Russia.

1988

1

New York, United States of America,
February 25th, 1988

Wells rubbed his hands with glee: Frankie Quattrone would lead the I.P.O. for DNAW. And to think that just a few weeks earlier he thought he was finished! Contradicting the apocalyptic predictions made by some, the sky did not fall, technological businesses did not go bankrupt, and the NASDAQ was almost untouched: *Black Monday* did not open the way to a severe recession. Alan Greenspan, the tough President of the Federal Reserve, was not mistaken: The U.S. economy was in a growth phase, and even though the crash caused immense losses, impoverished thousands, and unleashed a collective hysteria, it did not provoke a global catastrophe.

No one understood why on a Monday like any other, with no political or natural disasters, the Dow Jones had suffered the worst debacle in its history. Some blamed the computer system, others linked it to esoteric phenomena—economic cycles connected to planetary confluences—and still others accepted the conjunction of multiple factors, none of which on its own would have been powerful enough to nullify recovery.

Wells had lost fabulous quantities of money—his personal account was down to zero—but thanks to the financial engineering he'd developed, DNAW hadn't suffered irreparable damage. He wouldn't even dare imagine what would have happened if the company had gone public in September, as originally planned. At long last, everything would be taken care of: Frank Quattrone, eccentric numbers magician—always wearing his pink and orange-tinted sweaters—was the right person to inject money, lots of money, into the company. After graduating from Wharton, Quattrone studied at Stanford and then went to work for Morgan Stanley as an expert in technological investments. Starting then, he was the man behind the I.P.O.'s for the sparkling Silicon Valley startups: In just a few years, he'd brought in millions of dollars for them, for his bosses, and for himself.

Wells knew that the I.P.O. was the most delicate phase for a business like DNAW: Now he would be able to pay off the investors who until then had put their confidence in him, stabilize his finances, and perhaps receive the first benefits. A successful I.P.O. would guarantee his survival in the competitive pharmaceutical world. Convinced of the importance of this step, Wells was not hesitant about supplementing Quattrone's commission beyond the legally-mandated 7%: Having Quattrone on his side made any sacrifice worthwhile.

Unlike other businesses, biotechnology companies produced dividends only after a long fallow period. A company would begin operations by buying the patent for some product, process, or theory from a university or individual scientist, having faith in its possible therapeutic uses. This would be followed by an intricate series of technological and bureaucratic steps until it could be commercialized. For the moment, all of DNAW's products were in the testing stage. The expectation was that the tests would show their possible application in fields as varied (and lucrative) as vaccination or cancer treatment. But a new medication could only be sold to the public if, and only if, the Food and Drug Administration approved it—and that happened only rarely.

Before returning to DNAW, Wells asked his driver to pass by the Stock Exchange: The Greek columns outside the trading floor aroused an almost addictive anxiety in him. His fate would be decided in that place, where every single day people crossed the border between wealth and poverty, luck and disgrace. Very soon, on May 16th, according to Quattrone's calculations, the future of DNAW would materialize on its screens. Thousands of people would depend on its initials, its rises, its falls, its hits and its misses. Wells saw the market as a gallery: He was going to show a work of art—DNAW—and the experts would judge it with a critical eye. Or maybe the Market was more like a strip-club, a place where exhibitionists like him stripped naked in exchange for money. Comforted by that metaphor, Wells asked his driver to change course and go to Chelsea, to the secret address he visited when he needed an adrenaline injection: the loft of Erin Sanders, the nineteen-year-old daughter of Christina Sanders, with whom he'd begun an intense romance. For Wells, risk was the greatest aphrodisiac.

2

Moscow, Union of Soviet Socialist Republics, February 27th, 1988

I hate him, I hate him, I hate him: Oksana whispered into the pained face of her mother. Finally the catastrophe Irina had been fearing for so long had occurred, and not even she knew the cause. The gap between her husband and her daughter had become permanent. Overly obsessed with his struggle, Arkady had no patience to fight with Oksana's sensibility. It was a war of egos: Both wanted Irina to choose a side. Ultimately, without knowing for sure why, out of inertia or fear, or because her link with the democratic movement kept her from distancing herself from Arkady, she chose her husband. Betrayed, Oksana abandoned all prudence and dedicated herself to provoking them for no reason.

When Irina came home that afternoon, she noticed the echo of the most recent insults exchanged by Arkady and Oksana. Neither would tell her the cause, but a look at their faces—her daughter's dry tears, her husband's rictus—revealed the seriousness of the fight. Arkady used it as a pretext to leave, claiming he had a meeting to attend, and Oksana again muttered: I hate him, I hate him, I hate him. This time, Irina did not attempt to reason with her. She'd tried that so many times, and with such poor results, that she was no longer willing to waste her tenderness. She feigned a serenity she didn't feel and simply made dinner. Oksana barely ate anything, got up, and took refuge in the bathroom.

While her mother washed the dishes, Oksana spread a sheet of paper out on the floor: A poem by Aleksandr Kushner, recently published in *Novy Mir*, that Yulia Simeonova had just lent her:

Like an excited young man who reads a note from his girlfriend,
that's how newspapers are read these days:
as if time itself
were airing out dressers and bedrooms.

News about Moscow . . . If only you knew
how tensely Leningrad awaits you.
Oh swishing of pages, you eclipse the swishing of leaves.

Make noise, in the name of God!

Like Kushner, Oksana hated news from the paper, the agitation, her father's proclamations, the changes; in a word: the present. That was her principle conflict with Arkady. She avoided movement, speed, the need to transform herself; in sum, she despised that omnipresent word, perestroika. Just as Kushner evoked everyday life in Leningrad, she too wanted the world of Sverdlovsk returned to her, the peace and silence of its streets, its coldness and anonymity, the protection her distance and forgetting offered her. No sooner had they arrived at Moscow than she said to her father: I don't want to stay here, this city scares me, it frightens me to death, let's go back, please. He didn't even try to reason with her. Instead, comparing his twelve-year-old daughter with a Party commissar, he launched into a violent harangue in favor of human rights and the future of Russia.

Arkady could not stand the idea of his daughter giving up so soon, or that she considered his struggle irrelevant. Oksana, for her part, never accepted his reprimand: Her nostalgia for Sverdlovsk had nothing to do with politics, she wasn't trying to rebel or question her father's sacrifice, all she wanted was that peace, that anonymity. If it was true he was concerned abut the freedom of others, as he said day and night, then he'd have to let her go.

Oksana felt so frustrated, so impotent, that she picked up her pencil and, almost without realizing it, confronted the whiteness of a page, simply allowing her bitterness to flow through her hand. Nothing complicated came out, just a few verses, bad copies of the ones she read and admired: her first poem. She talked about her childhood, about the dryness of Sverdlovsk, about the moon among the mountains, and in secret also spoke about her pain, about the wounds she inflicted on her arms and legs, about the sinister joy they gave her. That was all, without moral lessons or details. Only a few lines that gave as good a picture of her as a photograph. Dizzy, she bent over the basin and vomited. Then she looked into the medicine chest and found the razor blade she used to cut her flesh. She raised her skirt and made an almost surgical incision on the inside of her right thigh, where the scars were lined up like war wounds. A scarlet droplet slid down her skin. Oksana held back a moan and discovered that this time she hadn't done it to purge her rage or sadness but to celebrate her writing. That day she became a poet. And poetry was linked to her blood.

3
Baku, Union of Soviet Socialist Republics, February 29th, 1988

Then past became present and war broke out. For months I'd been noticing that one of the most unexpected and terrible consequences of perestroika and glasnost was the exacerbation of national disputes and quarrels, all of which had been held in check by force for more than seven decades. The reforms carried out by Gorbachev, shepherd of men, opened Pandora's box. In an increasingly disordered environment, rancor spread like an epidemic and reached even the most distant corners of the empire. And it was in Azerbaijan, in the industrial neighborhood of Sumgait, not far from my house, where violence broke out during three days in February.

The Caucasus had always been a laboratory for apocalyptic scenarios: A permanently disputed territory, subject to the power of great empires and divided into diminutive ethnic communities who were all at odds with one another. The rivalry between Christian Armenians and Muslim Azerbaijanis always split the zone, especially after Stalin's decision to give the autonomous territory of Nagorno-Karabakh to Azerbaijan. After Gorbachev came to power, the Academy of Sciences and the Supreme Soviet of Armenia sent myriad petitions to Moscow, seeking to reincorporate that territory into their republic, but with no result. Tired of waiting, on February 20th, 1988, the Armenian deputies of the Nagorno-Karabakh National Council voted to be reincorporated into Armenia, eliciting the immediate response of the Supreme Soviet of Azerbaijan. Thousands of people—though the Armenians of the diaspora would say a million—gathered in their capital Yerevan to show their support of the NKNC.

As an Azeri Russian, I viewed these nationalist quarrels with horror: The region was so scarred by past conflicts that it mattered very little who was right. The harassment of Armenians in Azerbaijan and of Azerbaijanis in Armenia became routine. I myself witnessed the waves of Azerbaijani refugees who escaped from Nagorno-Karabkh and moved into desolate shacks on the outskirts of Baku, especially in Sumgait, on the northern shore of the Caspian Sea. Calls for prudence went unnoticed. Even my wife Zarifa, an ethnic Azeri, until then completely secular and moderate, began to show a menacing hostility toward Armenians: They want to take over our country, she would say. I tried to explain that hatred only breeds more hatred, but she joined the Azerbaijani demonstrations—to insult the enemies of Yerevan—that took place on a daily basis in downtown Baku. For over half a century there had been no public demonstrations in the Soviet Union, and when they finally appeared didn't demand liberty or democracy—they only sought to insult their neighbors.

When I turned on the TV that February 29th, I learned that war had become inevitable. In an outraged tone that would have been impossible to imagine in the Brezhnev era, an announcer was reporting on the murder of three young Azerbaijanis in Nagorno-Karabakh and demanding the arrest of the perpetrators. While the channel did not show pictures of the dead, the reporter's tone of voice was an invitation to revenge. With no need to organize, moved by resentment, hundreds of Azerbaijanis, armed with pistols and knives, attacked the Armenian minority of Sumgait while Soviet authorities stood by passively. This began the orgy of ethnic conflicts that would devastate the last days of the twentieth century. By the end of the day there were thirty-two dead, including six Azeris, though no one really trusted the statistics.

That night, I wrote in my diary:

February 29, 1988

Ghosts of the past are reappearing.
Once again we have death, once again we're entering History.

We haven't learned the lesson. Armenians and Azeris no longer consider themselves Communists. The dictates of Moscow and internationalism mean nothing to them; they're ready for war, to kill one another as they did centuries ago. The State is vanishing, and individuals are exacerbating their differences. Since we've stopped being Soviets, there is no other choice except to be Armenian or Russian or Azerbaijani. And what if the Soviet Union wasn't, deep down, anything more than an anomaly, a passing evil that within a few years no one will remember with sorrow or nostalgia? Perhaps we humans are a cursed race: Nothing can save us from the blind will to destroy that is inscribed in our genes.

The Soviet Union was falling into the abyss.

The criminal indifference of the police and the army could not be understood except as the consequence of a general paralysis, our incapacity to react against the demons that were being set free day after day. Gorbachev, shepherd of men, thought he was invincible: His picture was shining in the West, where "gorbymania" resulted in the sale of thousands of masks and dolls with his face on them in London, Paris, and New York. He was sure that his authority as Secretary-General of the CPSU would allow him to overcome the enemies of perestroika and lead the nation to a rapid and efficacious democratization, but Gorbachev was not living alongside the common people of the provinces. He didn't visit the Caucasus, that land just on the other side of the mountains from his own birthplace. If he had, if he'd seen the fear and anger built up there, if he'd listened to the harangues of Azeri nationalists, perhaps he would have understood just how close the Soviet Union was to extinction.

On the other hand, I was observing the collapse on a daily basis in my own neighborhood and in my own house. My marriage to Zarifa was not a function of love or passion or even friendship: We'd known each other for so long that our union always seemed inevitable. In that era, her family wasn't religious (that would change very quickly), and, if they opposed our marriage, it was more for economic than ethnic reasons. Zarifa was timid and standoffish, though with me she was always understanding. And, when I came back from Afghanistan, she was the only person who put up with my fear, my skittishness, my mood swings, my alcoholism, and my simmering rage.

Perhaps her genes had predisposed her to tolerate impossible men. During the two years we were married we barely ever argued—I talked and she agreed. I don't know if it was because she was afraid of me or because she was waiting for the right moment to rebel. The explosion of the Nagorno-Karabakh conflict changed her spirit: Overnight she stopped being the submissive woman I knew (or at least thought I knew), as if the nationalist virus had stirred up every one of her cells. Suddenly the Armenians became the object of her rage and were guilty of every evil. Only later did I understand that for Zarifa those anonymous beings were only a pretext. Insulting them, she was actually insulting all men. That absurd hatred was the only one she allowed herself, the only one her family and I allowed her. But when I finally figured out what was going on inside her, it was too late: We'd both taken opposite paths—two kinds of disillusionment—and we would only find each other, in a fleeting way, staring at the ruins of our home.

4
West Berlin, March 13th, 1988

As she explained to Klara in one of their daily telephone conferences (they usually took longer than an hour), Eva's life had become as placid as the surface of the Wannsee. Her spirit was slipping into a state of apparent repose, almost she could say of peace, that was impossible to imagine in America. The first reason for the change was Ismet, her plaything, whose hand she held as she strolled around the lake. It was still chilly, but the little flowers, the greening trees, and the flocks of ducks foretold spring.

The second cause of her well-being was the Eli Lilly drug company, which had just marketed an unusual drug known commercially as Prozac, whose effects worked miracles on her spirit. Ever since her psychiatrist gave her some pills he had received from New York, Eva could contemplate the disappearance of her anxieties and fears. That activator of serotonin, a simple chemical manipulator, was transfiguring her existence: She hadn't felt this calm for ages, so at peace. Perhaps her libido had diminished, but her lack of erotic interest seemed to her almost a blessing: She'd finally reached the age when a stroll or a cup of coffee were just as pleasant as the clash of bodies. She had no fear of acknowledging the fact to Klara: She felt happy, or least as happy as her battered spirit permitted her to feel—happy enough to request a one-year extension of her contract with the Zuse Institute.

The third and final reason for her joy was Berlin. Stuck in the heart of Communist opacity, that city, or city fragment, stood as the final frontier of civilization, and that was visible in the freedom of its people, in its artistic will, and in its admirable egoism. If you want me to tell you the truth, Eva said to her mother, I'm more in love with this city than I am with Ismet: It fascinates me to get lost in the neighborhoods, to be surrounded by outrageous punks and *okupas*, to visit the boutiques on the Ku'damm or the alleys of Charlottenburg. On any given evening, you can listen to (actually look at) Herbert von Karajan leading the Philharmonic in the sinuous Hans Scharoun Hall, get a glimpse of the Potsdamerplatz waste land—few enclaves reveal the reality of the Cold War better—or wander, starting at sun up, the paths of the Tiergarten. You'd love it, mama, you should come. Only a little after a year after arriving, Eva thought herself a Berliner, as Kennedy proclaimed during the blockade of 1961. For her, Berlin wasn't only Berlin, an island surrounded by cannibals, but a metaphor for resistance, a utopia.

Eva barely noticed the city's problems, didn't see the growing unemployment, didn't see the corruption of its politicians (the Senate wasted millions of marks celebrating the 750th anniversary of the founding of Berlin), and of course was not afflicted by the *Mauerkrankheit* that bothered some of her foreign colleagues at the Zuse. Perhaps because she felt safe in the west, Eva spent hours walking along the Wall, that infamous mark. She liked the fact that being there, a few meters away, reminded her which side she was on and who the enemy was. Her fascination was so powerful that she carefully wrote down the graffiti on the wall:

KEYS LOST, INQUIRE WITHIN
MOMMY, WHAT'S THAT WALL DOING THERE?
"OPEN SESAME" OPENS THE WALL
MARX, ENGLES, LENIN, MAO, AND THEN WHAT?
MARX, WHERE THE DEVIL ARE YOU?
25 YEARS ARE ENOUGH
LOVE IS MORE SOLID THAN CEMENT
TEAR DOWN THIS WALL AND ALL THE REST WILL FALL

And the one she liked most of all: ONE DAY THIS WILL ONLY BE ART.

Ismet, her plaything, did not share her enthusiasm. For him, Berlin was an illusion, a substitute. This, he would say, can't last, this place has something phantasmagoric, sinister to it. He wasn't referring to the

Nazi past but to the hostility of the most conservative sectors toward immigrants. Though he'd spent his whole life in Berlin and didn't even speak Turkish well—his family had come at the end of the '50s when he was eight—he wasn't able to feel German. I *don't want* to be German, he said to Eva. Even if I got a passport, they wouldn't let me. That *they* alluded to nationalist politicians like Heinrich Lummer, people who were not ashamed to say: The Moors have done their job; it's time for the Moors to go home. After the construction of the Wall, thousands of Turks had been invited by the Senate to replace workers from the east, but thirty years later they made up 13% of the population. If Berlin's worthy citizens foamed at the mouth whenever someone said the city was Germany's madhouse, they fumed when they realized that the Turks had taken over their island.

When they finished their stroll along the banks of the Wannsee, Eva accompanied Ismet to his place, a small apartment not far from Oranienplatz, in Kreuzberg. Appropriately enough, the neighborhood was known as Little Istanbul: Its streets swarming with dark-skinned men talking or playing cards, its multi-colored balconies, its antique shops, its kebab stands, and the aroma of garlic and thyme reminded one more of an Oriental bazaar than a capitalist enclave.

But the most surprising thing was that, alongside that horde from *One Thousand and One Nights*, the city's radical youth also gathered in Kreuzberg. Since its population was exempt from military service—in theory it was an Allied protectorate and not a *Bundesland*—Berlin was a refuge for pacifists, ecologists, painters, musicians, dropouts, and squatters—*Hausbesetzer*, who took over its ruined buildings and turned them into drug distribution centers. The only thing that bothered Eva in that circus was its hatred of the United States—enormous signs blared out the usual *YANKEE GO HOME!*—when Kennedy and his compatriots had been the real saviors of the city. The punks, drug addicts, and beggars didn't look for trouble and showed more solidarity with their Islamic neighbors than the upper middle classes in Charlottenburg.

Ismet had bought some greasy kebabs for dinner. His apartment wasn't pretty, but the mix of colors and aromas aroused a vitality in Eva that didn't exist in her place in Schöneberg, not far from where David Bowie established himself in the '70s. Like the protagonists in "Heroes," Bowie's emblematic song, that night Eva and Ismet would eat, drink, kiss, make love (or not), and then she would insist on calling a taxi. Ismet would protest a little, as usual, and then with the face of a sad dog would watch her leave. For her, Berlin, an island surrounded by cannibals, was paradise.

5
New York, United States of America, May 17th, 1988

By the end of the afternoon, Wells felt as if he'd been run over by a steamroller, but he couldn't feel any happier: His calculations had been surpassed thanks to Quattrone's determination. During the previous weeks, Quattrone sent him on a road show—from Los Angeles to Philadelphia, from San Francisco to Washington, from Boston to Seattle—to arouse the interest of new investors. No matter where Wells went, he repeated the same words, carefully chosen for him by Merrill Lynch's assessors: DNAW was not just another biotechnological business; it was the biotechnological business of the future. He would segue into a discussion of the panoply of the products the company would come to produce, emphasizing their eventual pharmaceutical uses and their commercial possibilities. If DNAW was successful with its drugs for fighting multiple sclerosis, diabetes, or osteoporosis—to say nothing of cancer or AIDS—the earnings would be legendary. Wells's obligation was to make the miracle credible by showing with figures and hard facts—and an unlimited self-confidence—that DNAW would attain his goals. Wells was astonished by his public's reaction: He supposed that those capitalists must have heard the same promises from the lips of other executives, but all his audiences evinced enthusiasm, seduced by the idea of becoming rich by serving mankind. His success was total: In two weeks he raised more than $60 million, and DNAW shares, which opened at $18, closed the day at $29. On the way home, Wells could only think about the two parties he'd hold to celebrate his triumph: the first, private, with Erin Sanders, and the second, huge, with Jennifer. For the miserable wretch, this was paradise itself.

6
Kettle River, Washington, United States of America, June 29th, 1988

The idea of taking part in another Round River Rendezvous would have been reason enough to make Allison happy, but this time the spirit of

Earth First! was anything but festive. The enthusiasm and faith of other meetings was absent, and the old-timers deplored the growing hostility between the followers of Dave Foreman and Mike Roselle. The ideological battle between the *apocalyptics* and the *millennialists* was acquiring harsher and harsher tones, to the point that the two old friends barely spoke.

As all the participants in the Rendezvous knew, Foreman and Roselle, along with three other friends, founded the movement during a trip to the Pinacate Desert in northern Mexico, in April of 1980. Sitting back on the dry earth under a harsh sun—and stimulated by alcohol and drugs according to their detractors—the five decided to create a group with enough courage to face up to those who were leading the Earth to environmental disaster. Shortly thereafter, ensconced in a New Mexico ghost town, they unveiled an inscription in honor of the Indian Victorio, who, according to local legend, had opposed the whites who were destroying the beauty of the desert. Foreman and Roselle became the leaders of the new organization, but their differences soon began to grow: Foreman thought ecological disaster was inevitable, while Roselle believed that Earth First! should take it upon itself to educate the rest of society and postpone the destruction as long as possible.

Foreman defined himself as a radical biocentrist: The fate of mankind was irrelevant compared to the well-being of the Earth. His vision stimulated the publication of two articles in the *Journal* signed by a Miss Ann Tropía, which immediately aroused the hostility of Roselle's allies. In the first, Miss Ann Tropía ascribed to humanity all the ills of the planet, while in the second she asserted that AIDS was the Earth's natural defense against its attackers. For Foreman, social justice was a chimera. With the shadow of the catastrophe falling on them, Earth First! should concentrate on helping the Earth in its struggle against the human parasite.

Allison respected Foreman, held his intelligence and energy in high esteem, but she'd seen her San Francisco friends die of AIDS and could never accept the idea that their deaths were beneficial to the planet. Hurt, she gravitated more and more to the group led by Judi Bari, the new feminist and liberal star of the movement (Roselle had been arrested after participating in a Greenpeace demonstration at Mount Rushmore). Walking alone along the Kettle River, Allison again began to doubt her course of action. Even in a movement as lively and spontaneous as Earth First!, fights and envy undermined the best intentions.

In the distance she could see the camp, with its blazing torches, and could hear the echo of Sean's guitar—he was one of the *official* musicians of the movement. Suddenly she stumbled over the body of a boy she'd seen at other meetings. Zakary Twain was resting against a log, staring at the powerful Washington sky and its avalanche of stars. Sorry, she said. Don't worry, come here, look at this. The two of them stayed there for a couple of hours, saying nothing, not even touching. That was what Allison enjoyed most about Earth First!, the instantaneous connection among its members.

Allison ran into Zak again and again in the following days. If she hadn't promised to stay out of complicated relationships, she would have recognized that she liked him, that she was sure the feeling was mutual. Aroused by the music—it was the last night of the Rendezvous—Allison left her female friends and went looking for Zak. She found him in an isolated spot, a few miles from the camp. When she saw him, Allison took off her clothes. He seemed taken aback, but finally he embraced her.

The next morning, Zak explained that he had to go to Tucson, but gave no further explanations. She wasn't especially surprised at his behavior—she knew how men were—but at the end of the day she realized she couldn't stop thinking about him. The central office of Earth First! was in Tucson, and it wouldn't be difficult to find a pretext to visit. Was she in love? Allison had a metallic taste in her mouth and then burst out laughing. At her age! After all she'd been through, she was still behaving like a teenager! Yes, she'd look for Zak, her little paradise.

7

Washington, D.C., United States of America, October 8th, 1988

Jennifer woke up in a terrible mood. Her head ached—a hammering in her temples—and her blood pressure was (she thought) low. She had yogurt and an apple for breakfast, then weighed herself on the bathroom scale: She'd gained a kilo. She studied herself in the mirror and, of course, found herself fat, old. Sure, men still chased her, but her body had slid into unstoppable decline: She'd just turned fourty-three. Forty-three!, she howled. She tried to exercise at least one hour a day, first on a stationary bicycle and then calisthenics; she led a healthy life and didn't even smoke. But every time she spent a weekend with Jack, she filled up on carbohydrates and saturated fats: cheeses and ice cream, cake, the only things that restrained her anxiety. When she came back to D.C., she tortured herself with salads and boiled vegetables.

Jennifer sank into her bath, already prepared with salts and toning oils, closed her eyes, and tried to keep her mind a blank. Several times, she'd tried to follow the advice of her girlfriends and signed up for yoga classes, but every time she ended up fleeing them, irritated by so much silence. She tried to calm down. This time she decided to stay in Washington, axis of the cosmos, to annoy Jack, who fully deserved to be annoyed, but she didn't enjoy it. She got out of the bath, wrapped herself up in a towel, and ran to the medicine chest to get some tranquilizers. What was wrong with her? Menopause perhaps? A mid-life crisis? The pills didn't seem to help. She'd take a cold shower and go shopping: the perfect therapy.

After applying her usual battery of creams, dressing, and putting on makeup, she drove to a shopping mall. She stayed there all morning, wandering from one window to another, bored, unable to decide between a bag and a dress, investing in her purchases the same concentration she deployed at work. She always analyzed the market, verified prices and product quality, and got confused in complicated calculations before choosing a Chanel dress, Gucci shoes, or a Dior stole. At the end of the operation, she'd spent more than $2,000 and still felt unsatisfied.

Hungry, she went to the food court, where she bought a hamburger and a milkshake. She knew she'd be sorry, that this whim would force her to starve to death for weeks, but it didn't matter: The calories would help her survive until Monday. Could Jack really be thinking about leaving her? She didn't think he was that stupid: Erin Sanders might be young, very rich, and *very* pretty, but she didn't have a thought in her head. What would people say about a man who walks out of his marriage for an adolescent? Jack wouldn't dare; he was too afraid of gossip. He only went out with the child for the novelty of the thing, the glamour, and her mother's contacts. He would get bored quickly and come back to her.

She swallowed the last bit of hamburger, licked her ketchup-covered fingers, and got ready to leave. To go where? The afternoon had barely begun, and she had nothing to do. Whom could she call? Who'd want to see her on Saturday? Her women friends had their families and were at their sons' football games or their daughters' ballet performances. None would be free to go out with her. Maybe it had been a mistake to scream at Jack and tell him she wouldn't go to his damn party. In New York, she'd at least have had fun fighting with him. She considered going to the office, but immediately changed her mind: She had to be able to amuse herself on her own. She'd go to the movies, what a good idea, it had been years since she'd seen a film. She checked the time: 3:00 P.M. Perfect. She walked to the other end of the mall, where there was a seven-theater complex, and bought a ticket for *Dangerous Liaisons*.

When she left, she was even more deeply depressed. The plot was too artificial and exquisite, almost pornographic. The Vicomte de Valmont, the miserable John Malkovich (a character so like Jack), was a confirmed and perverse Don Juan who ultimately fell in love with his victim, the insipid and apathetic princess played by Michelle Pfeiffer. At the end, she died thanks to him. The moral was obvious: To triumph in life you had to be a son of a bitch. *Always*. Jennifer walked to her car, unable to blot out the image of Glenn Close, who the movie audience rejected and mocked. That's how she felt: betrayed, mocked. She and Jack had signed an agreement, each one was free to sleep with anyone they pleased, but they were to do so in secret, keeping the façade of their fidelity intact. They were never to be seen in public, were obliged to avoid scandal and rumor. And now the idiot had broken the agreement! Every time he went to a restaurant with Erin Sanders it was as if he were slapping her in the face. Why did he put himself on display? Could the fool have fallen in love? And, like Valmont, could he have lost control and suddenly bailed out of their marriage? Jennifer couldn't allow it: She would do anything—anything—to keep it from happening.

8

Moscow, Union of Soviet Socialist Republics, November 12th, 1988

After he left prison, Arkady was a different man; his character had soured, and his fear had hardened into pride. Even he noticed the change: Before, in an earlier life he almost couldn't remember, Irina had accused him of being too prudent, too thoughtful—to the point that sometimes he thought his wife was branding him a fearful man, perhaps even a coward. Arkady knew that bitterness had taken root in his spirit long before his arrest, but only now, thanks to a kind of internal glasnost, did he dare rip off the mask of civilization and reason.

After he left prison, Arkady had no reason to compromise, no reason to put up with the stupidity, the vices, or the mistakes of others. He'd lost patience! Now he had the right to express his opinions without fear. That was why Irina distanced herself from him and Oksana was afraid of him. Arkady Ivanovich could not hold back, didn't want to, couldn't go back. The revolution of his mind and body was now unfettered. Yes, now he was violent; yes, now he was intransigent; yes, now he was brutal. That was the price he'd paid, and he wasn't going to settle for the crumbs of freedom conceded to him by Gorbachev, shepherd of men.

Because of his harsh, direct character, his relations with other members of the democratic movement, and with the directors of the Memorial, were getting more and more tense. Even Sakharov, maker of light, seemed tepid towards him. Arkady wanted immediate changes, with no transition: He wanted a market economy, direct elections, a multi-party democracy, the same rights held by citizens in the West, wanted to travel, wanted a house for his family, a car, a bank account, money; yes, money as well—it was an indispensable condition for individual freedom. And he wanted it all *now*.

That radicalism won him the esteem of Boris Yeltsin, of strong arms, the most impatient of Russian leaders. After resigning from the Central Committee and being reprimanded by Gorbachev, he'd become a paradoxical figure: a disgraced *apparatchik*, stripped of power, given over to alcohol and oblivion, but a man who, without realizing it, was seen by many who were sympathetic to his cause as one of the few political figures that could speak the truth. Not a day passed without Yeltsin and his wife Naina receiving letters full of praise that urged him to return to public life. During this time, Arkady became one of his closest advisers: The people need you, Boris Nikolayevich, he would say, Gorbachev would never have the guts to demolish the old structures of the Party. He thinks he holds all the strings, but it's the bureaucrats who control him. Yeltsin enjoyed his friend's comments, but he didn't dare leave his isolation: He was still too pained, and he felt too weak to enter a new battle. He preferred to travel with Naina, play tennis, relax. But letters and telegrams came to his house by the hundreds; all he had to do was walk outside to be applauded, hear expressions of affection and solidarity. Perhaps Arkady was right: The time for revenge had come.

While on vacation in Estonia, Yeltsin gave an interview to a local paper. Thinking few people would read it, he spoke about the USSR's problems with clarity and firmness, as he hadn't done during his appearance at the Central Committee. A year of calm, of study, and of discussions with Arkady had caused him to modify his statements, rendering them more logical and serene—but no less impassioned for that. The interview was reproduced from one end of the nation to the other, and he again felt the spotlight on him, as if he'd just awakened.

A few days later, he accepted Komsomol's invitation to inaugurate one of its Moscow meetings. Its young members restored his confidence by inviting him against the dictates of the Party, resisting censure and threats. When he finished speaking, he was given an ovation. Yeltsin reasoned, shouted, and electrified his audience for three hours. At the end, a student addressed him: You are no less popular than Gorbachev. Would you be willing to lead the Party? The nation? Yeltsin did not have to meditate his response: When we have elections with more than one candidate, I'll participate like anyone else. A salvo of applause sealed his speech. Sitting in the audience, Arkady rubbed his hands.

9

Tucson, Arizona, United States of America,
November 12th, 1988

Several weeks later, Allision finally ran into Zak at Earth First! headquarters. He didn't appear to be very enthusiastic, as if she were the last of his concerns. What are you doing here?, he asked point blank. Nothing, she answered, offended. Peg invited me to join the group; I hope that doesn't bother you. Zak muttered: This is no job for beginners. Why don't you go back to California and do more useful things? Your hands are needed elsewhere. Without saying good-bye, he turned and left.

Who did that jerk think he was, talking to her like that? She had as much right to be part of Emetic, one of the most aggressive sectors of Earth First!, as any other militant. Aware of her experience with Greenpeace, Peg had asked her to join the group—whose name was an acronym derived from Evan Meechan Ecoterrorist International Conspiracy—whose record already included the destruction of twenty-nine electric towers that belonged to a uranium mine in the Grand Canyon. Its current objective: carry out simultaneous attacks in Arizona, California, and New Mexico.

Zak still avoided her, but Allison wouldn't give up. She recognized the power she had over him and had no intention of leaving him in peace until he explained his change of attitude and they were together again, like they had been that night by the Kettle River. Along with the destruction of power plants, she'd taken on a parallel mission: to bury the resistance that kept Zak from her body.

1989

1
Kabul, Afghanistan, February 2nd, 1989

A miraculous year, a surprising year, a memorable year. You might think, perhaps, of an avalanche: A tiny stone breaks loose on top of a hill and drags particles of dust and ice with it, then pieces of rock; little by little the quantity grows and becomes a mass of mud and snow whose velocity accelerates with the fall, dragging along everything in its path, until that insignificant, fractured piece of gravel becomes a landslide: tons and tons of material that flatten forests or villages, end the lives of animals and plants, and bury unsuspecting passersby.

In 1983, the Russian mathematician Vladimir I. Arnold wrote: Catastrophes are sudden changes that appear as unforeseen reactions on the part of a system that has been subjected to a regular variation of external conditions. Small causes are capable of producing gigantic effects. Thus, in an untimely way, without anyone's fearing it or foreseeing it, an accident, an irrational decision, a hesitation, a careless act, even an idea—a revolution: a rough or intemperate swerve—alters the equilibrium of a system, of a fabric that has kept itself in order for years or decades or centuries, and everything changes overnight, is altered, and daily life is buried in the past, inaugurating a hazardous era that is out of control.

What we take for granted becomes horrifying: A single act is sufficient, a single impulse carried out in the precise instant when it can change the world, end oppression or unleash a massacre (an epidemic). The last Soviet soldier to leave the bloody hills of Afghanistan behind, a young, inexperienced, and defeated boy who simply followed orders that derived from other orders, in a chain of command that reached the Ministry of Defense, the Politburo, the Central Committee, and perhaps even the pen of Mikhail Gorbachev, shepherd of men, had no idea that his departure was the point of inflection in a glorious year, a unique year.

That young man, inside a dusty armored vehicle or a rusty tank, was the pebble that unleashed the avalanche, the cause of the cause of the end of the Cold War, the end of the Soviet Union. Let's try to imagine him: As he observes the landscape that opens before his eyes, a space that after ten days of forced marches will lead him to the border, to the end of the Brezhnev Doctrine, that buck private thinks only of his family in Moscow, Tashkent, or Samarkand, about receiving proper recognition for standing on the brink of death for so many years, for his struggle on behalf of Communism. The miserable fool doesn't know, can't know, that he'll never get home. He'll only reach an unknown land where his illusions, his memories, his beliefs—all his beliefs—will collapse over the course of a few months. When, on February 15th, 1989, he finally passes the military checkpoint that separates Afghanistan from the Soviet Socialist Republic of Tadzhikistan, where there is no official authority present to receive him with a medal or an embrace, that young and anonymous soldier of the Red Army will have broken the order of the world once and for all.

2

Sverdlovsk, Union of Socialist Soviet Republics, March 27th, 1989

It took Arkady less than a minute to accept Yeltsin's proposal: Yes, he would be a candidate in the first democratic elections ever to be held in the Soviet Union. He didn't have to talk it over with Irina, it was a natural decision, the logical consequence of his battle. If they couldn't destroy the system with the stroke of a pen, they would have to undermine it from within. Arkady would infiltrate its corrupt cells like a virus and from there begin his labor of destruction. That's how Andrei Sakharov, maker of light, understood things, because he too had announced his intention to participate in the campaign, becoming the most respected and visible of the congressional candidates.

While the elections were far from being as open and fair as the democrats desired—only a third of the members of the Congress of Deputies of the People would be elected by direct vote, while the other two-thirds would be nominated by the Communist Party, Komsomol, and other related groups—Arkady believed that the movement should take advantage of the opportunity to make itself heard. That same night, he communicated his decision to Irina, who approved enthusiastically. This would mean that Arkady had decided to contain his rage or at least sublimate it. He would return to active life and abandon the silent rancor that had done so much damage to him and his family.

There's only one problem, Arkady explained. We've only been living a short time in Moscow, city of wide avenues. Nobody would vote for me here, so the logical thing would be to be a candidate from some district of Sverdlovsk. Move again? No, replied Arkady, but I'll have to commute between the two cities. Irina gave a sigh of relief: The move to the capital had been too traumatic to think of moving back to Siberia. Don't worry, Arkady Ivanovich, we'll fight on two fronts. I'll take charge of details and preparations here in Moscow. This is great news! I'm sure that if you speak with people, with our people, if you tell them your experiences, and give them hope, you will win. Arkady smiled for the first time in many days. He may have been ashamed to admit it, but he was excited. He felt young, willing to travel from neighborhood to neighborhood, transformed into an evangelist or democratic missionary and—yes, he'd already decided to talk about it—a champion of free markets.

Arkady embarked on a frenetic program to acquire the signatures that would allow him to register. The process wasn't simple, complicated by a thousand bureaucratic knots that had been inherited from the past. The Party men could not keep anyone from participating, but they had the resources to dissuade even the most enthusiastic. For example, Boris Yeltsin, of strong arms, had satisfied all the requirements to register in Moscow, but the Party had blocked his candidacy until the popular support for his nomination was so overwhelming that his rivals dropped out.

Arkady's success was harder to achieve. After all, he was only a scientist with a sketchy profile—his years in Biopreparat had taken him out of the public arena. And, while he'd been in jail, he'd moved to Moscow after being set free. Even so, thanks to Yeltsin's support—his influence in Sverdlovsk was still powerful—Arkady succeeded in garnering the support of four organizations (including his former laboratory, which had been transformed into a civilian center), and, thanks to his energetic and direct rhetoric, he earned a reputation as an intransigent reformer, which guaranteed that he'd appear on the ballots.

From January until May, Arkady never stopped commuting between Sverdlovsk and Moscow, where Irina had abandoned her other activities in order to devote herself full-time to her husband's cause. Once again she'd decided to forget about herself—and her daughter—to become his campaign director. Almost without resources, but using wisely the contacts she'd made over the past few years, Irina managed to get the majority of the democratic movement, including many people from the Memorial, to pardon Arkady for his excesses and to embrace him as one of their own. Sakharov himself, pained by some of Arkady's statements, gave in to Irina's begging and agreed to support him in public: A photograph that showed them together, chatting in the old physicist's living room, was more important for his victory than all his speeches.

Arkady insisted that Irina and Oksana come to Sverdlovsk the day the voting took place. Neither of them had been back to the city for quite some time, and they found it had changed for the worse—not because of the rusty old factories and military installations, the spirit of the inhabitants had disappeared. Still, it was Yeltsin's personal territory, and people quoted his words from memory, waiving his photos around like flags.

Thanks to Yeltsin, Arkady made a place for himself in public life, and he too was recognized and celebrated. For Oksana, on the other hand, the electoral agitation had a rotten smell to it. She only wanted to visit her house, recover her memory, and enjoy images of an idyllic childhood that arose from her imagination and not from the facts. While her parents visited civic centers and workers organizations, she wandered around on her own, allowing herself to be eaten up by a nostalgia that was fictitious but no less anguishing for that. On election day, she outlined a somber poem about childhood in which the blackened chimneys were castle ruins, the cement blocks turned into empty battlements, and the steel bridges became swollen arcades.

When she caught up to her parents, she found them holding hands, as if their were lovers—how horrible, how disgusting—celebrating their imminent triumph. The elections had confirmed Oksana's fears: She'd lost the struggle. She took no interest in the development of the campaign, resisted congratulating her father, and withdrew to her room—actually an attic in the house of some friends—convinced that the Earth was an inhospitable and depraved place. While the nation celebrated the election of men like Sakharov, Yeltsin, and Granin, and the defeat of the old Party fogies, Oksana felt more alone than ever. Everything that took place outside, in the hated, exterior, adult world, was repugnant. Disgusted, Oksana gave herself over, for the second time that day, to the purge she called her ceremony of pain.

3
New York, United States of America, April 2nd, 1989

I simply cannot believe you pay attention to rumors, Jack exclaimed in a frightened, brittle tone that infuriated his wife. It must have been that witch Gloria, am I right? Since her husband plays around, she invents stories to feel better . . . By then Jennifer's rage had turned into tears, but it again became fury. She opened and closed drawers, packed up her things helter-skelter, and then, out of control, she again stretched out on the bed, intent on not forgetting her most valuable possessions—jewels, photographs, documents.

She'd decided to leave, to abandon that damned Park Avenue apartment, which in any case she'd never liked and never considered hers: Wells had decorated it in an outlandish, vulgar style. But first she was going to make Wells's life miserable. She'd make cutting comments, she'd take him apart—she'd smash him, leave him half dead—with words that were daggers. How could she sink him, punish him, and inflict a humiliation a thousand times greater than the one he inflicted on her? This time she wouldn't hold back, wouldn't maintain the decorum that had allowed them to reconcile in the past. He broke the pact, dishonored her, and did not deserve mercy. How could he?

What annoyed Jennifer most was that Jack denied everything, that he didn't even have the nerve to accept his infamy. Did he think she was stupid, that he was going to fool her with his excuses, that he was going to convince her of his innocence when everyone—*everyone*—had seen him hugging and kissing that stupid girl, little Erin Sanders, the two of them practically naked on a beach in Cancún or Jamaica, on the front page of the *New York Post.* There were limits, and Jack had gone way beyond them. She wasn't as indignant about his betrayal as she was about his indiscretion: He'd made public something that should have remained private, and by doing so had tossed his marriage and his prestige out the window.

Calm down, Wells insisted, you're right, I was a fool, unfeeling, I admit it, what do you want me to do, get down on my knees and beg forgiveness? I would. I don't want to lose you, Jen, not because of something as silly as this? Silly?, she shouted, *silly*? I know, I'm a jackass, but we can get beyond this, you and I are partners, accomplices. Jennifer was angry with herself: Even though she hated him, even though she wanted to see him writhing in agony or being tortured, cut to ribbons, pus flowing from every wound, deep down she believed him. After all, Jack could leave her for Erin Sanders, who was twenty years younger and had many millions more, had an anorexic body and the brain of a fly (perfectly appropriate for her), and even so, he still wanted to keep her, his begging sounded authentic. Perhaps he didn't love her any more—Jen didn't love him—but there was no doubt he needed her. Erin was an amusement, a caprice, an attractive target, but Jack would never make her his partner and would never, ever marry her: He couldn't stand her for even a week. Even so, Jennifer wasn't going to forgive him. Not easily in any case. For now, she would move out, go back to Washington, axis of the cosmos, and enjoy the melodrama that would soon be taking place—when Christina Sanders found out that Jack Wells was *also* sleeping with her adored and innocent daughter.

Jack didn't think all was lost either: This wasn't the first time Jennifer, in a fit of rage or jealousy, had threatened to leave him. On two other occasions she'd packed her bags, the first time in Philadelphia and later in Manhattan. Ultimately she gave up, though not without making his life unbearable. Wells stopped justifying himself and simply, mechanically begged forgiveness. He was sure that after a few nightmarish weeks everything would go back to normal. Only that way, with this front in order, would he be able to invest his energies in calming down Christina and Erin. Oh yes, he'd eventually have to sacrifice Erin, but it would end in a more-or-less friendly reconciliation.

Unable to find the right words to destroy her husband's self-esteem,

Jennifer shut her bags: Help me carry them downstairs, she ordered. Sweetheart, please . . . I'm not asking, she bellowed, and walked more swiftly. This time she wouldn't reverse course, she was fed up with feeling disdained, with Jack's playing around, of pretending that they both had the same sexual freedom: She'd never used hers, out of fear of blackmail on one hand and fear of sexually transmitted diseases on the other. She was also fed up with thinking she was the weakest link in their marriage.

Wells dragged the suitcases into the elevator, then out to the sidewalk, right under the nose of the astonished doorman, who had no idea how to react to the drama. Jennifer wanted everyone to be aware of her disgrace, to see with their own eyes how she was leaving the model entrepreneur, the supposed benefactor of all humanity, who was in reality nothing but a liar and hypocrite. Wells hailed a taxi and placed her bags in the trunk. Jennifer couldn't hold back and, without giving it a thought, insulted him one last time.

4
Moscow, Union of Soviet Socialist Republics, May 26th, 1989

One solid proof of the chaos that threatened the Soviet Union in 1989 was the ease with which anyone could overcome a bureaucracy that until then had been impossible to circumvent. In theory, only someone with a special permit could leave his region and move to Moscow, but, ever since the ethnic conflicts had begun, thousands of Russians living in the provinces had moved into the already overcrowded housing complexes that stretched through the suburbs of the capital. A new and anachronistic *lumpenproletariat* was born, and very soon it was possible to find beggars or unemployed workers wandering the streets of Moscow, city of wide avenues: an unequivocal sign that the market economy had arrived.

After separating from Zarifa, I too moved to Moscow: I wanted to observe the changes close up, experience that environment of imminence and danger at its very center, feel the excitement and the challenge, become an eyewitness—a chronicler—of that mutation. It wasn't hard to convince some cousins to let me move in with them in exchange for a good part of my savings.

Under my arm I carried the enormous manuscript I'd been working on, my Afghanistan memoirs. After making my way through scores of magazines, whose editors would receive me politely and almost immediately send me on my way, I landed in the ramshackle offices of *Ogoniok*, a weekly that was emblematic of the era. Artiom Borovik, a young journalist educated in the United States and son of a powerful man in the KGB, had already published a long article on Afghanistan. Vitali Korotich, a bilious editor, speed-read the first chapter of my manuscript and, in one of his typical fits of inspiration, asked me to write an article about the second session of the Congress of Deputies of the People which was going to take place the next day. He warned me that it probably wouldn't be published—some of his best reporters would be covering the event—but he wanted to see how smart I was.

The Congress had been convened the previous day: 2,250 delegates from every region in the country were present, fully aware of their historical role. No one could imagine what it was going to be like. Despite the official controls, and the fact that the overwhelming majority of the delegates came directly from the Party, hundreds of writers, artists, former dissidents, activists, and critics of the system would have the chance to express their opinions in public, to be heard, to become, if only for a few seconds, the protagonists of change. For the first time, the powerful recognized their existence, for the first time criticizing our leaders would become *normal*. As if that weren't enough, Yeltsin insisted the sessions be televised. After decades of darkness and silence, anyone could see how the Party was losing its sacred aura, how its leaders were questioned, how the common citizens were raising their voices without fear of imprisonment.

The first speech was delivered by Sakharov, maker of light. As a sign of respect, Gorbachev not only yielded to him the honor of inaugurating the session but Sakharov was the only delegate he referred to by his name. Fully aware of the symbolic value of his words, Sakharov made a ferocious declaration in favor of democracy and human rights, a statement that could also be read as a devastating criticism of Gorbachev. The physicist demanded that the Congress become the supreme power in the Union—his proposal would be vetoed by the Communists—and then he explained how the changes could generate an open society.

Sakharov's reflections were followed by an avalanche of speeches, mostly by members of the Party who limited themselves to praising the virtues of the Secretary-General and the road that had been taken up until that moment. But then the citizens of the USSR witnessed the impossible: Yuri Vlásov, Olympic weight lifting champion—the strongest man in the world, according to official propaganda—blamed the KGB for its role in repression and stagnation. A delegate dared to interrupt Gorbachev, and another chided him for his extremely costly dacha in the Crimea. A historian demanded that Lenin's body be removed from Red Square and buried in a cemetery; scores of delegates complained about the poverty in their regions, their lack of input, the lack of food, abandonment, and the misery that reigned in their villages. Finally, a delegate from Georgia denounced, with millions of spectators looking on, the massacre that took place in Tbilisi on April 9th, when the Soviet Army attacked a group of demonstrators.

This was something absolutely new: None of us had ever seen anything like it. On the second day, the excitement was even greater. I felt disconcerted and anxious, felt that anything might happen, that everything was allowed. Sakharov requested that the Congress vote to elect its President, making it obvious that Gorbachev had no reason to occupy that position without the vote of the delegates. After a few minutes of confusion, a delegate from the north of Russia, Aleksandr Obolenski, registered to compete against the Secretary-General, and then another delegate, this one from Sverdlovsk—I soon learned his name was Arkady Ivanovich Granin, biologist, old dissident, and member of the most liberal wing—proposed Boris Nikolayevich Yeltsin. An authentic election with more than one candidate in the USSR? Ultimately, Yeltsin withdrew his candidacy, and Gorbachev won 95.6% of the votes. But the precedent was undeniable: The opposition was no longer a chimera.

That afternoon, the speeches again reached the level of euphoria and bravura of the previous day: Politics turned into spectacle, public property, and stopped being the privilege of the *nomenklatura*. No matter how crazy, erratic, violent, or execrable the speeches were, their mere existence was shaking up the nation. Maybe we aren't living in a democracy yet, perhaps the Party still held control of all institutions, but perestroika and glasnost had become real. Words once again were weapons, and anyone—anyone—could identify with those who, as I wrote somewhat banally in my article, slowly but surely leaned to stutter out their freedom.

As was foreseeable, *Ogoniok* did not publish my article. Vitali showed me that it was too flat, even naïve: I hadn't been able to stand back from the events and view them from a distance. I'd copied the point of view of the liberals without taking anyone else into account—a reporter's worst error, he warned me—but even so, he praised my style and told me that from then on I could consider myself a regular contributor to the magazine. Now, get out of here, Yuri Mikhailovich, he said, I want you to cover the Congress to the end—it will be good training for you even if we don't publish any of your pieces. Not only had I become a witness of History, but I was even going to be paid for it. In those days of excitement and surprises, I made a point of believing, dear oh dear, that my life would begin again.

5
Wenden, Arizona, United States of America, May 31st, 1989

Go back to town, Allison, we need that drill, Zak shouted, not giving her the opportunity to refuse. She didn't want to go, she'd gotten that far with the others, and wasn't inclined to stay out of the game simply because he told her to. Why did she get involved with him? She wasn't a teenager any more. Sleeping with her didn't give him any right to berate her or give her orders, he wasn't her husband, her boyfriend, or her boss; in Earth First! and in Emetic there were no hierarchies, they were all equals. Allison again protested, Why don't you go if you need it so badly? But he shut her up with a shout. Finally, Peg had to calm things down: Do what Zak tells you to do, take the van and go to town, find the drill and get back to us here while we set the explosives. Allison made a face, but she couldn't refuse without seeming capricious or egocentric. They'd spent more than three months planning this strike—for the first time they were going to cut the power lines of a nuclear power plant—and even so they hadn't been able to eliminate all of their mistakes! That jerk Zak was the one who was supposed to bring the drill, not her. It was *his* fault.

From the start of the operation, her relationship—if it could be called that—with Zak had been limited to four or five sexual encounters that had led nowhere: Afterward, neither called the other for days, as if their couplings had only served to satisfy a physical need. And that's how things were arranged between them right from the beginning: sex and pure sex, intense, passionate, sometimes more than that, with the understanding that neither would look for anything more.

In the beginning, Allison agreed to the terms; in point of fact it was she who formulated them aloud, but only to free herself of her fear: She knew she was susceptible to that sickness, falling in love. Sex with Zak was like nothing she'd ever experienced with a man: When it was over, she was annihilated, feverish, and yes, ethereal as well. She was convinced he experienced something similar: She could see it in his eyes, smell it on his skin, feel it every time he left his semen in her body. But he couldn't say it; it would mean a betrayal, the breakdown of their pact. Which is why in public they behaved like enemies, exchanging barbed jokes and insults. The other members of the group believed they hated each other, that only their commitment to the Earth kept them from destroying each other.

When the preparations for carrying out the big April maneuver began—simultaneous actions in Arizona, California, and Colorado—Zak became even more odious, dead set on getting her out of the mission. She thought she found in him the same machismo that was present in the other male members of Earth First! No matter how radical they were, they didn't hide their misogyny when the time came for fighting. But Allison was not going to allow him to exclude her: This was her first collaboration with Emetic, so she had no intention of standing on the sidelines.

Allison ran to Peg Millett's van and started the engine: At that moment she would have happily run over her lover. She turned on the radio full blast—the ominous lyrics of Bad Religion's "You Are the Government" resounded like a hammer—and drove to Wenden, where Emetic had its base of operations. She parked in front of the motel, ran up to Zak's room, looked everywhere for the damned drill—where the hell could he have put it?—and, not knowing what else to do, went to a hardware store and bought a new one. When she got back to the Palo Verde camp, it was deserted. Not a trace of her friends. The sons of bitches left without me. She went back to the van: Where could they have gone? Could they have walked to town? It was several miles away. Only when she got back to Wenden did Allison sense the tragedy.

She parked the van behind the motel, and taking care to hide the drill under the seat, went up to her room. Just as she was about to open the door, a pair of hands seized her from behind. A mellow voice announced: You're under arrest. Two policemen made her turn around, frisked her, and then handcuffed her. A detective read her her rights (as they always do in movies), made her stumble down the stairs, and stuffed her into the back seat of a patrol car. Minutes later, she was in the county jail along with Peg, Mark I, and Mark II. What about Zak?

Peg hugged her tightly: Zak is one of them.

The next day, the FBI raided the Earth First! offices in Tucson, and, as the culmination of Operation THERCOM, which had been in progress for several years, also arrested Dave Foreman, accusing him of conspiracy, sabotage, damaging private property, and terrorism. After a quick trial—they all pleaded guilty to the charges—Peg Millet, Mark Baker, and Mark Davies were sentenced to three years in prison. Allison, on the other hand, was only sentenced to a year and a half, the jury taking into account the fact that she hadn't been captured at the scene of the crime. They also took her condition into account: As she would quickly discover, she was already four weeks pregnant when she was arrested.

6
Washington, D.C., United States of America, August 27th, 1989

Have you gone insane?, Jennifer screamed, as if she were in the desert and not in her IMF office, as if the other people in the office were deaf or very interested in her family life. She usually shouted out her problems without the slightest consideration—in the worst cases, to accuse her subordinates of being lazy or inept—but not even Emily, her faithful secretary, dared point it out to her. One day she tried to explain to Jennifer, in the most delicate terms, that her stories were audible all the way up on the third floor, but Jennifer didn't believe her and imagined yet another plot against her, a new way of annoying her. It was perhaps for this reason that her staff rarely lasted for more than a few months. Despite the attractive salaries and the enthusiasm Jennifer displayed in her best moments, very few were immune to her telephonic howls and her calumnies. At the end of the day, everyone knew her problems and even the office boy knew her husband was fooling around with Erin Sanders, that she had just walked out on him, and even that her sister Allison—just imagine that, her sister—was in jail.

How could you possibly think of giving birth to a child in prison?, Jennifer whimpered. That question disconcerted even those who knew Jennifer's personal history from A to Z: Their boss's family was becoming more and more like *Dallas* or *Dynasty* every day. Just to dispel any doubts, Jennifer repeated: Allison, do you really want to have a child in prison? Last time you said . . . you said . . . Everyone realized Jennifer was sobbing. This woman is nuts, said Bill Stuart, a Chicago graduate who'd just joined the IMF as an analyst. Emily could only sigh, as if to say, you haven't seen anything yet. Meanwhile, Jennifer went on with her tirade: Alli, for the love of God, this isn't right for you or the baby, are you just going to leave the child with no father? And if some day the baby says he wants to meet his father, what are you going to tell him, that the son of a bitch had you thrown in jail?

Someone should put the two of them in the nuthouse, added Bill, the only person in the office who dared to criticize Jennifer openly. Recently hired, he was unaware of the law of silence that reigned in the office. Emily, on the other hand, lived in constant fear of an even greater reprimand. Jennifer was capable of anything. When she found out someone had been talking about her behind her back, she would not rest until she chased him out of the IMF.

Allison, this is the last time I'm going to say this to you, growled Jennifer, seeing the battle lost, what kind of future do you intend to give him? Alli, please . . . Alli . . . Allison Moore! It seems Alli has less patience than we do, laughed Bill. Jennifer ran out of her office to the bathroom. As usual, Emily quickly caught up to her. A widow with white hair, though she was only around fifty, she had the unenviable position of being Jennifer's sentimental adviser, assistant, secretary, and factotum, which garnered her no respect whatsoever from her boss, who scolded her over the tiniest infractions and constantly asked for her to be transferred.

Are you okay? asked Emily, taking her by the hand. Jennifer couldn't stand being touched, but this time she made an effort, and, moving away in a mild fashion, tried to calm down. She dried her eyes, and, using the handkerchief held out to her by her secretary, wiped away the eye shadow-darkened tears. This is one of the worst periods in my life, she confessed in a neutral tone. First, my idiot husband is involved with Erin Sanders, and now I find out my sister is in jail. And now the fool says she wants to have the baby. I don't understand, Emily. Years ago, she had an abortion, you know that, and now she insists on having the child of a . . . policeman. Tell me, would give birth to the child of a man you hate? Emily didn't know what to say to that. Of course not!, Jennifer declared. By then she'd recovered her spirit. Well, well, let's go back to work, more important matters await us. One more thing: I'm asking you to be discreet—I wouldn't want anyone to find out about this. Emily held back a nervous laugh. As they went back to the office, Jennifer could not banish an image from her mind: her sister, pregnant, in an Arizona prison cell.

7
Leipzig, German Democratic Republic, October 9th, 1989

An expert on computer networks, artificial life, and computer simulations, Eva thought the democratic movement spreading through Central Europe would soon reach Democratic Germany. She went into great detail on the subject with Klara during another of their extremely long telephone calls. In East Berlin, her colleagues at the Institute, the few local friends she had, and even Ismet Dayali, her plaything, spoke of nothing else. Gorbachev, shepherd of men, would have to stop supporting the senile Communist bureaucracy. Only Friedrich Hauser, her neighbor, who'd escaped from the East a few weeks before the construction of the Wall in 1961, thought otherwise: Honecker is a clever vulture, better not get your hopes up.

Eva wouldn't believe him, and she read the newspapers and spent hours watching television every day, seeking the first buds of revolt. As the weeks passed after the triumph of Solidarity in Poland without anything happening in East Germany, Eva admitted her neighbor might be right: The countries that made up the Communist block were not uniform. Hungary, Poland, and perhaps Czechoslovakia had powerful national traditions and a Catholic culture that was opposed to the ideology of their leaders, but Bulgaria was a mystery, Romania was still dominated by that miniature Ceauşescu, and Germany . . .

And suddenly the flame of discontent flared up in the least likely place, in Leipzig, the ancient Saxon city that had been transformed into a gigantic block of cement. At the outset of May, Reverend Christian Führer, pastor of the Nikolaikirche, had begun to organize "prayer meetings for peace" that brought together all sectors of society, believers and non-believers, nationalists and anti-communists—and agents of the Stasi—creating a group that was large enough to lead a protest against Honecker. Protestantism had begun in that same city 450 years earlier, and that tradition of dissidence had remained alive, despite the Nazis and the Communists. At the beginning of October, more than two-thousand people gathered in the Nikolaikirche, and they opened the way for the first large-scale protests in Berlin since the 1953 uprising.

On October 7th, during the celebrations for the 40th anniversary of the founding of the German Democratic Republic, Mikhail Gorbachev was received as a savior, an ally whose contempt for Honecker was obvious. To keep the enthusiasm the Soviet leader had unleashed from firing up democratic souls, the Party and the Stasi had dispatched its agents to the principal cities in the nation, ready not only to threaten but to arrest the demonstrators.

Gorbachev evinced impatience with his host's passivity, even if he hid it behind a façade of Communist civility. Without criticizing Honecker directly, he went out of his way to suggest the road to follow: Danger only threatens those who can't react to change, he said, tacitly signalling the East Germans to take charge of their own destiny. Hundreds of people were arrested in the days following his visit, but the democratic epidemic had already infected that totalitarian fortress.

On October 9th, Eva and Ismet turned on the TV and saw how thousands of people were shouting in the streets and squares of Leipzig, while numerous agents of the Stasi and the Party were surrounding the Nikolaikirche, ready to storm the place. It was then the miracle took place: Reverend Führer renewed his call for peace and then, like a *deus ex machina*, the robust figure of Kurt Masur, Director of the Gewandhaus, appeared, accompanied by the theologian Peter Zimmerman: Both asked the crowd to remain calm. From inside the church, six hundred of the faithful came out to the atrium, where they were received with songs, prayers, and burning candles. The police were ready to intervene, but they did nothing; the special forces, though they had orders to arrest the demonstrators, stayed put too. And even though Party members and Stasi agents were supposed to denounce the instigators, they remained silent. *Wir sind das Volk* was heard for the first time: *We are the people.* That chant was repeated constantly during the following weeks, but soon turned into something else: *Wir sind eine Volk*, *We Are One People.*

Aren't you afraid of a reunified Germany? After what happened under the Nazis, it's hard to be sure that nationalistic enthusiasm won't turn into a slaughter. There are no Jews any more, but there are people like me . . . Eva did not share her plaything's pessimism, but though she noticed the polite racism of the Berliners, her hatred of Communism was greater. The collapse of the Soviet block was a victory for the United

States, a victory for her country, a victory that also belonged to her. For now, the only thing that matters is avoiding massacres, like the one that took place in Tiananmen Square, and making sure that the new governments in those countries respected democratic principles. Eva was convinced that if History continued its course, Hungary, her parents' and grandparents' homeland, would also be a free country. I'm not afraid, Ismet, I think we've learned the lesson.

8
Moscow, Union of Socialist Soviet Republics, October 17th, 1989

It's been three weeks since anyone's seen him or heard from him, exclaimed Arkady Ivanovich, as if this were the best news he'd received in years. Do you understand what that means, Irina Nikolayevna? Vladímir is going to tell them everything, *everything*, understand? And then they'll have to recognize the truth, and I'll be free to tell it after all. One of the friends Arkady still had at Biopreparat had revealed the secret: Vladímir Pasechnik, Director of the Leningrad Institute of Ultrapure Biopreparations—and one of the highest level scientists involved in the production of biological weapons—had vanished during a work visit in France. Arkady had met him during his time in Sverdlovsk, many years earlier, but he never imagined he'd have the courage to escape to the West.

Pasechnik had been invited to visit a pharmaceutical factory in Paris, and, in the administrative disorder taking place in the USSR, his boss, Kanatjan Alibekov, not only gave him permission to go but later forgot that he'd done it. It was not until he received an imperious telephone call from the Sub-Director of the Institute of Ultrapure Biopreparations that Alibekov realized that, in point of fact, it had been several days since the Director had communicated with him.

When his official visit to the French plant was over, Pasechnik had said good-bye to his traveling companion (another scientist from the Institute) and gone to the airport—or so he said—but he never took the return flight to Leningrad. From that moment on, no one knew his whereabouts. For the Ministry of Defense and the KGB, this was the worst possible disaster. Unlike Arkady, who after all had always been stationed in the Sverdlovsk plant, Pasechnik was one of the few scientist who were completely informed about the gigantic structure of

Biopreparat and possessed sufficient information to cause an international scandal.

If his defection was authentic, as Arkady hoped it was, the world would soon know that the USSR had broken every single agreement it had signed about biological weapons and that for the past twenty years it had accelerated its research into anthrax, the plague, and other compounds. The only condition Gorbachev made before setting me free was that I should never speak in public about my work in Biopreparat, Arkady reminded Irina. And I've kept my part of the deal. I'm no traitor, and I have a moral responsibility to my country. But if Vladímir talks, if he makes what he knows public, then I too can tell my story. I assure you that if such a thing comes about, Gorbachev won't get a good night's sleep for weeks.

The recent events in Eastern Europe kept Arkady in a state of permanent watchfulness. He spent hours attending to spontaneous petitions, keeping an eye on every symptom of decadence, like a doctor waiting for a patient's death-rattle. For example, more than three months earlier, the miners in the Kuzbass region had initiated a strike that was not very different from the protests of the Polish shipyards. The miners, not at all interested in political issues, were fed up with their lack of food and medical treatment, their abandonment and misery. Arkady had spoken with one of their leaders, a man with arms like tree trunks and the face of a child, and immediately agreed to act as a spokesman for their cause.

At the end of June, Arkady joined the Inter-Regional Deputies Group, the first opposition organized in the Soviet Union, standing alongside Yeltsin and Sakharov. Although the group only numbered 388—out of the two thousand members of the Congress of Deputies of the People—its members were aware of its symbolic character and were already shuffling the proposals they were going to make during the sessions in December. Arkady met with them almost daily: His idea was to present a package of amendments to the constitution that would allow the immediate introduction of the market economy, would define the autonomy of the republics, and establish a multiparty system.

In principle, the Inter-Regional Group was merely advocating the acceleration of perestroika and glasnost, but Gorbachev recognized its creation as a challenge. From the moment of its first public appearance on June 29th in the House of Film—the Party refused to let them meet in the Kremlin—he sabotaged every one of their proposals. Within the Group, several leaders, aside from the venerable Sakharov, stood out: the moderate Gavriil Popov, the radical Yuri Afanasiev, and Yeltsin himself. Arkady was loyal to Yeltsin, though he felt a great affinity for the ideas of Afanasiev, a historian shaped by the French *Annales* school and former Director of the Institute of Historical Archives. Afanasiev behaved with the intolerance of a convert: He never tired of attacking the Party and Gorbachev and defended the need to rewrite History, freeing it from the lies of Stalin and Brezhnev. Arkady was close to them but without abandoning his close relationship to Yeltsin of strong arms, certain that sooner or later he would become the leader Russia needed.

9
East Berlin, November 9th, 1989

They strolled through Berlin like extraterrestrials. Eva told Klara when it all ended. They walked through streets that were once Klara's, that belonged to both of them but that they haven't set foot on in twenty-eight years: men, women, children, more astonished than moved, walking through the city as if they were making a trip to a planet they dreamed of but never saw. Thanks to an act of weakness or benevolence or perhaps simply an error in calculation, a power vacuum or a lack of coordination, the new authorities in East Germany had announced that starting from that day—yes, from today, confirmed Günter Schabowski, First Secretary of the Democratic Socialist Party, to a woman reporter—any citizen had the freedom, yes, the complete freedom, to travel anywhere, even to the Federal Republic, yes comrade, even to East Berlin, as long as they present a valid passport.

Why did Schabowski say what he said? Why with those concise words—an insipid administrative precision—did he topple more than forty years of socialism? The misunderstanding was sufficient for scores of East German citizens to congregate around the sentry boxes along the Wall and demand that the disconcerted guards let them pass. No one had warned these thugs, but the crowd was so euphoric that they opened the gates as if they were used to a constant stream of traffic, as if the Wall were a chalk line, as if the stones and barbed wire didn't exist, as if no one had died there, as if the fugitives the guards had shot to pieces had been mirages.

The shy figures crossed the control points without realizing that, in doing so, they had lost their character as citizens of the German

Democratic Republic; they were entering an unknown territory (capitalism) in the forgotten half of their country, a part that had been amputated decades ago. On the other side, the municipal authorities gave a few Western marks to each *visitor*, a small gift so they didn't settle for mere looking, so they didn't suffer the frustration of not buying, so that at least they could acquire a Western sausage or a Western beer, or Western tooth paste, or a Western chocolate bar, or a Western radio. Every time one of those *ossies*—that's what they soon would be called—passed the control points and entered the free zone, they were rewarded with applause (before it was bullets) and exalted as supermen.

A few steps away from the Brandenburg Gate, not far from the former Reichstag, Eva watched as the human tide fanned out on the modern avenues, entered the luxury neighborhoods, went into the Tiergarten, or looked into the Ku'damm boutiques. And Eva didn't stop crying, as if she too had been a prisoner, as if she too were part of this history, as if she too had a right to this party. She felt overwhelmed, happy, nostalgic—that's how she told it to Klara, moved—and imagined she would always remember that moment, that she would never forget the eyes of that child or the wrinkled face of that man, or the shouts of joy of those young people who felt free for the first time. It's madness, she thought, and then she corrected herself: No, the real madness was dividing the city, separating families with a barrier, inventing so many enemies.

Two weeks hadn't yet passed since Honecker had been removed from his position, since Egon Krenz had taken charge of the country, since the Leipzig protests had opened the way to similar demonstrations in Dresden and Berlin, but none of that mattered now: Without the bloodshed of Beijing, without using weapons or confronting the police, Germany was reunited. No authority in Paris, Washington, or London dared speak the word reunification (it still made people uncomfortable), but reunification was a fact; in the streets of Berlin, the island surrounded by cannibals, the miracle had been achieved, and now it would be impossible to stop the rejoining. We are one people: The slogan achieved its full meaning, and now leaders from both sides would have to discover the most rapid and effective means to reconcile the enemies and bury suspicion.

Surrounded by the noise and confusion, the toasts and the surprise, Eva walked the length of the wall: It must have been 11:00 P.M., and Berlin was a fairground. While most of the East Berliners were getting ready to go home—only a few would stay—hundreds of happy, drunk young people took control of the Wall. They were dancing and singing in front of it, profaning that prohibited zone to the shock of the border guards, who were unable to fire on them and unable to join in the celebration. Near Checkpoint Charlie, several men were smashing the cement with hammers: The fall of the Wall would not only be symbolic but real and irreversible. The crowd clambered on the rocks, some stuffed chunks of cement into their pockets, and others showed pieces to the photographers and journalists who were covering the spectacle: Concrete was becoming a relic. Eva picked up a piece and put it in her pocket: the amulet she would, alas, wear until the night she died. Then, caught up in the camaraderie, she started dancing with them, allowing herself to be hugged and kissed, dragged along by a passion she hadn't felt for months—since she began using Prozac. Compared with the mortuary everydayness of the Zuse Institute, that was life.

Like many of her companions in the bacchanal, Eva woke up on a sidewalk, hungover, surrounded by bodies that, like her own, had given themselves over to the orgy. Her head ached, and an intense throbbing kept her from concentrating. She looked around and confirmed that the infamous barrier was still standing. For an instant she thought everything had been merely an alcohol-induced hallucination, but when the first rays of sunlight passed through the holes in the Wall, she understood that the change would never be reversed. The "iron curtain" that had fallen across the continent in 1946, as Churchill declared, was history.

10
Moscow, Union of Soviet Socialist Republics, November 9th, 1989

Dear Anniushka, Oksana wrote on the first page of her blue notebook, I apologize for not having written before, even though for years your poems have been saving me. When I'm torn apart, I sink into them as if they were a swamp—I recite "Requiem" whenever I see the precipice—but I was never able to gather enough strength to thank you for the illumination you've granted me. I know a void separates us—your death, my agony—but that doesn't stop me from feeling you at my side every afternoon, guiding my hand and correcting the verses that slip out of my pen. I dream of you covered by the cold light of St. Petersburg—in your presence I wouldn't dare mutter the epithet revenge has imposed on it—sitting in a rocking chair, not far from the window, in your Fontanka prison, the old Shermetiev Palace, alone and thoughtful, imagining the verses you would never dare write, and I fly to your lap, throw myself at your feet, barely touching the lace on your dress, like a house pet, your guardian, your disciple.

Why did it take me so long to understand it? We share the same delirium: voices shouting in the roar of the storm, undesired messengers who, defying persecution or oblivion, insist on shaking up the living and saying what no one says. Now that I review your life—your dreamed youth, your loneliness, the murder of Gumiliov, the persecution of your son, your spiritual exile, your moment as the emblem of your besieged city, the years of hunger and poverty, the tyrant's jealousy and hatred, your old age and your death—I find myself attracted to you like the moth fluttering around the candle.

Anniushka, let me imitate your challenge. I need you to encourage me to rebel against so much hostility. Trust me, tell me your secrets and show me the paths I'm to take, what my steps are to be, how to transform myself into a writer. No, into a prophet. Tell me how you did it.

I read an anecdote about you when you were just a little older than I am now, sixteen or seventeen. Your mother brought you to Bolshoi Fontan, the house where you were born on the outskirts of Odessa, and as soon as you saw that idyllic and almost forgotten place, you said: Some day there will be a plaque here with my name on it. That's what you said, without modesty or shame. Your mother scolded your pride, how badly I've brought you up, she said, not understanding that your statement was not a sign of pride or vanity but the ascetic acceptance of your destiny.

Poetry is not a blessing; it's a punishment that cannot be refused. I too have received it, dear Anniushka, I too am damned, I too feel the same fury inside me, the same despondency that I've seen in your life and words: That's why I'm writing to you, why I'm disturbing your sleep, that's why I'm invoking you from the realm of the living. Save me from this loneliness and this discomfort, from this pain that invades my pores and transmutes my blood, the blood I give up every day, help me create a voice that will shake up my contemporaries, that will save me from death, from that death I feel so close, so pleasant. I too want there to be a plaque on my filthy Sverdlovsk house, a plaque that will sing of my birth. I renounce the world and its pleasures and aspire to become a prophetess like you. Anniushka, don't abandon me at night, in the cold, I promise to be faithful to you, always.

When she finished, she signed: Oksana Granin. Dissatisfied, she blotted out her father's name and substituted for it a pen name she would carry attached to her skin from that afternoon on: Oksana Gorenko.

11
Moscow, Union of Soviet Socialist Republics, December 14th, 1989

Arkady and Irina had seen Andrei Sakharov, maker of light, that morning: energetic and vital as usual, but more and more annoyed with Gorbachev and his double face. Although his sympathy for the Secretary-General wasn't completely broken—he'd accepted the invitation to participate in the committee charged with sketching out a constitution, even if there was no possibility of having their arguments carry the day in the presence of the Communist majority—he was becoming more and more irritated with his soliloquies, his inability to hear opinions that differed from his own, the polite pride with which he rejected all criticism. The last time he called him on the telephone he had to scold him, as if he were a child: No more excuses, Mikhail Sergeyevich, you're turning into your own worst enemy. Gorbachev rejected his complaints, as if the problem the scientist was submitting for his consideration—the survival of another persecuted ethnic group—were irrelevant compared to the weight he was carrying on his shoulders. Mikhail Sergeyevich is suffering from an excess of vanity, he reported to his comrades in the Interregional Group.

The second period of sessions of the Congress of Deputies of the People was to begin the next day, and Andrei Dmitrievich went home early to prepare his speech. He picked at his food and locked himself away in his study. Before dedicating himself to politics, he wanted to put the finishing touches on his memoirs. During his exile in Gorki, he'd begun to put his memories in order, but in Moscow he barely had time or energy to finish the job. He preferred to concentrate on the present or the future, or to read a new theory of physics, rather than review his lost years: There were too many battles to fight—the USSR was still a barbarous nation—for him to let himself be carried away by nostalgia. The only reason to finish off that monstrous tome was to please Liusia.

Andrei Dmitrievich sat down at his old desk and stared at the thick manuscript that summarized his existence: Would he really be there, in those pages? He'd never know: He was incapable of looking at himself objectively, incapable of judging whether he was just or unjust with his contemporaries. He revealed infamies and betrayals, but he was not rancorous toward any of his enemies, bore no ill-will toward those who'd persecuted or accused him. His colleagues at the Academy of Sciences, so cowardly and short-sighted when he needed them, seemed to him now nothing more than inoffensive old men, as beaten down by time as he himself. No: Those memoirs would not be a settling of accounts but the story of his own journey, his stubborn search for truth and balance.

Andrei Sakharov, maker of light, leafed through its pages: He only recognized a few names, as if his road were a straight line that connected existences and places. He considered this book to be his grave, a funerary monument he carved himself. He almost regretted having begun it. No, he wasn't interested in death. He'd always fought against it, against its irrationality and stupidity, against those who thought they had the right to inflict it on others. As the father of the hydrogen bomb, he knew what he was talking about: His life had been a kind of repentance, a prayer for forgiveness from the father of extinction. Exhausted, Andrei Dmitrievich raised a hand to his forehead: too many emotions, too many plans. I need to rest a bit, but before that he had to put the finishing touch on his memoir.

He picked up his pen and, his wrist trembling, wrote:

> *The most important thing is that my dear and loved Liusia and I be united: I dedicate this book to her. Life goes on. We are together.*

His lifetime on earth, with all its faults and errors, had one single justification: his love for Liusia. She was the theory of everything.

Andrei Dmitrievich took off his glasses and put them down on the desk. His eyes were burning because of his tears. He went into the next room, where his wife had been working for hours. He walked up behind her, placed his hands on her shoulders and whispered into her ear: I need a nap, but get me up in a couple of hours, I still have a lot to do. She rested her hand on the back of his. The minutes accumulated, infinitely. Life goes on, he whispered in her ear, and we are together. Then he went into his bedroom and stretched out. He closed his eyes. In less than a minute, he'd fallen asleep. Two hours later, Liusia came to awaken him. Andrei Dmítrievich Sakharov, maker of light, did not wake up. He died in his sleep.

1990

1

Tucson, Arizona, United States of America,
January 13th, 1990

She didn't feel sick, she felt uncomfortable: the sheets soaked with sweat, the smelly pillow under her tangled hair, and, at least in her imagination, her stomach still covered with blood and bits of tissue. Allison tried to get up, but vertigo nailed her down to her bed. She wanted to take a bath, stay under the water for hours, soap herself up slowly, feel the suds on her skin, imagine herself clean and untouched.

She lifted her robe and stared at the bandages. If she concentrated, she was even able to feel a tingling in her groin. She was still swollen: Before the operation, she'd supposed that at least the fatness would disappear, but the excess fat was still staring at her accusingly. She would never be the same. When the effects of the anesthesia began to wear off, she was sorry she resembled her sister so much: She was alarmed by how deformed her navel was, by the size of her breasts as they filled with milk, by the stretch marks on her pubis and her thighs, by the enormous scar on her belly. Allison hated herself; she was just another bourgeois like Jennifer, a little lady intent on rebelling, the typical black sheep of an aristocratic family. The Moore genes were betraying her: At the precise moment when her life was acquiring value, she had to admit she was a fraud.

Why make this decision? Why this insanity? After the abortion that had cost her a huge fight with her sister, Allison had decided never to have children, and now, with everything against the idea—the pregnancy had been the result of a defect, and the father was a son of a bitch who'd betrayed her—she'd said yes, that she would have the child, that the difficulties didn't matter to her and that she was not going to change her mind. A demented act. Jennifer was right: It was the stupidest thing that had ever happened in a life filled with stupidities. Why, damn it, why? If she now wanted to be a mother—and she had very right to want it—why didn't she wait until she got out of jail and search for a man who loved her or who at least wasn't a cop? At least that way she wouldn't have to tell her child the bizarre story of how he was conceived. Perhaps it might have been more prudent (even her lawyer agreed with her), but Allison was convinced that this child was the natural result of her mistakes. She simply wanted to have it. It just did not matter to her that the father was an FBI agent: The boy, because she always knew it would be male, was going to be hers. He agreed, not having the slightest interest in being a father.

Allison closed her eyes, but the confusion and terror drove her sleep away. Despite judicial and family pressures, and the growing hostility she felt toward the baby in her uterus—she sometimes dreamed it dead or mutilated—the opportunity to opt out never presented itself. So, in a process that was much easier to plan than to live, Allison accepted being a mother. The mere word gave her chills: Her panic grew at the same pace as her stomach. She had always been senseless, adventurous, impulsive. How was she going to bring it up? And if she wasn't even able to take care of herself, how was she going to protect Jacob?

She chose the name Jacob from the moment she realized she was pregnant. She knew no Jacobs and knew nothing about the biblical prophet. The choice was either phonetic or the result of an association in her subconsciousness. She called him Jacob from the first day, in secret, and whenever she felt more desperate or more dead, she would say his name aloud, as a blessing or to exorcise her fears. Jacob, she would say, your mother is crazy. Or: Jacob, you're going to be much stronger than I am. Or: Jacob, I hope some day you'll forgive me.

In practical terms, the only advantage she gained from her pregnancy was a reduction of her sentence, after Jennifer put a sizable amount of money up as bail. She was released just in time to give birth. Rejecting her sister's advice, she refused to travel to an opulent clinic in Philadelphia or New York. Jacob was conceived in the desert and would be born in the desert. The ill-tempered gynecologist in the Community Hospital said it was a high-risk pregnancy—she was about to turn forty-two—and delivered the child by caesarean section.

Allison drank some water and pressed the button next to the bed. A nurse appeared: How do you feel, Mrs. Moore? Like the rabbits we used to dissect in biology class, she answered. And my son? He's just fine, very cute, want to see him? Before Allison could answer, the young woman went to get the child and returned carrying a bundle: So cute, she repeated, and Allison seemed to detect a perverse, threatening tone in her voice. When she saw her son's tiny body, she almost fainted. Look at him, look at him, the nurse insisted, uncovering the tiny, monstrous face. She felt her stomach turn. Take him away, nurse, she confusedly exclaimed. Sometimes rejection is normal, the nurse calmed her, but you'll get used to him, Mrs. Moore, just look how he smiles . . . Take him away!, shouted Allison. I don't want to see him! Please. The nurse covered Jacob's little head and quickly left the room. Allison didn't even have the strength to cry.

2

Baku, Azerbaijan, Union of Soviet Socialist Republics, January 25th, 1990

A black month. The ominous signs had been appearing for weeks, but not even the most pessimistic—myself included—could imagine the magnitude of the barbarism. We hadn't even finished celebrating the fall of the Berlin Wall when the most reactionary sectors of the nations mobilized—nothing like that would take place within our borders. The Party hawks still had a lot to say, their networks extended throughout the Kremlin, and their capacity for action dimmed the faith of the reformers. With his back closer and closer to the wall—or I should say, isolating himself among his adversaries—Gorbachev, shepherd of men, yielded to temptation and became a tyrant, just like his predecessors. Unlike other cases—Georgia or Lithuania for example—Mikhail Sergeyevich couldn't even justify himself by alleging that the security forces acted on their own: He gave the order to shoot, he signed the decree, he was responsible for the deaths.

Like the other citizens of Moscow, city of wide avenues, I didn't find out about the tragedy until the next day. There was no state of emergency and no public announcement: Units from the Soviet Army, the Ministry of the Interior, and the special forces took control of Baku and numerous other cities in Azerbaijan at dawn on January 19th. Having taken position during the darkness, as they would have during the worst periods of Stalinism, the troops showed no mercy. Azerbaijan experienced its own Afghanistan, its own Tiananmen, without anyone noticing: after all, Baku is not Beijing, not even Riga or Vilnius. It's just a forgotten industrial town on the shores of the Caspian Sea, a well that had been poisoned, according to the official media, by Islamic hatred. One hundred people lost their lives in just a few hours, a hundred individuals who, as was proven later, committed no other sin than opposing the invasion of their country. The one hundred were executed without mercy, while another hundred were arrested or wounded and had their houses burned down.

Only the next day did the Supreme Soviet of the USSR declare a state of emergency, using the violence of the Caucasus as a pretext. The motives were different: to crush Azerbaijani nationalism and eradicate the independence movements once and for all. Although Zarifa hadn't communicated with me for months, she telephoned me at dawn on Saturday the 20th. She was crying, shouting, cursing me, and also begging my help: This is like nothing you've ever seen before, Yuri Mikhailovich, there is blood everywhere, the Army has taken all suspects away, even members of the Azerbaijan Supreme Soviet and known Party members. You have to do something, Yuri Mikhailovich, in the name of God, help us. My brother Ramiz is one of the disappeared.

I told her I'd try to get to Baku that very night, even though I supposed that access would be blocked by the Army. The best thing would be to go by train, which would take at least forty-eight hours, with stops in every town along the way, but it was a much safer option than planes or cars. When I reached the Baku station on January 22nd, I found a detachment of tall, white, and blond Russian soldiers guarding the tracks and arresting anyone who looked as if he were from the Caucuses. Thanks to my

Russian identity, I managed to pass by without being noticed, and, after an extremely long trek, I was able to meet with Zarifa and her family.

I'd just visited Baku a few months before, but the entire city now looked different: gray, tense, desolate. Its inhabitants could not understand why the Russians, their Soviet brothers, had ordered the attack, why they'd murdered and arrested hundreds of civilians. By that time, Zarifa had recovered: She wasn't crying and instead was wandering the entire city with her other two brothers, trying to locate Ramiz. You aren't an evil man, said Farman, the eldest, maybe they'll listen to you.

We went from one police station to another and from one hospital to another: There were scores of wounded, and the doctors could barely keep up. No one could give us any information about the fate of the arrested. Soviet tanks were stationed in various parts of the city, as if perestroika and glasnost had been a dream, as if we'd suddenly returned to the Berlin of 1953, the Budapest of 1956, or the Prague of 1968. The only difference was that then the Soviet Union was an efficient war machine, while now, despite the threats and infamies the Army perpetrated, it was a dying animal.

Finally we went to the morgue. The building was guarded by security forces, and only those looking for relatives had the right to enter—after being searched and roughed up. Thanks to my journalist credentials, they allowed Farman, as the family's first-born, to look for his brother. While we waited for him, I again felt part of that family which had once been my own. I couldn't go back, couldn't recover it—and didn't want to—but in that moment I was honored to be one of them. Farman came out after an hour. He didn't have to say a word. Ramiz's body was there along with the others. Adding insult to injury, he'd been forced to fill in dozens of forms: Being the brother of a rebel made the entire family suspects. Zarifa didn't cry until we got back to the house, when she burst into a deep, terrifying lament.

The next morning, I accompanied the whole family—grandparents, uncles, cousins, and nephews—to a demonstration in Shahidlar Hiyabani, the Cemetery of the Martyrs. Thousands of people were leaving red carnations on the graves as symbols of grief and resistance. I'd never seen such a melancholy spectacle, and I felt ashamed to be Russian. While I'd always had my differences with the Azerbaijani nationalists (that was, at least in theory, the reason why I separated from Zarifa), I found now that the war was unifying the victims, making them identical in their depression.

Back in Moscow, city of wide avenues, I found out that Geidar Aliyev, the corrupt bureaucrat who'd controlled the destiny of Azerbaijan in the era of Brezhnev, the cunning mummy—on every official visit he presented him with gold and jewels and even built him a palace for his own personal use—who'd fallen into disgrace with perestroika, had declared that Gorbachev, shepherd of men, was responsible for the massacre. Sensing that his resurrection was at hand, he resigned from the Communist Party and proclaimed himself the defender of Azerbaijani sovereignty. The whole thing was disgusting: Gorbachev had approved the extermination, and now a brutal, authoritarian lordling like Aliyev took the stage as a hero.

I sent my report to *Ogoniok* that afternoon, without much hope it would ever come out. Vitali Korotich promised to publish it, but several weeks went by without any news. Finally, I had no choice but to contact a German journalist—foreigners weren't allowed to travel to Baku—who promised to do what he could to have it appear in his country. A week later, it appeared, translated into German, in *Der Spiegel.* Overnight I'd become a recognized journalist. And a dangerous dissident. Both things made me happy: My pathway to celebrity was now marked out, and I would never be the same again.

3
Moscow, Union of Soviet Socialist Republics, January 31st, 1990

The Granin family entered Pushkin Square—what irony—where thousands of Muscovites were gathering to witness the great event, the irreversible proof of the market economy's triumph. Arkady Ivanovich was there for contradictory reasons: His new and absolute liberalism and his desire to satisfy, for once, the whims of his daughter Oksana. Irina Nikolayevna, on the other hand, didn't feel the slightest enthusiasm for the inauguration of the building, but she did experience a kind of shame. She couldn't stand the kitschy interior, felt a natural aversion toward that profusion of reds and yellows, and even hatred for that grim character, the sinister clown who was playing the part of ambassador of Western wealth in Moscow, city of wide avenues.

Each one could judge the spectacle as tragic, glorious, or even pathetic according to their ideological orientation: For the first time in sixty years, about thirty thousand Muscovites were gathering spontaneously, willing to put up with hours of waiting in the cold, as they did during the worst moments of Stalinism, but not because of hunger or even to protest authoritarianism, not to oppose the rage of Gorbachev, shepherd of men, or to glorify Yeltsin of strong arms, not to face up to the police or to demand a rapid democratic opening, and not even to express their solidarity or disagreement with the Lithuanian Parliament, which had just proclaimed its independence, but to receive charity from the United States, to taste a piece of dry meat, a slice of rancid cheese, and a pickle. Those thirty thousand Muscovites were standing there, freezing in an endless line, only to enjoy—or rather, *to buy*—a McDonald's hamburger.

Russia was always a stoic (or servile) nation, a country of patient men and impassive women, but this was too much: thirty thousand people waiting their turn to try that crap. Unlike the Hungarians, the East Germans, the Czechs, and even the Romanians, we still hadn't witnessed the collapse of Communism. Gorbachev had not announced the end of the Soviet ideal, the apparatchiks were still at their posts, and the Party was fighting to keep its privileges, so those bittersweet mouthfuls represented the only proof that things had changed, that there would be no going back, that the controlled economy and the Gulag were behind us.

Each hamburger represented a triumph of liberty, Arkady proclaimed, as confused as he was excited by the democratic serenity of his people (most had been there for two hours, and the line was growing). And, intent on giving his family and his compatriots a lesson—by granting metaphysical status to ground meat and ketchup—he added: This is an example of civic courage; each time someone buys French fries, he's saying to the Government: *I'm free, I have the right to buy whatever I want.* We are witnessing the end of the planned economy and therefore of the Soviet Union itself!

Oksana did not share his point of view. If she had insisted on coming to the opening of the first McDonald's in Moscow, it was not out of civic spirit, not to defend freedom, and much less to show her faith in the market economy. None of that mattered to her. And of course she did not believe hamburgers were appetizing. No, Oksana wanted to be there to be with other young people—young people who, like her, were bored with politics—who were taking refuge in that symbol of Western banality. Oksana was willing to wait for hours to eat a McDonald's hamburger in the same way she could spend all her savings on a pirated tape of AC/DC or Bob Dylan: She was trying to identify herself with the other young people on the planet, to share a lifestyle that not only opposed the Soviet Union but her elders as well.

Oksana didn't say a word about her father's rhetoric. Irina, on the other hand, couldn't stand his grandiloquence. Does this moment really seem memorable to you, Arkady Ivanovich? Is this what we fought for? Is this what you spent five years in jail for? So the Americans could flood us with their garbage, turn us into prisoners of publicity and multinational corporations? To change our model we need to change our way of thinking, Arkady explained to his wife in a somber tone. People have to learn to get along with the market, and they will, but we have to give them time. Soon there will be many establishments like this one, and then everyone will be able to choose what he likes best—hamburgers, hot dogs, borscht, or blinis. The important thing, Irina Nikolayevna, is that each individual have the right to choose his own preferences . . .

She shook her head. You don't agree?, Arkady spurred her on. No, I don't. This is unworthy of the people. We have to teach them to fight for freedom, not to give in to fashion. I don't understand you. You talk like *them*: They think we aren't ready for democracy, not ready for the market, not ready for freedom. But these people are real. Today they're buying hamburgers, and tomorrow they'll be out defending democracy.

I want to go! shouted Oksana. What? Let's go home, I don't want to be here any more. Please. But you insisted on coming, Arkady scolded her. Well I don't want to be here anymore! He lost his temper. I don't intend to put up with your whims. We're here, and we're not leaving. Irina, for her part, was uncomfortable and surly: Let's leave it for another day, she added. Arkady didn't bother to look at her and stubbornly stayed in line. Finally, he paid for his damn hamburger and handed it to Oksana with a violent gesture. Unhurriedly, she tore off the paper wrapper, as if she were pulling the petals off a flower, brought it to her nose, made a grimace of disgust, and disdainfully threw it on the ground. Irina could barely hide her smile.

4

Washington, D.C., United States of America, March 3rd, 1990

For more than three months, she'd had nothing to do with him. Jennifer had refused to telephone him, had rejected invitations from mutual friends: She wanted nothing to do with Jack, did all she could not to hear his name. To forget him, she took refuge where she always took refuge, in her work. She stopped attending social events, despite the fact that she received invitations every week, invitations for which it was becoming increasingly difficult to invent pretexts to turn down. She only went to shops and malls, which meant that during those months she accumulated all sorts of useless objects—jewelry, dresses, bags, shoes, and myriad decorations for her apartment in Washington, axis of the universe. She did not, however, go back to the movies alone. She made an effort to read the classic texts of economics and tried to mitigate her tedium at the IMF, her home.

Her outbursts did not diminish, but she at least tried to appear more cordial with her colleagues and subordinates, taking an interest in their lives and joining them at lunch and dinner. Emily was the only person who still felt sorry for her. They went shopping together and even to the opera a couple of times, though even that did not reduce Jennifer's disdain for her during working hours. With the good grace of an extremely serene mother, Emily accepted the scoldings as if they were a daughter's tantrums, and even though she suffered and secretly wept, she preferred her boss's tortuous company to her usual lonely nights.

Jennifer understood that things couldn't go on that way: She was being eaten up by curiosity. What was going on with Jack, did he miss her, had he made up with Christina, was he still going out with Erin in secret, was he seeing the two of them? Or had he found another slut? At first she could control her anxieties, but soon Jack's fate became her obsession and then her only objective. She had to find out what kind of life he could have without her. Suddenly she began attending every single party, cocktail party, or reception to which she was invited, and while she tried to appear haughty and distant, she cross-examined the people she knew to gather news about her husband. The rumors were contradictory: Jacqueline told her Jack had broken things off with Christina and was now going out with a secretary from DNAW; Bob Winger, who was on that company's board of directors, denied that story and told her Jack was still alone. Debra Wright confirmed Jacqueline's story, though she made it clear it wasn't a serious affair; and Dick Reynolds confessed that he thought Jack was very depressed.

If Jennifer couldn't tolerate financial uncertainty, she tolerated emotional uncertainty even less. She couldn't sleep thinking about exactly what she'd say when she finally called him—because she had decided to call him—how she'd manage to seem impassive and at the same time interested, serene and happy, a bit caustic. She even wrote out her speech and circulated it among her office mates, so each one of her collaborators could give an opinion. With the corrections inserted, Jennifer stuck to her script with the skill of a great actress. She wanted to shout and howl, but she sounded confident and tranquil. Wells was surprised both by the call and his wife's tone. Everything's going well, he said, DNAW's numbers are better than ever, and you? Jennifer evaded the question and went back on the attack. Yes, of course I'd like to see you, Jen, perfect, Dorian's at 8:00.

She'd done it very well. And Jack? His nervousness was so obvious that it covered his guilt, lies, fear, or repentance. She'd have to wait until she saw him in person to make a judgment. Jennifer arrived first at the restaurant, but chose to take a walk so she wouldn't seem anxious. When she got back, Jack was waiting with a whiskey. Wells stood politely, but did not kiss her. After exchanging banalities about the weather, he took it upon himself to talk about politics. How do things look down at the IMF? Until then he'd never been interested in macroeconomics or international politics, or only to the degree either might influence his business. This time, however, he seemed up-to-date about the world situation, about the fall of the Wall and the possible consequences that instability in Eastern Europe might have on the market.

I think the next step is inevitable, Jennifer explained reluctantly: Either the Soviet Union reforms quickly or its internal struggles will destroy it. Yes, yes, I understand that, he interrupted her, but what interests me is knowing what will happen with our economy and the economies of those countries . . . In one way or another, the free market has triumphed, it's something that can't be stopped. We've won the Cold War, Jack, without having to fire a single shot, and now the Russians are at our mercy. I'm almost sorry for Gorbachev. He won't wait a year before he asks to have the Soviet Union admitted to the International Monetary Fund. The USSR is bankrupt. Today it's a Third World country with atomic weapons, only that . . .

Wells gulped down his drink and asked for another. Let's see, think about this, he said: Two hundred million people, two hundred million consumers suddenly join the world market. Don't you think all those countries are splendid places for investment? Jennifer thought it over for a few seconds: Yes, Jack, marvelous places, as long as you're wiling to pay the price: corruption and chaos. The Soviet Union is on the brink of collapse, a tiny push, just a couple of centimeters, and it would topple over. Of course it's an ill wind that brings no good.

And with that remark she wanted the political phase of their talk to end. Now she wanted to talk about them. But Wells wouldn't give in. He ordered another round and started yakking about his most recent investments, the renewed surge in biotechnology, his future projects, his contracts, and New York nightlife. After an hour, Jennifer was almost as drunk as he was, the light around her had gone murky, and she felt an urgent need to kiss him or rather that he kiss her. Tell me, Jack, she whispered in his ear, do you want me to come back to you? Of course!, he shouted, your place is at my side. Jennifer kissed him desperately. Then they took a taxi: Take me to a motel, I want you to make love to me the way you do with your tarts. Wells laughed at his wife's hyperbolic request, but he gave the driver the address of a place in Maryland. Do you bring them here? Wells laughed again. It's a serious question. Enough, Jen, let's go inside. Are you crazy? How can you treat me this way? You asked me . . . Well now I don't want to, let me go! How could I be so stupid, leave me in peace . . . Jennifer went back to the taxi and ordered the driver to leave. Seeing her go, Wells stamped his foot so hard he hurt himself.

5
East Berlin, German Democratic Republic, April 24th, 1990

We are the people, we are *one* people. Over the course of those months, after that silent revolution they preferred to call "die Wande" (the rotation), Eva could appreciate the subtle variation the slogan had suffered in the mouths of East Berliners. As she told Klara, Eva was unable to define her feelings, to discern whether she was overcome by emotion, nostalgia, or sadness as she contemplated the contrast between the two sides of the Wall.

That day she'd walked with Edwin Ohlander, a mathematician from the Zuse Institute who was born and grew up in that part of the city and had taken refuge in the West just before the 1961 crisis. They spent more than three hours walking aimlessly, stopping so he could recount different episodes in the history of the city. It was a foggy, peaceful afternoon that suggested nothing about the disturbances of the last few days. The buildings that had survived the war, and the subsequent Communist negligence, hadn't changed overnight.

Less than a month had gone by since the first free elections in Democratic Germany had granted victory to Lothar de Maizières, the candidate of the new Christian Democratic Party—a copy of Helmut Kohl's CDP—and despite the Soviets' initial resistance, reunification had become a goal no one was likely to renounce. However, as Eva pointed out to Klara that night, not all Germans seemed enthusiastic about the idea. On both sides, the maneuver provoked reactions of rage or skepticism. The progressive intellectuals, the most severe critics, thought East Germany had sold out, that it hadn't figured out how to maintain its integrity and its principles, that it had let itself be corrupted by money and Kohl's promises. But, mother, what I find most interesting is that many intellectuals from the East have the same opinion.

As she'd read in the papers—Edwin confirmed the truth of the articles—the Soviet Union had only blessed reunification after Kohl agreed to send Gorbachev fifty-two thousand tons of beef, fifty thousand tons of pork; twenty thousand tons of butter; ten thousand tons of powdered milk; and five thousand tons of cheese which added up to the ridiculous sum of 220 million marks. There was no lack, as Eva reported to Klara, of critical voices, from both sectors of the city, who asserted that German reunification was the result of that shameful food blackmail. Günter Grass himself wrote in the *New York Times* that because of all its sins, Germany did not deserve to become a unified nation.

Nothing disturbed Eva during her walk with Ohlander more than the episode she witnessed near the wall. In East Germany, bananas had been luxury items, a privilege of the higher-ups in the Party—common citizens had to content themselves with seeing them on television. The spell that this exotic fruit aroused was so strong that, as Eva told her mother, there was even a joke about it. Two children meet in one of the holes in the Wall; the one on the western side says to the other: On your side there are no bananas. The one on the eastern side says: But we have socialism; and the one on the west retorts: Well, we could also have socialism. The other concludes: Only if you give up bananas. I know the exchange sounds pathetic, mother, but it doesn't compare with what I saw that afternoon: A handful of kids from the West throwing banana peels at people from the East who dared to cross the Wall.

This is not going to be as easy as people think, Ohlander explained to Eva: We can erase the physical border in a few months, but fifty years of psychological, social, and economic barriers will require years of demolition. Eva didn't agree, didn't want to agree: We have to be optimistic and think that anything is possible, that reunification is also a reconciliation, a way to erase the Cold War and rewrite European history. Don't misunderstand me, Ohlander said, I'm in favor of reunification, this is my country too, I'm only saying that it will represent the end of the German miracle. Many years, a lot of effort, and all our reserves will be necessary for the citizens of the East to acquire our standard of living. Kohl doesn't stop making promises, he announces that everything will be easy and swift, but it isn't true, and we all know it isn't true. And that will provoke disillusionment and bitterness.

Maybe not, Edwin. Look around you: Who would have imagined that all this was possible? The biggest optimists thought reunification would only take place after fifty years. I know, Ohlander admitted, but all this haste is going to create myriad conflicts. Look what Kohl has done with the mark: Monetary reunification sounds marvelous, but who would make the two currencies equal in value? It's silly. People are happy, they're thinking about everything they can buy with their savings, but it will be the end of businesses in the East. Now we're giving them alms, but in short order we'll all be ruined.

I don't understand, mother, Eva summarized things that night. Sometimes I feel I'm the only person excited about the fall of the Wall, reunification, the change in Europe over the past few weeks. There's time for cold-eyed analysis, for frustration, and depression, but I want to maintain my illusions until the very end. Because I don't dare imagine the hangover that will come after this binge.

6

Washington, D.C., United States of America, May 31st, 1990

Just when they were about to enter the White House, Jennifer took Jack by the hand: It was such a subtle movement, so natural—you just don't forget all those years of being married overnight—that neither noticed its importance. After a year of separation, of angry meetings and interminable arguments over the telephone, they again appeared in public as man and wife. Jennifer had been invited to the state dinner President Bush was offering to Mikhail Gorbachev, shepherd of men, and since she couldn't stand the idea of going alone, she asked Wells to accompany her. He immediately accepted, happy to be rubbing elbows with the political élite of Washington.

They passed the corridor, lined with the haughty, smiling, and pensive portraits of the Presidents, and finally reached the banquet room, a cube decorated with lavish candelabras, and ran to find their table, too far, in their opinion, from the high table. The upholstery, the curtains, the chairs, and the eating utensils were golden, and Jennifer maliciously thought such splendor looked vulgar: If I lived here, she said to her husband, I'd have a less pompous color scheme, minimalist, perhaps a muted green or pale blue.

Little by little, the guests took their seats: It was already 6:00 P.M., and the hosts would soon be making their appearance. It had been a long day for Gorbachev: In the morning, he'd met with Bush in the White House, then the two of them went to the Soviet Embassy for an informal lunch. They dedicated the afternoon to signing a long list of agreements, the most important among them the "Treaty on the Destruction and Non-Production of Chemical and Biological Weapons." Suddenly there was a burst of applause, and the entire company rose. The ladies' baroque hairdos blocked Jennifer's view of the head table. Gorbachev and his wife Raisa were accompanied by George and Barbara Bush, and for once the explosion of jubilation did not seem phony: Those men had changed History. Wells, small-minded as usual, tried to identify the other important guests. On other occasions, he'd had the opportunity to say hello to Vice-President Dan Quayle and Secretary of Defense Dick Cheney, and he was only thinking about finding the right moment to talk to them again.

She's not as pretty as they say she is, whispered Jen in Wells's ear. Who? Raisa Gorbachyova, she muttered: Maybe she's distinguished, but nothing beyond that. And Barbara Bush, poor woman, I have no idea who designs the first lady's dresses. Enough of that!, said Wells, trying to silence his wife's voice. Once everyone was seated, Jack made a point of introducing himself to the others at his table, an Under-Secretary from Health and Human Services and his wife. Forgetting her diplomatic experience, Jennifer said aloud: Has Gorbachev's wife really spent millions on her clothes? You wouldn't know it from looking at her.

To the joy of the others, the Soviet President went to the dais and interrupted Jennifer's impertinent remarks. Gorbachev spoke for several minutes, and no one could deny that the Soviet leader emanated an uncommon aura of confidence and energy. He not only praised the new face of the Soviet Union but referred to German reunification as well, stressing that it was still necessary to think the matter through from several points of view (a way to hide the urgent Soviet need for loans, Jennifer commented). Then, eager to ingratiate himself with his hosts, the Soviet leader praised Andrei Sakharov, maker of light, with whom he'd had differences of opinion in the past. After exalting the new relationship between the two countries, Gorbachev proposed a toast: To idealism and idealists.

When Gorbachev went back to the high table, Bush took his place at the lectern, and his speech went on until 9:00 P.M. Words, words, and more words. That's why politicians irritated Jennifer so much: In the cold world of economics, you made decisions on the basis of numbers and statistics, but these people had to trick out theirs with ingenious turns of phrase. Even so, she was fascinated by Raisa's wrinkles, the shadows under Barbara Bush's eyes, Cheney's inexpressive face, Marilyn Quayle's bitterness, the infinite defects of the aristocracy that controlled the Earth. Needless to say, Wells, as soon as the Bushes and Gorbachevs got up, went running from table to table to shake as many hands as possible, those hands worth their weight in gold. He couldn't get to Quayle, but he did manage to exchange a few words with Cheney, who rewarded him with a slap on the back: a perfect night. Mr. and Mrs. Wells left the White House hand in hand. Their fascination with luxury, the things that power could imply with winks and nods, had managed to reconcile them.

7
Moscow, Union of Soviet Socialist Republics, August 3rd, 1990

Dear Anniushka, Oksana wrote once more in her blue notebook, I'm with you once again. I suppose you'd let one your stentorian guffaws out if you saw what's going on now, in this world that has outlived you. The jail is collapsing! I mean it, Anniushka, the bricks are turning into dust, musty cranes are picking apart its fragments and carrying them off to the cemeteries, the chains are slowly disappearing along with the yokes, the torture racks, and the statues of Lenin and Stalin. All you have to do in Moscow is walk out onto the street, though I suppose that the same thing must be happening in your beloved Leningrad, to see the downfall of the executioners: The grand ideas are splintering just like the old Communist signboards, the world that oppressed you so much, that murdered your loved ones, is falling apart. How you'd laugh, Anniushka, reading the newspapers and listening to the rumors! And despite the joy produced by this revenge, I think you'd also get depressed. Too late, nothing can make up for the damage that's already been done, nothing can revive the dead. Memory is made of a spongy material, we think we can go back, correct the errors, and give people back what's theirs, but it's a lie. This revolution is an involution, a leap back, a retrocession. And the only way to do you justice, to reconstruct the past, would be by running toward the future! But there is no future here, dear Anniushka. The reformists are bad copies of my father: Resentful bunnies, laboratory rats thirsty for blood or money, creeps ready to replace the Communists. Which is, in essence, what's happening: The weak, the disinherited, the victims, and the conquered knock down the statues of their oppressors, but only to put up plastic figures that represent them. No one has any need to enumerate the crimes of Stalin, your executioner, and some are even pointing out Lenin's vices; soon none of our great men will be safe. We've even lost our enemies, Anniushka, and we're even more alone and desperate. How did you manage to put up with so much stupidity, so much treachery? I read another anecdote that involves you, tell me if it's true. Just before the start of the Great Patriotic War, Stalin got the idea of asking about you: What's become of Anna Akhmatova, our nun, has she stopped writing? The wretch had always prided himself on having intellectual inclinations, thought he was a linguistics and history expert, didn't want to limit himself to deciding the life and death of millions but actually thought himself able to dictate the norms of good taste. An academic answered: She hasn't published anything in a long time. Akhmatova is like a museum piece, a relic, though I have read two or three poems of hers that circulate in samizdat, and I have to say they aren't bad. Stalin thought himself a literary critic and ordered that she be allowed to publish once again. How kind, how magnanimous! And then you put together a new book, a collection that would allow you to forget the years of silence and agony, a book that would be like a shout, like a lightning bolt. In mid-1939, you had the proofs ready, and all that was necessary was the approval of the censors before you sent it to the printer. Then someone knocked at your door. As usual, the messenger brought bad news: As he was leafing through your texts, Stalin had noticed one of your poems, a veiled criticism of horror and barbarism. He felt betrayed. He didn't even realize that the poem was dated 1922, when he hadn't yet taken power: Your poems would never be published. For some reason I don't understand, Stalin felt a special attraction for you, had a certain weakness for your hieratic figure, your dignity or your grief. When the Germans besieged Leningrad, he sent one of his planes so you and Dmitri Schostakovich could be evacuated from the burning city and lodged in Tashkent. Why did he do it, Anniushka? Why didn't he allow you to stay in Leningrad, your beloved St. Petersburg, howling for your dead? Why did he pull you from the grave? Did he perhaps love you? Did he secretly love you? It's impossible to guess the fixations of beasts. I fear it was some kind of infatuation on his part, he granted you life like some obscure courtship: He wanted you to leave testimony to his goodness, his greatness, wanted you to fall in love with him. Oh, Anniushka, what could we have done to fall into this limbo that is Russia? Here the only inhabitants are ghosts. If you could see Gorbachev, a woodcutter in a bureaucrat's suit or Yeltsin, a violent, alcoholic peasant, your laughter would turn to weeping. But I can at least tell you one thing: Stalin, your demented lover, no longer arouses fear, his name no longer frightens children, his profile no longer causes shivers. Soon his name will disappear from the streets. And with Lenin, his squalid predecessor, the same thing will happen. And then, Anniushka, you will have triumphed.

Yours,
Oksana Gorenko

8
Moscow, Union of Soviet Socialist Republics, October 13th, 1990

Irina Nikolayevna realized she was becoming more and more impotent: Unlike Arkady, she was not satisfied with chaos, was not relieved by the erosion of Gorbachev, shepherd of men, or the rise of Yeltsin, of strong arms, and she was unable to get excited about the demolition of her nation. Yes, the Soviet Union had been a nightmare, a source of oppression and torture, but Irina could not imagine herself in the desert: She couldn't stand the blind will to erase the past that animated the reformers. How could they construct a future out of nothing, how could they try to erase a century of history with the stroke of a pen? She had exchanged positions with Arkady: In 1990, he considered himself a raging democrat—a hurricane, an avalanche—while she was indecisive, as was Gorbachev, who feared the voraciousness of the market and the old Communists equally.

Marx, in *The 18th Brumaire of Louis Bonaparte*, wrote that the great events of universal history take place twice, first as tragedy and then as farce. This was exactly what was happening with the Soviet Union: The worst vices of autocracy were revived by the new Russian nationalists. For example, Irina thought it vulgar and scandalous that religious ceremonies were again celebrated in the Cathedral of Saint Basil. She was a scientist, so God was not her concern, but she could not tolerate the idea that men as intelligent as Gorbachev and Yeltsin would participate in such ceremonies as a symbol of change.

Few institutions had subjugated the Russian people as harshly as the Russian Orthodox Church, which was guilty of inculcating resignation and meekness in its believers. Nothing justified the Communist Party's jailing of its priests and theologians, but restoring it to a place of privilege in public life was an assault on reason. To grant power to those ignorant, anachronistic old men seemed to her an unequivocal sign of the current demagoguery. The ideological void left by Communism was being filled by another absurd faith: First it was Lenin, now Christ.

During the past few years, Irina had distanced herself from science, but biology was her only passion. She considered her human rights work a necessary evil, an obligation she had to carry out, but she was certain that once the political situation improved—when Russia was an open society—she would return to her cells and cultures. She missed that world and wanted to get back to it as soon as possible. Unfortunately, all her time went into accompanying Arkady, helping him carry out his work, forging his image as a democrat, and returning to biology seemed a remote possibility. Behind every one of her husband's works was her hand: For years she hadn't lived for herself. Ultimately, she had no time to think about any scientific subject, not even to leaf through the Western magazines that were easier and easier to get. In her worst moments she thought she'd never recover her lost time, that her scientific career was over, that in the best case she be nothing but a second-rank biologist.

Her worst fears were confirmed when she read a back issue of the *New York Times* to clip out a Yeltsin interview. She saw that Western science was indeed superior. While she did nothing but type letters and speeches for her husband, the U.S. government had set into motion a gigantic project to map the human genome. The technique to carry out the plan had advanced at such a rate that it was no longer a mere dream. According to the newspaper, in 1990 the U.S. Health Department and the National Institute of Health had presented a program called *Understanding Our Genetic Heritage, the U.S. Human Genome Project: the First Five Years (1991-1995).* The decoding would be done by 2005. The Human Genome Project, whose inception was set for October 13th, 1990, would not only trace a map of the 100,000 genes human DNA was supposed to have, but it would also define that of other organisms, beginning with Irina's beloved bacteria. Congress had named James Watson, who discovered the structure of DNA with Francis Crick, Director of the new National Center for the Investigation of the Human Genome, concluded the *Times* article.

As she read this article, Irina became increasingly angry. Unlike what was happening in mathematics or physics, it seemed as if some curse had deprived the Soviet Union of a solid tradition in biology. First, because of the infamous Lysenko, and now, because of neglect and a lack of resources, genetics in the USSR was light years behind what was taking place elsewhere. The bureaucrats in the Defense and Health ministries had only been interested in producing biological weapons, and, now that Gorbachev had prohibited them, they hadn't even bothered to transform the obsolete military laboratories into modern research centers.

In the Soviet Union, science was declining at the same speed as its economic structures. So while its counterparts were engaged in deciphering the essence of humanity, Soviet biologists had to be satisfied with surviving, with finding food and clothing for their children, with struggling to retain their scant funding in the new political arena. Irina's disquiet knew no limits. Arkady had become a liberal and was as authoritarian as his enemies. Oksana was rebelling against both, the country was falling apart, and she couldn't even imagine herself back in her laboratory.

9

New York, United States of America, November 12th, 1990

Jack Wells was also taken by surprise by the announcement of the Human Genome Project, but his shock was very different from Irina's.

There was something febrile and exciting in the possibility of analyzing the complete structure of human DNA. A project this vast, this ambitious had never been taken on before: Humans had been inhabiting the World for millions of years, but only now would they be able to understand the rules that moved them. Wells quickly looked up the project's economic numbers and felt a shiver: the National Institute of Health had assigned $88 million, the Energy Department—where the project started—$44 million, and the Department of Agriculture, $15 million, which added up to $147 million. And that's only for fiscal year 1991! The total could reach three billion!

That dance of numbers only meant one thing: Though it was perhaps too early to determine how much, the genome could become the most lucrative database ever conceived. After dedicating, with varying success, more than five years to biotechnology, Wells knew that the results of the project would become a major instrument for medicine, capable of helping in the treatment or cure of the more than four thousand genetic illnesses. His competitors would no doubt be thinking the same thing: Biotechnological businesses like DNAW had to join the project as soon as possible, otherwise they risked losing the infinite benefits that would derive from its success. From that day on, Wells considered the genome a treasure map.

10
Berlin, German Federal Republic, November 20th, 1990

Now that the two Germanys were once again one—on October 3rd, the territory of the former Democratic Republic joined the Federal Republic—and euphoria had given way to dismay and even disenchantment, Eva finally found time to get back to work. Jerked out of her meditations by the windstorm of History, she imagined her new objectives. Her work with cellular automata was beginning to bore her—the results were becoming more and more predictable—and she needed to find a new area of interest.

It was just at that moment when, in a providential way, she was called by Jeremy Fuller, one of her friends at MIT. While they hadn't seen each other for a long time, they'd followed parallel paths: A mathematician by profession, like her, he'd been drawn recently to biology and had intervened in the creation of the computer program that made it possible to acquire the genetic sequence for Fago Φ-X-174 (a diminutive virus that only infects certain bacteria), and from that time on he'd stayed in the avant-garde of bioprogramming.

Without wasting time on preambles, Fuller, a solid man of fifty-five who looked like a rugby player, told Eva he'd begun developing a program for accelerating the mapping and sequencing of genes as a part of the Human Genome Project, and that, given the interest her work had aroused in James Watson, he was inviting her to join his group. I'm very happy in Berlin, Eva answered. Do you really want to throw away an opportunity like this?, Jeremy argued. Berlin will be there forever, you'll be able to go back whenever you like. But the genome is a race against time. Think about it, Eva: You'll be part of the greatest scientific project our species has ever undertaken. How long will you give me to think it over? One minute, answered Jeremy. Okay, count me in. Only when she hung up the telephone did she think that she would never see Ismet, her plaything, again.

1991

1

Moscow, Union of Soviet Socialist Republics,
March 15th, 1991

As soon as he saw him in the restaurant, one of those new and luxurious salons that were beginning to pop up like mushrooms in the old buildings of Moscow, Arkady immediately recognized his host: Like millions of other Russians, he'd seen that face—boyish, timid—hundreds of times in his ubiquitous TV announcements. Dressed with the propriety of a Party member—after all, he'd been a member since childhood—he stood before the cameras without the resources of Western publicity. Sober and firm, he smacked his fist on the table and shouted: My name is Mihail Khodorkovsky, and I'm inviting you to assure your future by buying stock in the Menatep Bank. Arkady had always wanted to meet him, but it was actually Khodorkovsky who'd invited him. For Arkady, the impresario was the prototype of the *novi russki*, though for him that term had no negative connotations: Those irredentist boys, intent on prospering and becoming wealthy, were the only ones who could save the nation from misery.

When Gorbachev came to power, Khodorkovsky was a twenty-three-year-old boy who'd grown up in a communal building in Moscow and had just entered the Mendeleiev Chemical Technology Institute. There, thanks to his talent for public relations, he'd become one of the most charismatic leaders of Komsomol. As vice-President of the young Communist group at the Institute, he'd approved the government's new ordinances, which allowed the self-financing of social organizations—this was called *jozrachot*—and began his meteoric rise. Realizing this legislation was a first step toward private property, Khodorkovsky founded his first business, a small, not very successful, café in the Mendeleiev Institute. Then he got a better idea: Under the formal cover of Komsomol, he established an association of scientists which, using the name Foundation for Youthful Initiatives, provided consultants for state industries. In this way, he not only amassed capital but also came into direct contact with managers. His Foundation became a Center for Scientific-Technological Creativity for Youth, his first profitable initiative.

According to rumors I verified years later while I was writing my novel *In Search of Kaminski*, Khodorkovsky found the way to turn enormous quantities of *beznalíchniye*, the paper money turned over to businesses as part of their state subsidy, into *nalíchniye*, hard cash. Then by means of a complex financial system, he turned it into strong currencies, and obtained huge earnings in the process. In a lugubrious apartment at Number 1 Tverskaia-Yamskaia Street, he diversified the functions of the Center and began distributing computers and other technological devices, as well as black-market shipments of cognac. The transactions of his fledgling business grew more complex by the day—and the bribes more onerous—and Khodorkovsky thought that the only way to leap over the bureaucratic peaks would be by having his own bank. With no opposition from the authorities, he registered Menatep in 1988, and from being a simple student of chemistry, he became one of the most celebrated impresarios in the USSR. Mikhail Gorbachev, shepherd of men, invited him to the Kremlin in mid-1990 as an example of perestroika.

Jodorkovksi shook Arkady's hand and sat down at the table. In the café's dim light—a box lined with gold-embroidered cloth, without windows, hidden on the fifth floor of an old apartment building—he looked younger and more withdrawn than on television. Arkady had to start the conversation, even though he had no idea what he was supposed to say.

While they ordered (Arkady hadn't seen a menu with so many options and such high prices in a long while), they chatted about the weather, childhood, and the recent events in the Balkan states—Gorbachev has lost control over the security agencies Arkady said—until the impresario relaxed and dared to express his opinions. Essentially, he agreed with Arkady: The Soviet Union was doomed to extinction.

It was then that the serious part of the meeting began: Given that Gorbachev's days were numbered, Khodorkovsky thought it urgent to establish an alliance with Yeltsin in order to gain some advantage from the financial winds that would sweep Russia. Briefly put, he wanted Arkady to be his intermediary with the Russian President: Both were interested in having the country open up as soon as possible to the market economy. Once he decided to speak, Khodorkovsky was clear and direct. He was willing to finance Yeltsin's campaign against Gorbachev, as long as the new government would help him acquire the debilitated state industries that would be sold off.

Arkady admired his frankness. As he devoured a plate of foie gras—foie gras in Moscow!—he felt that Russia's future depended on men like this one. If in the past he had moral reservations about such proposals, it now seemed a proper *quid pro quo* to him. Arkady believed that the liberal democracy of the United States depended on daring and ambitious men like Khodorkovsky, unscrupulous creatures who, if they enjoyed the necessary legal and financial conditions, could transform their personal wealth into a source of prosperity for the rest of the population. The State was the absolute evil, the State which devoured the best of every individual: It had to be made as small as possible, so creative, energetic individuals could take control of the economy. Using the indirect political language he detested so much, he promised to bring the proposal to Yeltsin's attention.

I'm happy we agree, Arkady Ivanovich, Khodorkovsky rejoiced during dessert (pineapple mousse!). Sometimes it's hard to find people as open and understanding to talk to, and I promise I will not forget you in the future. Arkady smiled: My faith in democracy is identical to my faith in free enterprise. Before we leave, said Khodorkovsky, allow me to give you this small guidebook we've just published. In it we explain Menatep's philosophy, I'm sure you'll be interested. Arkady examined the cover of *The Man of the Ruble* and read here and there: Our compass is benefit, and our idol is his financial majesty, capital. And further on: A man who can turn one dollar into a billion is a genius. Then: To be rich is a form of being. And finally: We are the defenders of the right of all to be rich. Arkady had finally found someone who thought the way he did. He proposed a toast to freedom. Raising his glass of champagne, the impresario seconded the motion: To freedom.

2
New York, United States of America, March 17th, 1991

It was 8:00 A.M. when the doorbell rang. Looking through the peephole, Jennifer was astonished to see her sister. As usual, she hadn't bothered to have herself announced. She opened the door, and Allison rushed in, pushing a hideous blue stroller. Jacob was now over a year old, but differences between the sisters had postponed the visit again and again. What are you doing here?, Jennifer blurted out. I wanted you to meet my son, said Allison. Where's Jack? At a work meeting, her sister answered, not coming any closer to the baby.

Allison extracted him from his stroller and put him in Jennifer's arms. He likes you! Jennifer was not amused: Ever since her doctors told her she was sterile, she'd developed a sincere aversion to newborns. It was untrue that women were prepared by their genes for maternity: Jennifer couldn't get used to the baby and passed him from one arm to the other, helping herself with her chest and chin, horrified at the thought of dropping him.

Suddenly, even though she'd done nothing, Jacob began to cry. His faint, almost timid groan quickly gave way to an unbearable howl. I did nothing, she excused herself. Of course not, Jen, babies cry for no reason or for reasons we'll never understand, maybe just to annoy us. Pat him on the back, let's see if he calms down. Jennifer tried to be tender, but the baby's wailing unnerved her. Okay, let me try, Allison intervened. Jennifer handled the baby as if he were a Chinese vase and ran to wash her hands. What Jacob inspired in her, more than discomfort, was fear. Allison lulled her son, and a couple of minutes later managed to quiet him. See? All you need is a bit of patience. Patience! thought Jennifer. Just what I don't have.

Once Jacob was asleep, Jennifer turned to her sister: Tell me the truth, why did you come over? Don't misunderstand me, I'm happy to meet my nephew, but you could have made a formal presentation months ago.

Allison hated the fact that her sister could guess her thoughts: You're right, Jen, I always come to ask favors. Do you need money? This time I don't, it's something more important. I need you to take care of Jacob this weekend. I've got no one to leave him with, and I can't bring him with me.

You're crazy!, Jennifer jumped to her feet. How can you think I'm going to take care of this baby? I'm not capable of doing it, as you just saw. Where do you have to go? What could be more important than your child? I didn't come over so you could chew me out, Allison pointed out, but to ask a favor. I'm begging you Jen, just for tonight. I have to meet with some people here in Manhattan, but I can't tell you what it's about, and I can't bring Jacob along. I hope you're not in trouble again. For God's sake, Alli, why don't you get an ordinary job and take care of the child you were so intent on having? I don't want to read you a sermon, but you're a big girl now, you can't go on with this nomadic life, you have to take care of Jacob, that should be your only goal, forget saving the world and look after the only person who really needs you.

Allison didn't even wait for her sister to finish. She put Jacob back in his stroller and got ready to leave. I'm fed up, Jen! It's always the same thing! I didn't come by so you could tell me what to do with my life. If you can't or won't help me, I'll figure out something. Okay, Alli, forgive me. You know how much I love you. I worry about you, that's the only reason I get mad, you're an extraordinary woman who . . . I know, I know, an extraordinary woman who's wasted her life, right? Alli, let's not fight any more, we only have each other. I'll be happy to take care of Jacob tonight.

Really? Allison's face lit up. You'd do that for me? Just this once, nodded Jen. This weekend we have no engagements, so Jack and I can investigate what it means to be parents, for a day. Don't worry, he'll be fine with us. Thank you, really, thank you. And now I should be on my way. I'm leaving you his food, it's all ready, and a sheet with instructions. Instructions!, laughed Jennifer, as if he were an appliance! Go on, I only ask that you call me tomorrow so I'll know you're all right, okay? Yes. Promise? I promise. They hugged. Can you lend me $200? Jennifer gave her the money without comment. Allison picked up her jacket, kissed her son, and disappeared at top speed.

Only then did Jennifer realize what she'd done: This defenseless and strange being needed her care and affection. For a moment, she thought about running after her sister to explain that she wouldn't be able to do the job, but it was too late. She cautiously approached Jacob, as if he were a dangerous animal: He was sleeping placidly, indifferent to her fears. Twenty-four hours pass quickly, she consoled herself. She caressed her nephew's head and felt at peace.

Two hours later, Wells walked in on the unprecedented vision of Jennifer trying to change the diaper of a baby who was howling as though he were being tortured. What's going on here? Jennifer explained. Her husband shook his head and muttered: Your sister always gets her way, she does whatever she likes, it's your fault she's never learned to take care of herself. Well, all I ask is that you keep him quiet, I have to work a bit more. After a few hours, the two of them realized there was no escape: Children are tyrants, and adults can only bend to their whims. Which meant that they spent the rest of the day taking turns with Jacob, feeding him, cleaning him, playing with him, or trying to get him to sleep. The night was no better: He woke up at 3:00 A.M. and again at 5:00, making a racket that would not be silenced. I only hope your sister turns up soon, complained Jack.

It was as if he'd uttered a curse: By 7:00 P.M. on Sunday there was still no sign of Allison. Jennifer imagined a worst-case scenario. She tried to find her sister by every means, but it was no use. There was nothing else to do but hire a nanny, and, overwhelmed by guilt, ask the IMF for a few days leave to take care of her nephew. Her sister didn't materialize until the next week. By then she had passed from fury to impotence and from fear to resignation. But at the end of that adventure—that test—she did not feel completely negative: Jacob had not only survived her inexperience but had grown accustomed to her care. He'd even developed a certain attachment to her, or at least that's what she believed. She was sad when Allison finally took him away.

3
Moscow, Union of Soviet Socialist Republics, June 17th, 1991

The incident, as I started calling it later, took place hours after Boris Yeltsin was elected as the first democratic President of the Russian Federation. It was about 8:00 P.M., and I was walking along Znamenka Street toward the Borovitskaia subway station. I felt someone grab me from behind. At first I thought it might be one of my colleagues from

Ogoniok, but I quickly registered the icy point of a knife about to sink into my neck. Just keep walking, said a hoarse voice with Caucasian accent. If you cooperate, nothing will happen to you. I followed his orders, trying not to see his face, though I did glimpse his stony profile and the shadows of two other individuals just behind us. They forced me around a corner, put me in a car—a broken-down, brown Lada—and they blindfolded me. On either side, two bodies, as bulky as they were smelly, made themselves comfortable. The stench of cheap alcohol heightened my fear.

I'd heard that such scenes had become frequent in Moscow and Leningrad, cities of wide avenues, but I never imagined their degree of violence. Could it be a kidnapping, or, more likely, was someone getting even? I had no idea how long we rode around the city through the heavy afternoon traffic. I suppose they wanted to disorient me. For a time, I thought they were driving me to the edge of town—if that was the case, it meant the worst—but after three or four hours we stopped in a lot that, given the level of noise, had to be in the city. During the ride, my captors kept quiet, refusing to answer my questions, punching me in the kidneys whenever I opened my mouth. A part of me insisted on talking, to initiate, if possible, a minimal contact with them so that maybe they wouldn't shoot me, but my efforts only upset them.

The yanked me out of the car, dragged me along a hall and then down a long stairway before throwing me into a basement. I figured I was about to die, but I felt neither panic nor anguish, as I did in Afghanistan, only rage. They left me there, alone and uncomfortable, for a long time. The dead time helped me recover my serenity: If they were going to so much trouble, perhaps they weren't planning to murder me, or at least not right away. During that immersion in the darkness, I didn't try to recall my life, I didn't balance off my successes against my mistakes, I wasn't sorry for anything, I didn't seek divine consolation, and I didn't even try to understand the psychology of my captors. My hyperactive mind jumped from one subject to another, from a distant memory to my present sorrow, from images of Baku to the corpses I'd seen in Vilna just a few days earlier, from Zarifa and her murdered brother to my desire to fight oblivion by telling the story.

A pair of men interrupted my stream of consciousness. I heard them throw things to the ground—glass, chairs, tools—preparing the scene for torture. I heard the sound of a whip, or perhaps I only imagined it, and then the working of pincers and hammers. What were they going to do with me? Only one thing was clear: If they weren't KGB men, my number was up. I detected in their movement a choreographed routine, certain implicit things only acquired after years of practice at subjugating souls and bodies. Then I felt a slap, and an almost pleasant warmth spread over my face. The lull was over, and I'd finally learn what they were going to do with me.

The thugs kept silent while they beat me to a pulp, working off their own anger and their well-paid contempt. They asked me nothing, didn't insult me or wound me. They just did their job with cold, bureaucratic efficiency. It wasn't personal: Someone had certainly paid them to teach me a lesson, they might not even know why, they weren't the kind who read newspapers or watch the news, they may have thought I was just another of the insolvent debtors who were proliferating in Moscow and Leningrad, another of those tricky gamblers who had to pay for their greed.

The pain became so constant, so unbearable, that it almost didn't hurt: They had to throw a pail of water on me so I'd recover consciousness and, with it, the ability to suffer. It was there I understood that I had neither soul nor spirit, that I was only this mass of broken bones and lacerated tissue, of blood and tears, that I was only my body. When they finished, they carried me out and tossed me in the Lada's trunk. I heard how they locked me in and thought, in my delirium, that this was how life should close.

When I woke up, I found myself on an empty street, twenty hours after the initial kidnapping. I couldn't see my face, but the burning sensation and the reddish stains covering my shirt made me imagine I was disfigured. I dragged myself to several doors before an old lady agreed to call me an ambulance. In her eyes I read the horror she felt seeing me. I wasn't wrong: It was a warning, a subtle hint. If I insisted on writing about what was happening in Azerbaijan and Armenia, in the Baltic countries and in Moldovia, if I persisted in documenting the ruin of the army, more sessions like the one I'd just had—or even worse ones—awaited me. Everything was clear. I'd broken the unwritten laws of the system, been unable to see the border line between what could be said and what could not be said.

But the worst, the most terrible, the most horrifying thing was that those faceless, unknown men had achieved their objective. They didn't intimidate me, but they did accentuate the worst of me. Without realizing it, I was storing up an irrepressible hatred inside me. Those men made me even more violent and vengeful, they stripped away the little humanity I had left after Afghanistan. They made me one of their own, they infected me with their hatred, and they transformed me into the bitter, cruel creature I continue to be until this very day.

4
London, United Kingdom, July 17th, 1991

When Michel Camdessus broke the news to her at the outset of April, Jennifer didn't know if it was a promotion or a punishment. She'd been concentrating for so long on Latin American matters that she imagined she'd be spending the rest of her life learning Spanish and Portuguese and battling with the obsequious politicians of the region. Suddenly she was ordered to leave that world behind, forget its noisy, sun-drenched cities, its greasy and dangerous foods and concentrate on subjects about which she knew nothing or almost nothing.

Why had the Director-General chosen her? The IMF had recognized experts in the socialist field, men and women who'd dedicated their lives to learning Russian and other Slavic tongues, who'd acclimated themselves to its polar cold, to vodka, to the extremely touchy nature of those peoples, who'd broken their heads to understand the functioning of five-year plans and the abstruse social organization of that part of the world. Why should she run around them? Jennifer's habitual paranoia kept her from seeing the post as a prize: There had to be a dark side to it. Perhaps someone wanted to root her out of the Americas Department, lots of people envied her, her transfer had to be the result of some intrigue.

The director-general gave her no opportunity to mull things over: We need someone with your profile—dynamic, willing to learn, not one of those old fogies who've spent twenty years trying to fathom Soviet logic and who are now themselves incapable of adapting to the changes. By studying Communist bureaucrats for decades, they've ended up looking like them. But I don't know Russian, and I've never been in Russia. That's not important; what does matter is your experience with complicated cases. And this one is certainly complicated. I want you to work up a complete study on the current state of the Soviet economy. The idea is to present it during the London meeting of the Group of Seven, which Gorbachev will attend . . . But that's only three months from now! That's why it's all so urgent, Jennifer. I'm relying on you.

Overnight, she changed geographical regions, work teams, and even her office. Except for Emily, no one regretted her departure, though everyone was careful to congratulate her. From that moment on, Jennifer didn't have a moment of rest. Not only did she have to familiarize herself with the subject but also with a logic that was completely different from her own. There was no time for her to impose her criteria on the documents presented to her, and all she could do was correct them until fatigue set in. Her new employees seemed as indolent and pliable as the old ones, but by now she was so used to laziness and inefficiency that she didn't bother to fire them. The only thing that mattered was turning in the report on time, because her recommendations would set the stage for the kind of reception the industrialized nations would offer their former nemesis.

Wells didn't see her for weeks at a time. Instead of going to New York, navel of the world, and taking care of Jacob on weekends—this had become a routine—she chose to stay in Washington, axis of the cosmos, dedicated to reading and re-reading communiques, archives, documents, summaries, and outlines. Dominated by her anxiety for perfection, she took Russian classes from 7:00 A.M. until 9:00 A.M., convinced that only if she learned the language, or at least learned how it worked, would she be able to understand its leaders.

Three months after she took on the mission, Jennifer was satisfied. Paler than usual, she handed Camdessus two hundred pages. In them, she not only examined the Soviet economy, but offered an explanation of its decay. She also projected its future development and speculated about its stagnation. The diagnosis was severe: Nothing in the Soviet social organization suggested that they would be able to implement a free market correctly. After years of battling governments in Africa and Latin America, Jennifer was used to bureaucracy, but she had never encountered anything like Soviet bureaucracy—it occupied every available space—and she had no idea how a society like that could function.

Ever since perestroika began, a few citizens tried to introduce a primitive liberal economy. There were some banks, some cooperatives and micro-businesses, and the elites agreed that only an out-and-out liberalization would save the country. But that would not assure the end of statism. The greatest problem was that industries were not governed by the law of supply and demand but instead by having to meet quotas set by the Party. Jennifer thought that the only way to accelerate the opening of the economy was through a drastic liberalization of prices. This would be an unpopular measure because it would send inflation through the roof, but it was the price we Russians would have to pay for our errors. Camdessus was very impressed by the statement. Jennifer was an impossible person—her fame in the Fund preceded her—but she was 100% reliable. To reward her for a job well done, he allowed her to present her conclusions during the meeting of ministers of the Group of Seven.

Forced to take more and more pills for her nerves, with her face twisted by anxiety, and feeling uglier and fatter than ever—she chewed peanuts all day—Jennifer travelled to London at the head of the IMF mission. For her, those days passed like a blink: The drugs kept her in a state of lassitude that made it impossible for her to concentrate. A sub-director of analysis had to answer the questions and calm the doubts of the functionaries. Meanwhile, she remained in a cautious silence, besieged by her fear of being found ridiculous. The ministers did not sense her insecurity; some thought Camdessus's envoy was more stubborn—and pretty—than convincing, but they praised her wisdom and efficiency, and they ultimately defined their position thanks to her. Satisfied, Jennifer went back to New York without realizing that instead of saving us, she was responsible for setting the terms of our failure.

5

Union of Soviet Socialist Republics, August 18th, 1991

For Mikhail Gorbachev, shepherd of men, it had been a dry and arid summer. The list of problems, reversals, and obstacles to his control had only lengthened. The opposition of Yeltsin, of strong arms, had become more and more ferocious. Half of the former Soviet republics had declared their independence, and the hardest sectors of the Party mocked his authority. Only at the end of July did a final hope to reconstitute order arise. After an agitated, tempestuous series of meetings in Novo-Orgonovo, the Presidents of eight republics had agreed to sign a new *Union Treaty*. Gorbachev would retain his leadership of the state and his control over defense and foreign relations, while Yeltsin and the regional leaders would attend to internal matters. It was the best possible arrangement: That's how all the signatories understood it, including the turbulent Boris Nikolayevich. On August 20th, 1991, the official signing ceremony would take place.

With the agreement settled, Gorbachev had time to return to Moscow to receive President George Bush, to whom he communicated the good news: His understanding with Yeltsin guaranteed the survival of the Union. Encouraged by these developments, he went off, on August 4th, to his summer dacha—a mansion valued at $20 million—on Cape Foros in the Crimea. He was accompanied by his wife, daughter, son-in-law, and small granddaughter. For Gorbachev, shepherd of men, that place was a sanctuary: The grayish waters of the Black Sea would tone up his muscles, the sun would strengthen his body, and the after-dinner chats with his family would inject him with the energy he would need to face the challenges of autumn.

August 18th began like any other day. Gorbachev breakfasted with Raisa, jogged on the beach, revised some official documents, and had even rewarded himself by beginning a novel. At 4:50 P.M., his chief of security informed him a visitor was about to arrive. I haven't invited anyone, he pointed out, and he wanted to know who was on the way. He picked up the telephone, but it was dead. He tried another with the same result. He had no need to test the others to know what was happening. He gathered his family in the living room and revealed the danger. His voice evidenced neither fear nor anguish, just disquiet. He hugged Raisa and his daughter. Now all they could do was wait.

A delegation from Moscow dashed into the house. It was made up of his own personal assistant, the Sub-Director of the Defense Council, the Secretary of the Central Committee, the Commander-in-Chief of the army, and a representative of the KGB. Who sent you here, asked Gorbachev, shepherd of men. The committee named to deal with the state of emergency, answered General Valentin Varennikov. And who appointed the committee? I certainly didn't do it; neither did the Supreme Soviet. I'm afraid you've only got two options, Varennikov chided him, either accept our authority or resign from the presidency of the Union. You're nothing but adventurers and traitors, and you'll pay dearly for this. What happens to all of you matters little, but you will destroy the country. It's suicidal to think of returning to a totalitarian regime. You people are bringing us to civil war! On the 20th, we have to sign the new Treaty of the Union, the only thing that may save us.

There will be no signing, Mikhail Sergeyevich, blurted out Oleg Baklanov, Sub-Director of the Council of Defense. Yeltsin will be arrested. We don't want you to do anything, Mikhail Sergeyevich, except remain here. We'll do the dirty work. He then revealed the identities of the other members of the State Committee for the State of Emergency—even the name of the committee is idiotic, thought Gorbachev. Among the names were others who'd been his collaborators, people like the President of the Supreme Soviet, his old friend Anatoly Lukyanov. Also involved in the plot were the Director of the KGB, the Secretary of Defense, the Prime Minister, and the Minister of the Interior.

But what disgusted Gorbachev most was that the members of the coup had elected Vice-President Gennady Yanayev, an inveterate alcoholic, as their leader. You're just a pack of upstarts—an alliance of corrupt military men and brainless functionaries! Gorbachev closed his fists: He was the one who'd appointed them, he was the one who'd placed his faith in them, he was the one who'd passed over his old comrades to elevate these savages, he and only he! And what were they going to do after establishing this absurd state of emergency?, Gorbachev, shepherd of men, attacked them. We cannot accept that separatists and extremists are taking over the country, answered Varennikov. I've heard that one before, retorted the prisoner. And he added: Do you really think the people will accept a dictator? And in a voice that rose from the depth of his being he added: Go to hell!

6

Union of Soviet Socialist Republics, August 19th, 1991

At exactly 6:00 A.M., a mellow voice spoke over the radio. The same message, lacking any logic, would be repeated from then on every hour on the hour:

> *With regard to the inability of Mikhail Sergeyevich Gorbachev to continue in his role as President of the USSR because of the condition of his health: Based on Article 127.7 of the Constitution of the USSR, I have assumed the position of acting President of the USSR beginning on August 19, 1991.*
>
> *G.I. Yanayev, Vice-President of the USSR.*

Arkady, Irina, and Oksana learned of the coup at 7:00 A.M., when an out-of-breath phone call from a member of the Congress of Deputies announced the bad news. At the same moment, Vitali Korotich, editor of *Ogoniok*, called my house and shouted, We're screwed! While Arkady tried to calm his family—these wretches don't understand that the country has changed, that a coup will never take hold—I went to the magazine. I wanted to meet with my comrades to plan a strategy against the censorship the Emergency Committee was attempting to impose.

Boris Yeltsin, of strong arms, was in his summer dacha in Usovo getting ready for breakfast when Anatoly Sobchak appeared with the news. On the way, he'd noticed troops moving toward Moscow, city of wide avenues. Except for Arkady Granin, his team was at his side, including the new President of the Supreme Soviet, Ruslan Khasbulatov, with whom he would soon have his differences. After listening to their reports, Yeltsin decided to go to the capital and oppose the coup with all the means at his disposal. Now, said his daughter Tatiana, everything depends on you.

Yeltsin ordered his limousine and moved to the White House, on the banks of the Moskova, at Krasnopresnenskaya pier, as fast as he could. His entourage reached their objective at 10:00 A.M. A small group of officials, deputies, and friends, including Arkady Granin, met him at the entrance. By then I'd left the *Ogoniok* offices and had also moved on to the White House, where I heard the public statement in which Yeltsin refused to recognize the Emergency Committee and called for a general strike.

Outside the Russian Parliament, a discreet crowd was gathering. You could smell the fear but also the will to resist: The people there were not willing to give up the freedom they'd won through such determination. The same question was asked by everyone: What about Mikhail Gorbachev? Some Yeltsin backers suspected he'd sided with the coup forces, but most imagined he was under arrest or, even worse, that he'd been executed in the old style.

Just after 12:00 noon, Boris Nikolayevich made his way through his followers, and, to the surprise of all, climbed up on top of a T-72 tank that remained loyal to his government. His demeanor was neither warlike nor majestic, but the fact that he left the White House to rally his followers transformed him into a national leader (the photograph of him on the tank would be reproduced in every newspaper in the world). Citizens of Russia, bellowed Yeltsin, the President of the nation has been removed from power. We are faced with a right-wing, reactionary, unconstitutional coup . . . The cheering drowned out his voice. For the first time, I spoke to Arkady Granin, who happened to be standing next to me. This is a different country, he said, and the world must learn that. When I told him my name and told him I worked for *Ogoniok*,

Arkady asked me to follow him: This war won't be won with weapons but through the media. We need soldiers like you.

Inside the Parliament, Yeltsin's advisors were coordinating the resistance in a haphazard way. With some exceptions, they were functionaries or academics without military experience. I helped as much as I could, but Granin insisted on locking me in an improvised press room where there were only two telephones and a fax machine. My job would be to coordinate the Russian Government's press communiqués. At 5:00 P.M., Yanayev went on television, speaking as acting President of the USSR. His image was pathetic: Eaten up by remorse and alcohol, he improvised a speech full of indiscretions and mistakes that in itself should have been sufficient to announce his failure. It was incredible that a clown like that could become leader of the nation. But at that moment it was still impossible to predict the stance of the Army and the KGB: Both were at the ready, waiting to see which side had the greater possibility of success. Arkady again came into the press room. Yeltsin would remain in the White House, he warned me, and the order is to resist until the end. The history of the country was full of sieges, as if they were part of our identity. Like Leningrad during the Great Patriotic War, the White House would become a symbol of resistance.

While the coup leaders could rely on the support of the most conservative sectors, there were media outlets that had not been closed down, and they continued releasing Yeltsin's proclamations. Drunks and idiots, Arkady summarized at midnight, but drunks and idiots who control our atomic arsenal. Even so, he remained optimistic. According to Yeltsin himself, more than 100,000 people had gathered in the center of Sverdlovsk to protest the coup. We will defeat them, Arkady declared as he settled into a chair next to mine. Tomorrow will be a decisive day: If we manage to last twenty-four hours, we will have won.

7

Union of Soviet Socialist Republics, August 20th, 1991

Arkady Ivanovich woke me up at 5:00 A.M. Day was just breaking. He was carrying two AK-47s, one for him, one for me. How many people are left outside?, I asked. About ten thousand, too few to stand up to a battalion, but we have no choice. I picked up my Kalashnikov and suggested a scouting expedition. Outside the White House, it looked more like a campground than a siege. The barricades did not alter the calm of the Moskova in the slightest. We went back inside because I was supposed to write a communiqué announcing the creation of the new Russian Ministry of Defense under the direct control of Boris Yeltsin. If the coup leaders would not allow a medical team from the WHO to visit Gorbachev in the Crimea, we would initiate hostilities.

At 10:00 A.M., an unexpected ally, the great Mstislav Rostropovich, on tour in Moscow, appeared at the White House. Instead of his cello, he too was carrying an AK-47. Half an hour later, Yeltsin appeared before the crowd, looking more and more tranquil and confident. He accused the coup leaders of having blood-stained hands—they were responsible for the massacres in the Baltic states and the Caucasus—and assumed control over the security forces in the Russian Federation. He was flanked by Rostropovich and Yevgeny Yevtushenko, of the sonorous voice, who had a rare ability to compose a poem for any situation:

No! Russia will not bow down again for interminable years,
With us are Pushkin, Tolstoy.
With us is the entire aroused people.
And the Russian Parliament, like a wounded marble swan
of liberty
defended by the people swims in immortality.

No one took notice of the quality of the poem: The crowd received it with applause and cheers. Taking advantage of the fact that the show was ending, Arkady told me he'd be leaving for a few hours to look for his wife and daughter. If, as was rumored, the attack by the coup leaders was imminent, he at least wanted to say good-bye to them. I stayed in the White House, composing new bulletins and making sure they reached Western press agencies.

And what was going on with the coup during that interlude? Yanayev, drunk and isolated, had no idea why he'd joined with the conspirators, who weren't even sure they'd win. Where were the implacable Soviet leaders of the past?, he wondered. Perestroika, or, rather, the market and its luxuries, had corrupted them, and now they didn't dare give a definitive order. To verify the collapse of Communism, all you had to do was look at its latest soldiers: Fearful rats, snakes with no poison, drunken porpoises. According to the latest rumors, Prime Minister Pavlov checked into a military hospital because of alcohol poisoning, the leaders of the Ukraine and Kazakhstan would not support the junta, many members of the KGB were refusing to follow orders, and even the miserable Lukyanov was trying to erase his participation in the plot . . . Even so, it was impossible to forget what had happened in Baku or Vilnius. What if these lunatics pulled off something similar?

I met up with Arkady, accompanied by his wife and daughter, in the afternoon. What are all of you doing here?, I asked. We too have the right to defend our freedom answered Irina Nikolayevna. The languid beauty of their daughter surprised me, along with her apparent distance from the world, her extremely black and vivacious eyes (eyes I'd never see again but which would be so important for me). The presence of this teenaged girl restored my hope: Unless the world had gone suddenly rotten, our soldiers would never fire on their families. The people involved in the coup must have gone insane if they thought Russians would be willing to murder other Russians. Meanwhile, the press continued rebelling against the Emergency Committee: After some hours of fighting, *Izvestia* was under democratic control, and even the state news bulletin *Vremia* confirmed the reclusion of Pavlov and the sudden illness of Aleksandr Besmertinj, Foreign Minister of the USSR, another who'd succumbed to repentance.

I was in one of the offices on the second floor of the White House when the shooting began. I ran downstairs as quickly as I could with my AK-47. Yanayev, it seems, had given the order to attack. The spectacle recalled the revolts in Prague or Budapest: The tanks sent by the coup leaders were received with a rain of Molotov cocktails. The young people were screaming: *Shame! Shame!*, and then *Russia! Russia!*. An acrid smell saturated Moscow, city of wide avenues: Three boys were run over by troop carriers. A group of women formed a human chain around the White House: Soviet soldiers, do not fire on your mothers!

Everything was ready for the final attack. The various elements of the Army and the KGB were merely waiting for the order to begin "Operation Thunder." Within a few hours, the White House and those of us defending it would be transformed into statistics, to be added to the millions of innocent people sacrificed by Communism. But nothing happened. *Nothing*. Yanayev was not ready to assume such a burden. Nor were the commanding military officers. Several generals, the respected Aleksandr Lebed among them, refused to fire. Without our knowing it, the junta was falling apart: A phony coup d'état, toy tyrants. The silent, rainy night announced our victory.

8
Union of Soviet Socialist Republics, August 21st, 1991

I spent the night outdoors, among the defenders on the barricades. At 5:00 A.M., we were still breathing an air of anxiety and surprise, the sensation that victory could not be so simple, that the three boys murdered at the intersection of Garden Ring and Novy Arbat would not be the first names on an interminable list. But we also had a whiff of hope and conspiratorial smiles were on many faces; bottles of vodka and cognac passed from hand to hand, accompanied by prudent toasts that foretold the dawn. Up on top of the Kalininski Bridge, a poster announced: TO HELL WITH THE JUNTA.

Burdened by so much calm, I began a new scouting mission through the halls of the White House. People were sleeping or resting on the rugs or on top of desks, giving the Parliament the air of a refugee center. I hadn't slept in forty-eight hours, but I wasn't sleepy. Fatigue was an additional weight, another load on my knees and other joints. Then I discovered that someone was following me: It was Oksana, Arkady Granin's daughter. She looked fragile, ethereal, like a ghost. Why don't you try to sleep a little?, I asked. She didn't answer, as if she hadn't understood my words. How old are you? Fifteen. Her voice had a deep pulse, impossible to reconcile with someone her age. She walked over. It seemed to me she was hiding something, though my fatigue my have been making me think absurd things. Are you afraid? She stared intently at me, scrutinizing me. Afraid of what? I don't know, I stuttered, that all this might turn out badly. Excuse me, I don't know what I'm talking about, you're right. There's nothing to be afraid of. There was something in her way of turning her face, of blinking, or half-opening her lips that disturbed me.

You're all alike, she suddenly said. What? Oksana wiped her lips with the back of her hand, as if she wanted to erase what she'd just said. Alike? Yes, alike. In those moments, any words echoed in my ears like prophesies or warnings. Who? We and they, she explained, pronouncing each syllable as if I were a foreigner or an idiot. There's no difference between the hyenas out there and the wolves here.

Oksana again seemed a little girl to me, a dumb, rebellious child. I had to show her how mistaken she was: We're defending the legitimate government of this country. Democracy and freedom are our side, your parents are putting themselves at risk right now so that you'll be able to live in a better place in the future.

Do you really think they're doing it for me? Oksana's voice gave off a macabre scent. You're saturated with the same violence you're fighting.

Then she turned around and walked off. I considered following her, convincing her of her mistake, showing her how unjust she was being with her parents, with me, with all of us. I also thought about slapping her, but I just stood there, stunned. I would never again meet up with that wise, needy creature, with that adolescent sibyl, but her curse would soon reach me.

The rumor that the coup's leaders had fled Moscow returned me to reality. As soon as I saw Arkady's face in the press room, I knew we were going to survive. Khrushchev has just spoken to Boris Nikolayevich, he revealed, and has suggested he travel to Foros to find Gorbachev. Does that mean we've won? Arkady hugged me: Democracy has triumphed. At noon, we confirmed that the withdrawal of the tanks surrounding the White House was definitive. The city was coming out of the swamp. People were out on the streets and cheering the troops. There would be no more bloodshed, no more riots. Moscow, city of wide avenues, where neither Napoleon nor Hitler could triumph, had escaped tragedy again.

Three planes flew toward the Crimea: One carried Yeltsin's envoys; another, the coup leaders who were still at large; and in the third was the tortuous Lukyanov, who still hoped to distance himself from this accomplices. Hours later, in Foros, an official announced to Gorbachev, shepherd of men, the arrival of the delegations. With an acrid aftertaste, Mikhail Sergeyevich announced he would see only the Russians. That's what he said: Only the Russians, as if the others weren't Russians, as if at that precise moment, the Soviet Union had ceased to exist. The President gathered his family and told them the coup was over. They were all relieved—but he wasn't. What came next would be as horrible as his captivity: From now on, he would no longer be a prisoner, but he would not be free either. He wouldn't be free ever again.

As soon as the Russians appeared outside the dacha, Gorbachev thanked them for intervening. Wearing a gray sweater and bone-colored slacks (he looked like a man in retirement), he explained that he never made any pacts with the coup leaders, that it had all been a calumny, that he had remained firm and had demanded an emergency meeting of the Congress or the Supreme Soviet. He told them he'd even thought about suicide. Aleksandr Rutskoy, Russia's vice President, almost felt sorry, but he quickly recovered his composure and his role as emissary of Boris Yeltsin, of strong arms, Gorbachev's enemy, who was now saving him.

Raisa Maksimovna came out of the house and stood at the head of the stairs. Unlike her husband, she looked emaciated, her nerves destroyed by isolation. She did not hesitate to kiss each member of the Russian delegation. Are you ready to travel tonight?, Gorbachev asked her. Yes, she whispered, we should leave immediately.

Before they did, Anatoly Lukyanov, already in handcuffs, insisted on speaking with his old friend Gorbachev. Trembling, he tried to explain his position, said he hadn't wanted to participate in the coup, that he hadn't been able to convoke the Supreme Soviet, that he'd created the story about his health. Mikhail Sergeyevich did not allow him to finish: We've known each other for forty years, he shouted. Stop lying! The other conspirators were also arrested. Only Boris Pugo, Minister of the Interior for the coup, elected to commit suicide.

9

Boston, United States of America, December 23rd, 1991

When her plane finally landed at Logan Airport in Boston, there was no one waiting for her. Berlin, the city whose resurrection she'd witnessed, was behind her. That clamorous year, along with the doubts and suspicions aroused by German reunification, was behind her. As was the Zuse Institute, where she spent so many hours in the company of cellular automata. Ismet, her plaything, also was behind her, that unknown figure, that shadow who had remained faithful to her, and taken care of her until the moment Eva had discarded, him just as she'd discarded all the men in her life.

Eva was barely thirty-five, but she felt like an old woman. There were too many cities piled up on her shoulders, too much information, too many men. Her existence was a constant transit, an escape. A curious way to put it, she thought, but perhaps the only meaning life had was to escape misfortune, an apparently modest, apparently mediocre goal but one that was a wiser choice than the cunning pursuit of happiness. In effect, Eva had no home; she was Hungarian, American, and German (well, actually a Berliner) and none of those things. She was a vagabond or a nomad—homeless was a word she liked to repeat—bearing the wandering gene of her Magyar ancestors.

From the air, Boston looked like a wasteland covered with snow. Only after she left the Lufthansa jet, crossed the airport's long corridors, went through immigration, and stopped to pick up her bags did she begin to feel less anguished. Whenever she arrived someplace, the same thing happened. At first, she would feel disquiet, but after a few days everything became natural, quotidian, and anodyne. Eva watched luggage pass her by on the carousel until she was all alone in the halogen-illuminated room: Her things had been left in Frankfurt. As she went through the procedure to report the lost luggage, she thought that the loss had been foreseeable, a perfect metaphor for her life. She only had herself.

Free of all burdens, she quickly took a taxi and asked the driver to take her to a hotel. Which one? Any hotel. In which part of the city? You decide, she muttered without conviction. She'd spend Christmas in her room, alone. She'd watch television, order a bottle of champagne, and sleep in peace. She was about to begin a new phase, and for the first time she wasn't afraid of herself.

10
Union of Soviet Socialist Republics, December 31st, 1991

Dear Anniushka, wrote Oksana just before midnight, I'm writing you desperately to give you the most insane, perturbing, and demented news: Today is the last day. I know it will be hard for you to believe this, to accept that the echo of the millions of corpses, the memory of privation and exile, the bellowing of the dictators, the diatribes of the bureaucrats, the terrifying dream of equality and justice so many held within them are going to vanish this way, from one day to another, in a few hours. And not because of an invasion or an atomic bombardment, not even because of a revolution like the one in 1917, but because of the silent decree of three miserable wretches. Just like this: poof! Now you see it, now you don't. Like magic, like a nightmare.

How simple, my dear Anniushka! A few papers are all you need to cancel the past, to erase memories, to invent a new country! And now what will we be, my friend? Russians? I'll confess: Beginning today, I consider myself a stateless person. I was born in a dead nation, in a territory that will lose its name, in an empty time the world insists on forgetting. I consider myself a citizen of Nothingness, I can flash a passport for Nowhere, perhaps I too no longer exist. I'm an illusion, a mistake, collateral damage—that's what they call it—a ruin.

No, no I have it! I'm an *anachronism*. I'm fifteen, and my name is No One. Here, meanwhile, everyone's going crazy: Everyone, everywhere, wants to be someone else, to *transform themselves*. I've heard about people who've burned their photographs, their insignias and documents, their Pioneers membership cards, their affiliation with Komsomol and the Party. As incredible as it sounds, Anniushka, I'm discovering I've lived in a place where there never were any Communists.

Do you remember the hundreds or thousands of pages of Lenin, Marx, and Engels we memorized? Do you recall the infinite theoretical discussions, the dogmatic subtleties, the twists and turns of dialectics, the dictatorship of the proletariat, the class struggle, the blind power of History? Well, no one remembers any of that any more, what a waste. All this hullabaloo bores me: I'm not interested in reinventing my life, presuming that I always believed in what I believe now, like my father, I'm not interested in lamenting what we've lost or what's been taken away from us, like my mother.

I'm neither optimistic nor nostalgic. I don't think about either the past or the future. Only this damned present, where they've trapped me, matters. As that song by Yanka Diaguileva, a depressive and crazy punk who committed suicide a few weeks ago, says: *My sorrow is radiant.* (You won't believe it, but the only worthwhile poetry in this shitty country is being composed by rock groups; if you were alive, you too would be singing your poems.) Okay: I don't know if this story is sad or happy or just indifferent. What happens to me there, in the vulgar universe of the politicians, in that place they call *the real world*, doesn't matter. But I had to tell you this story, Anniushka, only to you, because only you can understand its absurd cycles. After all, you initiated the Cold War, no? So you deserve to know about its conclusion.

I remember your words—I've already told you that I know "Poem Without a Hero" and "Requiem" by heart—your elliptical narration of that moment. Do you remember? How could you not! That visit changed your life: Thanks to that you became a hostage and an enemy of the people, a martyr, and a priestess. The Great Patriotic War was over and you'd just returned to Leningrad, to your place in the Sheremetiev Palace, that tomb. During the euphoria unleashed by the triumph, Stalin again allowed people to show you their admiration and tenderness. You were the soul of the city, one of its most illustrious survivors.

Then, a freezing November afternoon in 1945, the doorman told you that a gentleman—a *foreigner*, he noted—wanted to interview you. Who could it be at that hour? Who would dare to walk around in the cemetery the city had become? It was he: your future guest. You were surprised to receive him: a young member of the British Foreign Service at the embassy in Moscow (but born in Lithuania and brought up in St. Petersburg), by the name of Isaiah Berlin. It was almost 5:00 P.M., and your house was filled with people who were coming and going. From the first moment, the luminosity of his face surprised you, as did his perfect and anachronistic Russian, his lucidity and courtesy. He didn't show you admiration but reverence, though at first the intrusion of other visitors, especially that uncomfortable female student of Assyrology who studied under Vladimir Shilenko, distracted you from his words.

Intoxicated by the words of this stranger who knew you so well, you began to read your poems aloud. It was your gift to him for having come from so far away. He thanked you in silence, enraptured, while you took a chance and read a few stanzas of "Poem Without a Hero" and explained the persecution your son had suffered. And so the hours passed by, until the girl understood she had to go, and you offered to cook something for the Briton, yet another example of your enthusiasm for him.

At around 3:00 A.M.—you were a bit drunk, not from alcohol but from memories—your son Liev came in, and the three of you ate the boiled potatoes you'd prepared, a terrestrial and prosaic tribute to your future guest. Soon after, Liev said he was going to bed; it had been a long and tiring day, like every day in the moribund city. Isaiah Berlin tried to leave, but you told him not to, told him to wait, that there were still other stories to share, other memories to evoke.

What happened during those hours, Anniushka? Did you only speak with him, did you only love him in silence, did you only fall in love with his figure and his mind, or was there something more, a light touch, a caress, a kiss? Why have you never wanted to tell me about it? Or why have you told it to me this way?

Enough freezing me with fear,
I'll invoke Bach's chaconne
and a man will enter when it's over
who will not be my beloved husband,
but we together will be so fearsome

that the twentieth century will be shaken to the root.
Not wanting to I confused him
with the mysterious envoy of destiny,
the one with whom bitter suffering would arrive.
He'll come to my Fontanka Palace,
very late, on that night of fog,
to toast the New Year with wine.
And he will keep in his memory Epiphany night,
the maple tree at the window, the nuptial candles
and the mortal flight of the poem . . .
But it is not the first bouquet of lilies,
nor the ring, nor the sweet prayers:
It's death, that's what he brings me.

Did you love him Anniushka? Did you fall in love like an adolescent with that thirty-five-year-old boy when you were twenty years older than he? What is love? Tell me, Anniushka, I beg you! You know better than anyone! Very well, my friend, I respect your silence. Others, on the other hand, did not respect it. Stalin, transformed into a jealous lover, had your house watched and quickly learned that a man, a foreigner, a British philosopher, a damned spy!, had spent the night with you. Your nun has become a whore!, Stalin bellowed, as rabid as a dog. From that instant, his mercy ended, you'd betrayed him, as all the others had.

The next year you were expelled from the Writers Union, that pig Andrei Zhdanov spit on your poems, ignominy and shame fell on your work by decree. As if it were nothing, the tyrant ordered Liev arrested again. And then there was nothing you could do but fall on your knees before the tyrant, beg his clemency. You wrote horrible poems to praise him, to beg his forgiveness, to commend the life of your son to him. In vain. We began the Cold War, you told Isaiah Berlin twenty years later, when you saw him again in Oxford, shortly before your death. Today, forty-six years later, the confrontation you two unleashed that icy dawn in 1945 is over. Today is the last day of the Union of Socialist Soviet Republics, the last day of Communism, the last day of our era. Only a few seconds remain for our brutal and sterile twentieth century to end—almost ten years early. The past is dead. May it rest in peace. Yours, Oksana Gorenko.

ACT THREE

THE ESSENCE OF THE HUMAN

(1991-2000)

THE INVISIBLE HAND

Russian Federation, 1991-1994

I contemplated the end of the old world. It wasn't invaded by barbarians, its generals did not fall on the battle field, its spies were never captured, no secret weapon devastated its cities or factories, intrigues and threats had no impact on it: It ceased to exist from one day to the next, the way an old tree trunk falls, devoured by rot. Not one stone of it remained on top of another. All the feared Communist ogre needed was a shake—a last thrust—to die. Suicide? More like a drastic euthanasia: In the forests of Belovezhskaia Pushcha, the ambitious threesome—Yeltsin, Kravchuk, and Shushkievich—provided the coup de grâce for a dying dream.

What now, Arkady Ivanovich?, asked Irina. Now we're going to govern this country. She'd stood with him on the barricades at the White House, had served him as spokesperson and squire, had foreseen a massacre, and had finally found herself on the winning side. But Russia was nothing more than fallow land, a name forgotten in History's freezer. How was it to be revived, how was it to be inhabited again? Irina did not celebrate: No doubt, those behind the coup were criminals and fearmongers, but the victors, Yeltsin of strong arms and those who swaggered at his side, were no better.

She'd learned to recognize them: Czar Boris's court was made up of unscrupulous upstarts—phony democrats who thought only about getting rich—and haughty boys fresh from the schoolroom. Irina was more afraid of them than of the apparatchiks. Used to the voracity of the wolves, she didn't have any confidence in those wild pups. Arkady Granin on the other hand had adopted them like a father, the father he never was for his own daughter. Or actually they adopted him, the only person in Yeltsin's intimate circle over the age of forty. They saw him as the most violent and daring of their group: The defense of the White House had turned him back into an adolescent.

Those young men had known one another since 1986. At the urging of Anatoly Chubais, who'd recently entered the Institute of Engineering and Economics, they would meet on Serpent Hill, a vacation chateau on the outskirts of Leningrad. There, carefully watching their backs, suspicious even of the shadows, they shaped their conspiracy: The Soviet economy, they said in hushed tones, was heading for collapse. In those days, they couldn't imagine that Communism would fall in under five years, and they limited themselves to making calculations, revealing fault lines and uncertainties, questioning economic indicators, and reading Friedman and Hayek. To them, the economy of the USSR looked like a swindle: No one knew the true value of things, the artificial prices ruined factories and workers along with them. The State behaved like a stupid, insatiable chimera—it was unable to make the decisions that in a free society are made by thousands or millions. But it was still too soon to say so. They'd have to wait until 1991 for their intuitions to become Government programs.

The leader of these reformers was Yegor Gaidar, a skinny, fragile technocrat who wore sober glasses and had the stare of a vulture. A former member of the Pan-Soviet Institute for System Research, he was chosen by Yeltsin of strong arms to plan Russia's immersion in the market economy. Gaidar quickly enlisted Chubais, who in a single night drove his broken-down yellow Zaporozhets to Moscow, city of wide avenues. Between September and October 1991, while the Soviet Union was dying, Gaidar, Chubais, and the other conspirators of Serpent Hill gathered in a secret place, Dacha Number 15, to compose Yeltsin's economic policy.

Arkady Ivanovich attended those sessions regularly. He wasn't a specialist, but he agreed with the boys' diagnosis: The foundation of the old regime would have to be demolished in one blow and with no reservations. And it would have to be done as soon as possible. The measures would not be popular—they knew that—so it would be necessary to take the people by surprise and make use of Yeltsin's heroic aura to minimize resistance and criticism. Russia would never be able to join the world system unless seven decades of negligence and statism were eliminated completely. The young men made two proposals: Eliminate price controls and privatize industry. The consequences of both would be painful, but that was the price Russians would have to pay to leave their backwardness behind.

A day before announcing his new team, Boris Yeltsin met with Arkady Granin to convince him to accept a post in his government. Arkady refused: I'm a scientist, not an administrator. There are people better prepared for such tasks. What do you think of Gaidar?, Yeltsin asked. In my opinion, he's the best of all. Have you decided what his job will be, Boris Nikolayevich? The only one that really matters: to take charge of the economic reform.

Arkdai smiled: It seemed mad to allow a thirty-two-year-old man to control the destiny of all the Russias, but only someone unaffected by the rancor of the past would have the strength to accept the challenge. Gaidar lacked experience and charisma, but he was wholely committed to Yeltsin. Gaidar is our man, confirmed Arkady.

The next day, the smooth-faced Gaidar became acting prime minister. Anatoly Chubais took charge of privatizing Soviet industry, and Arkady Granin became the President's advisor. Their mission: to invent a country using the ruins of the past.

But do you realize what's going to happen if price controls are eliminated in January? Irina Nikolayevna's voice was a frozen wind. I do know. Inflation will be out of control. I know that. Millions of people will sink into misery. I know that. Well? Don't you and your people feel any compassion, Arkady? Don't you think about the common people, their needs, their hopes? We will free prices because we are thinking about them, Irina Nikolayevna. It will be hard, but there is no other way, as Yeltsin said.

On October 28th, 1991, during one of his last televised speeches that year, Boris Yeltsin addressed the heroic Russian people with the words of his boys: We need to make a reformist advance on a grand scale. At first, it will be tough, but people's lives will improve little by little starting next year. And, unaware of the poverty of millions, he announced the immediate end of price controls. Thus, in one stroke of the pen—as I would write in one of my articles—we Russians joined the ranks of the Third World.

Heading European Group II (EU2) of the International Monetary Fund, Jennifer Wells landed at Moscow airport on November 10th, 1991. A few months earlier, she'd coordinated the publication of *The Economy of the Soviet Union*, a detailed study written in collaboration with specialists from the World Bank, in which she herself prescribed: "Nothing will be more important in achieving the successful transition to a market economy than the cessation of price controls." Accustomed to the turbulence of Africa and Latin America, she wasn't expecting to find a paradise, but by the same token she wasn't expecting a disaster area either: For half a century, the USSR had been her country's nemesis, a rival of the same weight on the see-saw, and its levels of education and sanitation were vastly superior to that of Zaire or Mexico.

She was met at the airport by Anatoly Chubais himself, the man responsible for privatization. The presence of this high-level functionary could only flatter her. Tall, blond, Chubais wasn't even thirty-five, and looking at him, Jennifer understood for the first time that she was a veteran of international finance. She greeted her host in careful Russian—she wasn't really fluent in the language, but she wanted to repay his courtesy with courtesy—and he bowed to kiss her hand. That huge man, he was almost two meters tall, had to conquer her.

During the long ride to Moscow, city of wide avenues, Jennifer enthused about the wide variety of luxury cars—BMWs, Lincolns, Mercedeses, Grand Cherokees, Toyotas, Misubishis, Buicks, and Cadillacs—and the billboards that were invading the landscape; she made sure she congratulated Chubais and his team for their bravery when time came to open the country.

Resistance from the past is still powerful, he pointed out, but we must finish the job. We have to shake off the chains of the gigantic, ubiquitous, bureaucratic, ruinous, and inefficient Soviet state. Jennifer smiled: That man had guts. And when do you plan to initiate the privatizing? As soon as possible. If we don't do it, reality will overtake us. Ever since Gorbachev's time, thousands of people have dedicated themselves to robbing state industries. They dismantle them and sell them piece by piece. Those thefts are, we'd have to admit, primitive forms of privatization. It's up to us to bring that chaotic but positive force under control.

Never before has the complete infrastructure of a state, much less a state of the dimensions of the Soviet Union, been sold off!, thought Jennifer. Privatization, Dr. Wells, her host continued, will have to include as much as possible. Private property is an indispensable condition for individual freedom.

Ever since Gaidar recommended him for the post, Chubais and his men had been elaborating the policies for dismantling the state as rapidly as possible. After analyzing several proposals, they opted for the simplest—sell the industries to the highest bidder. But, given Russia's situation, who has the money to buy a barber shop or a food store, let alone a textile mill or a factory?, asked Jennifer. There have been capitalist enterprises in the Soviet Union, on a small scale, since the beginning of perestroika, Dr. Wells. We imagine capitalism began in England or the United States in the same way. The initial accumulation of capital in a market economy is virtually criminal in nature. There are always a few individuals ready to take risks and take advantage of the situation: Those are the enterprising people we're looking for.

Over the course of the following days, Jennifer talked with Gaidar and the young turks surrounding Yeltsin, and what she admired in all of them was their determination. Her ideas were as radical as theirs: The Soviet economy was a hoax, Russian citizens lived in an imaginary country, and they must be forced into the real world. From now on, they'd have to earn their bread by the sweat of their brow. I'm not fooling myself, Chubais confessed at the end of their meeting. People will hate me for being the man who sold Russia. That's the poison we'll all have to drink.

And, as Yeltsin ordered, on January 2nd, 1992, price controls on consumer items were lifted. Within a few weeks, 99% of Russians lost their savings. Panic, weeping, sorrow, and rage (the announcement of a winter of misery) flooded the cities, towns, and villages of the country. Meanwhile, the IMF team celebrated the measure as a great accomplishment.

Sent by *Ogoniok*, I managed to catch Jennifer Wells just after the announcement, as she was leaving Chubais's offices, which were in a broken-down building in Novi Arbat. I'd heard her name mentioned weeks earlier at an editorial meeting, and I immediately became interested in her career. The editor Vitali Korotich described her to me as the all-powerful and implacable envoy of the IMF—the person responsible for transforming the country, or what remained of the country, into a free-market economy. My research into her impressive CV (the press called her the sorceress of finance) confirmed her ruthlessness, and allowed a glimpse of her hidden vulnerability. One thing was certain: The photos did her no justice (her face always looked sour). At forty-six, she still possessed a cruel beauty, well-established with her years.

When I stopped her on the street (she was accompanied by a driver or bodyguard supplied by the Ministry, who was doubtless there to spy on her as well as protect her), she stepped back from me with an air of suspicion and told me she only had a few seconds because she had to fly back to Washington. Journalists clearly intimidated her, and she tried to give the impression she was not only aggressive but sardonic. May I ask you a few questions, Dr. Wells?

I noted that throughout the interview she never looked me in the eye, and that she would only recite her talking points without listening to my replies or reacting to my disquiet, as if she were speaking to an anonymous mass and not to a flesh-and-blood individual. Along with the immediate release of price controls and the privatization of medium-size and small businesses, she summarized, the IMF recommends raising the price of consumer goods, fees, and taxes, iron-bound fiscal austerity, and drastic monetary reform.

For Jennifer, the essential point was the creation of an authentic market. If we, the citizens of Russia, could manage to control the economy in a direct fashion, each of us subject to the laws of supply and demand, the rest would follow suit. Perhaps at the outset there would be imbalances, a few people would become millionaires while others would sink into poverty (that was, she pointed out, the way competition worked, both in free societies and in the jungle). There would be a period of inflation and unemployment, but the invisible hand of the market would close the wounds and bring benefits to the destitute.

What about the suffering of the people? Doesn't that matter to you?, I dared to interrupt her, perturbed by her dogmatism. It was the same question Irina had put to Arkady a few days earlier. Her face austere and haughty, Jennifer did not flinch: The money you were using wasn't real.

She said that. Without looking me in the eye.

On meeting him in 1988, Vladimir Guzinki struck Jack Wells as a naïve, provincial, nervous, not especially promising Jew. This was his first trip to the West, and he was accompanied by an obscure bureaucrat from

Moscow, Yuri Luzhkov. Everything dazzled him: the skyscrapers, the well-stocked shops, the tropical fruit, the clothing boutiques, the way teenagers dressed, the way each person did whatever he liked. To Wells, these two characters—one finicky, the other dull—seemed to come right out of an old-time comedy, the two country bumpkins who suddenly find themselves face-to-face with the big city.

From a poor family—his grandfather was shot by the Bolsheviks—Gusinsky studied acting, and for years he dedicated himself to putting on one play after another until he finally realized that his histrionic talents were not equal to his ambition. One night, after a performance as insipid and depressing as all the others, he stumbled on a gold mine: an enormous wooden spool around which dozens of meters of copper wire were wound. Eureka! Forgetting the theater, he set about cutting and assembling that mana from heaven, turning it into thousands of bracelets; young Muscovites bought them like hot-cakes, convinced of their mystical or therapeutic qualities.

With his earnings, Gusinsky rented a run-down factory on the outskirts of Moscow, where six stamping machines printed the label "METAL" on his ever-more-popular copper bracelets, which he could now turn out at the rate of fifty thousand per day. This meant a daily profit of 259,000 rubles (the salary of a team of workers). In 1988, he founded a consulting office that gained him contact with an investment group based in Washington D.C., axis of the cosmos. Thanks to that group, Gusinsky and Luzhkov travelled to the United States at the end of 1988 to make contact with potential investors.

Marjorie Kraus, who was closely linked with financial circles in Washington, arranged a dinner in honor of the two Russians, which was attended by business types and politicians, including Jack and Jennifer Wells. By then, Gusinsky had chosen the name for his new business: Most (he realized, while he was dealing with a cash machine, another device he'd never seen before) means "bridge" in Russian. Most will be our cash machine, he promised Marjorie. On that occasion, Wells was courteous, but he never thought that out-of-place little man would become one of the most powerful businessmen in Russia. Four years later, Most was a gigantic investment bank, and Yuri Luzhkov the all-powerful mayor of Moscow.

When do you have to go back to Russia?, Wells asked Jennifer in February of 1992. In a couple of weeks; we have to do something to contain the hyperinflation and discontent. If we don't, the reforms could come to nothing. Why do you ask? Remember Vladimir Gusinsky? He asked me to visit him in Moscow.

You should have gone, you can't imagine what it was like! Zhenia Alexandrovna was tall and full-figured, with bee-stung lips, hair dyed a reddish color, and thigh-length boots. She talked like a peasant; Oksana had never heard so many curses as she heard from her lips. Daughter of the head of a plastics factory—and for that reason always well-stocked with cash—she looked twenty-one or twenty-two, though she wasn't over seventeen. Oksana met her at a secret party she'd attended behind her father's back and had instantly attached herself to the whirlwind that was Zhenia.

Zhenia danced by herself, self-absorbed, with provocative, obscene movements. Sheathed in a tight miniskirt, her long legs bare and with round breasts she never tired of showing off, Zhenia was fascinated with the idea she was desired and admired, the untouched center of the world. But, despite the brusque eroticism her adolescent body emitted, she always rejected all offers and returned home alone, preserving herself as the untouchable black virgin of the Muscovite *reiveri*.

Oksana was dazzled by her tales of infinite parties, alcohol and hash (the latest fad), indiscriminate sex and crazed DJ's; she couldn't take her eyes off her. Zhenia was an irresistible magnet: Just knowing she was nearby made Oksana's stomach turn. Indifferent to her desire, Zhenia told her about the *Gagarin Party*, the greatest *reiveri* in history, celebrated in Moscow's Cosmos Pavilion on December 14th, 1991.

Insane, insane (her incredibly white hands were dancing). Just imagine: They had Yuri Gagarin's space ship hanging there, I swear, the real one, the real one. Zhenia had the habit of repeating each word twice: But don't cry, all is not lost, this spring they're putting on Gagarin Party II. Crazy, crazy!

The necklace Zhenia wore around her neck, her long, firm neck, was a clear symptom of the times: Alongside a medal with the hammer and sickle, perhaps hocked by a Hero of the Soviet Union, she boasted a hippie peace symbol, a medal of Saint George (dragon included), and a skull which only a couple of years earlier would have been impossible to see in Moscow. When Oksana asked what the meaning of those charms was, Zhenia said she hadn't the slightest fucking idea, that she simply liked the figures.

And why the hell are you looking me, stupid?, she asked Oksana the first time they met. Zhenia was used to stares of admiration or envy, but Oksana's stare managed to upset her. Sorry. Never be sorry, little girl, never, never. It's out of style.

Oksana started to walk away, ashamed, but Zhenia grabbed her arm. That contact lasted a lifetime. And what the hell do you do, if you don't mind my asking? You don't dance, you don't sing, you just stand there, staring at me like some strange animal. No not a strange animal . . . muttered Oksana. Well?

I write.

Oksana had never revealed her secret. It was the most closely guarded part of her intimate being, and she had no idea why she'd told this complete stranger. When she heard that, Zhenia's attitude changed; she set aside her volcanic histrionics—her favorite disguise—and examined her new friend from head to toe. And what do you write? Nothing. Forget about it. I'd like to read it, seriously, seriously. It isn't worthwhile. I *want* to see it. And what's your name, girl? Oksana Gorenko. Well, I'm Zhenia, but I think you knew that already. Come on, let's get out of here. These jerks make me crazy, crazy.

Zhenia walked Oksana all the way home. They walked together through the snow, ceaselessly exchanging stories. Oksana hadn't shared so many hours with anyone for a long time—she'd spent years fleeing other people, and she was shut away in her solitude and the icy togetherness of her parents. Now I'll tell you my secret, Zhenia said, when they were about to part company. I compose. Understand? You and I will create a band, a band. I'll write the music, and you supply the lyrics. What do you say? You haven't even read what I write. I'd like to, I'd like to, she declared, kissing her on the corner of her mouth.

The next day, Zhenia picked Oksana up and brought her to an empty warehouse on the outskirts of the city—it used to be part of my father's factory, but now it's empty, ready for us, she explained. Your new headquarters. Zhenia spent hour after hour there: There was left-over food, clothes, records, and pirated tapes, enormous photographs of Viktor Tsoi, the lead singer of Kino; Boris Grebenshikov, the founder of Akvarium; and Yuri Shevchuk, of DDT. Have you listened to them? Geniuses, geniuses, right?

Oksana's knowledge of music was scanty compared to Zhenia's, who called herself a living encyclopedia of Russian rock. She flipped through her cassettes, chose her favorite, and put it into a luxurious Japanese cassette player, which contrasted sharply with the filthy floor.

You know Tsoi, right? Too bad, too bad. Zhenia pretended to weep. He killed himself two years ago after recording his last album. The big problem with Kino is that everyone loves them, even me. I saw Tsoi in his last concert in Luzhniki Stadium. I don't know how many of us were there, let's say fifty thousand or one hundred thousand, it's all the same. Poor guy, poor guy.

Oksana knew some of the songs, but she'd never before bothered to learn the name of the singer. Enough, enough, now let's listen to something by Akvarium, very Western, very *stilagi*, I don't know, I don't know . . . Zhenia again changed the tape even before the first song was over: And this one by Shevchuk . . . Him I do know, for a while he lived in my hometown, in Sverdlovsk, where he played with a band called Urfin Juis. Well, well, you never cease to surprise me, girl. This song is from his last album, *Aktrisa Visna*. It looks like they're going on tour this year, we have to see them. Okay, enough fooling around, let's get to work. Show me your stuff.

Oksana dug around in her knapsack and brought out some typewritten sheets: Her friend snatched them away. They're worthless, I've got no idea why I'm letting you see them. But Zhena read aloud:

Rose of the Russian nation
you're cold and capricious
like poetry and prose
in the furnace of a locomotive
    like
a disaster under the summit
    open rose
    rose of the Russian nation
    thorn in my heart
rose of the Russian nation
I shouldn't pick you with my hands
trample you under my feet
you're armed to the teeth
    you're made of rosy flesh
    all silences and threats
    no metempsychosis in you
    you're the direct path to the heavens
of the neurosis of dawn
full of intimate phosphorescence

—like the marvelous and intoxicating
moment—: Rose

When she finished reading, Zhenia wiped away some tears. Then, saying nothing—Oksana was hanging by a thread—she left the room and came back with a guitar. She improvised a slow, foreseeable melody, but her harsh, tense, and out-of-tune voice seemed to Oksana the perfect complement to her words. It was only then she discovered in them some value. Zhenia polished them, Zhenia gave them life. Zhenia tranformed them, for the first time, into poetry.

When she finished, Oksana wept too.

Jennifer swore she'd never again take a small Aeroflot plane; subject to the whims of turbulence and sudden changes of cabin pressure, they were a perfect metaphor for the new Russia. Anatoly Chubais had asked her to come, as a special favor—that way she could confirm the status of privatization *in situ*, he explained—and by then she could deny the blond giant nothing. From their first meeting, a frank and direct relationship was established between them. It wasn't that they were pals—neither was known for being disposed to make friends—but there was a confluence of styles. They were both convinced of the validity of their ideas and were willing to put them into practice at any cost. But both also knew how to step back at the last moment. They were stubborn but never stupid.

After landing at Nizhni Novgorod—the former Gorki, where Andrei Sakharov, maker of light, spent years in exile—Jennifer Wells had to board a dumpy bus that brought her to Literacy House, where the historic auction would take place. The idea had come from Boris Nemtsov, the mayor, who was intent on transforming his city (that lugubrious and moribund city) into the leader of modern Russia. They were auctioning off all kinds of businesses: workshops, textile plants, grocery stores, beauty shops, shoe stores, hardware shops, newsstands, clothing stores. If we publicize the event properly, Nemtsov assured everyone, the example will spread throughout the nation. Jennifer recognized that the proposal wasn't bad: It would allow citizens who had no contact with business culture to begin at the lowest rung in the ladder.

When the Muscovite delegation reached the former Literacy House—I'd already been there for hours, along with dozens of journalists brought in from Moscow—there were no signs of the idyllic reception Nemtsov had promised. On the contrary: Hundreds of demonstrators were shouting slogans against privatization and reform. The shock therapy had produced its first victims, and workers of all ages were waving signs saying things like: GAIDAR AND GHUBAIS, CARRY OUT YOUR EXPERIMENTS SOMEWHERE ELSE! or DEMOCRATS: NOTHING BUT SPECULATORS AND THIEVES!

Timid and distant, Gaidar couldn't control his nerves and was surrounded by his bodyguards, like an old-time *apparatchik*. Stay near me at all times, Chubais ordered Jennifer, protecting her from the pushing and shoving. Is this the welcoming committee you prepared for us?, she joked, quaking in her boots. Follow me, Doctor, we'll do what we came to do no matter what.

The group moved to the rear door of the House, where they ran into another, even rowdier, group of demonstrators. Chubais lost his temper and began to throw punches. Jennifer protected herself as best she could, and Gaidar, suspicious, kept his distance. For a moment, I thought this would be the end of the architects of Russian privatization, Chubais and Gaidar. And the end of that good-looking and unbearable functionary from the IMF. Auctions? To hell with auctions!, shouted the workers. Are you from some other country?

They were. Gaidar and Chubais wanted to transform Russia into *some other country*. When they reached the auditorium, the mood had changed: While we could see the suspicion and mistrust of most of those present, we also sensed a certain expectation and, yes, perhaps a touch of hope. A thin, pale guy with a huge mustache, wearing a silk shirt and a red bow-tie, ascended the platform. Without waiting for the Moscow delegation to take their seats, he launched into his pitch: The bidding is now open for beauty shop number 19, located at 47 Pushkina Street. The silence in the hall lasted a century. Then an old man with yellowish thin hair raised his hand. One hundred thousand rubles. 150,000. 180,000.

Jennifer's heart leapt: She was witnessing a historic moment, the establishment of capitalism in Russia. You can see it for yourself, Chubais whispered, today we're leaving the Soviet system behind, it's a great victory.

A great victory, Jennifer confirmed some hours later, back in Moscow, city of wide avenues. She was to meet her husband in a luxurious restaurant in the center of the city, near the Lubyanka, the old KGB prison, where not long before a group of young people had knocked down the statue of Felix Dzerzhinsky, its hated founder.

It's incredible what's going on here, said Wells. In a single day you can walk from the Middle Ages to the twenty-first century. Just look at this place! We wouldn't be eating any better in New York! Jennifer did not like the idea of her husband accompanying her to Russia—she was also afraid of the celebrated beauty of our women—but when Wells went over his tightly-packed interview agenda, she thought that the two of them could perhaps join forces. Who better than her husband to help local business people. In the current situation, any transaction is good news.

While Jennifer was with Chubais and Gaidar in Nizhni Novgorod, Wells spoke in Moscow with a Russian-born U.S. citizen: Boris Jordan. Descended from an old aristocratic family that had emigrated to New York, Jordan investigated investment opportunities for Crédit Suisse-First Boston. Everything is still very uncontrolled, he revealed to Wells the first time they met, but in a few years this is going to be an ideal place to invest. The Bank still has reservations because the market has yet to stabilize, but when that happens we should take advantage of it. He then mentioned that he visited the Committee of State Properties, Chubais's domain, every single day.

What do you do there?, Wells asked. Nothing. Or a lot, depending on how you look at it. Setting things up, getting to know people. You have no idea what you get with flattery, some advice, or a small gift. The investment is minimal, but the results may be marvelous (as he spoke, Jordan showed off his perfect teeth). For now, Crédit Suisse-First Boston only gives advice about privatization, that's the deal with Chubais. And we do it for nothing. We don't charge a damn ruble. That way, if something goes bad, no one can accuse us of anything. But if things work as we hope they will . . .

I get you, muttered Wells, and I'm interested. Very interested. The big problem is information, Jordan went on. If you don't have high-level contacts, you don't find out about anything: How can you know what you should buy in this gigantic flea market? There are no reliable indices, no indicators, nothing, my friend, nothing. Which is why we have to do so much spade work to find out where the treasure is. We know it exists, but it's not easy to recognize.

Jordan finished his whiskey: What's your field, Jack, what interests you? Biotechnology. You're nuts, my friend! Here they're barely selling chocolate factories, it's going to take a long time to get to those levels. But we will . . . How right you are, we will. Let me tell you a secret: In Russia you can buy anything. If you've got enough money, you can get anything from an aircraft carrier to a nuclear missile, believe me. But you need to count on someone *inside*, someone who has the information you're looking for, otherwise you're lost. Can you recommend someone, Boris? Jordan was silent for a few seconds, more to accentuate his importance than to meditate. Maybe, I don't know. It's always possible . . . Around here, *everything* is possible.

Cheers!, Wells toasted with his wife a few hours later. I like this country, Jen. There's something magical to it, it's virgin territory, the possibilities are infinite. Boris Jordan is an authentic worker bee, and he knows what he's talking about.

Jennifer smiled. Her husband hadn't been so enthusiastic, so empathetic, for years: In Russia, they had a second honeymoon. Even so, I'd advise you not to get too excited, she warned him. I know through Chubais that the resistance of the *red directors* is still enormous. They want to take control of the businesses they're running and don't want foreigners meddling in their affairs. Chubais fights them, thinking that any outside buyer is better than those parasites, but I don't know if he'll manage to get rid of them. Wells's spirits didn't flag; he took another bite of his salmon and cleansed his palate with champagne.

You heard what Yeltsin said, she went on, they need millions of property owners, not hundreds of millionaires. People are suspicious, Jack, they think privatization will only benefit a few, and that can hurt the whole process. You're exaggerating, Jen, Wells contradicted her. From what I've seen, people here are crazy about capitalism. Just go out onto the street: The squares are packed with people selling things. It's the most powerful force in the universe, Jen, greed. Nothing can stop it. I hope you're right, she added. And when do you meet with Gusinsky? Tomorrow. Meanwhile, I'll be with Gaidar, and maybe I'll even see Yeltsin. Jack Wells raised his glass: To us! Jennifer seconded the motion: Yes, to us! A second honeymoon.

Irina's frustration was like a cancer invading her organs: first her eyes and ears, then her throat, and finally her guts. Perhaps the young technocrats were less corrupt and cynical than their predecessors, but they had inherited the same blindness. The worst thing about the Soviet Union is that it had never existed: The distance between the speeches of its leaders and daily life was an abyss. The Party men spoke of a rich and powerful nation, a country full of possibilities, where misery had been eradicated and the workers were the owners of the factories, where Communism was erasing injustices and the only passion of its citizens was solidarity: lies and more lies. In the world of facts, the ordinary citizen had nothing—not even freedom. The economy was in chaos, the *nomenklatura* hoarded all the privileges, and rot suffocated any hope of improvement. Now that façade had fallen away, but the face that remained in its place was even more unbearable.

Irina hadn't fought for that, hadn't abandoned biology (her only faith), and even her own daughter, Oksana, so that nothing would change. Arkady and his friends—those boys in pink undies, as Vice-President Rutskoy called them—were also founding an unreal nation. Instead of helping ordinary citizens, they were helping a small minority. Wherever she went, Irina would run into these *novi russki*, and she hated them. While Arkady saw them as examples of the capitalist mentality and praised their ambition, Irina considered them boors who were devoid of culture, consumption machines who only lived to show off their wealth.

The jokes about them that proliferated barely did them justice. A *new Russian* brags to another: Look, I bought this tie in Paris, and it cost me $400. The other retorts: I bought the same tie, and it cost *me* $500. That was their morality and their intelligence. They'd sell their souls to the devil, not for immortality but for an Armani suit and a Louis Vuitton bag.

Like most people, Irina celebrated the fall of Yegor Gaidar in December of 1992, but she felt no relief in seeing the rise of Viktor Chernomyrdin, the former Soviet Minister of Natural Gas, an obscure administrator who had risen from one position to another since the time of Brezhnev, the cunning mummy. Arkady, on the other hand, was still enthralled with Yeltsin and celebrated each one of his moves. His alcoholism, his mood swings, and his authoritarian streak mattered little to Arkady. In his eyes, Yeltsin's heroic behavior at the White House exempted him from any criticism.

In order to get the support he needed to pursue his economic policy, Yeltsin, in April of 1993, forced Congress to hold a referendum. After a feverish campaign—and millions of rubles scattered everywhere—the people again gave him their confidence. Disgusted, Irina decided to distance herself from politics. She wouldn't stop collaborating with the human rights movement, but she no longer felt she had the strength to face the Russian debacle. Thanks to Yelena Bonner, Andrei Sakharov's widow, she found work in a pharmaceutical laboratory, and, no matter how boring her work was—the era in which she was developing her artificial life project was now in the distant past—it at least allowed her to escape the present. Stepping aside, stepping back from newspapers and television (the nation seemed only to be waiting for the thousandth rerun of *The Rich Also Weep*), she would perhaps recover her scientific life, that placid and anonymous life that life History had torn away from her.

But History again shook Irina totally, when she discovered the results of the second stage of privatization the government had set into motion. After the first phase (public auctions), a measure that did not fascinate Irina but which she considered essential, the Committee for State Properties accelerated the mechanism that would transform all citizens into owners (in theory) of the wealth of the nation. To achieve this, Anatoly Chubais had distributed 148 million vouchers with a nominal value of 10,000 rubles—and a real value of 25. These vouchers would be distributed throughout the nation, and with them (in theory) any citizen could acquire a part of the auctioned-off industries. Yeltsin announced the measure in August of 1992. According to him, the measure would end the planned economy. No sooner did Irina receive the vouchers, sepia-toned stacks not very different from banknotes, than she tossed them into a drawer and forgot about them. She didn't touch them again until the scandal exploded in Moscow, city of wide avenues.

What took place during the interval? Everywhere, in metro stations and bus stops, in kiosks and food stores, huge signs reading WE BUY VOUCHERS appeared, while in the main squares there were people with loudspeakers asking, "What Are You Going to Do with Your Vouchers?" The boys in pink panties hadn't calculated that their market price concept would end up being controlled by the laws of supply and demand, which meant that those who had liquid assets could buy the vouchers cheap and sell them at a profit. Their inexperience had fomented a tumultuous speculation. As usual, a minority would take control of the industries, while the majority would have to be happy with the crumbs. For example: One man, Mikhail Khodorkovsky (the *Kaminski* of my future novel) managed to get hold of millions of vouchers and more than one hundred industries. Where was the equity? And where the justice? The already impoverished Russian people would be left without vouchers, without property, and without money.

Dogs!, exploded Irina. Couldn't these damn technocrats have foreseen this? Though she was not in agreement with the ideas of Vice-President Rutskoy or the President of the Congress of the Deputies of the People, Ruslan Khasbulatov, Yeltsin's principle enemies, Irina thought that in this case they were right. The Communists hadn't managed to destroy the nation in seventy years, but the democrats were on the verge of doing so in two!

As I was able to verify years later, Jack Wells, in June of 1993, made another trip to Moscow, this time without his wife. Unlike Jennifer, who was growing more and more irritated by the day with her Russian counterparts, Wells thought the Russian reforms were an absolute success. Of course the country was living through a period of turbulence caused by the voracity of primitive capitalism, but thanks to this shock treatment, Russia would soon join the global economy. And, while inflation was high—despite the predictions of the IMF, the authorities had not managed to control it—the fall of the ruble was just another lure for foreign investors,. The only disadvantage Wells could see in Russia was the growing insecurity of its capital.

When he reached Moscow, he was met by an armed driver at the wheel of a Mercedes S-600 and an escort consisting of three gorillas in an enormous black Land Cruiser—all courtesy of Bank Most, as I found out later. His partners never stopped lamenting the kidnappings, thefts, and murders that put their businesses in danger. Moscow was looking more and more like the Chicago of the '30s. Even a sort of Mafia had appeared: the Solntsevo Brotherhood.

According to Arkady's associates, the Brotherhood had become the absolute owners of southwestern Moscow, where its members shook down the local businesses and made money from prostitution, gambling, and stolen cars. The police didn't dare stand up to them, and it was said that their leaders, Mijas and Averia Sr.—the local versions of Lucky Luciano and Al Capone—owned a network of banks and legal businesses in Moscow and numerous other cities. The clashes between rival gangs, especially between Solntsevo and the Chechnyans, had already produced thousands of bodies: 1993 was still young, but there had already been twenty-three thousand homicides, not to mention the twenty-five thousand disappearances.

To compensate for all these threats, Gusinsky offered Wells his first plunge into the delirious nightlife that had grown up in the capital. Sex had been taboo under Communism—Brezhnev, the cunning mummy, was as prudish as an Orthodox priest—perestroika had not only loosened the ties on the economy but also those on the flesh. Thanks to the presence of myriad solitary businessmen, who suddenly found themselves thousands of kilometers from their wives (Wells, for example), the erotic shows, the *American Bars*, the sex-shops, the massage parlors, the saunas and *hamams*, the peep-shows, strip tease joints, call girls, and gay hangouts, to say nothing of the classified notices in magazines and newspapers, and even the matrimony agencies, had proliferated endlessly. This was the logical end of capitalism: You could realize all your fantasies, as long as you could pay the going rate. No sooner had Wells walked into his suite than he was visited by two young ladies who looked as if they'd just stepped out of *Andrei*, the Russian version of *Playboy*. All courtesy of Most Bank.

Thanks to incentives like these, Wells became even more enthusiastic about the exuberant Russian market. Boris Jordan had told him it was just a matter of time, that the country was going to turn into a gold mine, and that moment had come. The best example of how someone could become rich over night was Bill Browder, another American who'd moved to Moscow and set up a gigantic investment fund. His story was exciting and paradoxical: Grandson of Earl Browder, the celebrated leader of the U.S. Communist Party until 1945, he'd acquired an interest in the old Soviet factories at ridiculous prices.

By then, Wells was already active in several businesses, ranging from cosmetics to food supply, but his main objective was to dominate the biomedical industry. The multinationals would soon be on the scene, and his only advantages were time and the quality of his contacts. He repeatedly begged Boris Jordan to find him an advisor, until Jordan finally found him the ideal person: a scientist in Yeltsin's inner circle, a man, so he was told, with first-hand knowledge of the Russian pharmaceutical sector. A man who moved effortlessly through the corridors of power.

When Arkady Ivanovich Granin entered the Café Aist, Wells was not overly impressed, despite the fact that, according to Jordan, this man with extremely white hair and a steely gaze was a symbol of the New Russia. On the other hand, Arkady recognized Wells as the prototypical Western businessman, direct and ambitious, and he praised the fact that Wells was willing to risk his money in an industry that, after a reasonable amount of time, would benefit the ordinary citizen.

Biology, Arkady declared, was never a priority for Soviet science, especially compared to mathematics or physics. Even so, hundreds of factories and laboratories were built all over the country. There are plants in the most unlikely places: Our bureaucrats were obsessed with confining scientists in the most remote regions, like Adademgorodok or Novosibirsk.

From there he went on to tell Wells the tragic story of biology during the Stalin years, painted a picture of the perfidious Lysenko, recounted the arrest and torture of Vavilov, talked about Biopreparat and the biological weapons program—without, of course, going into details. He summarized his own misfortunes, his crisis of conscience, his rebellion, his capture, and his psychiatric imprisonment. He ended his speech with a vehement defense of private enterprise: The State ruins everything, the great scientific discoveries were made by exceptionally talented and tenacious beings, not by bureaucratic structures. In science, as in economic affairs, privatization is indispensable.

Wells had almost no interest in Arkady's jeremiad, but Jordan was not mistaken in choosing him. Despite his tendency to sermonize, Granin could become the ideal partner.

The current situation of science in Russia is lamentable, Arkady went on, not even taking a breath. Researchers who would be prominent elsewhere are barely able to feed their families here. Some, the best, emigrate to U.S. or European universities, while others become taxi drivers or business people. It's contemptible. If it weren't for George Soros's financial support, we'd be facing a total catastrophe. But make no mistake about it, Mr. Wells, Russia is a great nation, it was before and will be again in the future. But we have to allow individuals to reach their potential, support them so they can be free to do research and create.

That's exactly what I'm looking for, Jack interrupted him: to make scientific research in your country profitable. You have the human capital and the infrastructure, I can supply resources and know-how. Arkady calmed down and finally took a sip of vodka: Tell me how I can help you, Mr. Wells.

Wells launched into a summary of his plans, talked to him about DNAW, about the Human Genome Project, and about the infinite possibilities that would open once the human genome was fully mapped. Arkady listed with delight, happy to return for an instant to science, the world he'd abandoned to dedicate himself to politics. He had no doubts: He would do everything possible to help Jack.

Tell me where to begin, Wells pleaded. I've got an idea. Many of the old biological weapons factories have been converted into civilian installations. There is a small laboratory right here in Moscow, not very extensive, but very specialized. It may interest you. I can arrange a visit for this very week. Wonderful. And how can I thank you for your help, Dr. Granin? I'm not doing this for you or me but for my country. Besides, let me tell you that we have a superlative contact in that laboratory.

That's where my wife, Irina Nikolayevna, works.

The same building, the White House, proud seat of the Russian Parliament on the banks of the Moskova, symbol of resistance against Communist brutality, was now becoming an emblem of disenchantment. Boris Yeltsin of strong arms was proving that democracy was a mask capable of justifying any excess. The enemies of the President, the grim Alexandr Rutskoy and the upstart Ruslan Khasbulatov, were hardly models of liberalism themselves. To the contrary, they'd almost certainly be more despotic than Yeltsin, but at least in a formal way (and democracy is above all a matter of form). After all, they had been elected by the people. Nothing justified their arrest. In sum: In the useless and regrettable confrontation between Yeltsin and Parliament, there were only losers.

My article on the events of October 1993 was the last I wrote for *Ogoniok*. Like other magazines, it too was beginning to crack, and very little remained of the spirit that had animated it during perestroika. Now it was filled with advertisements, cheap photos, and frivolous articles. In a time when almost anything could be said—attacks on the President excepted—the media were becoming insignificant and banal. The best proof of our decadence were the naked women who now decorated our back cover. Even so, I attempted to write about the squabble between the President and the Parliament with the greatest objectivity possible.

I tried to reflect the frustration and anger that the events aroused in me. No one could accuse me of sympathizing with Yeltsin's rivals, but I also deplored the behavior of the police and the government. Even if the President was the least of the current evils, that did not erase his infamy. When Yeltsin ordered the attack on the White House on October 4th, 1993, our chance to be a civilized nation disappeared forever. In the clutches of barbarity, corruption, the mafia, and misery, only the idea of consolidating our incipient freedoms stirred us. And now even that faith had vanished. Nearly twenty thousand people were arrested by the police, without arrest orders. The newspapers that supported Rutskoy and Khasbulatov, or that held opinions contrary to those of the President, were shut down.

Ogoniok published my article but censored my personal opinions. Ultimately, it sounded like fiery praise of Yeltsin and "democratic forces." Disgusted, I resigned from the magazine and joined the editorial staff of NTV, the country's first private television company, recently bought by Vladimir Gusinsky, who promised to defend freedom of expression at all costs.

Lenia Golúbkov was short and chubby, with unkempt hair. He boasted an opaque metal tooth, a product of Russian social security. The only thing that differentiated Lenia Golúbkov from any other citizen was that he didn't exist, or that he only existed for the millions of viewers who, like Irina, saw him every day on television. Well, perhaps there was another difference between the slovenly character and the rest of his compatriots: Lenia Golúbkov had become rich overnight and had become the personification of the "Russian way of life."

Irina detested his vulgarity and his clumsiness, detested the way his creators got rich on the credulity of the people. Because Lenia Golúbkov, like his stupid family, was the last and most irresponsible publicity stunt concocted by Sergey Mavrodi, the owner of MMM. And what the devil was MMM? Irina, like most viewers, had no idea: the dazzling success of the business had its roots in that ignorance.

MMM's commercials had begun to appear a few years earlier, when hyperinflation reached its critical phase. Very quickly they captured the attention of my compatriots. In its first ad, a group of people saw the letters MMM in the sky, as if it were a divine sign. Then an announcer shouted: *Everyone knows us*. In the second, even more grotesque ad, a butterfly fluttered toward the MMM logo, while a voice screamed, "We're flying from darkness to light." In the final ad, Lenia Golúbkov appeared together with his brother, a tattoo-covered miner, and they were sitting opposite a bottle of vodka and a jar of pickles. Don't you remember the advice our parents gave us?, Ivan asked. They taught us to work in an honorable way. You just go from one place to another with your stocks, you're a parasite! And Lenia answered back: You're wrong, brother, I'm not a parasite. I use my bulldozer, I make money honorably and buy stocks that give me dividends. You were dreaming about a factory, but you can't build it by yourself. But if we all contribute, we can build one that will provide us with earnings and feed us. I'm not a parasite, I'm a partner. Then an announcer broke in: "It's true, we're partners. MMM."

According to the commercials, Lenia Golúbkov, thanks to MMM, was able to buy leather boots for his wife, then a fur coat; finally, he took her to San Francisco, to support the national team in the World Cup matches. If Lenia Golúbkov, a luckless bore, could prosper, why couldn't many others get rich? All they had to do was invest in MMM, whose stocks promised a 3,000% annual profit.

In June of 1993, Mavrodi got government authorization to sell 991,000 shares in his business, with a nominal value of 1,000 rubles each (in reality, he sold millions of shares without saying so). Up to this point, everything seemed admirably clear: In any civilized country, a company offers its shares for sale and submits them to the game of supply and demand. But in Russia no one had the slightest idea how the stock market worked. Irina almost exploded: The crook was selling stock in a company whose only product was its stock! Pure Capitalism! MMM only produced its advertisements!

In February of 1993, MMM's stock reached 1,600 rubles, and by July it had risen to 105,600. Why didn't anyone notice the fraud? Perhaps the reformists were too busy preparing the attack on the White House to watch out for the interests of the citizens. On July 26th, 1994, Irina joined the thirty thousand demonstrators who'd gathered outside the offices of MMM at 26 Varshavska Street to demand the return of their money. Pursued by fiscal authorities, Mavrodi had announced that the value of the stocks would go from 100,000 rubles to 1,000. After a few hours, the riot police charged the crowd. Irina suffered a hard blow to her back that left her in pain for several months.

What happened to you?, asked Arkady. Aside from domestic matters, they barely spoke. She couldn't forgive him for teaming up with Jack Wells to take over her laboratory. Thanks to the spurious laws passed by Yeltsin of strong arms, Wells had paid a few thousand dollars for an installation worth ten times that amount. As Irina told me shortly after, that agreement seemed to her an unforgivable betrayal.

Courtesy of *your* government's security forces, Arkady Ivanovich. The capitalism we so desperately wanted. First a successful capitalist steals people's savings, and then the police beat the crap out of those who dare to protest. Wonderful market economy! Calm down! Are we really fighting about this? I hate to say it, but we were better off before. How can you say that? How can you say what you're saying? You're blind,

Arkady Ivanovich. Blind and deaf, like Yeltsin and his ministers. They're not concerned about the citizens or democracy or freedom. The only thing that matters to them is selling off the country to the highest bidder. What you all are doing is vile. Are you going to tell me you helped Jack Wells for the good of Russia? Arkady turned away. How unfair you are, how irresponsible! In effect, they had nothing left to say to each other.

After the July demonstration, the new prime minister, Viktor Chernomyrdin, went on television to calm people down. And, as if they were people of flesh and blood, he addressed Lenia Golúbkov and his family, warning them of the dangers of investing in MMM. Meanwhile, Mavrodi broadcast more advertisements. Unlike the state, we have never tricked you, he affirmed in one, and we never will. Garbage on top of garbage! howled Irina. But that was merely the beginning of Mavrodi's counteroffensive. On August 19th, he sponsored a meeting in which thousands of people took part (in all likelihood the first beneficiaries of the pyramid). Standing before an adoring crowd, Mavrodi announced that he would present himself as a candidate for the Presidency of Russia: The state is incapable of carrying out its functions, he declared, it's time private enterprise replaced it. The state is jealous of us because MMM does things better.

On October 31st, Mavrodi announced himself a candidate for the Duma from the new Party of the People's Capital (another business) and won with relative ease. Irina couldn't believe it: Accompanied by his stupid wife, Miss Zaporozhoie 1992, the wretch celebrated his judicial immunity.

Luckily, just before he assumed his new role, the government decided to act against him. He was arrested for fraud and tax evasion. A man of infinite tricks, Mavrodi went on manipulating the media from his jail cell, presenting himself as a martyr to free enterprise. He even hired the Mexican actress Victoria Ruffo, the star of *Simply Maria*, to denounce his imprisonment. Mavrodi's arrest did not alleviate Irina's resentment—or her guilt: That damned swindler was not the cause of the problem, only one of its consequences. The democrats had set the monster free, and now they could do nothing to stop it.

Tomorrow is the big day, tomorrow, tomorrow! Zhenia kissed her on the lips, and Oksana blushed. They'd been seeing each other every day for over eight months, sharing everything—Oksana spent more time at Zhenia's den than she did at the university or her parents' house—dedicating themselves to composing and rehearsing until dawn. Zhenia kissed her or felt her up casually—that was part of what made Frontanka, the punk group they'd just founded, attractive. She often suggested they sleep, and even bathe, together, but their physical contact never went beyond that, perhaps because Zhenia was horrified by the scars that had accumulated on Oksana's skin. Zhenia teased her, toyed with her, just that. Oksana knew that her friend didn't desire her, or perhaps didn't dare to desire her. She only pretended to be androgynous—another of the masks she used to face the world. As they could see, it was one of the most advantageous: it gave her a mysterious, perverse air, and accentuated her oddness. And it protected her from men.

Oksana tried to seduce her friend bit by bit, but with no success. One night, while they slept in each other's arms, she slipped her hand under Zhenia's night gown and softly squeezed her nipple. Zhenia pretended she was asleep and let herself be caressed, until she changed position. The next morning she didn't make the slightest reference to what had taken place. Another time, in the shower, Oksana soaped up her friend's buttocks. Again Zhenia let it happen, but stopped Oksana when she got too close to her sex. Ashamed, Oksana never tried anything of the sort again and tried to be satisfied with Zhenia's diffuse sensuality.

We should celebrate!, Zhenia insisted in an expansive mood. I know what we'll do, come with me. She took Oksana by the arm and dragged her through the Moscow metro to a run-down neighborhood, one that was very much in her taste. Close your eyes, she said. Zhenia led her friend to a place that was illuminated in neon and full of pictures of motorcycles and designs for serpents, dragons, and skulls. Now you can open them. Where are we? Zhenia dragged Oksana in, where they were met by a tall, bald man dressed in black, with his arms, shoulders, and neck covered with tattoos. We're going to make this day impossible to erase, impossible to erase.

Accustomed to physical pain, Oksana was not afraid of the needle pricks the man might administer. What would you like, sweetheart? I don't know, Roy, you're the artist, answered Zhenia. Something special, the same one for both of us. Tomorrow we give our first concert in Beli Tarakán, so it has to be unique. In Beli Tarakán? You two sure are sophisticated, my angels. Okay, tell me where.

If we're going to do this, it has to be in a visible place. On the forearm, Zhenia, on the forearm. Are you crazy? On the forearm, Oksana declared.

Roy giggled: I think the little one has made her decision, Zhenia, but I swear you won't be sorry. Zhenia and Oksana spent the whole day with Roy, who traced out for them a special design, as they'd demanded: a pair of airy creatures with languid feminine faces, their hair woven together, sibyls with enormous, sad eyes, forever linked. The two girls cried a bit, and when they discovered those fearsome and ethereal images on their skin they wept even more. They'd become sisters, now nothing would separate them.

The next night, still in pain, they finished up their concert at Beli Tarakán with one of Oksana's favorite songs:

I see
your hands in my nightmares
they cause me unbearable pain . . .
even if they're only scattering the dust
from the pale mirror of my soul.

When they finished, amid the applause and howls of the audience, they kissed on the mouth. For Oksana it was ecstasy, her moment of greatest happiness. Zhenia too, completely loose, couldn't contain her emotion.

They were a success, and now a long career lay before them. They went on dancing and drinking until they returned to their den with the first light of dawn. Zhenia took off her clothes as she always did, drunk and uninhibited, but this time Oksana felt neither modesty nor shame, nor that disquiet that paralyzed her in the presence of Zhenia's sex. She pulled off her clothes and hugged her friend, who received her with caresses and disconnected whispers. They kissed again, but this time Oksana put her tongue into Zhenia's mouth. Completely upset: Zhenia remained impassive, not reacting. Then Oksana kissed her on the neck, the chest, the breasts. She kissed her nipples for a long time—by then they were both stretched out on the floor—and finally sank her face into Zhenia's sex. Zhenia began to turn away, slowly recovering consciousness, until she managed to kick Oksana away. Are you crazy? she shouted. Oksana wouldn't stop and held Zhenia's thighs. Leave me alone, you slut! You're disgusting. Let go of me! Whore! Furious, Zhenia rolled on top of Oksana. They fought, scratched each other, punched each other. Out of control, Oksana hit Zhenia so hard that she knocked her over, her lips and nose bleeding. I never want to see you again! Oksana got dressed and ran out of the room, running away from herself, a wreck, falling to pieces. Zhenia would never hear another word about her.

On November 27th, 1994, Boris Yeltsin of strong arms and the National Security Council of the Russian Federation met in secret and approved a decree that ordered the restoration of constitutional order in Chechnya, which had been governed in criminal fashion, and beyond Moscow's reach, since 1991 by the old Soviet general Dzhojar Dudaiev. On December 11th, Yeltsin sent forty thousand soldiers to the rebel republic. On the 31st, as a sinister New Year's gift, he began the assault on Grozny, a ghost town.

When I reached the combat zone, as part of a special group of reporters sent by NTV, I found a mountain of corpses. I stayed in Chechnya for several weeks, the worst in my life. What I saw there was not comparable to anything I knew, not even Afghanistan or Baku. It was a sordid and chaotic horror, ancestral, a clear revelation of the time that was beginning. When I got back to Moscow, my body was completely empty. I was just a skin swollen with alcohol and violence, a residue of my former self. Outwardly I went on behaving like a normal man—like the sharp, committed journalist everyone wanted to see in me—but I too was a corpse.

DOUBLE HELIX

United States of America, 1993-1997

Jack Wells looked around and confirmed that, with only a few exceptions, all the great names of genetics were present at that April 1st, 1993 cocktail party to celebrate the launch of *Nature Genetics*. Its directors, Sir John Maddox and Kevin Davis, had convened the leading lighto of the field in one of the most luxurious hotels in Washington, axis of the cosmos. Like other bacteriology czars (Jack loved that term), Wells would never miss the opportunity to be in the same place with so many of his colleagues and enemies. That's Marie-Claire King, from Berkeley, he whispered to his wife. She identified the gene for breast cancer. That man over there is Roy Crystal. He specializes in genetic therapies to fight cystic fibrosis.

Jennifer loved to rub elbows with these promethean figures. Wells, on the contrary, only seemed interested in two of them, the ones who would be giving the final speeches that night, warriors that were destined to duel each other: the reborn Christian Francis Collins, from the

University of Michigan, who'd isolated the gene for neurofibromatosis—a kind of deforming cancer—and identified the gene for Huntington's Disease; and, in the other corner, the implacable J. Craig Venter of the fiery eyes, a long-time researcher at the National Institute of Health. He was, perhaps, the biologist who had revealed the most genetic information and was now Director of the Institute for Genomic Research, better known as TIGR (its critics consistently called it Tigger, after the character in *Winnie the Pooh*).

Those are the two stars of the moment, Wells explained to Jennifer. Francis represents the establishment, Craig the rebels. And believe me, no matter how courteous they appear to be now, they will soon destroy each other. Who's going to win?, she asked. The one who knows how to adapt himself better. Our Craig, of course.

The adversaries stood watch over their weapons: They shook hands, smiled for the cameras, clinked glasses, and muttered incomprehensible toasts, as if they had no idea of their fate, as if they did not sense the imminence of the war that would bring their armies into confrontation. Collins and Venter could not be more different. Collins was affable and sincere, tall and ungainly. He was convinced his research was a divine mission. Venter, bald and haughty, a bit petulant, a surfer in his youth, and now passionate about sailing, also wanted to save humankind. But the only god he worshipped was himself.

Wells admired Francis Collins's dedication but felt much more comfortable with Venter, because he saw in him not only a friend but a kindred soul. Wells met him when he was still working in the National Institute for Neurological Disorders and Stroke. After studying the adrenaline sensor for several years, Venter had sequenced large regions of chromosomic DNA with the intention of finding interesting genes (those linked with some kind of pathology). But Venter was even more ambitious and impatient than Wells, and that system seemed too slow to him. If he invested years in sequencing a single gene, how many years would he need to sequence the more than 100,000 genes in the human body?

One day, in a plane flying back to the United States, Venter had an epiphany: Suppose that, instead of using the traditional method, he sequenced the so-called complementary DNA (or cDNA) his colleagues held in utter contempt? The idea was so simple it seemed incredible to him that no one had tried it before. He immediately went to work: He gathered a library of cerebral cDNA, selected a few bacteria colonies, purified the results, and placed them in his powerful machines. This produced scores of sequences, which he named Expressed Sequence Tags or ESTs. In mid-1991, he announced his system in the magazine *Science* and caused an uproar. In a single article, he announced the discovery of the the identity of 330 genes, more than anyone before. Soon after, in *Nature*, he revealed the identity of 2,375 more. His own genes, that part of himself which intrigued him so much, transformed him into an uncontrolled hunter.

Jack Wells quickly understood the relevance of his method: If in the future the patent office changed its opinion and accepted the copyrighting of each EST, the implications for the pharmaceutical industry would be formidable. Just like other businessmen in biotechnology, Wells ran to visit Venter in his offices at TIGR. He did not get him to join DNAW—his offer had been $30,000,000 while Amgen offered $70,000,000. He accepted neither, but there arose between the two an instantaneous camaraderie: Both loved luxury and risk. They began seeing each other regularly: Jack and Jennifer sailed several times on the *Sorcerer*, Venter's twenty-five-meter yacht, while Venter and Claire Fraser, his colleague and wife, became regular guests at Wells's New York parties.

When Venter finished delivering his talk, in which he referred to the most recent advances at TIGR with pride, his friends quickly gathered around him. Congratulations, Craig, Jennifer kissed him. Caught up in the excitement, Wells gave him a hug. It was then that Sir John Maddox, eternal editor of *Nature*, came over with a smile on his lips and gave them the news that would upset their future (and the future of genetics) definitively: I suppose you already know this, but Francis Collins has accepted the post. What!, exclaimed Craig. The rumors are true, Maddox added with a touch of irony: He will be the new Director of the Human Genome Project. You've got to be bold to direct that mammoth! Venter clenched his fists: I'll have to wish him luck, he muttered, because he's going to need it.

The duel between the two titans—we'd better nuance this, between the genes of the two titans—had just begun.

What kind of creatures are we humans? For centuries we depicted ourselves as central elements in the universe, children of an aloof God who turned control of the Earth and its resources over to us, the only species with the intelligence necessary to figure out the mysteries of life. Once we thought our planet was the navel of the cosmos, and only after countless disputes,did we dare to hand that privilege to the Sun, one star among millions. Our pride has no limits: The idea of being peripheral organisms, the result of chance or luck—mere accidents—still sounds like heresy. Irritated by this lack of meaning, we imagine that our existence obeys a supreme cause and deserves to be justified and reproduced. But neither the Earth nor the Sun is the custodian of the universe. Our misfortunes do not correspond to a pre-established plan or to the designs of a Superior Intelligence—vain consolation—and, in biological terms, we are barely distinguishable from the nematodes, to say nothing of the simians.

Like the other living beings, we humans are simply survival machines, ephemeral redoubts against chaos, docile guardians of our genes. *That and that alone.* Dust and shadow. Millions of years had to pass before we could understand that. What is, then, our essence? What is the essence of the human? What makes us blind, proud, fearful, cruel, miserable, astute, ambitious, sickly, fierce, compassionate, dishonest? Finding out is within our grasp: The answers are hidden in our genome, that insane database which, at least in theory, would allow us to reconstruct ourselves. As James Watson and Francis Crick suspected, all we'd have to do was read it to find out our secrets. An encyclopedia, yes, but a rather dull one; millions of letters, one after another, absurd:

> AGCTCGCTGA GACTTCTGG ACCCCGCACCAGGCTGTGGG GTTCTCT-CAGA TAACTGGGCC

Where to begin? Each one of our cells has twenty-three pairs of chromosomes: Twenty-two numbered one to twenty-two, and a final pair, in charge of defining the gender of each individual—and condemning him forever—represented in women as XX and in men as XY. In turn, the chromosomes are made up of a mass of proteins and DNA, a nervous substance that folds over itself again and again. In these strange books, the genes constitute the definitions, although the terms that shape them, called here *codons*, only contain three letters. The alphabet of the genes—the alphabet of our perdition—only possesses four letters, A, C, G, and T, which correspond to adenine, cytosine, guanine, and thymine.

Our internal grammar has another particularity, as if it were a system of inviolable castes: A can only combine with T and C with G. Using the metaphor put forward by Watson and Crick in 1953, these steps connect the DNA's double spiral. Each codon contains the code of one of the twenty existing amino acids, which join together to produce the thousands of proteins that sustain our bodies.

What does this mean? That the person who obtains the complete schema of the genome will be a hero. The first person to sequence short molecules of ribonucleic acid was the English biochemist Fred Sanger, two-time winner of the Nobel Prize. Working with Walter Gilbert, he found a system for examining DNA. In 1977, they presented the first map of a complete genome—the tiny adenovirus known as oX174. At that moment, it was clear that by using a parallel mechanism (and technology that did not yet exist), it would be possible to sequence the human genome and see the causes of multiple disorders. Because it occasionally happens that, in the process of duplicating a chain of DNA, a codon can be incorrectly written—for example GTG instead of GAG—and an amino acid will be defective. These mutations have determined the evolution of our species—have made us what we are—but they are also the cause of illnesses and deformations.

For that reason, a complete sequence of the human genome would not only allow us to define our nature better, but it would also help us to spot numerous maladies and possibly propose a cure. And that, in real terms, implies money. A lot of money. It was natural that men like Francis Collins, Craig Venter, William Haseltine, and Jack Wells, responding to the ambition dictated to them by their cells, would be willing to tear themselves to pieces to reveal our essence. Perhaps we humans do not live at the heart of the universe, perhaps the Sun is an insignificant star, and perhaps our DNA barely separates us from bacteria and gorillas, but there is something in us, irrepressible egoism or eagerness, that makes us into the only creatures who have wanted to get rich through their genes.

A new life. When she left Berlin, Eva Halász decided to begin from zero. She was no longer the child prodigy of other times, the promising young woman, the genial mathematician; the incandescent expert had just turned thirty-eight and had not satisfied the expectations she'd aroused as a girl. She was, no doubt, a respected scientist whose contributions to the field of artificial intelligence and computer programming were quoted in infinite academic articles—a few lines, sometimes a few paragraphs—but she had in no way transformed knowledge in her field. Nor had she entered the select club of the revolutionaries. So what good did her damned intelligence do her, her unmeasurable IQ, the favor of the gods? Insofar as she was concerned, her career was a failure. A more painful and cruel failure than any other, because only she noticed it. Until that moment, her existence had not been more than a succession of truncated episodes, of running away and escaping, leaps from one place to another—and from one man to another—all lacking purpose. How was she going to triumph if she was incapable of concentrating, if her mind pursued variety and loss of control, if calm and stability were forbidden to her? Her professors always recommended—correctly—she follow a traditional career.

People with temperaments as scattered as hers must impose limits on themselves, she recriminated herself, otherwise you run the risk of getting hopelessly lost. And that is what happened. Eva hated being ethereal and inconstant, but she could not avoid it: A demon—more like a legion of demons—within her yanked her out of any place where she began to feel comfortable, forcing her to seek new horizons and, of course, to lose whatever she'd gained. It was as if she couldn't stand the past, as if she could barely keep abreast of the present and only thought about the future. But the future didn't exist.

I can't avoid it, she would confess to Klara, weeping her eyes out. Her mother was the only one who pushed her frenetic career forward: You've done the right thing, Eva, she would console her, there's nothing worse than boredom, nothing worse than immobility, believe me. My biggest mistake was to set myself up with your father. Take advantage of your freedom, you've got no ballast weighing you down, look ahead, always ahead.

Why wasn't Eva like other people? Why couldn't she be normal? Why did her genes condemn her to being simultaneously luminous and obscure? She missed that monotonous existence for which her mother had so much contempt: a day without worries—or thoughts—sitting on a park bench, doing nothing, contemplating the trees and lawns, safe from herself. Impossible. Eva couldn't recall a single instant of calm, a single instant without that absurd urgency that forced her to resolve all sorts of problems, without that feeling of guilt and anxiety in the face of her lack of progress. Laziness was forbidden to her.

Now the curse was going to repeat itself—again. It hadn't been even three years since her return to the United States, where, thanks to Jeremy Fuller, she'd helped write computer programs for the Human Genome Project, and now she was getting ready to move again. Why? Because she'd already learned enough about this new discipline, bioprogramming;

because the hierarchic and bureaucratic structure of the HGP dampened her curiosity and innovation; because she loved risks and challenges; and above all—she had to recognize it—because Jack Wells had begged her.

And just who is this Jack Wells?, Klara asked her. Eva didn't hide anything from her mother, even her most turbulent adventures: a businessman. A *what?* Klara clapped her hand to her forehead in a theatrical gesture. You could have said engineer, even lawyer, but a businessman? For God's sake, Eva, you can't fall any lower.

For once her mother was right.

Do you love him? Eva erupted in laughter. Well then? Can't you find a more attractive lover, maybe a young athlete? The Turk wasn't so bad . . . In theory, Klara approved of her licentiousness, but in practice she never accepted any of her lovers: No man seemed the equal of her daughter, they were all too fatuous or timid or vain or stubborn or stupid—stupid especially—for her. In her worst moments, Eva agreed with her mother's assessment: How else could she explain that none of them was still with her? Why hadn't she found the right person? Why did she always choose the wrong man?

The answer was obvious: She didn't know how to choose, didn't recognize her own desires. She let herself be carried away by an initial attraction and then, dragged along by inertia, leapt into passionate relationships with strangers, fell in love like a teenager and only discovered her mistake when it was too late. And then began the disenchantment, the reproaches, the distance, until she again found herself where she was at the beginning, but even more dissatisfied. Was she condemned to be alone? Or, even worse, to the loneliness of interchangeable bodies? Eva, why can't you stop yourself? What fear pushes you on, what mania, what delirium? Where does the impulse to sleep with one man after another, cast them aside as if they were worthless, as if they were mere sperm providers, spare males, where does that impulse come from?

Eva met Wells at a bioengineering congress in Baltimore, during a recess. She accepted his offer of a drink, and that same night shared his bed. Again, Eva? Yes, again. What did you know about him? Nothing. And then? I couldn't stop myself. Are you that vain, that frightened? I don't know. Did you like it? A little, yes. Eva demented, Eva insecure, Eva miserable. And then. Then, the usual thing . . . Furtive meetings, weekend escapes, torrid emails, cyber sex. And the reality of it? What reality? We live in a virtual world: holographic lovers, video game characters, avatars. The perfect solution? No, not perfect, but yes, it is a solution.

And what kind of business does this Jack Wells of yours run?, Klara persisted. Bioindustry, designer drugs. Is he rich at least? Very rich, mother. I suppose it's a symptom of maturity. Don't be sarcastic, Klara. You know money never mattered to me. You're not a sweet young thing any more. What makes me sad is that at this rate I'll never have a grandchild.

Klara touched one of the most sensitive points on the agenda: Eva swore that she had no interest in children, that she was incapable of taking care of anyone, but she chose to avoid the subject. Her genes forced her to do thousands of things, made her twist herself into knots out of frustration or plunge into the abyss, have sex again and again to the point of madness, until she fainted, but at least she retained that last citadel of freedom, perhaps the only authentic freedom we humans possess: that of not reproducing, of sentencing the genes that have enslaved us all our lives to death. That's how Eva though of it, or perhaps she only intuited it.

Wells lost his head over her. From the first day, he recognized that she would not be just one more of his usual conquests but instead a woman for many nights, perhaps all nights. For once he didn't play tricks, he told her he was married, that he could do nothing about it, that those were the conditions. As usual, it didn't matter to Eva: She imagined that by the next morning they would have forgotten each other, he would be one more mark on her headboard. But when she woke up, she didn't forget him, and he didn't forget her. What the hell could she find in Jack Wells's decadent body, in his rancid odor, in his graying hair, in his incipient old age? If she was never interested in the men she slept with, if for her they were only adventures (even if they were long-term adventures), how could she be taken by someone so fatuous and vulgar? What weakness tied her to him, what perversion or vice linked her to Wells? I hate writing this part of the story because I don't understand the motivations of the actors. Or perhaps I hate seeing Jack Wells as a mirror. In any case, Eva and Jack spent every moment of the next four days of the congress together. They stopped going to the lectures and barely saw the sun.

And how long have you been with him?, asked her mother. Seven months, nine days, fifteen hours. Thank heaven it's just an adventure. Thank heaven.

Wells would fly to Boston whenever he had a free afternoon—usually he'd rent a small plane—but that wasn't enough: He wanted more, much more. He wanted to possess her. To possess her all to himself. To the point that he would put his marriage with Jennifer at risk? Perhaps not yet, but who could see into the future? After a few months, Wells suggested a solution to their problem: Come work with me at DNAW. Not for my sake, but for yours. From day one, you'd be making three times the salary MIT pays you, and in a few months you'd be getting stock in the company. The scientific possibilities are extraordinary.

Eva held out for weeks: How was she going to abandon her job again because of a man? But Wells was unrelenting. Every time he saw her he improved the offer. And he said again and again: Forget our relationship, I'm making you a professional offer, it's right for you and for DNAW as well. Eva could barely sleep, overwhelmed by the conflict between her interest and her obligation, between her guilt and her desire. Again, Eva? Yes, again.

I imagine you requested a leave of absence, her mother ventured. No, Klara, I can't go on playing, I have to be responsible for my acts. I resigned from MIT. Definitively. For that businessman? Yes, for Jack Wells.

For my nemesis. For my shadow.

That was the last trip Irina and Arkady made together. Ever since Oksana ran away, their relationship had been a mirage (pure inertia); they only stayed together because, as she told me later, because they shared the same despair. For Arkady, the mysterious and sudden escape of his daughter revealed his psychic weakness. For Irina, it only proved they'd been terrible parents. You never taught her to be a woman, he would reproach her, she's a child.

Arkady's rebukes stuck in her body like needles. You have to understand, Irina tried to exonerate herself, Oksana's world was destroyed twice. First when you were arrested, and then when you were set free. She suddenly had nothing to hold on to. And now for the first time she wants to be herself.

If Arkady suffered because of his daughter's behavior, he covered it up perfectly. Instead of seeing himself as a cause of Oksana's spiritual breakdown, he chose to feel betrayed. His own genes, that half of her that belonged to him, scorned him. I no longer have a daughter, he would say.

Despite their quarreling, Arkady and Irina flew to the United States together. For a long time, both had dreamed of seeing at the country against which the USSR had fought for so many years, and which was now its model, first-hand. It wasn't the first time they were leaving Russia—Arkady had given lectures in half of Europe over the previous few years—but it was the first time they were crossing the Atlantic. The circumstances could not be more favorable, because Arkady would not only participate in a meeting of DNAW's Scientific Committee, which he'd just joined, but he would take advantage of the opportunity to be granted an honorary doctorate by Cornell University.

Irina and Arkady landed at JFK on Saturday, February 5th, 1994. A limousine brought them to a suite at the Plaza—DNAW had reserved it for them. The luxury was overpowering, but in only three years the New Russia had achieved similar levels of consumption, so they were barely surprised. Irina was attracted more by the prosperity of ordinary people than by the abundance of the department stores, though she yielded to the temptation to buy handbags at Prada and shoes at Gucci.

Arkady for his part was indifferent to the commercial fever of the New Yorkers. He'd spent so much time imagining this cityscape and trying to transplant it in Moscow, city of wide avenues, that the original seemed coarse and insipid. His interest in the shops or Broadway shows was minimal—he was against going to a musical, as his wife suggested—and only after a lot of pleading did he agree to go to the movies (and he nodded off during the film). Capitalism was not that obscene proliferation of products, brands, colors, and tastes but something superior, something almost metaphysical: an abstract kind of life, a metaphor for freedom that barely corresponded to its real incarnation. The only thing that interested him in the United States were the scientific, political, and business contacts he could make, not this materialist avalanche.

Wells picked them up at 10:00 A.M. on Monday. The Council meeting would take place at 4:00 P.M., but he wanted to delight his visitors with a sightseeing trip through the city. Like any tourist guide, Wells accompanied them to the emblematic sites of the city—the Empire State Building, the Twin Towers, Times Square (the most horrifying place on the planet, in Arkady's opinion), Central Park, the U.N. building, and finally Wall Street and the Stock Market. So it's here where the destiny of the planet is forged, was the scientist's only comment.

Irina remained silent. Wells was upset by the coldness of his guests, but he imagined they were stupefied by the tour, and he set about singing the glories of the "American way of life." When he finished his speech, he invited them to lunch at the Russian Tea Room—what a stupid idea,

Arkady said to himself—where he had them eat a tasteless duck in cherry sauce.

Have you had any news about your daughter? She sent another letter a couple of weeks ago, Irina cut in. She's moved to Valdivostok, in far eastern Russia, thanks for asking. Now she says she's a singer! grumbled Arkady. Can you imagine that, Jack, a singer in a filthy port like Vladivostok? Who the hell will pay to listen to her? The sailors? Arkady's rictus went from bitterness to violence: There's nothing worse than a child. You don't know how lucky you are, Jack. Reproduction is nothing but an instinctive urge, the absurd desire of our genes to perpetuate themselves, no matter how miserable they make us.

Not at all used to such pessimism, Wells changed the subject: It's a shame Jennifer couldn't be with us, but she sends her most affectionate greetings. As you know, she's getting ready for another trip to Russia. According to her, the economic prospects for this year couldn't be better. Irina leapt: For whom, Mr. Wells? For the oligarchs?

Those Russians were really impossible. It was okay to do business with them, but nothing more. At 4:00 P.M. on the dot they were in the DNAW meeting room, in Soho, accompanied by the company staff (including Eva) and the dozen scientists who made up the advisory council (J. Craig Venter chaired the council). After calling the meeting to order, Wells profusely thanked Dr. Granin for coming. Starting then, he would be a full member of the council. Arkady was received with applause, and Irina was pained at being ignored, as if she weren't a scientist, as if she were a secretary.

I won't beat around the bush, Wells exclaimed. It's true that DNAW has recently suffered from the turbulence of the market, but you know that biomedical research, especially in complicated areas like cancer, requires intense, long-term effort before it yields concrete results. But when that does take place, and it's about to, the benefits will be incalculable.

Wells made a theatrical pause and then quietly announced: Today I wish to announce that DNAW has signed an exclusive contract with Dr. James Bartholdy and the University of Southern California which will allow us, exclusively, to develop and study the monoclonal antibody C225, perhaps the most effective compound for fighting cancer yet discovered. For reasons that can only be explained by the inefficiency of our health system, C225 has been consigned to oblivion by the authorities for almost twenty years, despite the fact that Dr. Bartholdy's studies show its effectiveness in treating malignant tumors. Now I'd like to ask Dr. Bartholdy to provide a detailed explanation of the prospects for this compound.

Arkady and Irina were as impressed with Bartholdy's exposition as the others: If he was correct, C225 could be the best treatment ever invented for treating several kinds of cancer. Through it, DNAW could become one of the most powerful biotechnological firms in the world. The road forward would be long and treacherous, because the Food and Drug Administration could take months or years to approve a new medication, but the hopes for C225 were more than simply encouraging.

The next morning, as they traveled to Ithaca, the frozen site of Cornell University, Arkady realized he'd recovered his enthusiasm for capitalism. The State, with all its bureaucratic detours, would never be able to produce a drug like C225. On the other hand, a small business led by a determined and ambitious individual like Wells could produce miracles. Even Irina forgot her bitterness—how she would have liked to take part in the laboratory testing!—and for an instant recovered her faith in humanity.

The nineties are going to be prodigious. What's going on in the markets is incredible: the economy of this country couldn't be better in anyone's wildest dreams, Eva. Not only have we left the '91 recession behind, but growth seems uncontrollable. She and Wells stood there holding hands—what horror, what impotence—breathing the cool April air. He was less and less prudent and had invited Eva out to his new house in the Hamptons, where he was surrounded by rich and famous neighbors, his darling Christina Sanders, of course, among them. How could Eva put up with people like that, how did she stand his monologues, how could she *touch him*? I have to accept reality: Perhaps she was fascinated by the boundless luxury, by those whims, by those vacuous pleasures, or not so much by the boundlessness, the whims, or the pleasures in themselves but by the novelty they constituted in her life. I don't know what to believe, Eva, really I just don't know. How many times did we argue over the same thing, how many times did I reproach you for that shameless frivolity, how many times did we fight because of this error?

Jack Wells had good reason to be optimistic: Except for the tiny bump caused by the rise in interest rates decreed by Alan Greenspan in 1994, the S&P 500 index had continued to go up, and at the end of that year its Market earnings had risen about 40%,on top of 1993's 16%.

Meanwhile, the Dow Jones had broken the 4,000 point barrier, and it was expected that at the end of 1995 it would be nudging 5,000.

You can feel the frenzy in the streets, he went on. Everybody wants to get rich, as they did during the Roaring Twenties. But the '20s ended with the 1929 crash, Eva counterattacked, recovering the cynicism that defined her. Wells took the blow cheerfully: This time there won't be any crash, my love, we've learned our lesson. Wealth is there, within reach. During the past four years, I've made more money than I did during my entire life. I'm so rich it turns my stomach! What you really are is so unbearable you turn my stomach, she retorted. Wells paid no attention: As Gordon Gekko says, "Greed is good."

What Wells *did not* tell Eva that afternoon in the Hamptons was that while he certainly did have a huge cash flow available to him, his wealth was a mirage, more an abstract concept than a tangible reality. DNAW did not deliver profits of the kind Wells proclaimed. In real terms, his firm hadn't produced *any* concrete results: All its products, including C225, were in the experimental phase, and none had been sent to the Food and Drug Administration for approval.

So how could Jack Wells spend so much money? By getting cash from here and there, especially from the exclusive contracts he signed with multinational pharmaceutical corporations. By convincing his shareholders that his products had a great likelihood of being approved by the FDA, he'd raised the value of DNAW stock from $18 to $28.50. And, after announcing that C225, now known as Erbitex, was perhaps the most effective anti-cancer drug ever discovered—the *New York Times* and the *Washington Post* put the news on their front pages—that value had doubled, reaching $56.40 in April of 1995.

As was discovered during his trial, Wells pocketed thousands of stock options (his adored options) as a reward for his magnificent leadership. In 1994, he convinced the DNAW board of directors to turn over a package of 275,000 shares to him. Which meant, as he bragged to Eva in the Hamptons, that he was both rich—and corrupt—to the point of turning anyone's stomach. If everything worked out according to his plans, his options would triple in value once the FDA approved Erbitex.

Using that pretext, he diversified his portfolio both in the United States and abroad. In a direct way, he helped build three other bioindustries: Merlin Pharmaceutical Corporation, Morgana Pharmaceutical Corporation, and Arthur Pharmaceutical Corporation (he had a weakness for tales of the Round Table), acquired Moskvie Medical Laboratory (where Irina worked and which Arkady Granin managed behind the scenes), took control of Cadmus, a Swiss medical instrument factory, and participated in businesses as diverse as the restaurant Bello in New York (his partner was none other than John Travolta), the movie producing firm Sunlight, the magazine *W*, the New York gymnasium Kya, and, with his friend Christina Sanders, was owner of the online cosmetics site iColors.com.

But that afternoon in the Hamptons, Wells also neglected to confess to Eva that his debts—the result of bad investments, lost lawsuits, and old loans—amounted to about $30,000,000, an insignificant figure in view of his expectations but one that would always be a concern to a cautious investor. Thank God, Wells was not cautious, and his carelessness would end up burying him.

At that time, only Allison seemed to have an idea about her brother-in-law's maneuvers. Perhaps she knew little about numbers—and she was probably incapable of explaining how the stock market worked—but her contempt for Jack and his businesses made her think something was rotten in DNAW. While she spent most of the year in Palestine or attending alternative forums in Europe, she never missed a chance to spy on him: Wells for her had become a symbol of imperialist abuse of power and theft. Where does his money come from?, she asked her sister again and again.

Jennifer was disturbed not by her husband's sudden wealth but by his infidelity. Once again, their pact had fallen apart. She couldn't understand why she'd been so credulous: She imagined that after what happened with Erin Sanders, Jack would be more careful. She never thought his amorous lapses would ever stop—that was his damned temperament, and she had learned to tolerate it—but after the good period they'd gone through, she was sure he'd be ultra-careful. And instead, he went right back to his old ways in the most cynical and impudent fashion. She still didn't know who his latest lover was; she'd been told it was one of his employees at DNAW—Wells always chose stupid young women—but this time he seemed to do everything possible so she'd catch him *in flagrante*. Where did he get off bringing this slut to the Hamptons? The neighbors wouldn't let ten minutes pass without spreading rumors to Manhattan!

Greed is the ruling passion of the day, Jennifer, her sister would say. Important executives like Jack will do anything to get rich. They think it's normal to cook the company books, you saw what happened with Nick Leeson in Thailand, the idiot caused one of the oldest banks in England to fail.

Meanwhile, Jacob was jumping from one place to another, indifferent to the discussion between his mother and his aunt. I'm talking about DNAW, I'm talking about Jack. You don't matter to him, the cancer patients don't matter to him, nothing but money matters to him. His damned money. Very well, little sister, I've heard you out, thanks so much, I'll take your advice into account. Happy now? Allison stared at her, not understanding why she insisted on masking her husband's outrages.

To balance the invitation Wells had extended to him, Craig Venter asked him to join the administrative council of TIGR. That kind of *quid pro quo* was common practice during those years, despite the fact that such executive inbreeding undermined the notion of boards as independent overseers and advisors. Often, partners or even tennis partners were made members. So it seemed normal that a CEO would be on five or six boards, thanks to which he could receive compensation of about $70,000 a year.

Accompanied by Eva, Jack introduced her as DNAW's computer officer, he visited TIGR's installation in Rockville, Maryland in April of 1995. The building had been designed to house a ceramics factory, but, as Venter quickly bragged, he'd turned into the largest genetics laboratory in the world. Proud, he showed them his thirty ABI 372 sequencers—the jewels of his empire—along with the seventeen ABI Catalyst stations. Eva was astonished by the database installed in a Sun System SPAR Center2000, the most advanced hardware of the day.

Over the past few months, we've created an enormous library of human EST's, Venter explained—he was fascinated with himself. No other center on earth possesses as much information as we do.

Venter showed them to his office, where Hamilton Smith, winner of the 1978 Nobel Prize for Medicine (he always said he didn't deserve it), was waiting for them. Smith had joined TIGR a couple of years earlier. The scale model of the Sorcerer stood in the center of the office like a totem; the walls were covered with newspaper and magazine articles. Eva glanced at a cover of *Business Week* that featured Venter and Haseltine with the headline "The Kings of Genes," while Wells admired, not without envy, a 1994 article from the *New York Times* according to which Venter's stock was worth more than $13 million.

Venter dropped into a huge bordeaux-colored leather chair. Ham, why don't you tell Jack and his enchanting computer officer about our recent advances? Unlike Venter, Smith was withdrawn, even a bit surly—he could destroy someone with a single sentence—and preferred to focus on practice. Before he could say a word, his boss intervened: Hamilton is the magician of TIGR. Without him, we'd be just one more genetic information center. You urged us to take the crucial step, right, Ham? Smith mumbled again, and Venter again stepped in: One day I invited him to a meeting of the TIGR council and asked him if he had any innovations up his sleeve. And then he said . . . What did you say, Ham? That . . . He said that, if we were so proud of being an Institute of Genomic Research we should sequence a complete genome. What insight! As obvious as it may seem, no one had thought to do anything like that. *No one.* And we decided to do it, didn't we, Ham? That's right, Craig. How many months have we been working on the project? Since the end of 1993. Perhaps the normal thing would have been to choose a typical bacteria, *E. Coli* for example, but we decided to take chance with a more amusing organism, and it just happened that Ham had worked with the *Haemophilus Influenzae*, the pathogen that causes otitis and infantile pneumonia. A stupendous idea. The only one who didn't like the idea was that jerk Haseltine.

Are you still having problems with him, Craig?, Wells asked. He's dead set on destroying me, but I won't allow it. Isn't that right, Ham? We're living in a crossfire: That idiot on one side and Francis Collins on the other. Do you know that the National Institute of Health refused us financial aid because they considered our project inviable? Fools! When we finally got their answer we were about 90% finished. We haven't slept for months. Ham's ruined his eyes on this project. Finally, a team of eight, using fourteen ABI372 sequencers, carried out twenty-eight thousand reactions with about 500 DNA letters each. On average, each letter was sequenced six times.

That's a lot of work! You said it, dear Eva. But all we needed were three months to have the experimental results ready. Now all we need . . . is a program capable of connecting the separate pieces, Eva interrupted. And which did you use? Our computer officer is not as attractive as the one from DNAW, answered Venter, but he does a good job. His name is Granger Sutton, from the University of Maryland. After solving a few problems, he managed to group the twenty-eight thousand individual sequences into 140 lots which we were then able to join, using a bit of faith and a bit of patience. And we finally have it ready, dear friends! Isn't that the case, Ham? It hasn't been easy, Haseltine insists that we not make the complete sequence of this genome public, but I don't intend to pay any attention to him. As the article we're going to publish in *Science* proves, the results are astonishing. Why don't we give them a preview, Ham?

The genome of *H. influenzae*, stuttered Smith, contains 1,830,137 DNA letters. Each one of these bases forms 1,749 genes, with an average density of a thousand bases per gene. That means there is almost no junk DNA and that all the genes codify some important substance, Venter clarified. Now our objective will be to sequence *Mycoplasma genitalium*. And then? Then, said Venter, licking his lips, we'll be ready to take on the only project that is really worthwhile. Am I right, Ham?

Stimulated by what she'd seen at TIGR, Eva decided that while she'd certainly continue working at DNAW, she would also try to develop a new program to assemble DNA sequences. Granger Sutton had, no doubt about it, done excellent work in completing the sequencing of *H. influenzae*, but his system was too rigid to take on more complex organisms. And of course it would never pass the test of assembling the three billion million letters the human genome was supposed to have. Without even talking it over with Wells, Eva Halász contacted James Weber, Director of the Marshfield Medical Foundation in Wisconsin, and, and Eugene Myers, from the University of Tucson.

In February of 1996, Weber attended a seminar organized by the Human Genome Project in Bermuda, where he suggested completely changing the programming focus for sequencing DNA, but the participants rejected his ideas. Unlike them, Eva thought his intuitions were correct. As they said, ordering the fragments of each chromosome before sequencing them was a slow and messy process. Instead, they proposed working on loose fragments of DNA chosen at random which they would then gather together through a new program.

The solution she conceived was terse and elegant: to generate a maximum of information in a minimum of time, leaving the more problematic regions open for the scientists. Using that criterion, it would be possible to sequence 99% of the human genome long before 2005. Few experts thought her proposal valid, either because they thought it wasn't viable or because the task of filling in the holes looked like a nightmare to them. Eva's call was like a balm for Weber and Myers: For months they'd received only criticism, so they were delighted to know that someone actually agreed with them. We should get together as soon as possible, Myers said.

In short order, the three found themselves working toward a common goal: to design the program that would re-order DNA by random sequencing or, as Jim Weber termed it, sequencing it shotgun style. Their computer simulations had a pristine, ethereal beauty. Eva enjoyed Myers's visits especially because, unlike most of the mathematicians she knew, Gene (a perfect name for his work) revealed his eccentricities without undo self-consciousness—he usually wore a yellow foulard and an earring, and he never let himself be guided by political ambition or professional jealousy. After several months of work, the three had finished an article in which they presented their theories: "Shotgun Sequencing of the Complete Human Genome." It would be published in *Genome Research* at the outset of 1997.

The idea is brilliant, Wells shouted when Eva told him about their results. Too bad not everyone agrees. Bioprogramming experts think we're insane. Forget them, Eva. As usual, those science bureaucrats can't see beyond the end of their noses. But do you know who would be very interested in talking to you three? Venter. It's time to pay him another visit.

It was a cold, luminous afternoon, too cold for the end of March: A vague and imprecise sun—barely a whitish disk—shone on the neat façade of the DNAW building in Soho. The weather report announced an unseasonal snow storm, but for the moment there were no other signs of bad weather than the frozen wind that struck Jennifer's face. Wearing an impeccable black overcoat and a magenta Hermès scarf—she wanted to look relaxed—she walked into her husband's building and, without allowing the receptionist to announce her, walked up the stairs to the third floor. No one tried to stop her. Half-way there, she met a biochemist she'd met at one of her husband's parties. I'm afraid Mr. Wells isn't here right now, he said, I think he had a meeting with the Bristol-Squibb people. I know, she answered, and kept going.

Jennifer didn't stop until she found the office of the computing officer. It was, she told herself, inevitable I'd come here today. And then: It's not my fault; it's Jack's fault. She opened the door decisively (she'd rehearsed it a thousand times) and strode into the office deliberately, wearing an expression that reflected neither ill-will nor surprise (this too she'd practiced), just an indubitable determination.

Yes?, Eva looked up. Jennifer needed only a second to take her measure in detail, as if she were the biologist observing a bacteria under the microscope: Her firm, fresh, very white skin, her almost-yellow eyes—hardly spectacular she noted—her haughty neck, her slightly ungainly shoulders, the outline of two breasts, still firm, and the obvious vulgarity of the total picture. Eva Halász, right? Yes, and you must be Mrs. Wells.

As Eva told me later, Jennifer did not expect such a rapid response, so she made an effort not to lose her advantage. They shook hands longer than necessary—Eva's grasp tight, but Jennifer's tighter still—and compared their relative strengths. Eva was no fool: An expert in game theory, she'd foreseen her meeting with Jack's wife. This too she took to be the inevitable consequence of her acts, which is why she tried to appear tough but cautious. It would be counterproductive to pretend or to try to dance around the issue.

You know that Jack is not in the building, she blurted out in a dry but not sarcastic tone. That's why I'm here. Well then, Mrs. Wells, what can I do for you? I wanted to meet you, Eva—I may call you Eva, no? As long as you'll let me call you Jennifer. How nice we agree! Jennifer too wasn't going to waste her time on nonsense: I've only come to say one thing to you, don't appear with Jack in public, don't visit his friends, and don't humiliate me in any other way, understand?

I'm sorry, Jennifer, but this is something you should talk over with your husband. I'm not asking you to stop seeing him, sleep with him all you like, but just limit yourself to your own part in this story, and we'll all be happy. I'm the wife, you're the lover.

Eva smiled. She liked that blonde, nervous woman: Behind her vehemence there was an insecurity that made Eva almost feel sorry for her. How could she fight someone who was so fragile? Good wives don't usually disturb their husbands' lovers during working hours, she said. If you want to talk about intimate matters, consult Jack, and, if he accepts, the three of us can get together. Jennifer squeezed one hand in the other, hurting herself. Maybe this woman was cleverer than the others, but she was no better. Right now she thought herself invincible, absolute mistress of the heart—actually the balls—of Jennifer's husband, but ultimately what always happens would happen. Jack would get bored with her, in the same way he'd finally had enough of the others.

You're very brave to come here like this, said Eva. I admire you, Jennifer, but now I have to ask you to leave, I've got a lot to do. Jennifer got up brusquely, intent on showing her superiority to the end: I take your remarks as a declaration of war, she exclaimed. A declaration of war, Eva repeated. I like you, Jennifer, I like you a lot.

Over the course of the weeks that followed, the two women gave each other no respite and were certainly generous when it came to low blows and betrayals. Wells became a pretext, an abstract goal in their struggle. Jennifer was not going to allow this parvenu to steal her husband, and Eva was ready to fight merely for the pleasure of stealing him.

Just as Jack predicted, William Haseltine's Human Genome Sciences and J. Craig Venter's Institute for Genomic Research announced their separation: Their founders' ferocious egoism excluded any possibility of peacemaking. Almost at the same time, Wells made an equivalent decision: He would separate from his wife, this time voluntarily, and follow through with his whim of taking control of Eva Halász.

Jennifer invading his Soho offices was the perfect pretext for getting rid of her. Despite her frequent attacks of jealousy, she'd always respected his space, fearful of creating a public scandal. But this time she'd broken a barrier, and from that moment on she'd never stopped annoying Eva and, in the process, him in all possible ways. Have you gone mad, Jennifer?, the wretch recriminated her. This time you've gone too far, you've got no right to persecute the people who work with me.

Wells didn't even try to make his arguments sound plausible: What he was trying to do, advised by Eva, was to get his wife to burst like a balloon. He could no longer stand her. But even so, the coward had to end their relationship like a victim. Just as Eva had planned things, Jennifer wept, screamed, wept again, shouted again, even gave him a couple of slaps, which he received with joy, and finally demanded divorce, yes, divorce, you son of a bitch, I don't want to see you in my life ever again, ever, understand? For the first time, Wells savored those insults, not so much because they would allow him to stay with Eva, but because, finally, they would allow him to be free, rich and free, richer and freer than he'd ever imagined.

Is that what you want, Jennifer?, he went on provoking her. Yes, that's what I want. Ultimately, Eva won the day: She defeated Jennifer and rubbed it into her face day after day by going with Wells to all the dinners, openings, concerts, galas, and social and academic gatherings in the city. A great triumph! Each used the other, relying on their lucky star, not knowing that at the end, when tragedy and crime became part of their lives—when *I* became part of their lives—they would be the losers and Jennifer the only survivor in their triangle. But for the time being, Eva and Wells had no fear of the future and enjoyed themselves as if they had all the time in the world.

At the end of the year, Eva gave up her place as computing officer at DNAW and, with the enthusiastic approval of Wells, in whose loft on 58th Street she spent the weekends, she joined the team that Gene Meyers was assembling at Celera, the company Venter had founded after the breaking up of TIGR. Her mission was to obtain a complete sequence of the human genome before the scientists working at Francis Collins's government-funded institute did so. On all fronts, war. Damned war.

THE TRIUMPH OF FREEDOM

Russian Federation, 1995-1998

Russia was a bargain: A couple of years after joining forces, Arkady Ivanovich Granin and Jack Wells had become the third largest pharmaceutical investors in the country. After the acquisition of Moskvi Medical Lab in 1993, the laboratory where Irina worked, the two men went on an acquisition campaign that included factories that manufactured both medication and hair dye, cleanliness products and substances used by the petroleum industry, perfumes and body creams. Even, beginning a promising stage of diversification, toy factories and plastic container factories. In legal terms, Arkady only appeared as an advisor to DNAW-Rus, the new holding company, but, as I was able to discover, the biologist and fighter for human rights had stock in almost all those companies. And, thanks to those stocks, he was now a rich man.

The appropriation of broken-down state-owned plants had accelerated with the program of Credits for Stocks. At the outset of 1995, the Russian government was on the brink of bankruptcy and urgently needed fresh capital. Vladimir Potanin, owner of Uneximbank, understood that he possessed that money—at least in a nominal form, since a good part of it was in bonds sold by the government itself—and considered lending it to Yeltsin of strong arms in exchange for a satisfactory counter-loan. Potanin proposed the idea to Boris Jordan and Steve Jennings, Wells's partners, who had just founded Renaissance Capital, an investment group with a wide network of official contacts. They delivered a program to Potanin: The banks would lend money to the government, which would guarantee repayment with stocks in businesses it still held. If the government failed to pay the money back within the agreed term, the banks could sell the stocks and get a solid commission. A perfect plan!

When Potanin presented the plan to Yeltsin's economic cabinet—he was backed by Khodorkovsky and other oligarchs—the concept had changed a bit: A consortium of commercial banks would deliver 9.1 billion rubles to the Russian government in exchange for stocks, but if the government did not pay back the loans, the banks themselves could auction them off. Also, the offer would be limited to Russian citizens. The message was clear: In case of default, the lending institutions would take over the businesses. Despite the aroma of corruption, Prime Minister Chernomyrdin and Vice-Prime Minister Chubais sanctioned the plan. And then Yeltsin too gave his approval.

How the loans were assigned and the stocks doled out, no one knows for certain. But Tatiana Diachenko, Yeltsin's ambitious daughter, certainly had a central role in the settlement. On October 17th, 1995, the decree that placed sixteen of the largest industries in the nation in the Credit for Stock program was made public. His dream now coming true, Potanin obtained 38% of Norilsk Nickel, the largest smelter in the world; Boris Berezovsky got control of 51% of Sibneft; and Mikhail Khodorkovsky took over 45% of the Yukos oil company. And who intervened on their behalf? The celebrated and incorruptible Arkady Granin, who had just been nominated for the Nobel Peace Prize.

This is scandalous, Arkady Ivanovich, Irina berated him. What are we doing with Russia? Would you prefer that the Communists return to power, that Ziuganov take us back to the stone age? Anything is better than that, Irina Nikolayevna. Perhaps the procedure hasn't been completely clean, but I assure you the investors will manage those industries better than the government. Do you really think the oligarchs are after the well-being of Russia?, she insisted.

Their old arguments had led to a dead end. Irina turned away from her husband and withdrew to her room. She'd reached her limit. That night she made an irrevocable decision: She would no longer keep her mouth shut, would no longer be a prisoner, people had to know what was going on, learn about the pact between the businessmen and the government, know who the real bosses of the country were. Even if this meant destroying her marriage, she had to free herself of this burden, she had to denounce the deals and corruption.

The next day she got the number of NTV and asked to speak with me. Her voice rang like metal.

At the outset of 1996, Yeltsin was a sluggish, sleepy beast. Little remained of the choleric spirit that challenged Gorbachev, defeated the coup of 1991, or bombarded the parliament in 1993. His health was poor (a heart attack precipitated an emergency stay at the Barvija Sanatorium), his mental faculties diminished, and no one would bet a penny on his re-election. According to the most recent polls, only 3% of the population was thinking of voting for him, as opposed to the 40% in favor of Gennady Ziuganov, the new Communist leader.

During the meeting of the World Economic Forum in Davos that year, Boris Berezovsky had personally experienced Ziuganov's fiery oratory and understood that if Ziuganov won, the system that protected his wealth would cease to exist. He immediately contacted Guzinksi, who had also come to the Swiss town. We've got no choice, Berezovsky declared, we have to join forces to support Yeltsin. I can't defeat you, and you can't defeat me, so the only sensible thing is for us to unite. We need someone who can shake Yeltsin out of his lethargy. Chubais? Yes, Chubais.

The man formerly in charge of privatization had been out of work for months: Yeltsin had to fire him because of pressure from the Duma. Berezovki himself interviewed him, saying the elite of the business world was relying on his ability and talent, that he was the only man who could save Yeltsin and, in the process, all of them. Chubais accepted with one condition: The businessmen had to provide his new Center for the Protection of Private Property with a $5,000,000 grant. Without anyone realizing it, the oligarchs, hidden in the shadows during that dark winter of 1996, decided to invest in Boris Yeltsin. They decided that the best way to control a corrupt, inefficient government like his was by buying it.

At the age of sixty-four, Irina Nikolayevna Granin possessed a timeless beauty, the severe gaze of a mother in despair, and the vitality of an adolescent. The wrinkles at the corner of her eyes and mouth emphasized her daring, while her dry and slow gestures conferred on her the distinction of a vestal virgin. I'd met her in another terrible moment—Russian history is made up of calamities—when the democrats, myself included, gathered inside the White House to defend Yeltsin from the 1991 coup. Only five years had passed since then, but it was as if those heroic days were part of a distant past. How many hopes had flowered with the defeat of the Communists! And how many of them had been betrayed in just five years!

Irina and I met in a desolate café and spent hours reciting our frustrations. She gave me a summary of her life, spoke about Arkady, about her passion for biology, her years in Sverdlovsk, about Biopreparat, about her husband's doubts, about his fight against the system, his arrest, his psychiatric internment, and his freedom. We fought for so many years just to change everything and now it's worse, she apologized. I'm so sad, so confused. Irina looked even more vulnerable than she said and looked more beautiful than before as well: The living picture of the Russian matron. Then she spoke about Oksana, about Oksana's pain, about Oksana's pointless life, about her guilt at having lost Oksana, that harsh, fragile girl whose eyes had impressed me so deeply.

She needed me, needed me more than Arkady did, but I didn't know how to help her. I chose the simplest path, to fight to save my husband from jail: Who would reproach me for doing that? I focused totally on Arkady and left her alone. I left my child alone. You have no idea how many times I've reproached myself for that! You just did what you thought was right, Irina Nikolayevna, don't be so hard on yourself. Thank you for your words, Yuri Mikhailovich, but I'm not looking for consolation. I recognize my mistakes, and what I did with her is unforgivable. Arkady forced me to choose between them, and, stupid me, I accepted his conditions. I never should have tolerated that dilemma. If I'd been firmer, perhaps Oksana wouldn't have left.

Have you heard from her? She sends a note every once in a while, only that. Irina dried her eyes: You don't know how much I miss her voice. Maybe she needs distance to grow up. Irina recovered her composure: Forgive me, Yuri Mikhailovich, I didn't come to talk about my daughter. Making an effort to show she was calm, she went back to talking about her husband: His hatred of Communism had turned him into a free market fanatic capable of forgiving all Yeltsin's errors. And capable of taking advantage of them.

I can understand unconditional loyalty, even admire it, but not blindness or lack of principle. Arkady Ivanovich justifies all Yeltsin's measures out of fear of the Communists. Meanwhile, his oligarch cronies take over the country. Russia has turned into a bazaar, you can buy anything—influence, favors, sinecures. In a word, impunity. That isn't the capitalism we sought, Yuri Mikhailovich. Yeltsin's daughter hands out state industries to her favorites.

Have you any proof, Irina Nikolayevna?

I can give you the clues, but you'll have to investigate on your own. I do know that a few months ago Arkady Ivanovich and Jack Wells, his American partner, made deals with Mikhail Khodorkovsky. My husband knows the illegal maneuvers Khodorkovsky carried out to take over Yukos and other state companies, I may be able to get you some documents.

You've got to be careful, Irina Nikolayevna. Are you sure you want to go forward with all this? I have to. What about your husband? Each of us shapes his own destiny. You're very brave, I told her. She didn't even attempt a smile. She simply stood up and walked away. There are no more women like her: I admired her and felt sorry for her. So I set aside my articles about Chechnya and concentrated on ferreting out the financial tricks of Mikhail Jodorkovsky and Arkady Ivanovich Granin. Those tricks would lead me to Jack Wells and Eva Halász.

Boris Yeltsin looked like a rag doll, but the oligarchs didn't rest until the weakened President agreed to join up with them at the start of March.

The situation is very complicated, Boris Nikolayevich, Anatoly Chubais warned him. Your approval ratings are at about 5%. Yeltsin bristled: The polls taken by his subordinates gave him a more than 50% approval rating. Well I think your figures are mistaken, the President mumbled.

The room sank into an ominous silence. The surveys prepared by your people are filled with lies, Gusinsky interrupted. And how the hell do you know that? I know it because you're behaving imprudently. The oligarch paused: If the Communists get back into power it will be your fault. We're here to avoid that. The Communists will hang us from the lamp posts, Alexandr Smolenski pointed out. Unless we change the situation, within a month it will be too late. What do you want?, snorted Yeltsin. You need us to win the elections, Berzovski interrupted. We suggest you put Chubais on your campaign team.

Yeltsin just sat there, silent and surly. How was it possible that these wretches, who'd gotten rich because of him, were now trying to order him around? Vermin! But finally, knowing he'd already lost, he gave in to them. He didn't fire his former associates, but he did create a parallel structure for Chubais, who set up his office in the Bank Most building. This fact was the first public indication of the alliance between business and government. But the pact became even clearer when the oligarchs published a manifesto about the elections.

And as if that weren't enough, Yeltsin's daughter turned up that same week at NTV's offices. Her mission was to convince Igor Malashenko, the head of the station and my immediate boss, to take on the task of public relations for her father. When Malashenko accepted, he asked me to go with her. The reputation we've earned for independence will disappear over night, I told him. Sometimes you have to sacrifice one thing to get another, Yuri Mikhailovich. If the Communists take control, we won't even be able to imagine the possibility of being independent, and you know it.

Did I know it? Would Ziuganov's Communists behave like their predecessors? Was it proper to use the resources of the state to destroy a candidate? The democrats were going insane. Reconsider my offer, Yuri Mikhailovich, he insisted. I don't have to reconsider. Just as you like, only I think you should be careful. We're at war, and in a war freedoms are restricted. I was on the verge of quitting NTV at that instant, but something stopped me: fear of the Communists, the need to measure the limits of our feeble democracy, inertia.

Malashenko was convinced that if Yeltsin accepted his suggestions, he could carry off the victory. He wanted the President to get into a campaign in the western style. Not only would he have to appear on television, but he would also have to travel all around the country, give speeches, visit factories and schools, renew contact with the people. In a word, he would have to copy Reagan, sovereign of heaven.

For their part, the Communists were not willing to go down without a fight. On March 15th, the Duma approved a non-binding resolution that undid the Belovezhskaia Puschcha agreements which dissolved the Soviet Union. Just as it had in 1993, the parliament was rebelling against the President. Yeltsin felt insulted. If the Communists won, they'd have his head. As far as Aleksandr Kozhakov, his head of security, was concerned, this was a provocation they could not allow. The only way out was to postpone the elections or, if things got really out of hand, to dissolve parliament.

The oligarchs didn't agree. If the President allowed himself the luxury of violating constitutional order again, he would unleash a civil war—this would impact their investments negatively. The Kremlin was boiling: The two sides torpedoed and accused each other, each one vying for Yeltsin's favor. The President was in a state of doubt and took refuge in silence. Ultimately, his daughter's pleas convinced him that postponing the elections would be a huge mistake, and, against all expectations, she placed her confidence in Chubais and the oligarchs. Like a bear whose period of hibernation had come to an end, Yeltsin gave up alcohol and even seemed to recover from his various illnesses. He could spend months vegetating, alienated from himself, but when the situation became desperate he was able to rise from his own ashes. Soon the rumor began to circulate: Boris Yeltsin of strong arms was not only alive but intended to climb in the polls. And win.

Jennifer went to Moscow in mid-May 1996 with good news for Yeltsin and his team. After six months of negotiations, the International Monetary Fund had approved the structural reform program for the two-year period 1996-1998. Jennifer worked harder on the task than she'd ever worked before, convinced that the country would emerge from recession and become a stable economy. The program designed by the IMF and the World Bank contained provisions of all kinds: The essential point was the introduction of a system of modern legislation and supervision over private banking, over capital markets, and over foreign trade. At the same time, it proposed redesigning the fiscal regime, making privatization transparent, and improving the education and health care systems. After myriad delays and reversals—Jennifer swore in secret—the Russian negotiators agreed to follow the plan to the letter. But, like negotiators from every country, the Russians were lying. They were barefaced liars, fully knowing they lacked the support necessary to put the plan into practice. In exchange for these vague promises, the Executive Board of the the IMF rewarded Russia with the largest loan in its history: $10.2 billion, payable in three years. To close the deal, Jennifer flew to Moscow, city of wide avenues.

As usual, Anatoly Chubais invited her to dinner. Communism is the most malignant form of government ever created by human beings, he blurted out on first seeing her. It only functions by means of concentration camps and terror. Those are the enemies we're facing today, Jennifer dear (by now they were on familiar terms). Yeltsin must be re-elected, no matter the cost.

Jennifer adored the blond orangutan who had become a key player in Russia's political and economic structure. I hope that's the case, she said, toasting him with champagne. But she couldn't imagine that in fewer than six months, the IMF's gigantic loan was going to evaporate. How was it possible to spend that much money in such a short period of time? Easily. On Boris Yeltsin. The strategy had been created by Berezovsky: Instead of paying for re-electing the President out of their own pockets, the oligarchs would use the resources of the IMF. The end justified the means. No price was too high to avoid the return of Communism. Could the directors of the IMF and the World Bank know what would happen to their money? It would pain her, but Jennifer had become an accomplice of the Russian President and the oligarchs.

There is nothing as outrageous as television. In the USSR it had been an instrument of Party propaganda, and now the private channels monopolized the truth: Russian citizens had no other means to find out what was going on except TV. And every channel backed Yeltsin. His public relations people spent millions on advertisements and interviews. Not noticing the damage they would inflict on the nation, Berezovsky and Gusinsky placed their channels at the service of the President, while Ziuganov was paid barely any attention at all—his ads were prehistoric. Yeltsin's swollen face clogged prime time. NTV, the station that bragged about its freedom and lack of political commitments, also succumbed. Instead of its long-standing programs on Chechnya or ferocious criticism of the President, the chain dedicated itself to praising Yeltsin's talents or stirring up fear at the possible triumph of Communism. Not even *Kulki*, the comedy program that thrashed the government, escaped the indulgence Gusinsky bestowed on his new ally. Fed up, I quit my job at NTV and concentrated fully on Khodorkovsky.

The clues Irina gave me did not point so much at Khodorkovsky's maneuvers to take over Yukos, but to a loose thread I could pull that would take apart the whole sweater: a small, nearly invisible fertilizer company named Apatit. In theory, four businesses had competed for 20% of its stock, but, following the information Irina gave me, all four belonged to Khodorkovsky. The financial structure created by the oligarch (with the consent of Arkady Granin) was almost impossible to take apart. It seemed that one of his companies had resold the Apatit stocks to other phantom companies created in different fiscal paradises—Cyprus, the Isle of Man, the British Virgin Islands, the Turks, and the Caicos. I spent weeks pulling apart his net, figuring out his schemes, establishing his biography.

I knew from the start that I couldn't make my discoveries public until after the elections: No medium would risk threatening one of the President's main allies before knowing how things would turn out. But it was during those astonishing weeks, while the country again yielded itself to Yeltsin, that it occurred to me to transform my investigation into a novel. At first, it was an amusement, a pastime. Then the work became so absorbing that tracing Khodorkovsky's history, which was also the history of the end of the Soviet Union and the history of the triumph of capitalism in Russia, made the days simply vanish.

The subject and the characters absorbed me to such an extent that I became their hostage. Mikhail Borisovich Khodorkovsky, whom I renamed Vladimir Vladimirovich Kaminski, became my daily challenge. The superficially imaginary nature of the text goaded me into saying things I would never say on the news. I was writing for myself, indifferent to the destruction those pages could cause me. Against all logic, a fiction, a crude political thriller, could turn out to be more powerful than the truth.

On June 16th, the results of the first electoral round were announced. Boris Yeltsin got 35.28% of the votes; Gennady Ziuganov, 32.03%; General Aleksandr Lebed, an Afghanistan veteran, 14.52%; and Grigori Yablinski, an impeccably honest liberal politician, a mere 7.34%. It was a great triumph for the President. The oligarchs had rescued him and rescued themselves.

While Yeltsin celebrated his triumph—and had multiple by-pass heart surgery—the oligarchs presented the bill for their services. Khodorkovsky received immense fiscal benefits and won absolute control of the industries his bank had managed under the Credits for Stocks system. The same day that the results of the second round were announced—Yeltsin's majority was even greater—I finished the first draft of my novel. Picking a title was easy: *In Search of Kaminski.*

Yeltsin's second term was an authentic interregnum. Sick and alone, he governed with the indifference of a czar, while the oligarchs prospered as never before. Except that, as was only to be expected, they returned to hating each other. It didn't take long for the former allies to begin to intrigue against one another. The prize was too desirable for anyone to want to share it. The cleverest was Mikhail Khodorkovsky. Without getting involved in the government, as his other colleagues had done, he got everything he wanted.

Acting as an intermediary—that was the role he played, as the papers Irina gave me confirmed—Arkady convinced a languid Boris Yeltsin to sign a decree allowing Yukos to issue new stock, so creditors could be paid. In practice, this gave Khodorkovsky absolute control over the company. All told, Khodorkovsky paid out $350 million for a company whose market value would soon reach $6.2 billion. And to top things off, he announced at the start of 1998 that Yukos would merge with Sibneft, Berezovsky's company, to form Yuksi, which would become one of the largest oil companies in Russia—controlling 22% of all production—and possess the largest crude oil reserves in the world.

In Search of Kaminski was published in September of 1998 and provoked an instantaneous scandal. My success did not derive from the ten printings the novel went through in just a few weeks, or in the innumerable articles, reviews, and newspaper pieces published about it—the most important in *Der Spiegel*—but in the myriad death threats I received. I thought I was used to pressure, but the fever of those weeks overwhelmed me. Trapped in my sudden fame, in my sad, ephemeral fame, and fearful of how my powerful enemy would react, I again drowned myself in alcohol.

Thanks to the piece in *Der Spiegel*, some twenty foreign publishers expressed interest in translating the novel, and I began to receive invitations to give lectures in Europe and the United States. My life stopped. For months, my existence was reduced to speaking a thousand and one times in different cities and languages—at times I couldn't even recognize which they were—about the infamous Vladimir Kaminiski, who not only consumed Khodorkovsky but did the same to me. I came to hate that obtuse and pretentious character as much as I hated his real incarnation.

To palliate this disagreement with myself, and to heal a guilt that would never go away, I became involved in all kinds of beneficent campaigns. I wanted to show that neither celebrity nor money had changed me in the slightest, that I was the same man I had always been, that no one could accuse me of getting rich off of my political beliefs. I gave a good part of my income to non-governmental organizations, defended all just causes in public, became the greatest enemy of the new Russian *nomenklatura*, signed ecological manifestoes (especially those protesting the desiccation of the Aral Sea), and was the scourge of businessmen and politicians. None of the journalists who at the time fought to interview me, none of the TV talk-show hosts who smiled at me on camera, none of the academics who invited me to their universities, none of the activists who requested my presence at their congresses, and none of the French graduate students who wrote doctoral theses on me, none of them could have imagined that the great hope of Slavic literature, the post-Communist Solzhenitsyn, the conscience of the New Russia, the admired and celebrated Yuri Mikhailovich Chernishevsky, would become a murderer.

How could you dare do something like this? Arkady was screaming in rage, desperate. How could you betray me this way? Irina was besieged by remorse. Her eyes and throat were burning, and chills made her tremble as if she were afraid. She may well have been afraid. We were a team, Irina Nikolayevna. How many years have we been together? A lifetime. I don't understand, I don't understand you! Why did you destroy a loyalty that had lasted for so many years? What you've done is infamous, Irina Nikolayevna. Arkady Ivanovich actually thought himself a victim: I didn't deserve this from you. Perhaps I was mistaken in some things, perhaps I was stubborn or naïve, but you know I love Russia, that I've done everything I could to save this country.

In Search of Kaminski was transparent for him: One of the characters was a scientist—in this case, a nuclear physicist—named Arseny Volkov, whose life was Arkady's. Like Granin, my Volkov worked in the Soviet arms program; like Granin, he refused to collaborate with his superiors; like Granin, he was accused of treason and sent into internal exile; like Granin, he was pardoned by Gorbachev; and, like Granin, he'd joined the human rights movement. Like Granin, he joined with Yeltsin; like Granin, he'd sold out to Yeltsin; like Granin, he'd linked himself to the oligarchs—especially to Kaminski of course; like Granin, he'd become a millionaire by partnering with a cynical American capitalist.

But what pained Arkady most was the intimate portrait of Volkov. My character had a son instead of a daughter, but, like Oksana, he fled Volkov. Volkov seemed like a rock, an ambitious and tortured being, an absolute egoist full of ideals and desires, full of anger, pride, and the need for revenge. In a novel shot through with monsters, Volkov wasn't the worst of them, but he came off as a tortured and blind figure.

I could no longer remain silent, Irina muttered. If the novel has irritated you so much it's because you recognize yourself in it. It's a mirror, and you don't like seeing yourself in it. You revealed our intimate life, our secrets, he complained, you *exposed* me. I only told the truth, the truth you don't want to hear. Perhaps you are a good man, Arkady Ivanovich, it's not for me to judge, but you've made some big mistakes. With this country, with Oksana, with me. With yourself.

And are you perfect? You used a mercenary to destroy me and, in the process, to destroy Russia. For years, you haven't listened to anyone, Arkady Ivanovich. Ever since you returned from exile, you've only heard your own voice. Anyone who tries to talk to you is met with indifference or silence. Enough, Irina. Your behavior has broken what little remained of our love. For me, you no longer exist.

Irina wept in spite of herself. She didn't want to end up this way, she never imagined living alone, without her husband. But she wasn't sorry. For a long time you haven't existed for yourself, Arkady Ivanovich. And, still sobbing, she turned on her heel with a neutral, barely violent motion. She wouldn't see her husband until three years later, a December night, at the side of her daughter's body.

OTHER WORLDS

The Jenin Refugee Camp, the West Bank
Birmingham, Great Britain; Seattle, United States of America
Moscow, Russian Federation, 1997-2000

Jerusalem, thrice-holy city, cradle of the three great monotheistic religions, was a cursed city. Whenever Allison caught sight of the rocky, dry hills surrounding it—a landscape as harsh and hostile as its history—she felt the same oppression in her chest, the same metallic taste in her mouth, the same throbbing in her temples. All that spirituality made her nauseous, as if it were a heavy wine or a highly-concentrated stench. Unlike the pilgrims who visited the area—she contemptuously called them divinity tourists—she preferred to get out of the Old City as soon as she could: She couldn't stand its sublime perfection or its blood-chilling past.

Only on her first visit, during her initial tour of Israel and Palestine in 1992, did Allison dare to see the obligatory sights: First, the Wailing Wall, then the Al-Aqsa mosque, and finally the Church of the Holy Sepulchre. The three sites were as impressive as they were ominous, as evocative as they were iniquitous. If it were up to her, someone would destroy them once and for all, flatten them with the efficiency of an Israeli bulldozer demolishing Palestinian homes! None of them had the proper construction permits, none deserved to stand at that crossroad, stirring up anger and causing death!

Allison considered herself religious but without religion, and she felt more and more contempt (and fear) for official religions. Those pilgrimage sites were nothing more than that: rocks and sand. It was ridiculous that people were willing to give their lives to preserve those carcasses from obscure times. The Holy Sites only fanned anger and served as pretexts for intolerance. To the contrary of what the tourist guides said, Allison didn't feel the slightest trace of faith among the sanctuary guards, only a mixture of pride, ignorance, and prejudice.

But the most indecent thing—she had to call it indecent—was that the suspicion and fighting were not limited to Jews, Muslims, and Christians. Within each group there proliferated myriad battling sects: Sephardic Jews and Ashkenazi Jews; Orthodox Christians, Catholics, Armenians, and Copts; Shiite Muslims and Sunni Muslims. Jerusalem was the Babel of hatred, the plaything of a malevolent God who mocked His creatures by imposing absurd dogmas on them. It was like no other place in the world: on a daily basis, you could see identical human beings, possessing the same genetic code, warily regarding each another as enemies. These enemies shared a common history, and even bragged about honoring the same Supreme Being, but that didn't keep them from hating one another. What virus made each group think it alone possessed the truth? All that was necessary to turn them into predators was for an idea to grow in their brains: the conviction they were the chosen people. They'd spent so many years insulting one another, accumulating offenses and revenge, that there was no longer any room for either forgiveness or oblivion. Allison said it proudly: Jerusalem wounded her.

Like many Palestinian cities, Jenin held no surprises for the visitor. It was an enormous village of thirty-four thousand inhabitants, to which it was necessary to add the approximately thirteen thousand refugees counted up by the UNRWA, the United Nations Relief and Works Agency. Even though the horizon presented an arid, irregular profile—a succession of whitish shacks flanked by dirt roads and laconic bushes just a few kilometers from the Jordan valley, Allison always felt a rapid relief contemplating it in the distance. Unlike the Jewish settlements that, since 1996, proliferated like mushrooms in the occupied territories—solid, cement structures protected by fences—the Palestinian villages clung to the foothills in a natural, almost spontaneous way.

The refugee camp, founded in 1953 to house the Palestinians expelled after the 1948 war, was a square kilometer in size and abutted the city. For a few months now it had been under the nominal control of the Palestinian Authority. From the moment she saw it, Allison understood that now she had indeed found a home. Nothing reminded her of her boring existence in the United States: The camp was a gigantic prison, an odious and terrible human experiment—a world in miniature—but no less energetic and vital because of that. What would her compatriots give to possess just a little of the strength and charm of these people! As paradoxical as it may sound, Allison felt much freer in the enormous jail the West Bank was than on the Mall in Washington, axis of the cosmos. Here each of her acts lost its irrelevance, here she could be useful, here her life acquired meaning, here she was able to fight imperialism and help others. Although there were so many things lacking, there was a world of things to do.

During her first visit to the camp, Allison found herself trapped in a scene that was to become part of her routine: Dozens of children surrounded her, begging for money, besieging her with their shrieks, their smiles, their embraces, and their pleas. Me, me, please, please, me, me! She'd never experienced such powerful emotion: These children needed her, required her attention and her affection. Moved, Allison wanted to give herself to them. Any privations she might have to suffer were unimportant, as long as she could relieve their despair. Me, me, me!

According to the last census, 47% of the camp's population was under fifteen, and the combined numbers of women and children reached 67%. These figures alarmed her—and filled her with secret joy. She now knew where to concentrate her energy. In March of 1995, Allison joined the Coalition for Children/Palestine Section, a non-governmental agency established in 1992, whose main objective was to protect the rights of children in Gaza and the West Bank and to mobilize and supply the local and international community to defend those rights, as its declaration of principles stated.

Two years later, Allison had become a familiar presence in the camp. While she still spent time in the United States—she usually shared her summers with Jacob, who spent the rest of the year in a pompous Montessori School in Washington—and while she still tried to attend alternative forums in all parts of the world, the center of her life had shifted to that hodgepodge of shacks in the wastelands of the West Bank. She loved the Palestinian people and the family she'd gathered around her. While her superiors in the Coalition recommended she not become too emotionally tied to particular children—it might arouse the suspicion of others—she hadn't been able to elude the charms of Salim, Alaa, Walid, Yehya, and little Rami.

Salim and Alaa were brother and sister. He was fifteen and she fourteen, and their clean smiles simply melted Allison. Walid, thirteen, was more timid and introverted, Allison could barely pry a few words out of him—it seemed his parents had been murdered in the Sabra refugee camp in Lebanon. Yehya was twelve, and already the outlines of a dark, captivating beauty were beginning to show in her. Rami, a spoiled child, somehow related to Walid, was only five (the same age as Jacob).

The children followed her constantly and served as intermediaries with the rest of the community. Allison thought of them as her guardian angels, as if they were responsible for taking care of her and not the other way around. The five children competed for her attention, covered her with kisses and flattery and, except when their relatives made them come home, never left her side for a single moment. Starting during her second year in Jenin, when she was finally able to string together complete paragraphs in Arabic, Allison spent hours telling them stories and fairy tales. The children listened in fascination and asked her to repeat the yarns again and again.

If it hadn't been for them—Salim, Alaa, Walid, Yehya, and little Rami—Allison could not have withstood conditions in the camp. The misery was so scandalous—so offensive—that she had to fight each morning not to wake up sobbing. While it was true that a high percentage of the adult men had more-or-less fixed jobs, their salaries barely allowed them to feed their families. Almost all the women collaborated in the domestic economy, most baking bread in their own homes and selling it in the markets, though some specialized in breeding chickens, preparing milk products or sweets, or baking little cakes.

In general, the women married—were obliged to—when they turned fifteen. According to the UNRWA statistics, almost half had had at least one miscarriage, sufficient proof of the lack of information and medicines in the camp. Allison had become used to working with few resources, but refused to tolerate the jealousy, suspicion, and ingratitude of so many of the refugees and the rivalry and envy other people like her displayed. Sometimes the humanitarian workers had very little humanity.

The first person she got to know when she came to Jenin was a French doctor named Henri Soldain, who'd been working with Palestinian refugees for more than ten years. They're sons of bitches, Allison, he blurted out by way of greeting. Be careful with them. You leave everything you have in your country to help them, and they never thank you. Those words offended Allison: If Henri took that attitude toward the victims, the best thing he could do would be to go back once and for all to the Paris he missed and let someone with more spirit take his place.

Allison quickly discovered that the community of expatriates—as the members of the non-governmental agencies called themselves—was saturated with eccentric, embittered, and stubborn people just like Henri. Many saw themselves as messiahs, exceptional beings who deserved the recognition (and, in the process, the submission) of the victims. Others seemed to think of their time in these miserable and exotic places, the occupied territories—the same thing happened in Africa, southeast Asia, or Haiti—as if it were a vacation that provided them with entertainment and allowed them to show off their altruism. Still others were just like bureaucrats everywhere and doled out aid with the same ill-will with which they would have stamped forms at a customs office.

Allison was shocked by the appearance and attitude of some of her colleagues: They would arrive at the refugee camps in the brand new Jeeps, surrounded by drivers and helpers, dressed as if they were going on safari and blasting their stereos. They spoke an incomprehensible dialect, stuffed with ambiguous and euphemistic terms—beneficiaries, developing nations, persons with nutritional deficits—overflowing with abbreviations and unknown initials. It was not uncommon for the participants to mock one another and give new meanings to the acronyms: SC (Save the Children) became Shave the Children or Save the Chicken; DWB, Doctors without Borders, became Doctors without Brassieres; ACF (Action contre la Faim) became Action contre les Femmes, or DOW (Doctors of the World) became Doctors of the Whores.

Luckily, among this embarrassing humanitarian fauna, there were always two or three dedicated and critical individuals who, without losing sight of the contradictions their task involved, still considered it valuable and indispensable. Sven Sigurdsson, an Icelandic giant with a whitish beard, was one of them. We are not superheroes, he told Allison, and we certainly aren't special. We do a job like any other, and that job is to distribute aid. And we don't do it for free, our philanthropy is not that great, except that instead of money we prefer to feel comfortable with ourselves, which is no small thing.

Gesine Muller, a German development expert, was more lucid: Our mission is very ambiguous. We work to alleviate the plight of the dispossessed, but if they were to disappear, our labor would cease to have any meaning. We need them as much as they need us. Worse than that, intervened Ruth Jenkins, the only Jew working in the camp as part of the B'Tselem human rights organization, we want to give and want it known that we give. They don't want our aid, but they have no choice, and prefer it not to be known: it's a perfectly mismatched relationship.

Allison hated being the typical neurotic First World inhabitant who, in order to heal her guilt, moves to the Third World, even though she recognizes that many of her attitudes coincided with the stereotype: She dressed like the Palestinian women, took Arabic lessons, had a small apartment decorated with the work of local artisans, and adored grape leaves, olive oil, hummus, and tabouli.

Does all this make me a fraud? Maybe not, Alli, Ruth consoled her, but some day you'll have to recognize that you will never be one of them. You come here for a while and know that you can leave whenever you want. They can't. If one fine day you get bored with the privations and the local color, you can go to a shopping center or discotheque in Tel Aviv. They can't. That's where the difference lies, Alli: We're here because we choose to be, and at any moment we can leave, but they'll be here forever. And they know that as well as we do.

Allison could not accept being dispensable, another dumb blond from America in the humanitarian anthill. Her mission was unique and important. She was indispensable for Salim, for Alaa, for Walid, for Yehya, and especially for little Rami. Don't fool them, Gesine reproached her. No matter what you do, they will never become *your* family.

A disenchanted Allison quickly discovered that, in effect, many of the people she was helping only tried to take advantage of her. Yehya's parents, for example, never stopped lamenting their sicknesses, their privations, their poverty; after listening to that litany of misfortune, she was unable not to give them a few dollars—what did those dollars mean to her, a rich bourgeois from Philadelphia—though they barely meant anything to the recipients. But there were worse cases, professional victims who were experts in the art of looting non-governmental organizations. Just two days before, she'd heard the story of two young men who destroyed the road to their houses every night, so they could demand money to repair it the next day. And that was just one example: Con-games and frauds abounded in the camp, though nothing could compare with the greed and corruption of the Palestine Authority. Taking advantage of the chaos, the absence of laws and controls, they diverted money to their own accounts, sent aid to relatives and friends, and only helped those who agreed to give back a percentage. On one occasion, Allison, fed up with bribes and blackmail, faced up to one of those bureaucrats.

For God's sake!, she shouted in a fury. How can you profit from the poverty of your brothers? You'll never get out of your misery and will never be able to become an independent state! The representative of Al-Fatah in Jenin shrugged his shoulders, as if he himself had asked the same question in the past. The Jews will never let us be independent, he said, turning on his heel.

Disillusion made Allison feverish. At the end of her first year in the camp, she was on the point of quitting. What use were her efforts, her enthusiasm, her altruism? What meaning could fighting have when everyone else assumed they were beaten? The world was a repugnant place: a miserable planet lost on the fringe of the Milky Way whose inhabitants weren't capable of living in peace.

The statistics gathered by the Coalition for Children and other non-governmental organizations were sufficient proof of the stupidity of their fellow human beings: Each year more than thirty thousand children died in underdeveloped nations of diseases that had been eradicated in the West. The cost of providing health services rose to $13 billion, four billion less than what the Europeans and Japanese spent on pet food! The inequities were so monstrous they gave you goose bumps: the 900 million people lucky enough to be born in developed nations garnered 79% of the world's income, were responsible for 89% of its consumer expenses, 47% of its carbon emissions, consumed 58% of its energy, and possessed 74% of its telephone lines. By comparison, the 1.2 billion people who lived in the poorest countries shared only 1.3% of the world's telephone lines and were responsible for only 5% of the world's meat and fish consumption. How was it possible not to grow indignant and despair, how was it possible not to hate U.S. and European politicians, who were the ones responsible for this hell?

Why are you sad?, asked Rami, staring at her with his deep black eyes. For no good reason. Allison wiped away her tears. We love you.

Those simple words saved her. Allison took the boy in her arms and covered him with kisses. What did it matter what happened to the rest of humanity? Alone, she would never manage to eliminate the gap between rich and poor, between the powerful and the disinherited, but she at least could see to it that five or ten people, maybe twenty or thirty, could become aware of their situation and learn to survive on their own. And I love you, she declared.

As she did each week, Allison sat down to write a long letter to Jacob, this time about his eighth birthday. She'd begun this practice when he was five, convinced that he'd quickly learn to decipher her handwriting on his own. Meanwhile, she'd asked Jennifer to read them to him. What did she tell him? Everything. She tried to be precise and explicit, as if a detailed picture of her life in the refugee camp, of the turbulent landscapes in Gaza, of the purple tone of nightfall, of the sweetness of the little cakes, the scent of the jasmines and oranges, the desolate faces of the old and the beauty of the young could draw him to her, as if with those pictures and scenes she could transport him from his innocuous and frigid school in Washington to the fiery precariousness of Palestine.

Allison was neither stupid nor malevolent: She knew that each one of her words bore witness to her guilt, that nothing in the world could make her feel less wretched about the absence of her son. So why didn't she have him at her side? Why did she leave him in the hands of her sister?

He's still too little, but as soon as he grows up a bit more I'll bring him with me everywhere, she repeated daily. It was her habitual answer, the one she always gave whenever someone asked about him. But more than three years had passed since the first time she recited that excuse, and she still hadn't brought him along. Once she tried to take him away from Washington, to separate him from Jennifer once and for all. She fully intended to reject her sister's blackmail: She'd go to the Montessori school where they held him prisoner, pack up his toys and the things he needed (she'd given him a knapsack he always used), and together they'd take the first plane out of the United States.

What are you doing here, mom?, Jacob asked. Aren't you happy to see me, Jako? Allison ruffled his hair: You and I are going on a trip, it's going to be a lot of fun, I promise. Won't Aunt Jen get mad? I'll have a talk with Aunt Jen. Just as Jacob had foreseen, the clash of the sisters was not pleasant. Freshly separated from her unbearable husband, Jennifer was not in the mood.

Why didn't you tell me you were coming? He's my son, Jen, I can pick him up whenever I like. Jennifer was shaking: You're completely thoughtless, Allison. First you ask me to look after your son, and now you reproach me for it. How can you be so egoistic? I've already told you: Jacob is my son, and I've come to take him way. Where? With me. It doesn't matter where.

Jennifer ran her fingers through her hair, destroying her hairdo: You've never been capable of being responsible for yourself, what are you going to do with a seven-year-old boy? Do you want him to become a nomad like you? To sleep on the floor, to have no education, to get cholera? Alli, you've got to see things clearly. If you want to lead the kind of life you lead, fine, but don't make an innocent child give up all he has.

Since you put it that way, Jen, what does he have? The best education, the best books, the best health system, security, protection, affection. *Your* affection, Jen. He lacks for nothing here, don't you dare hurt your own child, Allison. Don't let a whim ruin his life. It isn't Jacob's fault, you can't use him as a hostage in our arguments.

Even though they'd taken care to lock the child in his room so he wouldn't witness their fight, Jennifer's shouting made him cry. His sobs reached the kitchen. Now do you see what you've done?, Jennifer bellowed. How can you be so insensitive? Jacob will never be better off than he is here. This is his home.

Allison finally gave in: She didn't want to deprive her son of the possibility of happiness. Perhaps Jennifer was right, and she shouldn't expose him to the dangers of Palestine. At least not yet. Jacob was born in a developed country and was too used to its benefits. Expelling him would be an incomprehensible punishment. Allison wept for a week, only stopping when she returned to Jenin and opened her arms to Salim, Alaa, Walid, Yehya, and little Rami.

Unlike the majority of her colleagues in the Coalition and the members of the other NGOs in Jenin, Allison chose not to talk about politics with the children. The poverty of the Palestinian people seemed so obvious, so intolerable, that she barely felt the need to point it out. Israel was no doubt the enemy, the great villain, the colonizing power, the first guilty party in the oppression and misery of the camps, but she felt no need to accentuate the hatred, to prolong a war that was catastrophic for everyone. Lots of her friends in the anti-capitalist movement were Jews, so she felt the need to mark the difference between ordinary citizens and the government, especially since that rhinoceros Netanyahu was in power, surrounded by serpents like Rehavam Zevi, who never stopped calling the Palestinians a cancer. Her more radical friends, like Gesine Muller, considered her attitude hypocritical. Doesn't it seem obvious to you who the executioners and victims are?, the German hectored her. How many U.N. resolutions does Israel violate every single day? And who cares about it? If an Arab nation did the same thing, your country would bombard it mercilessly.

Allison hated being confused with *her* country, but had by necessity gotten used to it, was used to receiving the constant reproaches of her humanitarian colleagues, as if she were the ambassador from Washington. I know, I know, she excused herself, it makes me indignant as well. The only thing I can say is that Arabs and Jews will have to learn to live together, there's no other way out. Turning up the hatred serves no purpose.

If Israel were to withdraw from the occupied territories and recognize the creation of a Palestinian state, the problems would be over, that's the only valid solution, Allison. Instead, Netanyahu sends his colonists to take over Gaza and the West Bank in order to build Greater Israel. But the Oslo accords . . . You know as well as I that the Oslo accords are as dead as the Dead Sea.

The accumulation of offenses was so huge that there was no space for moderation. Gesine and those who thought as she did simply didn't understand her. Allison didn't remove a speck of responsibility from Israel: Sharon, Netanyahu, and the Likud party personified absolute evil for her, but there would never be a solution as long as Jews and Palestinians did not see one another as equals, as human beings forced to live together in that inferno that people on both sides called the Holy Land. The discussion became even more bitter when the Palestinians from the camp joined in. While the rage of the expatriates responded only to an abstract feeling of solidarity, it was impossible to have a dialogue with those who'd suffered injustice, discrimination, violence, or the death.

The Nazis should have done a better job, she heard Walid say one day. You can't say that!, Allison reprimanded him. I know what you've suffered, Walid, but for that very reason you ought to understand the suffering of others. Nothing can justify the death of innocent people, *nothing*. You don't understand. Of course I do. You're angry and you have reason to be, what they did with your parents is terrible and the guilty parties will have to pay, but there are thousands of Jews on your side, looking for peace, trying to punish the guilty. They won't rest until they expel us from our land, we have to kill them before they kill us.

No, no!, Allison insisted, that's not the answer. That leads to a chain of revenge that never ends. Believe me, Walid, we've got to find other options, dialogue with them, try to find peace. No one was looking for peace when they murdered my parents.

Allison tried to hug him, but he stepped back: Don't let hatred eat you up, Walid. I . . . You're just like them, he rebuked her. Why don't you go take care of your son instead of coming here? Get out, we don't need you!

Unable to contain herself, Allison slapped him. She'd never hit any of the children, never let herself be carried away by the very violence she wanted so much to repudiate. Walid raised his hand to his cheek as if he wanted to measure the size of the insult, spit at Allison's feet, and dashed out. She just stood there under the imperious Middle Eastern sun, weeping. Weeping for Walid, for Palestine, for herself. And weeping for Jacob.

The obstinate and eternal rain, an obvious image of Seattle, did not frighten away the demonstrators. They all stood at their places, ready to put up with the bad weather and, in just a short time, the attacks of the police. I'd been awake for hours, but I wasn't sleepy or even tired, just feeling a kind of vertigo, as if from alcohol or hashish. It was 5:00 A.M., November 30th, 1999 (by then I'd spent months going back and forth to the United States chasing down Jack Wells and Eva Halász), and the sky had a acquired a rat-like color. The immense clouds were barely moving, paralyzed in time. This would be different from Birmingham. This time I was attending as part of the Direct Action Network, the collective that coordinated protests, so my job would not only consist in observing the spectacle and writing about it in my articles but also in directing operations (or at least that was the official reason for my trip).

According to the plan set weeks earlier, a contingent of students, workers, and activists from developed countries would move toward the center of Seattle from the north while representatives from the poor nations would mobilize from the south. The idea expressed an impeccable symbolism: Both groups would block the two halves of the city and meet around the Washington State Convention Center, where the summit of the World Trade Organization was to be held.

Hundreds of groups of all stripes and ideological positions had congregated there, not only to oppose the economic policies of the rich nations but to express their discontent about all areas of public life.

There were students, members of innumerable NGOs, members of trade unions, housewives, left-wing politicians, independent journalists, academics, and even—yes—extreme right-wing groups who were also opposed to free trade. The crowd of activists, along with a large number of students from the University of Washington, hoped to stop the delegates from attending the opening ceremonies in the Paramount Theater by blocking them in their hotels.

At 9:15, I was standing at the corner of Sixth and Pike, one of the key intersections in the city, when a small group of demonstrators dressed in black and wearing ski masks began to throw trash and garbage cans onto the sidewalks. Worried about this outburst by provocateurs, the members of the Network tried to stop them while the crowd chanted NO VIOLENCE, NO VIOLENCE. The masked group withdrew, but that was the first sign that something wasn't right. Not very far from there, another group of masked rebels—there couldn't be more than a hundred, compared to the seventy-five thousand peaceful demonstrators—disobeyed the ground rules set by the Net, broke shop windows, and spray-painted enormous "A"s on public buildings. Several of us tried to convince them to stop, but it was useless. By contrast, in a spontaneously orderly fashion that astounded me, the rest of the contingent blocked the entrances to the Paramount Theater and the Convention Center without any disturbances. We had achieved our first objective: At 10:00 A.M., the directors of the WTO had to postpone the opening ceremonies.

Just minutes later, I saw how the police, inside their armored vehicles on the flanks of the convention center, fired tear-gas grenades at the demonstrators. The fine order immediately collapsed, plunging the center of the city into an uncontrollable chaos. Trapped within the crowd, the security forces were unable to protect the delegates or open a path to the official locations. Numerous activists chained themselves to the doors of the convention center and refused to leave, despite being doused with toxic agents. Covering my face with a handkerchief, I avoided the riot police and offered the protestors some water. While the provocateurs on Sixth Avenue went on breaking the windows of McDonald's, Banana Republic, Nike, Planet Hollywood, and Warner Brothers, the formal opening of the WTO convention was postponed for a second time. The Secretary of State, Madeleine Albright, and the representatives of the WTO couldn't even leave their hotels.

Despite the fact that the arrival of new contingents of demonstrators made holding them back impossible, the plenary session of the WTO finally took place at 2:00 P.M. Meanwhile, I found myself back at Fourth Avenue and Pike, where a group of anarchists from the town of Eugene, Oregon was engaged in hand-to-hand combat with the security forces. Overwhelmed, the security forces put aside the tear gas and turned pepper spray on the young people and even shot rubber bullets at them. I was hit on the shoulder and had to run away from the toxic cloud rolling toward me.

At 4:00 P.M., Paul Schell, the mayor of Seattle, declared a state of emergency and imposed a curfew on the city center. Because of the imminent arrival of President Clinton, imperial seducer, the state governor ordered the National Guard to join the police. In pain and exhausted, I withdrew from the scene at around 8:00. But skirmishes between the security forces and the rebels—by now not only the anarchists but those who'd been gassed or hurt—went on for another hour, until at 9:00 the police withdrew from Capitol Hill.

The next day was no quieter. While the meeting took place, thanks to unprecedented security measures, the street fights went on all day. In his usual fawning style, Clinton asserted, in an interview with the *Seattle Times*, that he condemned the actions of the violent but was happy that the rest of us had shown our discontent in a peaceful way. The President always said what he had to say, the perfect tricky, fast-talking Don Juan. The liberalization of world trade was the biggest hoax in history: the WTO and its allies, the World Bank and the International Monetary Fund, demanded the elimination of subsidies and export taxes, while the industrialized nations, with the United States, Japan, and the European Union leading the way, did nothing else but protect their own. Why this double standard? Why all this impunity? Good intentions would mean nothing until the world made a definitive turn and developing nations could negotiate as equals with the great powers. The Seattle protests revealed this disproportionate relationship, and it was perhaps for that reason that the delegates from the southern nations did not succumb to the blackmail, bribery, and pressure from the great powers. After myriad hours of discussion, the WTO closed its doors without having reached any clear agreements.

We won the battle, I said to a blond, energetic activist. A few thousand unarmed, peaceful activists have brought down the WTO. It's a banner day for the whole world. There may still be space for hope. Her hair was a mess, and she was covered with sweat, but she answered me with a short smile: But this is merely the beginning.

It was Allison Moore. A few weeks earlier, I'd discovered she too was part of the Network and that, taking advantage of one of her trips to the United States to visit her son (she spent most of her time in Palestine), she traveled to Seattle to take part in the demonstration. There was nothing accidental in our meeting, but I knew how to disguise my intentions. There was nothing suspicious in this dialogue between two anti-globalization militants. In the humid, dark, afternoon setting, echoes of the fights were still audible, embers of the fire we'd just lit, a fire, according to our predictions, that would never go out. Of course she knew who I was (our microcosm fatally linked us), and she barely raised an eyebrow when I suggested that we have dinner together: a typical act of camaraderie between revolutionaries.

We went into a tiny Vietnamese restaurant and took a table in the rear. We used the first hour to review the fury and dedication of that week, the dizzying joy of the protests. Though we both preferred to appear skeptical, our excitement revealed the sense of a shared victory: Yes, perhaps another world was possible. Then in a long walk that took us to the docks and the aquarium, she told me about her experience in Palestine—especially about her children—while I, with some necessary omissions, told her about Russia, Azerbaijan, Chechnya, Yeltsin, and the oligarchs. And about my novel, which, she confessed, she'd read with enormous difficulty. Fiction has never been my strong suit, she told me, perhaps because the facts are always more horrifying and terrible.

Four hours later, we could take up, without fear or suspicion, the only subject that really interested me, the only subject that, setting aside my social commitment, had led me to Seattle and to her. We started talking about environmental matters, then genetics, and finally biotechnology. As was to be expected, Allison was alarmed about the commercialization of the genome. The idea that scientists were trafficking in the secrets of life irritated her, as did the contempt they felt toward nature—her time in Greenpeace and Earth First! had marked her forever—and their infinite arrogance. They're determined to be gods, she went on, but millionaire gods. I shared her fears, and, encouraged, she continued her harangue: We're like Dr. Frankenstein, we're trying to create a society of perfect beings, it won't be long before we turn out designer children and abort the deformed, the technological dictatorship is swallowing us up, we barely have any idea what we're playing with, and we rush out to sell it, we respect nothing, nothing, and at the end we'll turn into monsters, that's right, monsters.

After that jumble, it was inevitable she'd end up mentioning Jack Wells's name. She didn't hold back a single criticism of her brother-in-law: The miserable bastard not only cheated on her sister (ultimately that was the least of his sins) but tried to mock the entire world. Wells swore he'd discovered a miracle drug, a cure for cancer, a panacea, but Allison was convinced it was just a hoax, a lie just like all the other lies he'd told over the course of his life.

Why are you so sure?, I asked. I know Jack Wells better than I know myself, I know that something's not going right in his business, his arrogance will never lead him anywhere. But do you have concrete proof? Unfortunately I don't. Allison thought for a moment: If only my stupid sister would have the nerve to talk . . . I know she suspects something, but she refuses to face the truth. Your sister is a very hard woman. Do you know her? I interviewed her in Moscow a few years ago. As you know, she was the one responsible . . . For dragging your country into ruin, I know. Do you think I should talk to her just once more? Could you convince her to be interviewed by me? No one can convince Jennifer of anything, she's her own advisor.

We went on strolling the streets of Seattle until the rain and wind forced us to seek shelter. The night had stretched out over us, dense and ethereal, covering us with its lack of certainties. We said good-bye at a bus stop, frozen stiff. The next day, she would fly to Los Angeles to meet with her sister and son for the last time, and I was heading for New York to keep on plotting my somber battle against Jack Wells.

After a few months of ominous calm, on September 28th, 2000, Ariel Sharon, leader of the Likud party and the mastermind of the Sabra and Shatila massacre, had the strange idea of visiting the Temple Mount, in the Old City of Jerusalem, perhaps the most religiously charged site in the entire world. In a space less than a square kilometer in size were the holiest place in Judaism, the third most sacred place in Islam, and one of Christianity's holy places. Sharon, a savage seal, insisted that the Oslo Agreements guaranteed the right of free passage to Jewish citizens to visit the Wailing Wall. He assured everyone he was going to pray like any other believer. It was not his intention to provoke the Palestinian people, he blared out again and again to the press, but instead to send a message of peace and reconciliation. Besides, he pledged to carry out his pilgrimage in the most circumspect way possible.

A careful man, that one!, lamented Allison: The swine knows his presence will be taken as a sacrilege. His incursion will never go unnoticed, not just because of his ostentatious girth but because of the thousand or so armed guards who will accompany him. His faith will bury the peace process forever. And that's just what happened. Hundreds of Palestinians flooded the streets of East Jerusalem to protest against the infidel. Gathered at he edge of the Esplanade of the Mosques, they threw stones at the human wall protecting Sharon. Fights between the police and the demonstrators went on all that day, at the end of which a dozen Palestinians were dead, shot by the Israeli Defense Forces. Thus began the Al-Aqsa Intifada, a new period of street rioting similar to those that took place between 1987 and 1993.

Allison followed the news from Jenin: once again violence, once again horror, once again the angel of death. Within days the camp turned into a beehive of revenge and conspiracy; even the outside aid givers became radicalized and shared their irritation with the refugees, who said they were ready to die in order to expel the occupying forces. The first statistics were harrowing: scores of dead and hundreds of wounded, many of them minors. As a reprisal against Palestinian attacks on civilians, the Israeli Security Forces reoccupied the zones that were under the control of the Palestinian Authority, placed controls on all highways and roads, including those inside cities—at times people had to wait seven or eight hours to travel from one neighborhood to another—and enforced curfews that kept Palestinians from getting to work or shopping for groceries. Both the city and the Jenin camp were surrounded by the Israeli Army, under the pretext that many of the attacks that took civilian lives in Jerusalem and Tel Aviv were planned there.

One afternoon, Allison discovered to her horror that Salim, Walid, and Rami had disappeared. No one knew anything about them, and Alaa and Yehya refused to tell her where they'd gone. You must tell me where they are, begged Allison. They're just boys! Just a few days before, she'd seen Walid with Mahdi Ali Zgohoul, a refugee who led a group linked to Hamas, one of the most radical sects in Palestine. Salim is grown up, answered Alaa, he knows what he's doing.

In point of fact, age in Palestine barely mattered. According to the reports of the Coalition for Children/Palestine Section, the Tsahal was authorized to kill any suspicious person above the age of twelve. Allison feared the worst. And that's what she got. Like the rest of the world, she saw on television, live, as if it were a cowboy movie or a cartoon, the murder of a twelve-year-old child, Muhammad al-Durra. Like the rest of the world, she saw that he and his father were caught in the crossfire between the Israelis and Palestinian commandos. Like the rest of the world, she saw Muhammad's eyes when a bullet pierced his chest. Like the rest of the world, she saw how the boy tried to calm his father as his clothing became soaked with his blood. Like the rest of the world, she listened to the wailing of his father, and, like the rest of the world, she saw Muhammad collapse on the ground, dead, dead.

But Allison did not see little Rami die, the television cameras didn't see him get gunned down; Yehya and Alaa told her about it, weeping in mourning. It seems Walid convinced him to serve as a messenger between two Palestinian detachments, and an Israeli sniper had shot him in the stomach. A regrettable error, according to the press office of the Israeli Defense Forces. He was only ten years old.

Television couldn't turn him into another symbol of the Intifada, as it did with Muhammad al-Durra, so his name was merely added to the list of minors who had been killed or wounded by the Israeli security forces that the Coalition for Children compiled. In just the first weeks of the revolt, ninety-four Palestinians under the age of eighteen lost their lives.

Allison thought humanity was a plague, a malignant and perverse species that wasn't even able to protect its own progeny. But the madness was far from over. To avenge the death of Rami, Walid loaded himself with explosives one December morning, and, getting around the Israeli police and the various security controls, he walked into the Dolphinarium, a discotheque in the coastal area of Tel Aviv and blew himself into a thousand pieces. Twenty-one Israelis, most of them high-school students, died in an instant. As a reprisal, the Israeli Defense Forces decided to demolish the house belonging to Walid's uncle in Jenin. When she found out about it, Allison had a nervous crisis: How could they punish innocent people for a crime committed by a family member? What kind of justice was that? And how could the international community tolerate it?

Furious, Allison spoke with the Director of the Coalition for Children and urged them to take measures. Their superiors told her there was nothing they could do. But she was not going to stand there and let this happen. No more. In Jenin, she contacted members of the Movement for International Solidarity, a new NGO whose mission was to stop extreme punishments against Palestinians. These activists offered themselves as human shields. Allison would never allow Israeli bulldozers to knock down her family's home.

EGOISTIC GENES

United States of America, 1999-2000

Feelings are an evolutionary scruple, declared Eva, drunk and naked, a pathology of the intelligence, in the best case a self-preservation manual. Love is the glue of reproduction, anger a detonator in times of danger, fear a follow-up to pain and perhaps death. She just wouldn't stop repeating these statements, as if they were aphrodisiacs. She took advantage of these tirades by invading my private zones, invading my passivity. Then she laughed wildly and threw herself over my sex, a victim of the euphoria that swept over her after every period of depression.

The glow of morning turned her skin into a bonfire and then into an underwater image: The red and blue rays tinted her thighs and hips, stripping away their humanness, while her face remained among the shadows, barely visible. I rested my head on her belly, next to her navel, and let her caress me in silence. Two bodies, completely intertwined, two masses of muscles piled up. Carbon machines governed by despotic cells whose only desire was to feed and reproduce themselves, indifferent to our passions, to our standards of proportion and beauty. Our genes govern us, Eva concluded, we allow ourselves to be led by their whims.

I listened to her in a daze. Her sex gave off a bitter, fascinating scent: An avalanche of chemical reactions that provoked sudden electric discharges in my brain, according to her. Our genes insist on surviving at all costs, she went on, their only objective is to remain on the earth by means of our descendants. They need sex, not us. If we copulate, it's only to keep ourselves satisfied. Meanwhile, I was kissing her pubis, ignoring her speech, like someone who recognizes a way out of the abyss. She shuddered, then stretched her legs and received me resignedly. A biological imperative, a simple hormonal or glandular order? Absurd: It was I who wanted to be there, not my genes. It was I who wanted to sink between her folds. It was I who, barely knowing her, imagined her to be mine.

We slept for more than ten hours. When I woke up, I studied her features, that profile I'd touched and outlined but barely glimpsed. She opened her eyes: Her extremely black pupils seemed framed by an almost yellow aura. I felt around on the night table until I found my watch. Noon. Both of us should have taken our respective return flights three hours earlier, she to Washington, axis of the cosmos, and I much further, to Moscow, city of wide avenues. I don't think you'll be having dinner at home today, she joked, kissing my hands. Do you still remember my name?, she teased.

And you are, she paused, that Romanian photographer . . . No, no, now I remember, that Russian novelist . . . Yuri . . . Yuri Something or Other. I threw myself on top of her and kissed her hard. She seized my wrists and bit my lip. That hurt, I complained. And that's only the beginning. Her skin was a refuge from the world, it protected me from cold and wind. Her skin saved me. We spent the whole day in that lugubrious New Haven hotel, and the next, and the next. In the morning, we said it would be the last, and at night we postponed the date of our return. Not paying too much attention, I heard her mumble awkward excuses into the telephone: I still felt I had no right to demand explanations from her. All that mattered to me was being with her.

At her suggestion, we didn't share personal stories. Nor did we allow hope for the future. That encounter—a collision she called it—would be unique in both senses of the term: unforgettable and unrepeatable. An adventure? Yes, an adventure. On the other hand, I had no one I had to lie to: For months I'd had no other boss than my own obsession, and the women in my life were merely stopping points, names and addresses that never impinged on my schedules.

I'd gone to the United States to learn more about DNAW—the thread that linked Arkady Granin with America—never imagining that I'd end up spending three nights with Jack Wells's lover. She was taking part in an academic congress at Yale University, and at the end of her paper (much too complicated for my tastes), I made a point of approaching her. I told her I wanted to write a journalistic piece about the biotechnical industry (that was no lie, though I neglected to tell her why), and I requested an interview. Somewhat surprised, she agreed to meet me in the lobby of her hotel at 6:00 P.M., and she told me about her career and the work she was doing at Celera at that time. Then we chatted a bit, had a few drinks—I couldn't pull myself away from her eyes—and with no formalities she invited me up to her room.

Perhaps falling in love was only an evolutionary pretext, as she said, a foundation-less emotion, a justification for a biochemical confusion caused by genes—a desire to possess the genes of the other—but the effects brought about by that disorder quickly appeared on my body. I wanted to go on seeing her as long as possible. We had to lie to other people in order to sleep together, Eva warned me when we parted, so it's not necessary that we fool each other. Instead of kissing me good-bye, she held out her hand. It's been a pleasure, Yuri Chernishevsky. And she walked away, just like that. Eva. Eva Halász.

The Celera building, an 18,500 square meter construction in a scruffy industrial park in Rockville, Maryland, looked like a ruin just months earlier. Its façade was blackened by pollution, and its windows were opaque from dust. Craig Venter supervised the reconstruction with the same ardor he bestowed on his new yacht, the Sorcerer II. His wanted to captain a starship—a miniature city, his Deathstar—and reach the twenty-first century before anyone else. He scrutinized every detail, intending to show that Celera was a part of the future. With its stainless steel facing, its metallic-blue carpeting, and its logo—that sought to evoke the intertwined strands of DNA—the vestibule transported visitors to a parallel dimension controlled by the chimeras and deliriums of science fiction.

Assuming the role of an intergalactic warrior, Venter constructed a command bridge straight out of *Star Trek*. Opposite his enormous control chair were the curved monitors, where every new bit of information about the genome flashed in real time. The fourth floor was set aside for the largest sequencing center in the world: a vast tangle of connections, cables, and halogen light where the 300 ABI PRISM 3700 computers, Celera's secret weapon, were housed.

Every time a new one was added to the business, the techies working for Venter (Darth Venter) gave it a nickname like Princess Leia, Han Solo, or Luke Skywalker. Each of the $300,000 cubical monsters was given a mechanical arm—making it a kind of R2D2 that could sequence up to a million DNA bases per day. Thanks to that army of androids, Celera, a small private business, would smash the proud forces of the Human Genome Project.

If Celera was a space ship and Craig Venter its captain, then Gene Myers and Eva Halász were its navigators. They owned Celera's third floor, a tennis court sized space where Compaq had installed one of the most powerful computers on the planet—only the Department of Defense had one like it, which they used for simulating atomic explosions—the Alpha 8400, valued at $80 million. Perhaps Eva wouldn't come to understand the secrets of intelligence, as she'd always dreamed, but now she could contribute to an even greater objective: She and Myers had designed the program, the only one of its kind, that would reassemble the genome once the PRISM 3700s had disassembled each one of its bases. Eva saw herself as the person responsible for introducing order and intelligibility into that chaos. How paradoxical and correct her career turned out to be! The mission of an unbalanced woman like her would be to fight anarchy and to contemplate, before anyone else, the essence of the human being.

Before taking on such a great task and assuring his entry into History, Venter decided to test his automatons—and the assembly program—on a simpler organism, *Drosophila menanogaster*, the fruit fly that was the delight of biologists. Though its genome didn't contain even 5% of the information in the human genome, it was composed of around 120 million letters. If the PRISM 3700s produced sequences of 500 pairs, the program created by Myers and Halász would have to put together a puzzle with about 240,000 pieces. And, for the results to be reliable, they would have to repeat the experiment at least ten times. In an interview, Venter expressed his certainty that Celera would achieve its goal in record time, much faster than the Sanger Institute had sequenced the nematode *Caenorhabditis elegans*, the public program's greatest success. Yet another slap in the face to his rivals! He'd also declared in a

New York Times article in 1998 that Celera would finish mapping the human genome while his rivals were still struggling to get started. He went on to suggest they re-direct their efforts to discovering the genome of the mouse.

The Human Genome Project militia felt offended, and even if Francis Collins, its general, did not want to be combative at first, and even though he welcomed Celera to the competition, his collaborators were less prudent and never stopped insulting Venter. The most restrained called him the Bill Gates of biotechnology, but most referred to him as a cheap peddler and a hypocrite. And even James Watson, the father of DNA, had compared him to Hitler. In their eyes, Venter had sold his soul to the multinational pharmaceutical companies.

To place the project in the hands of a private company, whose only objective is making money, seems to me the height of stupidity!, bellowed Michael Morgan, the Director of the Wellcome Foundation, which was responsible for financing the British section of the Human Genome Project. Starting next month, we'll double the resources of the Sanger Institute. The Institute will sequence a third of the genome on its own. And humiliate that science vendor.

Morgan's announcement showed the level to which things had risen: It was unthinkable that a single man—much less a villain like Venter—should get all the credit. Every means possible would be used to keep him from perverting the meaning of science forever. To respond to such accusations, Venter published an article in *Science*, where he declared that the data obtained by Celera would be made public in no more than three months—the HGP demanded it be done immediately—and assured everyone that his company would retain only 1% of the genetic information they obtained.

The article was not enough to calm the suspicion, hatred, and envy. Even Francis Collins lost his composure and suggested that the shotgun sequencing proposed by Venter would be full of holes and end up looking like an issue *Mad* magazine. For this reason, Venter needed Gene, Eva, and the rest of Celera's biocomputing team to give him the *Drosophila* results as soon as possible: It was the only way to shut those loudmouths up.

While Eva cohabited with the fruit fly, Jack Wells had more important things to do: His desire to possess her hadn't diminished, but nothing could compare to the excitement of making a deal. And he was on the verge of signing the most lucrative agreement in his career, perhaps the most lucrative in pharmaceutical history. In April 1999, he received a strange visit from James de Priest, a neat, restrained individual who promoted DNAW's interests in the financial community. The only sign of ambition in him was the incessant fluttering of his eyelids. I won't beat around the bush, Jack. Yesterday I got a call from Branford-Midway Stern. Wells's cells released monstrous doses of adrenaline: An offer? They want exclusive rights to C225 and a substantial package of DNAW stock.

This was the news he'd been waiting decades to hear. An impatient Wells set up an interview with the pharmaceutical giant in the bar at the Plaza. He left his nervousness behind: Now he would have to appear assertive and energized. In his entire career as a businessman, he'd never felt so powerful, so sure of himself. He was the owner of the most promising drug ever created—the elixir of life—and now the rest of the world would have to kow-tow to his demands. Wells delivered the first blow.

I'm flattered that Branford-Midway Stern is so interested in our little firm, he smiled, but I've always wanted to maintain DNAW's independence. We've had to make countless sacrifices to reach this point, and we wouldn't want to be swallowed up without guarantees.

Brian Markinson, Branford-Midway Stern's negotiator, immediately detested Wells's vanity. They exchanged niceties for half an hour until, a couple of bourbons later, they returned to the subject at hand. Perhaps we could make an exchange of stock, Markinson finally proposed, but we would need time to study the matter. As you like, gentlemen. But time is the one thing I do not have.

Wells left savoring his triumph: Those punks had taken the hook. A week later, accompanied by Eva, he attended the 37th Meeting of the United States Society of Clinical Oncology, held in San Francisco, where more that twenty-five thousand experts in the field had gathered. There, before the creme-de-la-creme of the scientific community, he announced that C225 would be the emblematic drug of the twenty-first century. According to our most recent studies, he said, the combination of Erbitex and Irinotecan has a 22.5% success rate with patients suffering from refractory rectal cancer, the highest recovery rate ever recorded. Those grandiloquent words were enough to turn DNAW into the most sought-after and admired company at the meeting. In Wells's opinion, those pedants from Branford-Midway Stern would now have no option but to give in to his demands.

Listen to this, Eva, almost all the Wall Street analysts have given DNAW an A for performance. Wells wasn't wrong: After his visit to San Francisco, DNAW stock went up 40%. Wall Street was living in another period of euphoria, and C225 had become the last hope for scores of desperate patients and a gold mine for thousands of investors.

I met up with Eva Halász again in July, 1999, two months after our first encounter. This time it was a hotel in Washington. Why did she take back what she said and see me again? What was prolonging our story? Why did we both persist? Then, trapped within those anodyne walls, we sealed our fate. We should have foreseen it: Two creatures who resign themselves beforehand to defeat. I seized her frozen body and kissed her eyelids: Our genes longed to be eternal. We began the experiment, that rending she refused to recognize as passion.

Eva sat down on the bed and looked me over pitilessly. I obeyed her order and stripped in front of her with the same impatience I'd felt the first time, awkward and vulnerable. Her gaze could have no other meaning: Only here am I yours. Soon I would be defenseless, at her mercy. There she was again, identical to the character I'd constructed during her absence: Eva Halász. Her skin stood out in contrast to the darkness of the sheets. She moved toward me, grazing me with her thighs, her hips. I tried to kiss her, but she covered my mouth with her hand. Obsessed, I made another attempt to reach her neck, but instead I slipped to the floor. Then she leapt onto me, pinned me down, and ran her tongue over my skin. She paused for an eternity on my chest until she achieved her objective: a ruddy shadow, her mark.

I tried to slip free, awkward and excited as I was, but Eva wouldn't let me escape. I closed my eyes. I wanted to sink into her and wanted her lips on my sex. Was there no love in our encounter? Was everything a crude chemical reaction, the result of the insane avidity of our cells? Eva quickly got dressed, as if in that second she'd forgotten what had taken place between us, as if those hours had vanished, as if they'd been erased while she was cleaning the semen off her lips. When will I see you again?, I asked. I don't know, Yuri Mikhailovich. I don't know.

Assembling a fly wasn't a biological problem, it was a mathematical one. Craig Venter and his team, those experts in genetics with their sequencing machines and their Nobel Prizes, were nothing more than artisans, simple initiators of a labor whose culmination would only be reached thanks to the beauty of numbers. Gene Meyers and Eva Halász, on the other hand, thought of themselves as shy but powerful architects. From their cave on the third floor of Celera, far away from the tidy lawyers, the eccentric biologists, the slender secretaries, and the elegant businessmen, they would determine the success or failure of the project. If their algorithms worked, the *Drosophila* genome would pop up on their screens: a living being digitalized, a chimera composed only of numbers.

Imagine a program for putting puzzles together, Eva explained to me the previous afternoon. The system begins by recognizing the form, the size, and the colors of a given piece, then it compares it with the others, and, starting with their similarities, places them in order. Little by little it constructs the complete image, even if there are a few holes that will have to be filled in later. The most dangerous thing is that we can believe that one piece fits with another when it really doesn't. We have to be right 99% of the time! On August 25th, 1999, the assembly process was on the verge of concluding. I never imagined that instead of conceiving a child, I'd end up conceiving a fly!, she joked.

Eager to show off the results as soon as possible, Craig Venter held an urgent meeting on the Celera command bridge. Well? I'm afraid we've obtained a rather strange number. Myers looked calm, but Eva was trembling. What are you talking about, Gene? 802,000, Eva mumbled. What does that mean? That the assembler didn't give us a complete sequence of the "Drosophila" genome but 802,000 separate fragments. Something must have happened when we ran the program. But don't worry, Craig, we'll figure it out.

Venter didn't even look at them: If they didn't correct the mistake within a week, Celera stock would sink. And that would be end of his race. Eva worked through the night trying to identify the error. When she went back to Celera the next morning, her face pale and purple shadows under her eyes, she found Myers sunk in despair. By the end of the day the situation was no better. Nor was it the next or the one after that. The two felt like criminals on the way to the gallows, unable to stop the march of time. Could they have failed? I really don't understand, Eva confessed.

On Friday morning, the assembly team was on the verge of a nervous breakdown. Myers suggested the staff take the afternoon off. Everyone gathered up their gear and left. Eva pretended to do the same, but at the last moment decided to check the calculations one last time. At one in the morning, she had yet to find the error. At one in the morning, she answered the thousandth missed message on her cellphone. It was Wells, with whom she had a date at 8:00 P.M. Where were you? I'm busy. I can't stand being stood up like this! Eva never permitted reproaches like that, so without saying another word, she ended the call and turned off the phone. She needed sleep.

On Saturday she went back to Celera, and on Sunday as well. She examined the assembly program again and again. Wells called again, and she again didn't answer. At 11:00 P.M., she looked carefully at line number 678 in the program. She looked up and down and went back to 678. Incredible: A first-year student wold have found the error! A single badly constructed line, out of 150,000, had wrecked everything. When they solved the problem, she and Gene quickly dominated the insect.

The next morning, Celera's attorney presented an application at the Patent Office: "Primary Sequence for Nucleic Acid in the Genome of *Drosophila*, Discovery Systems that Contain the Sequence of *Drosophila* and Possible Applications." Thanks to Gene Myers and Eva Halász, J. Craig Venter, master of the cells, was on the verge of becoming the owner of a fly. Not bad for a start.

The Christmas vacation of 1999 would bring them together one last time. Months earlier, Jennifer had arranged a trip to Disney World, and, as usual, invited Allison at the last moment, when it was too late to change plans. Allison hated her sister's tyranny. Jennifer knew that the last place on earth Allison would ever want to visit with her son was Disney World, which she considered a sanctuary of mild-mannered and naïve conformists. What a small, small world, chanted a chorus of wooden puppets. So small that the United States could make it into a private hunting preserve, muttered Allison. For God's sake, Alli, relax and enjoy yourself. Can't you put aside politics even for a second.

The two women flanked Jacob, who stared in embarrassment at the false castle rising before him. Forced to make his mother and his aunt happy, the boy stood stock still, waiting for a signal.

I want Jacob to become critical, starting now. But just look at him, Alli, he's happy, don't destroy his illusions. Sooner or later, he'll have to learn to deal with the real world. I don't want to educate him the way our mother educated us. When he finds out he doesn't live in a fantasy world, that we're not in a fairy tale with a happy ending, he'll reproach us for having lied to him. To the contrary little sister: He'll thank us for having shielded him a little from the horror. He's only ten! Why do you want to make him into an adult? Give him a chance to grow up, to be like other children his age. Maybe happiness is just a hoax, but we don't have any right to destroy his.

Jacob turned toward his mother and shot her a forlorn look. Allison's stomach turned. All right, let's go in. Allison was violating her own principles, but she wasn't strong enough to say no. How could she explain to her son that week after week she lived next to death, the real danger of Jenin, and that by comparison the make-believe danger of an amusement park seemed vulgar to her? Jacob took her by the hand and dragged her to half a dozen attractions, some boring or disappointing, others unbearable, some almost intelligent. Allison didn't want her son to remember her as a monster. She might feel stupid and superficial riding on a phony rocket or a make-believe pirate ship, but her son's enthusiasm was authentic.

Was it really all that awful, Alli? Jacob was playing around with a phony gigantic mouse while they argued over their food: salads, no dressing, their only shared taste. It wasn't bad, but I wasn't wrong either, Jennifer. Tonight I'll try to discuss a few concepts from today's experience with him. Jennifer burst out laughing, and Allison couldn't stop herself from doing the same. After so many fights and disagreements, the sisters were still able to have a good time together. They hugged for the last time. Jacob came over to them, worn out. And without thinking about it, he threw himself into his mother's arms. This was the best day in my life, he concluded.

When I made out the grim skyscrapers of New York, navel of the world, rising above the mist, I tried to convince myself that the move had been voluntary, a natural step in my career as an activist and writer, the natural consequence of my research. Eva Halász has nothing to do with this trip, I repeated, her eyes don't lead me down my road, her lips never invoked me. If I've come here, its to continue tracking down Arkady Ivanovich Granin and Jack Wells, not to look for her. Six months had gone by since our last encounter—our collision—and she had barely answered any of my messages. In theory, my idea was to visit the United States for only a few weeks, the time necessary to finish my investigation into DNAW, and then go back to Europe, the only place where I felt comfortable and safe.

I didn't let even a single day go by without looking for her. At first she wasn't very enthusiastic—she hated feeling pursued—but that didn't stop her from meeting me in a Gaithersburg hotel, near Rockville. I can't get this damn program to work right, she said, so I'll only have a few hours. The excitement of seeing her near Celera made me forget her conditions. The only thing that mattered was being with her as soon as possible. Eva came an hour late, but she never uttered a word of apology. We leapt at each other without saying a thing.

She stipulated that I banish my demands, and I obeyed without making a fuss. I almost wish that meeting had been a disaster, that our skins had stopped attracting each other, but that didn't happen: A secret impetus united us and condemned us. I have to admit it, Yuri Mikhailovich, Eva said before leaving, unlike me, my sex still needs you.

The anonymous and neat Holiday Inn in Gaithersburg, Maryland, became my home for the next few weeks. It's stupid to set yourself up in that hole because of me, Yuri Mikhailovich. I can write here or anywhere else, I explained, and at least the decoration doesn't distract me. And that was the truth: I spent hours focused on my computer, oblivious to the death rattles of the world, as if I'd gone into a monastery. It had been a long time since I enjoyed so much calm and so much silence—I finally felt that my fame, my vulgar and ephemeral fame, was now behind me—and I thought I could perhaps begin a new life, a life different from my own. During the first days, I didn't even have to drink to get inspired or to cancel out the echoes of Afghanistan or Chechnya: I had at my disposal an infinite and placid stretch of time inhabited only by my words. Though she never promised me anything, Eva turned up at the Holiday Inn every day at lunch time.

Those were—I know it now—our only moments of something that I won't call happiness, I wouldn't want to betray her skepticism. What it was was tranquility. Could we have gone on that way indefinitely, without questions or commitments, in pure improvisation, subject only to the rhythms of our flesh? Why can't we humans recognize well-being at the right moment? Why do we always want more? Why are we simultaneously greedy and insatiable? At the end of those three weeks, whose perfection I can only glimpse at this distance, I told Eva I could no longer stand being locked away like that, that the Holiday Inn was becoming a jail (when in fact it was paradise), and I revealed that I intended to rent a cabin not far from there. I saw the advertisement in the local paper, and I'd already worked out an agreement with the owner, I told her. If you think you'll be more comfortable that way, Eva muttered, and it seemed to me she smiled. You'll soon see, you'll like it, I promise. A cabin on the bank of a river.

At a press conference that looked more like a birthday party, Jack Wells and the representatives of Branford-Midway Stern publicly announced their association: The pharmaceutical giant would pay one billion dollars for fourteen million shares of DNAW, and another billion for the development and exclusive commercialization of C225. According to the terms of the contract, BMS would buy the DNAW stock for $70.00 per share, even though the market currently valued it at $50.00. As was revealed thanks to my research, Wells, as President and CEO of the company, was authorized to buy a new stock package at the preferential price of $8.00. At the end of the day, Wells deposited he equivalent of $111 million in his bank account. The press almost unanimously celebrated the pact, convinced by DNAW prospects, BMS's seriousness, and the fabulous nature of the drug. Never before had a biopharmaceutical product fetched such a price.

To celebrate the event, Jack organized a sumptuous party at the Ritz-Carlton Hotel. He invited the entire *who's who* of New York, navel of the world: Wall Street financiers, Soho artists, Hollywood stars, television hosts, bankers, brokers, scientists (including six or seven Nobel laureates), aristocrats, business figures—Christina Sanders topped the list—and celebrated journalists. I begged Eva to get me an invitation: I swore I'd be discrete, that my only interest was to experience the momentous event first-hand. At first she refused, because she did not want to go on mixing our worlds, and perhaps she feared my imprudence and my jealousy. After myriad requests, she finally accepted.

That night, I witnessed the alliance between frivolity and humanitarianism: The crowd celebrated in equal doses the most promising scientific advance of recent years and the fortune Jack and his partners had amassed in a single afternoon. Very few were concerned about the veracity of Jack's statements. None of the guests doubted DNAW's success. None except me. Restraining myself with all my might, I approached the host.

Congratulations, Mr. Wells. He glanced at me for an instant and pretended to recognize me. Thank you, thanks a lot. I hope you're having a good time. Suddenly Eva joined us, incredibly beautiful in her red dress. Allow me to introduce you to Eva Halász. Yuri Chernishevsky, delighted. I leave you in good hands, Mr. Chernishevsky, Wells concluded, and walked away. Wearing a top hat, he stepped onto the dais and took the microphone. He looked like the master of ceremonies in *Cabaret*. Don't be afraid, I have no intention of giving a speech. Music, maestro, please!

On the television screens, hung in the four corners of the salon, appeared the image of Frank Sinatra, and Wells belted out his personal version of "My Way." He was singing to shut me up, to silence the doubts about his triumph, the doubts about his wealth, the doubts about his fame. After destroying another two songs—by Britney Spears—some young ladies disguised as Las Vegas chorus girls distributed enormous posters to the guests so they could follow the choreography of "YMCA."

How can you stand this?, I whispered into Eva's ear. Let's get out of here! Contrary to my expectations, she said yes. She made no sarcastic remarks, didn't wound me with her contempt. She looked at me, tranquil and bright, as never before, as never again. I took her by the hand, taking advantage of the hullabaloo, and dragged her to the coat check. We got our coats and slipped away, happy and hysterical, like children committing some bit of mischief. Drunk on his triumph and wealth, Wells didn't seem to notice our escape.

My relationship with Eva twisted a bit, as if a foul odor emanated from the depths of my cabin on the river, as if the murmur of the current already contained the announcement of death. Outwardly, the setting was idyllic: Luminous, tranquil, set in an almost frightening natural beauty. It was hard to believe that it was only fifteen minutes from the highway and an hour away from Washington, axis of the cosmos. But from the moment she laid eyes on it, Eva was uncomfortable: Something bothered her, the color of the furniture, the afternoon rain, or the sound of wind beating against the roof, or perhaps her mood had become more vacillating and erratic since Venter ordered the assembly of the human genome. Her visits became sporadic, and I, sunk in that solitude, that void, became irritable and blind.

Where before nothing mattered except the hours Eva spent with me, now I suddenly wanted her all to myself. And instead of concentrating on writing about Wells, her lover, I began to worry about the time Eva set aside for him, the time she did not set aside for me. I thought my situation was not only gloomy but unfair: There I was, stuck in that damn forest, thousands of kilometers from my country, only for her sake.

Was it too much ask that she appreciate the gesture, that she reward my sacrifice a little? Our times together, shorter and shorter but no less searing—fights and shouting had replaced the preliminaries—always ended at the same point.

Why don't you leave him? My voice sounded like a warning and not like a question. Even though our shared madness had gone on for weeks—an eternity—Eva refused to abandon Wells. Don't you love me? Yuri! I know, I know, I bit my lips, love doesn't exist. But in that case what the hell are you doing here? You know why I'm here, I don't have to tell you: Because what we have is absurd, absurd and clear. Then why do you go back to him, what can a person like Wells give you? He's *contemptible.* Yuri, you don't have to . . . You know that as well as I do, Eva: The only thing that matters to him is money. You're just another of his properties, the best piece in his collection.

We couldn't avoid it: Alcohol and cocaine became our life raft. I've told you my life story a thousand and one times, Yuri Mikhailovich. Eva stretched her naked skin over mine: You know what I've lived through. I'm fed up with perfect stories, romantic loves, absolute yielding, and outsized passions. None of that is any good, none of it lasts. They're tricks, sweetheart. Why fool ourselves? You and I have something unique and impossible. That's where its value lies. We're here because we want to be, because we desire each other, because we couldn't stand being elsewhere. It's grandiose, but it's everything. And you know it, you know it as well as I do.

I emptied another glass of vodka and sank my face into her sex, my antidote against the present. Ever since my separation from Zarifa, I thought I was immune to jealousy and suspicion, and I roundly condemned men who tried to take control of women as if they were farms or cars, but faced with Eva's harsh freedom, faced with her daring and her lack of answers, I thought of nothing else but possessing her. Just thinking of her in Wells's hands was unbearable. The only thing we need is right here, Yuri Mikhailovich, she calmed me. You and I are this, the humors of our bodies, the acid smell that envelopes us, our cells, our saliva. Nothing else.

I loved her, and I hated her. How could she keep on being so sure of herself? Do you really want to go on this way, Eva? Having to hide, taking note of the minutes left to us? I know what I want, Yuri: the chance to be like this, with you, from time to time. To think about you as an inducement. To miss you. To lose you and to find you again, understand?

Yes, I lied. We humans are alone, we're born alone, we love alone, and we die alone, there's nothing to be done, she insisted. If we accept that from the start, we avoid infinite disappointments. The combination of vodka and coke was making me stagger. I was fed up with her rationalizations, fed up with her equanimity, fed up with her words. I only wanted her body.

Why don't you just leave me in peace!, I shouted at her one afternoon. Isn't it you who says we're always alone? She didn't even look at me. I got up, ready to leave, to go back to Russia, to forget the whole story. She took me by the arm. I twisted away from her arm and forgot myself. I lost my head and slapped her face. Her beloved face. An accident. There was a dry sound. My hand burned, as if I'd placed it on a burning coal. Eva did not cry, did not shout, did not insult me. She didn't even walk out. She just stood there, impassive, barely surprised. She ran her hand over her cheek in a gesture that was almost sweet. Why didn't she do anything? Why did she just stay in that damned cabin, at my side, soft and ethereal, sad, perhaps resigned instead of running away, instead of escaping toward freedom and life? Why the devil did she stay with me? Stupid, a thousand times stupid! She should have expelled me from her life, spit on me. But it was I who wept. I fell down on my knees before her and cursed myself, begged her not to abandon me, promised I'd never touch her again, asked for another chance. Eva listened in silence. She took my face in her hands and forgave me, and forgave me.

Jennifer stared into the mirror, scrutinized the shadows under her eyes and the wrinkles at the corner of her lips, counted the stains on her skin, which had first appeared on her cheeks, and thought: I'm ridiculous. She filled her hands with water and splashed it over her face as if she wanted to erase it or wash off her makeup. Ridiculous and old, she repeated in a low voice, determined to hurt herself. Where had her youth, her grace, her beauty gone? She'd never been this way, never let herself be beaten, had never given in to misfortune, perhaps because the world never seemed a welcoming place to her, because she never believed happiness was possible. Her father educated her to carry out orders, not to feel satisfied. The Senator condemned her to a life of stubbornness, of contention, of self-sufficiency! What use had her prosperity been? Day after day she'd debated about how to be the best, and she'd attained that goal. And then? Who applauded her sacrifices? Who celebrated her triumphs?

Not only was she ridiculous and old: She was useless. Her work at the International Monetary Fund? More emptiness: None of her efforts had brought about results. Zaire was still a cesspool; Latin America, a robbers' cave; Russia, a cemetery. The adjustment plans, the millions in loans, the structural reforms, the shock treatments: Nothing worked. The whole planet was a stinking, sad, swamp. She violently dried her face: She needed a bit of physical pain. Thank heaven no one could see her in those moments: hidden in her desolate apartment in Washington, axis of the cosmos, an unknown force was making her go from one place to another without breathing.

She walked toward her nephew's room, peeked through the partly-open door and confirmed for the thousandth time that he was sleeping peacefully. How she envied that innocence! She tiptoed away and went back to the kitchen. She poured a cup of tea and drank a sip that was as tepid and tasteless as her life. She'd just turned fifty-five and had nothing. *Nothing.* A job at the IMF. Mere routine. A broken, non-existent marriage. Genetic sterility. And Jacob? Jacob wasn't even hers. Jacob was the burden imposed on her by her sister to make her pay for her success: Instead of hating or cursing her, Allison had given her her only son—so she'd be forced to see him every day, to grow fond of him, to confirm the impossibility of ever being a mother, of being the mother of *that* child.

Jennifer glanced at the clock: 8:00 P.M. She still had five or six hours of insomnia before her. The buzzer went off. May I come in?

After an absence of several months, Wells turned up again, as inconsiderate and irascible as always. Where do you get off turning up here without warning? Jennifer opened the door and let him walk into the living room, straight for the shelves where the bottles were lined up. Wells poured himself a bourbon, swallowed it, and poured another. It was obvious he'd been drinking for hours.

What do you want? Wells collapsed into an armchair: I've got good news and bad news. Which would you like to hear first? I don't want you in my house, Jack. Okay, first the good news: Eva's been unfaithful to me. Wells's words had no effect on Jennifer: I hope you don't expect me to console you. I thought you'd be happy, said Jack, gulping down another glass of whiskey. Happy? You're a stranger to me.

Wells took the blow with ease. He knew his wife was enjoying the moment as she enjoyed few things. And now the bad news: The Food and Drug Administration has refused to evaluate our anti-cancer drug.

They wouldn't even accept the formal request. But Jack, just a few weeks ago . . . ! DNAW is headed for ruin, Jennifer. One day we're the most promising biotechnical company in the world, and the next we're garbage. What about your partners? What about the BMS people? Wells raised his hands to his brow: His gesture suggested fatigue rather than despair.

They'll slit my throat. You know them, Jennifer. No one likes to lose millions overnight. How could this happen? The idiots at the FDA say our clinical results are not reliable. That we haven't treated enough patients. So what happens now? For the first time in my life, I do something the right way, and it all goes to hell. C225 is the best hope we have against cancer. That's true, I swear. And I fucked it up, Jen, I fucked it up! I'm sorry, she barely sweetened her voice. Tomorrow morning tell your broker to sell. It's that serious? More serious than you can imagine. And I also want you to do something for me, Jen. For old time's sake.

No, Jack. And that's final. I've already given orders to have some stock transferred to your account, Jennifer. You have to sell all of it before the news comes out! It's illegal, Jack. I don't want to be involved in this. I'll lose everything, and so will you. If only from the legal point of view, we're still man and wife. You have to do it, Jen, I'm begging you. No! Do you want me to get down on my knees? Humiliate me all you like, I deserve it. And then give the order to sell that damned stock! Jennifer got up, impassive. It's time you left, Jack.

He knew his wife well enough to know it would be useless to insist. He'd tossed the dice, and now all he could do was hope that a night with her demons would soften her. It was his only hope. As soon as she was alone, Jennifer felt the tears run down her cheeks. The idiot didn't even give you the chance to enjoy his defeat. Now she'd spend a sleepless night, debating with herself about whether she should save him or dig his grave.

Eva confirmed my suspicion, as if it were a mere trifle. It was at the end of yet another of our amorous fights—we let ourselves be tempted by violence without really realizing it—a story like so many others, a tale among myriad parallel tales. Not an accusation, not a denunciation but a marginal comment, a slip: the trail I'd been on for months, the trail that had led me to America, the trail that justified my suspicion, the trail that had injected Allison Moore into me, the trail that would bury Jack Wells. Without knowing it, innocent and placid (also naked and hot),

Eva Halász confided to me the key that would allow me to terminate her lover's career and perhaps send him to jail. The miserable wretch deserved it: That was my only excuse and my only consolation.

I pretended not to ascribe much importance to Eva's words—to Eva's slip—and I didn't start unwinding the skein. I didn't make her add any details; I changed the subject, and put away her comment as if it were a secret weapon. What did Eva Halász say? What was her indiscretion? The day before, Wells had spoken with her over the telephone—the jerk kept calling her at all hours—a rapid, mysterious conversation. The businessman sounded beaten down and tense, or perhaps just frightened, and he confided to Eva that the FDA had stopped him dead in his tracks, that C225 would have to wait for a better moment, nothing more.

Only someone fully aware of what was going on, only someone who'd followed, day by day, week by week, month by month, the highs and lows of DNAW, someone, that is, like me, could figure out the true meaning of his words. Wells was going down. And even more seriously: He knew he was going down. And knowing that, knowing that before anyone else—knowing it before the public found out—he would do everything he could to avoid sinking to the bottom. It was his nature. I'd been studying him for months, I'd pursued him with the same determination and courage I'd pursued Kaminski, so I could guess how he'd react.

After so many years of fighting, after all the effort he'd put into becoming rich and famous, he wouldn't be willing to return to poverty and anonymity, to the mediocrity his father had predicted for him, the mediocrity he deserved. No, Jack Wells would not sit back and watch the slow death of DNAW, his creation. He'd try to save whatever he could, even if that meant breaking the rules. All I had to do was hear Eva's innocent words to put two and two together. Now I knew where to look. And I'd have to move quickly: Time was the only advantage I had. I'd have to track down Wells's accounts and penetrate his inner circle. That, inevitably, would lead me to Jennifer Moore.

Why should we have to team up with them? Eva's tone was more one of repulsion than annoyance: What do we get out of it? Gene Myers wasn't surprised at his colleague's aggression. Both had dedicated themselves body and soul to Celera and to what Celera represented—the challenge, the triumph of will, the absence of official support—and they didn't want to ruin things at the last moment. Why should they listen to Eric Lander, from the Human Genome Project, one of their enemies? Why arrange a truce? Even if for the moment the HGP was ahead, the situation would reverse itself in a few months, and Celera would win. The press was already calling the two projects the tortoise and the hare: There was no way that Collins and his team would beat them. Why discuss anything with them?

Celera's leadership had gathered in the Wye River Conference Center, where just a few months earlier Yasser Arafat and Benjamin Netanyahu met with Clinton, imperial seducer, in a new and vain Middle East peace initiative. Venter himself was commanding the expedition, accompanied by Hamilton Smith and other members of his team. The image of Eric Lander, of the Whitehead Institute, one of the most efficient centers in the public project, one that had just acquired 125 PRISM 3700s, identical to those at Celera, blazed from a screen at the far end of the hall.

Let's listen to their proposition, Venter declared. If he'd agreed to participate in this video-conference, it was not for fun. To finish the sequencing of the genome in 2001, as he'd promised, Celera would have to use the data the HGP posted every day on GenBank, its internet site, where anyone could consult it. Just as Francis Collin's guard dogs suspected, if Celera published the complete sequence of the genome, it would have to cite all the members of the public program as co-authors.

Greetings to the scientific team that's faster than lightning, Eric Lander introduced himself. The Celera executives took the joke coolly. I promise that when we discover the humor gene, you'll be the first to know, Eric, replied Venter. Fun time was over.

Before getting started, I'd like to know who in the public program is abreast of this conversation, Smith interrupted. Francis knows about our conversation, but I'm not authorized to speak in his name. Not yet. And I still haven't spoken with any of the other members of the HGP. To do so at this time would only cause trouble. I think the only obstacle to our coming to an agreement is the publication of data, intervened one of the Celera lawyers. Would we be able to deliver the genome on a DVD, as we did with *Drosophila*? Francis prefers immediate publication, but, yes, we could accept that. Lander cleared his throat. But there is one matter that isn't up for debate: If Celera uses data from the public project, the final article has to be a joint publication.

An article or two, what's the difference, Venter pointed out. No, there's a big difference, Craig. The difference is huge! I'm not going to produce data so you can publish it! Okay, okay, Eric, don't get upset.

We'll think it over and give you an answer as soon as we can. They said good-bye and hung up.

Venter was scratching his chin. Who do these jerks think they are? Eva blurted out. Eric Lander giving us lessons in morality? If we listen to him, we'd have to include Gregor Mendel as one of the co-authors as well! We can't give in, Craig, they just want to take advantage of us. The scientific community thinks we're the bad guys and they're the good guys, but it isn't true. We're as good as they are: We don't need them. Venter shared Eva's rage, but he intuited that at this point an agreement was their only option. If the authorship problem became complicated, the war between both projects would get to the press, and that would panic the stockholders. Sometimes the only way to win is by abandoning one's principles. Or pretending to. Because, no matter what happened, Venter intended to win the race no matter how it shaped up. To do it, he kept an ace up his sleeve.

A couple of months earlier, Jennifer had begun using her maiden name again. I called her early in the afternoon, and, despite my expectations, she remembered me very well: Yes, we met in Moscow a few years ago. Could we meet somewhere? For what purpose, Mr. Chernishevsky? I have to speak to you, a personal matter. I'm not in the habit of meeting anyone without knowing beforehand what it's all about, Mr. Chernishevsky. Just a few minutes, I promise not to bother you again. I have to know what you expect to learn from me, Mr. Chernishevsky, otherwise we can consider this conversation over. Okay, I want to talk to you about your husband. You mean my ex-husband. Exactly, Mr. Wells. I've got nothing to say. Please, Mrs. Moore, I'm certain you'll be interested. And I'm certain I've got nothing to say to you, Mr. Chernishevsky. This was a dialogue of the deaf: I should have made her trust me, forced her to be more explicit. I knew she hated Wells, but not to what degree. Would you like to get even with him? Or are you going to protect him to the end?

I know something's not right with C225. That's none of my business, Mr. Chernishevsky. Have you spoken to your ex-husband recently? That's none of *your* business, Mr. Chernishevsky. I think this matter is important to both of us, I forced the issue. Mr. Wells has just signed the juiciest agreement in pharmaceutical history. He promised to produce a cure for cancer, and I suspect the whole thing is a fraud. You may suspect whatever you like, Mr. Chernishevsky. Mrs. Moore, if you know something, tell me, it would be better for you. Are you threatening me,

Mr. Chernishevsky? Of course not! What do you take me for? I think this conversation has gone too far, Mr. Chernishevsky.

That damn family: Despite the fact that they all hated one another, none of them was willing to talk. They were trapped in an iron-bound code of silence. But I had no intention of giving in. All afternoon I made calls, begged favors, made promises that were impossible to keep, risked my reputation—and perhaps more than that—without getting any conclusive results. Furious, I went back to the cabin by the river to chew my frustration until Eva showed up. It must have been 9:00 P.M. when the telephone rang. It took me a few seconds to recognize Jennifer Moore's metallic voice. She'd spent the whole afternoon thinking over her options and had decided to look for me. This time her tone did not intimidate me: I now controlled the situation.

In her harsh voice, she told me she had to speak with me in person to clarify certain points in our conversation. Tomorrow, at 3:00 P.M., in the Promenade Café. It's in Washington, do you know where? I can find out. I'll see you there. And she hung up. My excitement kept me from sleeping that night, I was getting closer and closer to my objective: the end of Jack Wells.

What made her change her mind? Why did it take her so long to plot her revenge? Or did her vacillation correspond to a well-formulated plan whose only goal was to arouse my curiosity even more? Despite her apparent nervousness—she never stopped moving her long fingers the whole time we spoke—the IMF's star negotiator knew what she was going to do: If she was talking to me now, it was not because she suddenly believed in me but because she'd discovered that I was an agent sent by providence, the perfect instrument of her rage. I was of no importance in this game; I was a mere secondary actor in the duel of husband and wife. If Jennifer would confide her secret (just a piece of her secret) it was not so she could protect herself but so she could break completely with Jack Wells.

No, she was unaware of any malfeasance. No, she had never taken any interest in her husband's business. No, she didn't believe he was involved in anything illegal. No, she had nothing to tell me about that. What then? While Jack had always been a very intuitive man, it's true that he's been very nervous during the past few days, Mr. Chernishevsky. I think that for that reason he believes the value of the stock in his company will fall despite its spectacular growth over the past weeks.

Did Jack Wells suggest you sell your DNAW stock?, I asked. Yes, but of course I didn't want to do it. In my opinion, the company is in one of its best periods, and the nation's economy couldn't be better. But on the other hand that fool Christina Sanders . . . That was the key. Has she sold her DNAW stock?, I persisted. Jennifer smiled, knowing her words had erased her husband's future and, at the same time, that of the celebrated Ms. Sanders. That's right, Mr. Chernishevsky, she sold all she had. Confirm it for yourself.

A draw?, asked Craig Venter. Ari Patrinos, the Director of the genetics program of the Energy Department, had managed to bring the two warriors, Craig Venter and Francis Collins, together under the utmost secrecy. Hostilities between Celera and the Human Genome Project had become even more inflamed recently. Despite attempts to find common ground, both entities had done even the impossible to blow each other up, wasting a good part of their energy in the process.

Thanks to the PRISM 3700 the public project bought— from Celera's sister company, one of those paradoxes that are endemic to the business world—its sequencing capacity had accelerated at a dizzying rate. Celera was running at top speed, but was suffering a financial storm that threatened to destroy it. If everything went according to the plans Gene Myers and Eva Halász had set out, Celera would be able to have a complete version of the genome by September of 2000—one year earlier than they had planned. Unfortunately, the HGP press people had announced that they would present a final draft in April.

So, who would win? That would depend on which group had the greatest ability to convince the public, the media, and the investors that they had the authentic model. Venter was afraid that even if his army achieved the victory in absolute terms, the triumph would be rendered ambiguous by the HGP announcement. For his part, Francis Collins was delighted with the results generated by the network of official laboratories, but he knew that Celera would go on using his data. Both men were caught in the same trap. Neither relished the idea of collaborating with the other—they'd spent too much time hating each other—but that was they only way they could save themselves.

Call it whatever you like, answered Patrinos. The important thing is that you two recognize that, despite your differences, you'd now prefer to work together to discover what the human genome really means. After years of competition, doubts, suspicions, back-stabbing, skirmishes, and battles, a damned draw.

What the hell can he want from me? What's the hurry? Wells asked to meet with me in a luminous Soho coffee shop not far from DNAW. I suppose the glass tables, the ocher and silver on the walls, the windows facing the street, and the frenetic traffic of university students made him feel sure of himself, and anonymous. In a place like that I wouldn't dare threaten or blackmail him (the first thing he thought after my call) or unleash a scandal. When I got there, he was nursing a cup of coffee. He looked at me confidently and with an ostentatious show of contempt. His strategy was simple: He would say nothing, make no mistakes, wait to see just what my intentions were. His histrionic talents were above average, but it was clear he wasn't living his best days. I'd just have to touch one of his weak points to make him hysterical. When I sat down, he waved to a waitress to bring me a cup of coffee.

Think I don't know who you are?, he began. Yuri Mikhailovich Chernishevsky, journalist, writer, novelist to be more precise (perhaps that's why you like fictions so much), protector of the helpless, champion of just causes. And if that weren't enough, the bastard who's screwing Eva Halász behind my back.

He was talking in a calm tone, as if he were discussing the weather or sports, not making a fuss, holding in his hatred so it would sound like indifference. Every once in a while he sipped his coffee, burning his lips. I didn't think the conversation would become personal so rapidly. I'd underestimated him.

I haven't come here to talk about that, Mr. Wells. I'm here to talk about your business. You don't give a damn about my business, what you want is to get something from me, like all the rest. Over the course of my life, I've seen scores of men like you, Chernishevsky, men who appear to be principled and full of good intentions, but who are just waiting for the right moment to take advantage of their closest friends. You and your kind are repugnant. I, at least, don't fool anyone. No one?, I counterattacked. And what about your shareholders? What about the sick people who rely on you? What about FDA? The Government? I wouldn't be so sure of myself, Mr. Wells.

What are you after, Chernishevsky? Let's be frank. Money? Money doesn't matter to me. I get it, what you want is Eva Halász, right? Okay, she's yours, Chernishevsky, all yours. Satisfied? Can we leave now?

He was trying to distract me from the only important matter, the confidential information he used to his own advantage, in violation of the rules of the Securities Exchange Commission. Can you tell me why you've gotten rid of thousands of shares of stock in your prosperous company, owner of the most promising anti-cancer drug ever discovered, only five days after you closed the most lucrative deal in the history of the pharmaceutical industry? Doesn't that seem odd, even to you? There's nothing illegal about it, I can do what I like with my stocks, he exclaimed. Of course, Mr. Wells, but if it happened that the FDA didn't approve C225, your transaction would acquire a macabre logic. The rat had his back to the wall. Let me ask you again, Chernishevsky, what do you want?

Wells shifted as if he were getting up (pure fakery) and again collapsed in his chair. He looked me up and down, smiling: Are you upset that Eva Halász is about to ditch you? He paused to note the effect of his question. Oh! She hasn't told you yet? I'm sorry to rain on your parade, Chernishevsky, but Eva Halász isn't in love with you. Or me. Or anyone else. That's the way she is. By now you should have learned that. Surprised? Let me see if I remember her exact words: I can't stand him any more. Yes, she was talking about you, Chernishevsky. I can't stand his jealousy, his rage. I think I'll break things off with him this week, as soon as the genome is announced.

I didn't believe his lies, not for a second. His pathetic strategy was proof of his desperation. Eva would never leave me like that. She could be volatile, irrational, but she was always direct. It was impossible she'd rely more on Wells than on me. I understand that you don't believe me, Chernishevsky, but just think about her. Hasn't it occurred to you that maybe she's so afraid of you that she'd rather leave you just like that, before you try to stop her? In my opinion, violent men are the most contemptible creatures in the world, don't you agree? You know nothing about me, Wells, nothing, I said without getting excited, in the same slow, tranquil tone he used. You're saying all that to save yourself. But when it all comes down around you, you'll end up in jail. Completely calm, I got up, tossed a couple of dollars on the table, and discreetly escaped from that hell.

On June 26th, 2000, Craig Venter and Francis Collins formalized their obligatory alliance in the White House in the presence of President William Jefferson Clinton, imperial seducer, who by then was ending his term in office. Mired in his sexual scandals, he saw no better way to clean up his name than by standing behind the event. Among the guests were all the great names of twentieth-century biology. In the first row, the leadership of Celera, with Hamilton Smith, Gene Myers, and Eva Halász heading the list, then the members of the public project, with whom they'd collided so many times. It was supposed to be a memorable day (one of the most important in the history of humanity according to the HGP press releases), but the scientists did not look exultant. Oh yes, they smiled for the cameras, but in their hearts they mistrusted one another. On the highest stair stood the priestly figure of James Watson, the patriarch of DNA, wearing a white suit, watching over his creatures like a surly Moses who'd shown his disciples the promised land.

Far from the floodlights, I was taking notes, never taking my eyes off Eva. A good part of the triumph belonged to her, to her perseverance and courage, to those weeks when we beat each other to death every night. Jack Wells was there too. And he was also looking at her. But Eva didn't look at me. She looked at him.

In the end, the life form that had best adapted to the environment, as Darwin postulated, had defeated its rivals.

REQUIEM

Valdivostok, Russian Federation, 2000

It's not me, it's some other girl who's suffering, Oksana told herself when she opened her eyes. Dawn spread over her, turbid and milky, much like the ocean that was devouring the port. She rubbed her eyes until she hurt herself; only pain allowed her to withstand the moonlight that filtered through the window. One more day, she muttered. They took you away at dawn, she then prayed, and imagined herself transformed into an ice floe, an iceberg. Finally she got up.

That place did not belong to the world. It was the vestibule to hell, a cold and stormy hell. She walked a few steps and turned on the lights. Nothing. This was the worst time of year. In mid-winter, her neighborhood only had electricity and heat three or four hours a day, and the temperature barely got above zero. She couldn't understand how the old people of Valdivostok, the ghost port, didn't freeze to death in their houses, what insane strength (the Russian soul) kept them from dying in winter. Oksana bundled herself up, walked to the kitchen, and turned on the gas, running the risk that she might be using up her last bit of gas. The tea seared her throat. Death is gliding over our heads, she said to herself.

She sat down at the desk—a bouquet of dry carnations at one end, a postcard from Anniushka in the center, the rest covered with pieces of paper of different colors and sizes, all filthy or covered with drafts. She grasped her pencil as if it were a dagger. She could spend the entire morning like that, her mind a blank, numb (a buoy in the middle of the ocean), not noticing the hours that passed. She lit a pair of candles, the only glow allowed her, clenched her teeth, and tried not to think about the Korean, to keep his memory—his rancid smell, his pallor, his indifference—from distracting her from her music.

After two hours of cold, her fingers finally scratched out a few lines:

. . . if it rhymes with blood
it poisons the blood,
and it's the bloodiest thing in the world.

Nothing truer or more precise. She looked at her scar-covered arms, that rigorous count of her days. Each mark represented a triumph, a sign of survival. She took another swallow of tea, that salty, barely tepid liquid, picked up her guitar, and rested it on her lap. She strummed the strings with the same precision she used to slit her skin: For her, music was another kind of crying. The sounds shook the half-light. She tried the same notes again and again, the same chords, the same dissonances: If it rhymes with blood . . . Soon she was distracted by the pounding on the other side of the wall. The neighbors didn't share her passion and had already threatened to call the police and throw her out of the building. She ignored them; the grimy tenth-floor apartment on Chasovitinga Street had been her home for four years.

Her fingers again drew a senseless calligraphy:

What's lurking in the mirror? Pain.
What's moving around behind the wall? Calamity.

The Korean's shadow came back into her mind, his long, delicate hands, his colorless skin, his soft, barely perceptible muscles, his silence. His fierce silence. Oksana missed that Oriental fatigue, that whim he seemed to practice so well. Thinking about his touch turned her stomach.

The Korean was like a jade idol, a funerary statue, a god. Which is why she'd put up no resistance and had accepted becoming the board on which he played his game.

Oksana had been singing in a dive at the port for almost a year before he burst in one night, surrounded by an entourage of Russians and Mongols, with the indolence of someone who knows he's the owner of lives and destinies. She supposed he was probably just another of those anachronistic foreign investors who were still sure they'd get rich in Vladivostok, the ghost port. When she first got to the city, Japanese men with cellphones and attaché cases stuffed with money were buying everything they found in their path—hotels, casinos, shops, laundromats, and bordellos—but after a few years of war, they were wiped out by the *vory-v-zakonie* and the local mafiosi. And the dream of transforming the far Russian east into a new Hong Kong vanished like mist. From that time on, only a few Chinese and Koreans with no memory or scruples dared to walk its streets, protected by gorillas who were armed to the teeth.

Surrounded by his men, the Korean shot her a gaze like the point of a needle. Oksana didn't avoid it. When she finished her song, an explosion titled "Back Home," one of the thugs ordered her to come to the Korean's table. The chief of the group didn't speak to her (perhaps he spoke no Russian) and slowly looked her over as if her were a collector. Oksana detected no lust in his manner, as if the Korean were planning a mere business transaction. Close up he seemed young and lost, barely older than she—his Asian features were tricky—and she imagined him as some lost teenager, a boy disguised as a gangster. The Korean snapped his fingers and his bodyguards all stood up at the same time. A drunk, redheaded giant grabbed Oksana by the arm, dragged her out of the bar, and put her into a black car. I'm going to give you some advice, he said: Don't say a word, don't even think of opening your damn mouth. If you take my advice, you may be alive tomorrow. After half an hour of riding around the city, the Russian deposited her at a downtown hotel, not far from the plaza where miners and students usually protested the perennial cuts in electric power.

The Korean received her wearing a purple robe. With no preamble, he signaled her to undress. Oksana did it carefully, without fear, as if she were going to take a bath. She barely trembled. The Korean approached, sniffed her armpits and sex, then felt her muscles, her nipples, and her buttocks, as if he were examining a horse. His fingers were long and cold, but the rest of his body possessed a sweet, almost feminine warmth.

Oksana couldn't resist. It was the first time she would sleep with a man. The Korean paused to observe the scars on her thighs and forearms without understanding their meaning. He measured the wounds with the tip of his fingers, as if they were still open. Only then did he lead her to bed.

Oksana never protested: She would have followed him anywhere. She tried to kiss him, but he covered her mouth. What could he want? He then placed her on the sheets as if she were a doll, removed his robe, and, sweaty, stretched out on top of her. Oksana tried to caress him, but again he rejected her. She barely felt the Korean's body on top of her own; he was weightless, like a phantom, like a newborn. He rubbed against her skin awkwardly, vainly trying to excite himself. Finally he leapt off the bed, put on his robe again, handed Oksana a $100 bill (she'd never seen one before), and let her leave.

That night Oksana dreamed of a tiger without claws.

The next day, she waited for the Korean to reappear in the dive down at the port. She looked for him among the shadows, blinded by the lights shining on her face and guitar, and even tried to invoke him with her songs.

Waiting for him gives me more pleasure
than having a good time with someone else.

Oksana was ecstatic because of the Korean: She imagined him on top of her, alone and sad, mute, denied pleasure. Who could this unfortunate creature be? Why would he take notice of her? Why would he choose her? Why had he paid for his consolation? Ever since she came to Vladivostok, Oksana had drowned herself in the skin of other women, pale, moribund females with no identity or history, typical frontier types. Most were, like her, artists (or at least that's what they said), but there were also workers and secretaries, mothers and wives, and even a model who was married to a celebrated mafioso. All of them had satisfied her desire, all of them had revived her, all of them had allowed her to discover herself, but none had obsessed her as he did: a powerful impotent man, a male who in bed was no different than a woman.

Who was that Korean who came in here a few days ago?, she asked Kornei Ivanovich, the owner of the dive. It's probably better you don't know, he answered, as obtuse as usual. Know where I can find him? It's probably better if you don't look for him.

It isn't you who comforts me,
It's not of you I ask forgiveness,
It's not at your feet where I'll fall,
It's not you I fear at night.

Vladivostok, the ghost port, is the last port in the world, Oksana wrote in her blue notebook, the far end of civilization, the end of the world. More than a diary, Oksana was writing a mixed series of aphorisms, poems, songs, stories, and scattered fragments, all addressed to her adored Anna Akmatova, whose picture (a worn-out postcard with Anniushka's picture on it) watched over her work. The poet was still Oksana's guide, her model. A woman who could withstand the windstorms of History, a woman who could stay on her feet like the last wall holding off barbarism, when all the others were falling. And now Oksana not only knew her poems by heart but, barely modified, she made them reappear in her songs.

Three weeks after their first encounter, the Korean returned to the dive with the same impudent ease. Oksana sang him the verses she'd dedicated to him:

Don't give me anything to remember you:
I know how short memory is.

The Korean didn't smile, didn't change his expression, paid no attention to her words or the echoes of her guitar. He didn't even fix his needle-like gaze on her. Oksana wanted to forgive him: Now she possessed his secret, and he could not see her as he had before. After three or four songs, she went over to his table herself. The Russian giant blocked the path to his boss, as if she were a murderer or beggar, but Oksana would not allow herself to be intimidated. The Korean stopped the physical exchange, whispered a few words to the Russian, and he translated for Oksana: at midnight, same services, same price.

The Korean didn't stay until Oksana finished her set, so he missed one of her best songs, about a teenager who'd gone missing and a tiger without claws. When she finished, the black car was waiting for her. The Russian glared at her with contempt, almost with sorrow. You're either a nut or a jerk, he said between his teeth. Oksana ignored him and remained silent during the ride, focused on the snow-covered sidewalks and the darkened buildings. The wind flowing in from the Sea of Japan scourged the street lamps and the trees, as if it wanted to pull them up by the roots. The sky was black, black.

The Korean again received Oksana in his purple robe. She stripped diligently, following the pre-established ritual, and allowed him to touch and sniff her. He seemed even more needy than before. Then Oksana stretched out on the bed and waited to receive him on her belly. But he tried to excite himself on his own before getting into bed with her. His erection only lasted a few seconds. He moved to the side and sat on the bed. Oksana approached him very delicately (he looked as if he might fall apart) and caressed his cheek.

Pretending it was a transaction like any other, the gangster took out his wallet, removed two $100 bills, and handed them to Oksana. She shook her head in refusal, but he forced her to take them. There was no emotion in his eyes, not even a hint of sorrow or shame. Nothing. Oksana quickly dressed, and it wasn't until she reached the street, whipped by the gusts from the Sea of Japan, that she felt the painful need to shout.

Back in her apartment, she discovered that her lungs hadn't stood up to the wind: Fever was burning her skin. This time the heat was working (outside it must have been ten or twelve degrees below zero), but her body was shivering as if she were outdoors. Her joints ached, her chest, her throat. She was delirious. For a moment, she thought she was in a room in the Fontanka palace and thought that she too had brought about the end of an era. Then she dreamed that the tiger without claws was leaping on her.

When she awakened the next morning (the sky was still uniformly gray), she found she was covered with sweat. She was no longer feverish, but she was coughing as if her lungs were filled with worms. She washed her face, looked in the mirror, and thought she would die. She quickly made some tea and sat down at her desk. Anniushka was waiting for her there, sober and brave, with her blue dress and her orange shawl covering her arms. Oksana thought she was looking more and more like her.

Her fingers revived.
. . . And they seemed like fires
that flew next to me until dawn,
and I never managed to find out what color
those strange eyes were.

All around, everything trembled and sang,
and I didn't know if you were friend or foe,
if it was summer or winter.

For two weeks, Oksana couldn't sing. The doctors at the regional clinic told her that antibiotics were scarce and only gave her enough for a couple of days. Her voice sounded like the bellow of a dying animal. It might well have been. The days she spent in bed, locked up with the shadows and moisture of her Chasovitina Street flat, Oksana regretted not being able to make her date with the Korean. As absurd as it seemed, she felt she was betraying him.

But she wrote as if possessed. She filled the blue notebook and had to use the back of the pages she'd already covered with writing. Now she no longer spoke about lost love or Vladivostok, the ghost port, or about the Korean, but about an idea that began to slip through her verses. What if she were the only surviving member of the human species? The last woman on Earth? What would it mean to sense the absolute extinction of the race? The idea was so disturbing that she barely managed to control herself. What would that silence hide?

Her fingers took control of the pencil once again.

But there is no power more formidable, more terrible in the world than the prophetic word of the poet.

On her thirteenth day of convalescence, Oksana went back to the dive. The Korean and his entourage arrived punctually, though she couldn't know if he'd come on the nights she'd missed. The temperature had fallen to twenty-eight below zero, and the sky shone with a strange luminescence. It was as if time had petrified, as if the universe had used up its minutes. Even the wind from the Sea of Japan had stopped blowing.

Except for the Korean and his bodyguards, there were only two other customers in the bar, a bald, toothless man and a thick, greasy stevedore, both attracted by the heat and the alcohol, not by the music. The audience barely mattered to Oksana. This would be the best performance of her life (she decided), and nothing could change that. Before beginning, she looked for the Korean and focused her gaze on him. The halogen lights made Oksana's skin go from blue to blood red. Her voice still sounded harsh and cavernous. She sang some of the poems she'd written during her convalescence: It was the gift she was preparing for the Korean.

Oksana held her guitar as if it were a flotation device and howled with all her strength.

> *And that would be for the others*
> *like the times of Vespatian,*
> *and that was a wound*
> *and a cloud, above, of storms.*

This time there was no need to come to an agreement on price. The Korean left halfway through her set, and the Russian giant waited for Oksana in his black automobile. The sky was still ablaze with a whitish glow. Vladivostok, the ghost port, never seemed so peaceful. The branches on the trees were not supposed to move, and didn't. The night birds were not supposed to flutter around, and they didn't. The night was supposed to seem eternal, and it was. Why do you do it?, asked the Russian as he drove her to the broken-down hotel downtown. She shrugged her shoulders and stared at the empty streets and distant shinning.

The Korean received her wearing his purple robe. Oksana undressed calmly. The Korean sniffed her armpits and her sex. Oksana got into bed. The Korean took off his robe and leaped on top of her. Oksana caressed his back and the nape of his neck. The Korean remained erect. For an instant, their eyes met, and both knew what would happen next. The Korean went to the bathroom. When he came back, he was holding a knife. Oksana admired its shine.

> *Like prisoners who leave jail,*
> *we know something about the others,*
> *something terrible. We find ourselves in a circle of hell*
> *perhaps we aren't even ourselves.*

And she thought about Zhenia, her mother, and Anniushka, and about the world as a wasteland. And she said to herself: Season of ash.

THREE WOMEN

1

Moscow, Russian Federation, December 31st, 2000

Those aren't her eyes. Irina Nikolayevna mutters those words to herself, oblivious to everything happening around her. Her hands barely shake, the pain is so intense that she doesn't even feel it: It comes over her more like a vertigo than an oppression, more like nausea than a wound, more like disgust than sorrow. She wishes she could become enraged—against Arkady, against herself, against her country, against her daughter—explode in insults or hysterics, throw herself on the coffin, as she's seen people do in films, curse heaven and hell, but instead she stands still, turned to stone. The snow that muddies the cemetery does not render it sadder or more pathetic, just filthier. The December air is saturated by the sulphur of the neighboring factories; the stench contaminates the bodies of the living as well as the dead. All that fatigue. All that waste. Irina only wants to leave that place once and for all, end the ceremony, take refuge in solitude and sleep. Hours before, Arkady made her take a tranquilizer, and now Oksana's body no longer belongs to her; she contemplates it in the distance as if it were already part of some another world.

An absurd priest from the Russian Orthodox Church—Arkady called him against her wishes—reels off a tangled litany. She too would like to pray, to have the courage to fool herself with an afterlife, to console herself with the idea that Oksana is traversing the empyrean, transformed into an angel or a spirit. But her despair, while it has made her vulnerable, has not made her stupid: She's a scientist, an unfortunate Soviet biologist—that's right Soviet—and not even the death of her daughter will convince her to abandon reason. This is the end: There is nothing beyond the death of the cells. Oksana no longer exists, and will never exist again. It's that simple.

Meanwhile, Arkady Ivanovich Granin is crossing himself. He himself doesn't know if he's doing it out of habit, inertia, or fear: God always seemed an unsolvable problem to him, a question it wasn't worthwhile asking, a matter alien to thought. Even so, he invokes God's mercy, appears exposed, adrift, though perhaps his pain has something official to it. Unlike Irina, who wipes away a tear from time to time, he has a parchment-like face that contracts out of anguish. He looks like a sick man, a father who has finally been beaten down by guilt. Is he suffering? Perhaps he only needs others to see him this way, overwhelmed. Is he in any way responsible for this death? Did he force his daughter to live in danger? He tries not to believe it, but he has his doubts. And those doubts eat away at him. And they will do so forever.

The priest obstinately goes deeper and deeper into his prayers.

Only a few invited guests—respecting the wishes of Arkady Ivanovich—have attended: a representative of Boris Yeltsin, of strong arms (he telephoned his condolences), two or three members of the civil rights movement, and the administrator of DNAW-Rus. All of them maintain a silence that Irina considers irreverent. They have no business being there. Her loss means nothing to them, it would be better if they left. Not imagining what she is thinking, these anonymous beings approach her, take her hand, brazenly kiss her, or whisper treacherous words in her ear. Irina puts up with them as if they were vermin and secretly wishes them atrocious suffering, suffering much like her own.

Arkady, on the other hand, expresses his thanks for their show of sympathy. He nods his head in resignation each time one of those men hugs or comforts him. There is the great difference between Arkady and Irina, the line that divides their destinies: He always tried to get along with others, always submitted, with pleasure, to the gaze of others. Even in his times of rebellion, he never stopped seeking the approval of others. Irina never tolerated compromise. Her struggle did not have fame as its goal: If she persevered through so many years, it was because she had no choice.

As soon as the priest ends his chanting, two men lower the coffin into the grave. To Irina, the gravediggers seem perfect inhabitants of her century. The snow mixes with the dirt to form a turbid mass. The men pile it up around the edges of the gravesite and then toss it onto the coffin by arduous, violent shovelfuls. It's been the longest night in their lives. It began when Irina and Arkady met in the morgue, and it's ending only now, thirty-five hours later.

The autopsy results revealed a painful death caused by ten or twenty knife wounds. Not a single part of her body escaped the brutality of her attacker. The cuts reached her thighs and arms, her breasts, and her stomach, her face, and her sex. Who could do something like this?, asked Arkady. A criminal or a lunatic, answered the pathologist. The mafia controls Vladivostok, Dr. Granin, you must know that. The answer didn't satisfy him, but there was no other. It didn't even make sense to speculate about a possible arrest or even revenge: Every year, there were hundreds of crimes like this in Russia, and only one out of ten or twenty cases reached the courts. It was useless to demand a rigorous investigation or a clear answer. But not all the scars on his daughter's body came from the attack. She had caused many of them herself. The pathologist showed Oksana's arms and thighs to Arkady. There are dozens of small cuts, Dr. Granin. Your daughter must have begun hurting herself when she was a child. I don't want my wife to find out about this. And it shouldn't be part of the report, understand?

For Arkady it was impossible to erase the image of his ten- or twelve-year-old daughter cutting herself. How could she? And how could they not have stopped her? How stupid, how blind parents can be! The image seemed almost pornographic. Obscene. What had he done to bring this about?

During the long hours between the autopsy and the burial, Irina refused to accept the facts. Those are not her eyes, not hers, she said over and over. A daughter dying before her parents is unnatural, perverse. Oksana couldn't have punished her parents that way. Just seeing her face in the coffin—her immaculate, little-girl's-face—Irina understands. She discovers that she has no future. She's just turned sixty-eight and can't go on any longer. She was born and grew up in a country that no longer exists, she married a man she no longer loves, and she's just lost her only child. A triple failure: as a scientist, as a wife, and as a mother. What sense is there in going on? Despite everything, Irina knows she won't kill herself. She has neither the courage nor the strength. The life she still has within her, that life governed by cells and genes, fights against death.

When the gravediggers finish patting down the mud on top of his daughter's grave, Arkady Ivanovich experiences a sudden relief. Finally, it's over. Now all he wants to do is to take a shower, to stay under the hot spray for a long time, wash himself unhurriedly and then sleep, sleep all he possibly can. Unlike his wife, he does have other things to worry about. The death of his daughter swept away the little faith he still had, but it hasn't closed his existence. There are still matters he must resolve, other battles to fight.

The very existence of DNAW-Rus is in danger because of the accusations made in the United States against Jack Wells. Even Arkady's honesty has been called into question. Little by little, the rumor has spread: Arkady Ivanovich Granin, a biologist of the highest caliber, former Soviet dissident and recognized defender of human rights, has sold himself to foreign capital. Arkady Ivanovich Granin made all his money illegally. Arkady Ivanovich Granin is facing charges in the United States. Arkady Ivanovich Granin has become corrupt, like so many others. Oksana's death came at the worst moment: His enemies will use it against him, his detractors will take advantage of it to vilify him. After everything he went through, everything he withstood, no one has the right to accuse him of anything! No one has any right to smear his good name!

The ceremony concluded, and the guests leave, little by little, until they disappear in the snow. Only Oksana's parents remain standing at the grave. They look into each other's eyes: Perhaps they can still console each other, perhaps a reconciliation will be granted to them. They're fooling themselves. They became strangers a long time ago. Feigning a deference he does not feel in his heart, Arkady goes to Irina and tries to embrace her. That would be the natural thing: They've just lost their daughter. His wife's coldness keeps him from carrying through his intention. His arms remain in the air, stretched toward her. How ridiculous he is, she thinks, cruelly.

Can I give you a ride home? Irina looks him up and down. I loved this man, she thinks. Then: I don't know who he is, I don't know him and never met him. For me, he was always a stranger. No thanks, I'll get a taxi.

Arkady shrugs. Both would like to disappear immediately, forever, but they still have to walk side by side to the cemetery's entrance. Their steps are short and dry; they barely look at each other, can barely stand each other. Neither lags behind or moves ahead, as they had synchronized their steps for all time. Their footprints in the snow mark their last meeting. Arkady waves to his driver to meet him at the gates to the cemetery. Irina is not surprised that it's an enormous black limousine, the same kind the old apparatchiks used. Sure you don't want me to drop you off? No.

They don't kiss, there's no embrace, they don't even shake hands. Arkady gets into the car and loses sight of her in a second. She stands there a few minutes, indifferent to the afternoon cold. Finally, she hails a cab and tells the driver her address. Only now, seated in the back seat, the windows covered with her breath, does Irina become fully conscious. Only now does she tremble, only now does she shake. She tries to remember Oksana's eyes, in vain. She isn't even sure what color they were, doesn't know if they were black or brown or copper-colored. Her bosom bursts.

Are you all right, ma'am?, asks the driver. When she steps out of the taxi, she is not the same woman who entered it. What a huge mistake!, she whispers. She has trouble climbing the stairs, as if she were climbing a mountain. Her breath is short. She takes off her shoes and leaves them on the landing, weighed down by her haste. The keys slip out of her hands and fall to the floor. She barely recognizes her apartment, as if she'd never been there before. Out of breath, she pulls a package out of her bag and puts it on the kitchen table: a bundle of Oksana's last belongings.

Irina unties the strings and finds three blue notebooks. *Season of Ash by Oksana Gorenko.*

Oksana Gorenko?

Irina spends the next few nights submerged in those manuscripts. It's all that's left of her daughter.

Her eyes ravaged by weeping, she puts the notebooks back in the original wrapping and places them in a box. The next morning, she goes to the post office and sends them to the mailing address Yuri Mikhailovich Chernishevsky keeps in the United States. Now those notebooks are here, next to me. After sending hundreds of petitions, the guards have allowed me to keep them.

2
New York, United States of America, December 31st, 2000

His tiny blue eyes glitter with the promise of another life, another world. From time to time, those eyes wander from their miniature Middle Ages—the towers, battlements, castles, and drawbridges he's been building since 6:00 A.M.—and look up at her just to make sure she's at his side. His hands are almost as dextrous as an adult's: They dance through the battle field with the agility of cranes, carefully pick up the bodies of the dead and wounded, work the catapults and combat machines, barely interfere with the unfortunate fate of the defenders.

How could he learn so soon that the world is an accumulation of wars and battles? Jennifer asks him, with a mix of shock and apprehension. The boy could never answer her question and doesn't imagine anything more exciting and amusing could exist. Even though Allison tried to keep war toys out of his hands, Jennifer always gave in to her nephew's whims. Now he owns blank pistols and air guns and historical armies—Roman legions, barbarian hordes, Viking fleets, Renaissance pikemen, Napoleonic dragoons, machine-guns and biplanes from World War I, aircraft carriers and bombers from World War II—even though his favorites (he's collected more than two hundred different figures) are medieval knights.

To assure his loyalty and love, and to make her sister foam at the mouth in rage, Jennifer has spoiled him to an unheard-of degree. Aside from his collection of soldiers and weapons, Jacob has also become the envy of his schoolmates because of his video games. At the age of ten, he considers himself an expert strategist and defeats adversaries twice his age. As if that weren't enough, Jennifer, after one of her visits to Russia, gave him a complete suit of armor, his size, with chain mail, sword, and helmet. To go with it, she gave him a shipment of military paraphernalia from the Soviet era: medals, ribbons, canteens bearing the likeness of Brezhnev and Gorbachev, pistol grips decorated with a solitary red star, and even a Red Army captain's cap.

Despite his fascination with violence—huge posters of Sylvester Stallone and Bruce Willis decorate his bedroom—Jacob is the most peaceful boy in the world. Jennifer has never heard a complaint or a reproach from his teachers, who, in any case, think he's too introverted. Jacob is neither stubborn nor impetuous and has no problems with anyone, though he barely has any friends and spends most of his time in the company of his generals and soldiers. As withdrawn as his mother and as nervous as his aunt, he's yet to develop the irascibility or rebelliousness of either. Sometimes Jennifer forgets he's there: He barely makes any noise, concentrating on his computer or his simulated battles. When Jennifer urges him to invite a schoolmate over to the house, Jacob looks annoyed: They're very boring, he answers, I always beat them. The typical pride of the Moores flows in his veins. His loneliness is not a function so much of his timidity as of his awareness of his superiority.

You're turning him into a monster, Allison berated her whenever she came back from Israel. I don't want my son to be one of those spongy Park Avenue rabbits who only worry about accumulating more and more things. And I also don't want him to be a spoiled freak. If you give in to all his desires, he'll never learn to be self-critical. Jennifer had learned to remain silent during her sister's tirades: After all, Allison turned up once every two months in the best of cases and had no way of knowing what her son's real needs were.

Now Jennifer is contemplating him, horrified: The boy smiles at her, and she feels a chill. Jacob suspects nothing, can't even imagine that today, the last day of the year, the century, the millennium, he's about to lose his innocence. She smiles back, eaten away from within. She knows that very soon she'll have to say the damned words, that very soon she'll have to hurt him, that very soon she'll have to deal with his rage. And above all, she knows—no, she doesn't know it: she feels it—that she loves him. Jennifer loves this boy as she's never loved anyone. She'd do anything to protect him; she'd even give up her career to dedicate herself to him body and soul.

Instead, she now sets about lying to him. She'll tell him his mother died for her ideals. She'll be forced to invent a different Allison. She'll have to set aside her egoism, her instability, and her distance. And in spite of herself, she'll transform her sister into a saint. Why can't she tell Jacob that his mother abandoned him right from the start, why can't she tell him that the wretch preferred to save Palestinian children instead of him? Why can't she tell him the truth? The answer is simple: It's because Jennifer has won the game and feels obliged to cede this posthumous reparation to her sister. That way, Jacob can keep her in his memory without hating her, that way Jacob will be able to accept her absence, that way Jacob will stop asking questions, at least for a few years. There is nothing altruistic in Jennifer's decision. She'll defend her sister's memory only in order not to feel guilty about sullying it, in order to take control of the boy without remorse.

For the thousandth time that morning (it's after eleven), Jennifer thinks the time has come to make the great leap and talk to him. She knows the strength of his character and guesses he won't fall apart. If she hasn't dared tell him until now it's been out of fear of making a mistake, of not finding the right words or the most convincing explanation. Sitting in the living room, Jennifer again goes over that story which has no resemblance to the fairy tales she whispers to Jacob at night, although perhaps it should begin this way: "Once upon a time there were two sisters . . ."

The doorbell yanks her out of these reveries. It's Jack Wells. It couldn't be anyone else. Now what?, she greets him angrily. I've come to say goodbye, Jennifer. The shadows under her ex-husband's eyes have become two purplish grooves. Hi Uncle Jack, says Jacob from the floor. Jack goes over and ruffles Jacob's hair: How's it going, champ? Who's wining? The Franks, as always.

Jack dear, you look awful, Jennifer interrupts. Let's go to another room. Both feign an impossible tranquility. Well, do you know what happened to Allison? A bulldozer or something ran her over when she tried to protect the houses of some Palestinians. What shit, Jennifer. Do you know when the body will get here? Not yet. Wells stutters: But I haven't come to talk about that, Jen. It's something more serious. More serious than the death of my sister? A judge has ordered me and Christina Sanders arrested.

Jennifer can't repress a smile: Christina Sanders in jail? We've got the best lawyers, but not even they are sure they can get us out. You're not serious, Jack. I've never been more serious in my life, Jennifer. I'm sorry. A tense, ominous pause. Is there anything I can do for you? She's never seen him so beaten down, so miserable. And, against all her expectations, she's not enjoying it. Not at all.

Come back to me, he asks her. She smiles, this time tenderly. But you're on the way to prison! There's no irony in her words. For that very reason, Jennifer. I confess I made lots of mistakes, but I always thought you and I would end up together, always together. It's in our nature. After what happened with Eva . . . Wells's voice cracks.

I'm really sorry, Jack. Really. What happened with that woman was horrible, I was never happy about it. And I'm sorry for what's happening to you, and even to Christina. But it's too late for us. Too late. But we only have each other, Jennifer! That's how it was before, but things have changed. Allison is dead, and I have to take care of Jacob. The three of us could be together, be a family. Jennifer shakes her head. Please, Jen! She caresses his cheek, a gesture she'd never imagined making, and then she takes him by the hand. It's time you were leaving, Jack.

Wells has lost the battle. He gives Jacob one last hug, picks up his coat, and leaves without looking back. When he finally closes the door behind him, Jennifer knows her time has run out. The time has come to face Jacob. He looks at her with his small blue, almost transparent, eyes. The secret of life seems to hide within them. Life, or a new life. Jennifer goes to him in silence, and takes him in her arms. She caresses his cheek impatiently. Kisses his eyelids.

And she thinks: Now I'm your mother.

3
New Jersey, United States of America, December 31st, 2000

In this grave, it is not darkness that reigns: An incisive shaft of yellowish light is on all day, a way to be sure that no tricks or fights take place in the shadows. The silhouettes change shape. A person could confuse his own hands with claws and his feet with hooves. Little by little, we become beasts whose only goal is to sleep and eat. Perhaps that's a good thing: After all, as Francis Collins and Craig Venter proved, our genome barely separates us from rats.

I've finally been left in peace. Jeffrey, a Latino who weighs a hundred kilos and has teeth like a camel, who was sentenced for raping and murdering three teenage girls, snores shamelessly in the middle of the night. He made me listen to his stories until dawn and only now has succumbed to his own boredom. I barely grinned at his jokes: That we have to live together, like a bitter married couple, is a calamity I try to push out of my mind. Jeffrey seems like a good person, at least to the point where a murderer can be a good person, but I can't stand his curiosity or his manners.

When we got back from our exercise hour—we're forced to take laps like donkeys—I found him going through my papers. I snatched them out of his hands in a fury and told him to keep his hands off my things.

Even though Jeffrey could kill me with one punch, he seemed to take my threats seriously, and his sausage-sized fingers released my notebooks. I'm sorry, he bellowed, and stopped bothering me. Now the bars have taken on an orange-like tinge: It's been more than fifty hours since I slept. The silence is broken only by Jeffrey's deep breathing, which sounds like a roar. The other prisoners are sleeping too. I'm the only man awake in this morgue. I'm waiting for dawn. My mission is to stay alert. And to write, as I've already said, *Season of Ash*. And to remember, until my death, that night.

Once the announcement by President Clinton, imperial seducer, is over, the crowd scatters at top speed. Legions of journalists, cameramen, and reporters leave the gardens of the White House, hurrying to release the good news. The scientists and the special guests, except for Francis Collins, Craig Venter, James Watson, and a few others, also dash out, happy or annoyed (each one has his own reasons), trying to assimilate the consequences of the announcement. Even if it's a first draft, an outline, just guess work, the first complete sequencing of the human genome represents a milestone. It's no exaggeration to speak of it as a landmark, which is what the President called it, or even to mention the end of History. No discovery can be compared to this one: It's the first time a life form knows the substance of its life.

At the end of the ceremony, you come over to me, incandescent, and kiss me on the cheek, intoxicated with your triumph, the triumph of Celera, the triumph of Craig Venter, the triumph of our species. Perhaps we can still save ourselves, I think. Let's you and I celebrate, I whisper in your ear, you and I alone, in the cabin. I take your hands and kiss them again and again. I have to leave with the team, you excuse yourself. Then we could meet at your place, I suggest, at about five. That way we'd get to the river before dinner. Okay, you whisper without enthusiasm, at five.

I have a sandwich for lunch and spend the rest of the afternoon buying wine, vodka, caviar, blinis, and sour cream. I want us to celebrate with an authentic Russian meal. Then I call Jason and ask for the best things available, everything should be perfect. I dedicate the hours to concluding my article on DNAW—the definitive accusation against Wells—but I can't concentrate. Alcohol barely allows me to calm down, so I have no choice but to help myself with some cocaine. I scribble out three or four pages and throw them in the wastebasket. I check my watch: It's almost time. You'll be here soon.

I stop working and, after having another vodka, go into the study and turn on the television. I find the news: Clinton's image appears, flanked by Francis Collins and Craig Venter. The announcer repeats the usual clichés, summarizes the competition between Celera and the Human Genome Project, spells out the advances, summarizes the words of the President and the scientists . . . The camera makes a panoramic sweep, and I think I spot your profile, your ephemeral smile. After the commercials, the woman reads another bulletin, one I've been waiting weeks for, the one I've provoked: After the FDA rejected the anti-cancer drug produced by DNAW, Congress created a subcommittee charged with investigating the company's CEO, John H. Wells, who may have benefitted from internal, prior information concerning the sudden collapse of his company.

I again check the clock. I switch channels, growing more and more nervous. Before me, a parade of games—hockey, American football—the strident colors of an MTV video, the yellow skin of The Simpsons, a reality TV show where two women are in a fistfight, urged on by the announcer. Finally I stop at a comedy series, intrigued by American humor. When I look at the clock again, it's 6:00 P.M., and you still give no signs of life. You're just late—I calm myself. I suppose you're celebrating with Venter and your Celera pals or being interviewed again. Fed up with the program, I continue my channel surfing until I stop at an old Hollywood film. I amuse myself for a while, but at seven, I dial your cell number. It rings. And rings. And rings. Finally I hear your voice: Leave your message after the beep. Your voice, frozen forever.

I can't stand the screen any longer and make my way to the kitchen, another vodka, a spoonful of caviar, and more cocaine. I traverse the house from one end to the other, a prisoner. I can understand being late, but why the hell don't you call me? The kitchen clock mocks me. I hear the motor of your car at around nine, four hours late. It's obvious you've been drinking too, your eyes sparkle and your complexion is rosy. It's been a great, great, impossible day, Yuri Mikhailovich, you say by way of apology. You kiss me, and I, excited, kiss you. I caress the back of your neck and try to unbutton your blouse. Maybe it's better we stay, since it's so late, you suggest. I don't scold you for being late, my desire is greater than my anger. You caress me, but without letting me take your clothes off. Let's go to the cabin, I insist, you don't work tomorrow, we're in no hurry. I smell the alcohol on your breath, and I get even more excited. It will be perfect, I promise.

The starless night makes us imagine we're inside a gallery. You play a CD as loud as possible: It keeps us from talking and submerges us in madness. The empty highway, barely illuminated by the headlights, arouses a feeling of disgust, a reflection of myself. Outside an uncomfortable drizzle is falling, making it hard to see. What shitty weather, I become annoyed. You languidly fix your hair and give yourself over to the music, oblivious to the turbulence of the landscape and my resentment. We get to the cabin long before midnight, just as I predicted. It shouldn't rain, and it doesn't rain. Inside it should be arid and hostile, and it is. Do you smell that?, you ask, that rotten stink? It must be some dead animal, I answer.

I don't even let you turn on the lights and grab you. I pull off your clothes, rip your blouse and the stockings you wore to the White House to shreds, and I kiss you as if I wanted to suffocate you. I don't want to love you, only possess you, possess you completely. I run my tongue over your stomach and your breasts and seek out your sex. You put up with my attack with resignation or prudence, but I can't excite you. An eternity goes by before I can enter your body. I sense no pleasure in your eyes.

We collapse on the floor, worn out, and we stay there who knows how long, ruins after an earthquake, ruins of an extinct civilization. We stop being ourselves, transformed into two exhausted, anonymous bodies. Why the nonsense and the distance? My head reposes on your pubis. I examine your belly in the thin shaft of light that filters in from outside; I see the tiny lines on your thighs, the soft perfection of your navel. I think: You're mine. And I wonder: Why this pain, why? You caress me indolently. The cold makes us cuddle together. We don't recognize each other.

You get up and go to the bathroom. I hear the noise of the water falling on your skin. I light a fire: The sudden flame yanks me out of my lethargy. I recover an instant of consciousness, the warmth enfolds me little by little. I open another bottle of vodka and take a long drink. For the first time that day, I feel lucid and safe. You leave the bathroom with wet hair and whitish spots on your nose. Now it's you who jumps on my sex, now it's you who uses it as she pleases. My pleasure disappears in a second, nonexistent. The brightness of the flames enables me to see the tears held between your eyelids. I take you in my arms and try to console you. You're right: Both of us are alone. There's no way out.

Búskomorság, you suddenly mutter. Again? Always. I know I can do nothing for you. I kiss your eyelids and forehead, uselessly. The distant noise of the river is no consolation whatsoever. It only makes the anguish worse, more intolerable. We drink more vodka. More. More. More.

Where were you all afternoon?, I finally ask. You turn over, you can't stand being touched, you move away from me. Nowhere. Now I move away. Two identical forces that repel each other. Nowhere, I mock you. What do you want me to say, Yuri Mikhailovich? I raise my hand to your head, or rather I observe, from an unnamed place, how a hand moves toward a head. Not mine, another, there, far away, in a parallel world. I want you to tell me the truth, I demand. Too much cocaine, too much vodka, too much night. The truth? You laugh, you laugh at me, you no longer touch me, you open your hands and place them closer to the fire.

I spent the afternoon with Jack Wells, you finally confess. Your tone no longer sounds contemptuous. You used me to get to him, you reproach me, you used me to destroy him. Is that what the bastard told you? It's a lie, Eva. He just wants to separate us, don't you understand? I love you. I forgot that in your world love justifies everything, and you step away. I can't control myself: You went to bed with him, right? You're crazy, Yuri Mikhailovich. I sense your fear, but you feel you must confront me. Your nature makes you do it, your damn genes. Answer me, Eva! You jump to your feet, defiant. I look at your naked body, the reflections that illuminate you, the fragility of your silhouette. Your beauty. Your smile shows your disdain. The last request of the condemned man, I hear you say, his last wish before going to jail: to go to bed with me one last time. The stink of rot becomes more intense.

Okay, Yuri, want to hear it all? Yes, I went to bed with Jack, again and again, the whole fucking afternoon. You must have noticed his smell on my skin, his semen in my sex. A lie, a bad lie to make me angry. But I, in an explosion of rage, of jealousy, or anger, push you away violently. Since I can't believe you, since I can't stand your past, since cocaine and vodka are clouding my mind, since I love you and can't hold back, since I love you as much as you love me, I throw you into the shadows and the silence. You slip, but I manage to grab your hand. For an instant. And then I just let go of you in midair, forever.

An accident, Eva. An accident.

Your head hits the table. The blood flows from your right temple and little by little reaches the floor. Luminous and soft, perfect, you remain that way for hours, until I recover from my shock and run out to get a doctor. That's all, the absurd, inevitable end. The season of ash. Eva, if I've told this story, it's been so that I can hold your hand for another second.

Rome–Ithaca–Cholula–San Sebastián, 2003–2006

CHARACTERS

I. Chernobyl

Olexandr Akimov, *Team Chief*
Boris Stoliarchuk, *Assistant*
Viktor Petrovich Briujanov, *Director of the Center*
Boris Chenina, *Head of the Government Commission*
Nicolay Fomin, *Adjunct Director and First Engineer*
Anatoly Diatlov, *Adjunct Engineer-in-Chief*
Boris Rogoikin, *Director of the Night Guard*
Olexandr Kovalenko, *Director of the Second and Third Reactors*
Yuri Lauchkin, *Gosatomnadzor Inspector*

II. Soviets

Irina Nikolayevna Granina, *born Sudayeva, biologist*
Arkady Ivanovich Granin, *biologist and dissident, husband to Irina*
Oksana Arkadyevna Granina, *daughter of the above, singer and poet*

Ivan Tijonovich Granin, *Arkady's father*
Yelena Pavlovna Granina, *Arkady's mother*
Nikolai Sergeyevich Sudayev, *Irina's father*
Yevgenya Timofeia, *Irina's mother*
Vsevolod Andronovich Birstein, *friend of Arkady at university*
Yevgeny Konstaninovich Ponomariov, *Irina's first husband*
Olga Sergeyevna Karpova, *Arkady's lover*
Mstislav Alexandrovich Slavnikov, *Irina's teacher*
Iosif Dzhugashvili, *known as* Stalin, *Secretary-General of the Communist Party of the Soviet Union*
Lavrentiy Beria, *Head of the NKVD*
Nikita Khrushchev, *Secretary-General of the Communist Party of the Soviet Union*
Leonid Brezhnev, *Secretary-General of the Communist Party of the Soviet Union*
Yuri Andropov, *Secretary-General of the Communist Party of the Soviet Union*
Konstantin Ustinovich Chernenko, *Secretary-General of the Communist of the Soviet Union*
Mikhail Sergeyevich Gorbachev, *Secretary-General of the Communist Party of the Soviet Union, later President of the USSR*
Raisa Maksimovna Gorbachyova, *wife of above*
Trofim Denisovich Lysenko, *biologist, protegee of Stalin*
Nikolai Ivanovich Vavilov, *biologist, murdered by Stalin*
Aleksander Jvat, *torturer working for the NKVD*
Piotr Burgasov, *Arkady's boss*
Aleksandr Ajutin, *Arkady's cell mate*
Andrei Sakharov, *father of the Soviet hydrogen bomb, dissident*
Sofiya Kalistratova, *defender of human rights*
Kira Gorchakova, *defender of human rights*
Sergey Kovaliov, *dissident*

III. Americans

Jennifer Wells, neé Moore, *functionary of the International Monetary Fund*
Jack Wells, *husband of the above, businessman involved in biotechnology*
Allison Moore, *sister of Jennifer, antiglobalization activist*
Jacob Moore, *son of Allison*
Edgar J. Moore, *U.S. Senator, father of Jennifer and Allison*
Ellen Moore, *mother of Jennifer and Allison*
Mary Ann Moore, *first wife of Senator Moore*

Theodore Wells, *father of Jack*
Cameron Tilly, *Allison's first boyfriend*
Susa Anderson, *friend of Allison*
Christina Sanders, *businesswoman and partner of Jack*
Erin Sanders, *businesswoman, daughter of Christina and lover of Jack*
James Carter, *President of the United States*
Ronald Reagan, *President of the United States*
George Bush, *President of the United States*
William Clinton, *President of the United States*

IV. Lovers

Eva Halász, *Head of Computing, Celera*
Klara Halász, *mother of Eva*
Ferenc Halász, *father of Eva*
Philip Putnam, *first husband of Eva*
Andrew O'Connor, *second husband of Eva*
Ismet Dayali, *Turkish lover of Eva*
Yuri Mikhailovich Chernishevsky, *writer*
Zarifa Chernishevskaya, *ex-wife of Yuri*
Ramiz, Farman, *Zarifa's brothers*

V. In Hungary

Imre Nagy, *Prime Minister, sought to renovate Hungary*
Mátyás Rakosi, *First-Secretary of the MDP, pro-Soviet*
András Hegedüs, *Prime Minister, pro-Soviet*
Ernő Gerő, *Prime Minister, pro-Soviet*
János Kádár and Ferenc Münnich, *plot against Nagy*

VI. Scientists

Norbert Wiener, *mathematician, creator of cybernetics*
John von Neumann, *mathematician*
Marvin Minsky, *expert in artificial intelligence*
John Conway, *expert in artificial life*
Arturo Rosenblueth, *physiologist*
Warren McCulloch, *neurobiologist*
Alan Turing, *mathematician*

Edward Teller, *physicist*
Hans Bethe, *physicist*

VII. On Wall Street

Gerry Tsai, *expert in investment funds*
Andy Krieger, *expert in options*
Arthur Lowell, *broker of Jack Wells*
Frank Quattrone, *financial strategist, in charge of OPI and DNAW*
Roy Vagelos, *CEO of Merck*

VIII. Economists

John Kenneth Galbraith
John Maynard Keynes
Harry Dexter White
Jacques de Larosière, *Director-General of the IMF*
Michel Camdessus, *Director-General of the IMF*
James Baker, *Treasury Secretary of the United States*

IX. Ecologists

Jane, Albert, Susan, Marie-Pierre, Davy, and Pete, *crew of the* Rainbow Warrior
Fernando Pereira, *photographer for Greenpeace*
Dave Foreman and Mike Roselle, *founders of Earth First!*
Edward Abbey, *radical ecologist, author of* The Monkey Wrench Gang
Zachary Twain, *member of Earth First!*

X. In Zaire

Mobutu Sese Seko Nkuku Ngbendu wa Za Banga, *dictator of Zaire*
Jean-Baptiste Mukengeshayi, *assistant to Jennifer Moore in Zaire*
Erwin Blumenthal, *head of the IMF mission to Zaire*

XI. In San Francisco

Teddy, Sonia, Ge, and Victoria, *female friends of Allison*

Season of Ash

Kevin Reynolds, *lover of Allison*

XII. In Afghanistan

Hafizullah Amin, *President*
Ghulam Dastagir Panjsheri, *traitor*
Babrak Karmal, *pro-Soviet President*
Gulbuddin Hekmatyar, *warlord*

XIII. Strategic Defense Initiative

James A. Abrahamson, *project director*
Fred S. Hoffman, *participant, Eva's boss*
James C. Fletcher, *participant*

XIV. Plotters

Gennady Yanayev, *Vice-President of the USSR*
Oleg Baklanov, *Sub-Director of the Defense Council*
Anatoly Lukyanov, *President of the Supreme Soviet*
Vladimir Kryuchkov, *Director of the KGB*
Dmitriy Yazov, *Secretary of Defense*
Valentin Pavlov, *Prime Minister*
Boris Pugo, *Minister of the Interior*

XV. The New Russians

Boris Nikolayevich Yeltsin, *President of Russia*
Aleksandr Rutskoy, *Vice-President of Russia*
Anatoly Chubais, *head of privatization, Vice-Prime Minister, oligarch*
Ruslan Khasbulatov, *President of the Russian Duma*
Yegor Gaidar, *Russian Prime Minister, liberal*
Viktor Chernomyrdin, *Russian Prime Minister*
Boris Nemtsov, *Mayor of Nizhni Novgorod*
Sergey Kiriyenko, *Russian Prime Minister*
Alksandr Korzhakov, *Yeltsin's security chief*
Gennady Ziuganov, *leader of the new Communist Party*
Igor Malashenko, *Director of NTV and later Yeltsin's image advisor*

XVI. The Oligarchs

Vladimir Gusinsky, *oligarch, owner of Most Bank and NTV*
Mikhail Khodorkovsky, *oligarch owner of YUKOS*
Vladimir Potanin, *oligarch, owner of Uneximbank and Norilsk Nickel*
Boris Berezovsky, *oligarch, owner of Sibneft*
Sergey Mavrodi, *owner of MMM*
Boris Jordan and Bill Browder, *investors*

XVII. The Poets

Anna Akhmatova
Marina Tsvetaeva
Bella Akhmadulina
Polina Ivanova
Yunna Moritz
Natalia Gorbanevskaya
Aleksandr Kushner
Yanka Diaguileva, *rock singer*
Viktor Tsoi, *rock singer, lead singer of Kino*
Boris Grebenshikov, *rock singer, lead singer of Akvarium*
Yuri Shevchuk, *rock singer, lead singer of DDT*

XVIII. The Activists

Henri Soldain, *participant*
Gesine Muller, *participant*
Ruth Jenkins, *participant*
Jeff Perlstein, *creator of Indymedia*

XIX. Children of Jenin

Salim, Alaa, Walid, Yeha, Rami

XX. The Genome

Oswald Avery, Colin MacLeod, and Maclyn McCarty, *discoverers of DNA*

James Watson and Francis Crick, *Nobel laureates, discoverers of the structure of DNA*
J. Craig Venter, *founder of Celera Genomics*
Claire Fraser, *wife of Venter*
Francis Collins, *Director of the Human Genome Project*
James Bartholdy, *biologist, creator of C225*
James Weber, *Director of the Marshfield Medical Foundation of Wisconsin*
Eugene Myers, *Director of Biocomputing, Celera*
William Haseltine, *Director of Human Genome Sciences*
Hamilton Smith, *Nobel Laureate, Scientific Director of Celera*
Eric Lander, *Director of Whitehead Institute*
Ari Patrinos, *Director of the genetic program of Energy Department*

XXI. In Vladivostok

The Korean
Kornei Ivanovich, *bar owner*

FINAL NOTE

The poems that Oksana reads or writes in the Second Act derive from Valentina Polujina, ed. *Russian Women Poets*. Modern Poetry in Translation, No. 20, Kings College, University of London, 2002, translated into Spanish by the author. The poem by Oksana that becomes the first song of her group is a free translation of the poem "Wild Rose," by Vitalina Tjorzhevskaia (Sverdlovsk, 1971), while the second is "I See," by Yekaterina Vlasova (Slatojusk, 1976).

For the other poems by Anna Akhmatova that Oksana quotes or sets to music in the Third Act, as well as the poem "To Alia," by Marina Tsvetaiva, I have used translations by Monika Zugustova and Olvido García Valdés included in *El canto y la ceniza*. Galaxia Gutemberg/Círculo de Lectores, Barcelona, 2005—except in a few instances whose free versions derived from Russian and English were made by the author based on *The Complete Poems of Anna Akhmatova*, Robert Reeder, ed., Judith Hemschemeyer (trans.), Zephyr Press, Brooklyn, Massachusetts, 2000.

ACKNOWLEDGMENTS

This work was written thanks to a John S. Guggenheim Foundation grant along with the support of the Sistema Nacional de Creadores in Mexico. Edmundo Paz Soldán and Debra Castillo, who invited me to spend a semester amid books and snow at Cornell University, and Pedro Angel Palou, who held me prisoner for another six months at the Universidad de las Americas in Puebla, are all responsible for the completion of this book.

I also want to thank for their help or support the following people: Ximena Briceño, María José Bruña, Carmen Boullosa, Nuria Cartón de Gramont, Alejandra Costamagna, Svetlana Doubin, Denise Dresser, Amaya Elezcano, Yuri Fanjul, Indira García, Blanca Granados, Natalia Guzmán, Juantxu Herguera, Gabriel Iaculli, Elizabeth Hernández, Vicente Herrasti, Flavia Hevia, Amelia Hinojosa, Héctor Hoyos, Maité Iracheta, Antonia Kerrigan and Ricardo Pérdigo, Gerardo Kleinburg, Paty Mazón, Gesine Muller, Luna Nájera, Guadalupe Nettel, Nacho Padilla and Lili Cerdio, Marie-Pierre Ramouche, Martín Solares and Mónica Herrerías, Ana Pellicer and Enrique Vallano, Elena Ramírez, Marisol Schulz, Daniela Tarazona, Rafael Tovar and de Teresa, Eloy Urroz and Lety Barrera, and, of course, my parents.

Jorge Volpi is a doctor in law and a teacher of Mexican literature at the UNAM (Autonomous University of Mexico); he received his PhD in Spanish Philology from the University of Salamanca. The author of nine novels, including *In Search of Klingsor*, for which he won the Spanish Premio Biblioteca Breve prize and the French Deux-Océans-Grizane-Cavour Prize, Volpi is one of the founders of the "Crack" group—a Mexican literary movement that seeks to move beyond magical realism and mimics the ideals of the 1968 Latin American literary Boom. He has received grants from the John S. Guggenheim Foundation and is a member of National System of Creators in Mexico.

Alfred Mac Adam has been a professor of Latin American literature at Barnard College-Columbia University since 1983. He has translated novels by Carlos Fuentes, Mario Vargas Llosa, José Donoso, Juan Carlos Onetti, and Julio Cortázar, amongst others. Between 1984 and 2004, Mac Adam was the editor of *Review: Latin American Literature and Arts*, a magazine that presents work by Latin American writers to English-speaking audiences.

Open Letter—the University of Rochester's nonprofit, literary translation press—is one of only a handful of publishing houses dedicated to increasing access to world literature for English readers. Publishing ten titles in translation each year, Open Letter searches for works that are extraordinary and influential, works that we hope will become the classics of tomorrow.

Making world literature available in English is crucial to opening our cultural borders, and its availability plays a vital role in maintaining a healthy and vibrant book culture. Open Letter strives to cultivate an audience for these works by helping readers discover imaginative, stunning works of fiction and by creating a constellation of international writing that is engaging, stimulating, and enduring.

Current and forthcoming titles from Open Letter include works from Argentina, Austria, Brazil, France, Iceland, Lithuania, Spain, and numerous other countries.